THE SHADOW
ON THE QUILT

The Quilt Chronicles

STEPHANIE GRACE WHITSON

BARBOUR
PUBLISHING

Print ISBN 978-1-61626-444-4

eBook Editions:
Adobe Digital Edition (.epub) 978-1-62029-104-7
Kindle and MobiPocket Edition (.prc) 978-1-62029-105-4

Cover design: Müllerhaus Publishing Arts, Inc., www.Mullerhaus.net

Published by Barbour Publishing, Inc., P.O. Box 719, Uhrichsville, Ohio 44683, www.barbourbooks.com

Our mission is to publish and distribute inspirational products offering exceptional value and biblical encouragement to the masses.

 Member of the
Evangelical Christian
Publishers Association

Printed in the United States of America.

CHAPTER 1

Save me, O God; for the waters are come in unto my soul.
I sink in deep mire, where there is no standing:
I am come into deep waters, where the floods overflow me.
PSALM 69:1–2

Lincoln, Nebraska
April 15, 1883

Juliana Sutton stood before her husband's mahogany dresser, staring down at the gold locket. What was it doing nestled in the leather box where Sterling kept his diamond studs? She glanced back at the bedroom door, feeling almost guilty for having found it. He was probably planning to surprise her. Ah, well. She would pretend to be surprised and tease him about how she'd come to find it.

"It's not my fault my husband doesn't pick up after himself," she would say. "I was sitting at my dressing table, brushing my hair before retiring last night, when something glinted in the lamplight. I glanced over, and there it was: one of your diamond studs languishing against the baseboard. It must have gotten lost when I...when we—" And she would blush as she was blushing now, remembering her part in—*things* just last night. Her response to Sterling's hand at her waist when he pulled her close. Her removing one glove before reaching up to rake her fingers through his hair. Her unfettered joy at his kiss.

She turned the locket over in her hand. *He's had it engraved.* She

3

shouldn't read the inscription, but now that she'd discovered it, she couldn't help herself. And so, leaving the dresser drawer open, she retreated to her dressing table and held it close to the lamp and—gasped. She sat down.

> *To my P. L.*
> *S. T. S.*

Her mouth went dry. She didn't know anyone with the initials *P. L.* Sterling was Sterling Theodore, *S.T.S.*

Maybe it's an estate piece. He was going to have it reworked for me. Perhaps the initials are a coincidence. She reached up with her free hand to touch the locket that hung around her neck. *He knows how I love lockets.* She already owned half a dozen, all but one gifts from Sterling.

She opened the locket and looked down at the portrait of a young woman holding an infant in her arms. But it wasn't the portrait of the woman that sucked the air out of her lungs. It was the curl of white-blond hair that dropped into her lap. And Sterling's profile behind the glass on the left.

God help me. For the first time in her life, Juliana wished she was the kind of woman who fainted away in a crisis. If she could only faint, the pain would stop. At least for a moment, she wouldn't have to feel as though some evil specter had reached inside her chest to squeeze her heart with a ghostly hand.

Steady. Breathe. Hold on. She looked at herself in the mirror, willing the glimmering tears away. *Be strong. You are no wilting violet.* She lifted her chin. Stared into her dark eyes to remind herself. Juliana Regina Masters Sutton was a graduate of Mt. Holyoke Female Seminary. On the board of directors of the Society of the Home for the Friendless. A respected member of First Church. Not a woman to act the role of the wounded martyr.

She would not wail or accuse. She would. . .think. *Think. This is no time for hysterics. It will only drive him further away.* But as the lamp flickered and the moments passed, thinking didn't really help. Thinking reminded her of all the nights Sterling "worked late." Thinking reminded her of Aunt Theodora's protest just this morning.

"I might have to work late tonight," Sterling had said as he laid his napkin aside and rose from the breakfast table. "Finney's having trouble with the ledger. Could be a while. Don't wait supper." He'd kissed the top of her head on his way out of the dining room. "And don't wait up."

Juliana hadn't protested, but Sterling's Aunt Theodora had not been so accepting. "Successful businessmen need efficient help, dear boy," she'd called after him. "If that Irishman can't handle the job, then—"

Aunt Lydia had interrupted her. "Now, now, Sister. Let's not suggest poor Christopher Finney should lose his position. The man has five children and a wife to feed."

Children. Juliana looked down at the infant, little more than a smudge of sepia swathed in lace. Once again, tears threatened. She and Sterling had longed for children for all of their ten years of married life. She'd seen more than one specialist, even traveled to Philadelphia in search of help. No one gave them hope. Through it all, Sterling had been steadfast. Loving. Everything a husband should be. *"We have each other,"* he'd said more than once. *"That's all that matters."*

Juliana closed the locket. She swiped her tears away. She shouldn't be surprised. Not really. After all, in recent years, a great many things had seemed to matter more to Sterling than she did. More business mattered. More land. More investments. More employees. More buildings. More professional accolades.

Oh, he'd included Juliana and his two elderly aunts in his life, but now that Juliana thought about it, perhaps they merely served as excuses for his quest for more. More jewelry. More furs. More horses. A grand piano for Aunt Theodora. Generous donations to all of Aunt Lydia's pet causes. A summer house in Wisconsin so the aunts could escape the Nebraska heat.

5

He'd pressed Juliana to go with them last summer. Now she wondered if there'd been a hidden reason for his sudden willingness to have her gone for a month. How old was the child in that woman's arms?

She bowed her head and closed her eyes. She'd thought last night meant a new beginning. They'd weathered the storm. They were going to be all right.

The locket burned into her palm. Opening her eyes, she put it down on the cool marble surface of the dressing table and stared at it. What should she do? She took a deep breath. Then another. Finally, her racing heart began to slow. Somehow she managed to force shock and betrayal, hurt and dismay back. In favor of anger. Anger could be useful. Anger would keep her strong until—until she knew what to do.

Rising, she crossed the room and dropped the locket back into the satin-lined case with the diamond studs. She closed the drawer. Firmly. And began to pace. As she crossed the carpeted room, she reached up to grasp the locket around her own neck. Reaching the closed door, she spun about to head back toward the opposite wall where Sterling's dresser loomed. She yanked on the chain. Once. Twice. Finally, it gave way.

Locket in hand, she paced out of the bedroom. Through the sitting room on the upstairs landing. Out onto the upstairs porch and to the ornate railing that graced the Italianate home she had grown to love. She looked toward Lincoln and the warehouse district. Wondered where Sterling was really "working" tonight. And with all her strength, she launched the locket into the night.

—⁓—

Juliana stayed out on the balcony, pacing back and forth, willing herself not to give in to tears, until she felt that she could retire without wailing and waking the aunts. They both doted on their only nephew, and Juliana had grown to love them. Whatever she decided to do, it must not involve them. Aunt Lydia was sixty-two; her sister, Theodora, seventy. They didn't deserve heartbreak. Juliana would do what she could to shield them from it. How that would work out, she didn't know, but she would find a way.

She headed for the door to the upstairs hall, hesitating for one last glance toward town before going inside. Sterling had taken her for a gullible fool. He would learn that that was a mistake.

She'd just opened the door when the fire bells sounded in town. Was it her imagination, or could she smell smoke on the spring breeze? She looked west. Tongues of fire lapped up the darkness hovering over what appeared to be the warehouse district. Frowning, Juliana let the door close and stayed outside, returning to the railing to gaze toward the western horizon.

Moments later, Aunt Theodora came out onto the porch. "We heard the alarm."

"It's a big fire," Juliana said, nodding toward town.

"I tried to call Sterling at the office. He didn't answer."

"I didn't realize you even knew how to use the telephone."

"Just because I didn't want the dear boy installing one in my private sitting room doesn't mean I have remained willfully ignorant. Although it obviously doesn't solve all the problems in the land, now does it. In this case it doesn't solve a thing. Sterling didn't answer. We are still left to worry."

Juliana looked behind her at Aunt Theodora, her profile illuminated by the amber light spilling out of the house. Tall, slim, and somehow managing to look regal even though she must have hurried to dress.

"Lydia went to rouse Alfred," Theodora said. "He's hitching up the buggy. I knew you would want to check on Sterling, but you must not go alone. I shall ride with you while Lydia stays here. If anyone calls or brings word while we're away, she'll send Alfred with the news." She motioned for Juliana to come inside. "It is fortunate that you haven't changed yet this evening."

Aunt Theodora was a force to be reckoned with. There would be no way to keep her at home. The best Juliana could do was to drive the buggy into town and hope that Sterling would have a good story waiting in the morning. Perhaps he really was at the office. Perhaps he was merely. . .distracted. The mental image that created made her shiver as she swept through the doorway and went inside.

"Everything will be all right, dear," Aunt Theodora said. "We'll probably know it's another building before we're halfway there. And Sterling will have called before we get back—or perhaps he'll be home by then." She led the way downstairs, all the while muttering against "that Irishman in the office" whose incompetence forced Sterling to work such long hours untangling his mistakes.

When the older woman hurried into the kitchen, Juliana hung back. She didn't want to go chasing after Sterling. Not tonight. Not with the image of another woman and her child taunting her. She blinked back tears. *God, help me. I don't know what to do.*

A glimmer of strength returned. Aunt Theodora came to the kitchen door and called out that the buggy was waiting. Juliana headed for the kitchen where Aunt Lydia stood, her gray hair tumbling down her back, her hands clasped as she nodded at whatever Aunt Theodora was saying.

"All right, Sister." There was a slight edge to her voice. "I think I can be trusted to stay awake and send Alfred with word if Sterling— or anyone else—turns up with news. It's not like you've asked me to translate a passage of Greek poetry."

"You were never good with the Greeks," Aunt Theodora snapped, then glanced at Juliana. "Ah. Here you are." She led the way outside.

Aunt Lydia reached for Juliana. Taking both her hands, she gave them a squeeze. "Prayers ascending, my dear."

Juliana kissed the old woman on the cheek. Once outside, she thanked Alfred for being so quick about hitching up the buggy, then climbed aboard and took up the reins. As Fancy moved seamlessly into a trot and headed up the road toward the warehouse district, Juliana peered at the flickering light in the distance.

What kind of woman saw something like that and almost hoped it was her husband's business feeding the flames? She couldn't help it. If the business burned, if they had to start over, maybe Sterling would come back to her. Maybe they could start over as lovers, too.

And if not, maybe she'd strangle him with the gold chain attached to that confounded locket in his dresser drawer.

—∞—

Awakened by the fire bell, Cass Gregory had been content to throw up the sash and watch as a team of Belgians charged past with the new Silsby engine in tow. The hose team raced after it, half-a-dozen men pulling the two-wheeled cart bearing a giant spool of fire hose. But then Cass heard someone shout, "It's Goldie's!"

Tonight, the childhood lessons in fast dressing taught by the painful end of his stepfather's buggy whip served Cass well. In no time, he was bounding down the stairs of his rooming house. Once outside, he tore off up the street, dodging the merely curious and coming to an abrupt, skidding stop when he rounded the corner and saw that it was, indeed, a fire at Goldie's lighting up the night sky.

For a moment, it felt like someone had knocked the wind out of him and stopped time itself. The building would be a complete loss. There was no doubt of that. Cass scanned the crowd. He looked up at the flames leaping from the second story toward the back alley. Was Sadie's room in that part of the place? He didn't know. Hadn't wanted to know. Ma's was just off the kitchen. Had the fire started there? *God in heaven. Please. Not this. Not this.*

The hose team went to work attaching the fire hose to the water tank. As the men began to work the pump, a stream of water fought the crackling flames. A shout went up from the crowd as a soot-streaked figure stumbled out the front door.

Cass shoved his way through the crowd, ignoring the curses spewed at him. Before he could get close enough, the girl collapsed into the arms of a fireman. He carried her to a waiting wagon and laid her—none too gently, Cass thought—in the wagon bed. Cass recognized Dr. Gilbert as the doc bent over her. *Blond hair.* It wasn't Sadie. He turned his attention back to the burning building, his heart hammering in his chest, his fists clenched at his side.

Inhaling the acrid scent of the fire, he coughed. Again, he

scanned the crowd. The curious onlookers' faces shone red and yellow, reflecting the flames. Someone just behind him muttered that the demise of Goldie's wasn't exactly a terrible loss for the community. Cass nearly punched the man. In the wake of lives possibly lost in the most horrible way a person could die, he thought a little common grace might be extended. He didn't say it, though. He just stood watching, his emotions a mixture of panic, rage, and grief. *God in heaven. Please.*

He'd just raked the back of his hand across his face to scrub away tears when someone tugged on his shirtsleeve and called his name. One look and he engulfed the older woman in his arms. "Ma! Thank the Lord! I thought—" A sob swallowed the rest of what he was going to say. Without opening his eyes, he whispered Sadie's name as a question.

"I'm here, silly."

He opened his eyes. She stood wrapped in a flamboyant blue silk robe, her Titian red hair half pinned up, half tumbling down her back, her vibrant blue eyes as defiant as ever, a smirk uplifting one corner of her mouth.

She held the silk robe closed and nudged him with one shoulder. "You don't think I'd be stupid enough to die in a fire? I was out before the alarm rang. In fact," she said, "I'm the one who raised the alarm." She looked up at the building and shuddered. "I've been telling Goldie to forbid smoking upstairs ever since she opened. Would she listen?" She shook her head. "She'll regret it now."

"If she lives to regret anything," Cass muttered.

"Aren't you the dramatic one?" Sadie nodded toward the saloon across the way.

"Ernie Krapp might be blackhearted, but he took us in when we ran for cover."

Cass followed her gaze to where Goldie stood in the saloon doorway, smoking a cigarette and watching her building burn. Her stoic expression revealed nothing of what she must be feeling. He turned back to Sadie. "Everyone's all right then? Everyone got out?"

Sadie shrugged. "I didn't exactly wait at the front door and check names off a list."

It wasn't until Sadie shivered that Cass wished he'd taken time to grab his jacket on his way out the door. Suddenly, he was aware of the men in the crowd leering at Sadie, the outlines of her body all too apparent beneath the thin silk. A male voice sounded from behind them.

"S–Simone? Is that you? Oh, thank God!"

The speaker was at least an inch shorter than Sadie—Cass could not make himself think of his own sister by the name she'd taken for herself. Wiry blond curls framed the stranger's round face. Dark eyes glimmered behind spectacles. He shrugged out of his coat and draped it across her shoulders. Then he spoke to Cass. "You must be the brother." He thrust out his hand and introduced himself. "Ludwig Meyer."

Cass didn't quite know what to say to that. Sadie talked about family with her clients?

"It's him, all right," Sadie said, looping her arm through Meyer's and looking up at him with a familiarity Cass found embarrassing.

But Meyer's expression was all devotion as he smiled, first at Sadie, and then at Ma. "You must both come home with me tonight."

Ma hesitated. She glanced across the way to the saloon. "I'm sure Goldie will have made arrangements."

"Come with me," Cass said.

Sadie's voice sounded disbelief. "Unless you've moved, your landlady might have something to say about that."

Just as Cass opened his mouth to retort, the back wall of the burning building fell in. The crowd gasped and moved away as one as a shower of sparks and a cloud of soot shot into the night sky.

Ludwig Meyer tightened his grasp on Sadie. "Please, *mein Schatz*. Come with me." He fended Cass's protest off. "I have a small house. They will be comfortable." He patted Sadie's hand. "Have I not been saying as much for weeks?" Then he smiled at Ma again. "Allow me to help you."

11

Ma looked to Cass. "You know Sadie's right about your landlady." She glanced at Sadie. "If Sadie's in agreement—"

"I'm in agreement with anything that will get us away from all these holier-than-thou sightseers."

Cass glanced around them, not knowing whether to feel embarrassed or defensive on Sadie's behalf about the mutterings and the leering glances.

Sadie nodded toward the saloon. "We'll have to tell Goldie." She led the way across the unpaved road.

Cass hesitated before offering Ma his arm and following. Then he cursed himself for being a hypocrite. *They wouldn't be in this situation if you hadn't run off and left them to—* A familiar horse and buggy just crossing the street to the north caught his eye. Cass frowned. What was Mrs. Sutton doing down here? And was that the boss's aunt? Neither woman was the kind to chase a fire out of curiosity.

"What is it?" Ma followed his gaze, but the buggy was already out of sight, headed east.

"I just saw the boss's wife. And one of his aunts, if I'm not mistaken. Headed east, which means—" His heart sank. It meant the boss wasn't home. The Suttons had a phone, one of only a few hundred in the entire city of twenty thousand. For Mrs. Sutton to have driven down here. . . The boss must have told his wife he was working late. They'd probably called to check on him when they heard the fire alarm. And if he hadn't answered— What that probably meant sent a flash of anger through Cass as he glanced toward the office and the adjoining lumberyard just a few blocks away in the warehouse district.

What was it Jessup had said a while back? Something about seeing the boss's horse tied up at a farm house over by Yankee Hill. When Cass said the boss was always looking to buy property, Jessup had grinned. "Sure he is. And everybody knows it takes a man several lo–o–ong visits to inspect a place and make a decision. Especially when there's a pretty girl involved."

"You want to keep working for Sutton Builders," Cass had snapped, "you'd best shut your imagination and your mouth. Permanently."

"Didn't mean any harm," Jessup had said, and that had been that. Ma's voice brought Cass back to the moment.

"Well," she said, waving a response to the salute Goldie sent in their direction, "that's settled."

"This Meyer fellow—" Cass began.

"A good man, from what I can tell," Ma said. "He was dragged into Goldie's by a bunch of wild friends. He paid Sadie to *talk*— and then begged her not to tell his friends that's how they spent their time. It's been that way ever since." She paused. "I think Sadie genuinely likes him."

When the couple came to where Cass and Ma stood talking, Meyer offered Ma his arm. She took it with a smile at Cass. "Don't worry about us. We'll be all right."

"Come to supper tomorrow," Meyer said, and mentioned an address in the tidy neighborhood called the Russian Bottoms.

Cass promised to come and stood for a few moments, watching the three make their way toward Meyer's neighborhood. Cass didn't know Meyer, but Sutton Builders employed plenty of Germans from that neighborhood, every one of them God-fearing and hardworking. At some point in the past they'd emigrated en masse from Germany to Russia. But they'd kept their heritage and their traditional faith alive. They were pacifists, and when the Russians began to force their sons into the army, the Germans were forced to either leave the region or betray their conscience.

Conscience. The things conscience could demand of a man. Cass thought again of the boss. What caused a man to betray a woman as beautiful and accomplished as Juliana Sutton? *What causes another man to remain silent when he knows it's going on?*

When Cass had finally realized that Jessup's suspicions were true, he'd told himself it wasn't any of his business. Maybe it wasn't, but that wasn't why he ignored the obvious, and the real reason shamed him. Confronting the boss would almost definitely amount to firing himself. And Cass didn't want to lose his job.

Coward. You ignore what's going on right under your nose and let your own mother, your own sister— He corrected himself. He wasn't *letting* Sadie or Ma do anything. He'd begged Sadie to leave Goldie's, but she refused. And as long as Sadie wouldn't leave, neither would Ma. He was doing the best he could. Working, saving money, and hoping for better things. He'd even started going to church a couple of years ago, not only surprised at how well he remembered the Bible stories Ma had read to him when he was a boy but also comforted by the sermons. Pastor Taylor was a humble man who had a way of scattering hope across his congregation. And hope kept Cass coming back. Hope that God hadn't abandoned him. Hope that someday he'd be able to make it up to Ma and Sadie for running off. For not being there when they'd needed him most.

Cass turned back toward the ruined building. The fire was almost out, the crowd dispersing. Shoving his hands in his pockets, he headed for the rooming house. He'd only taken a few steps when a shout sounded and Dr. Gilbert jumped down from the back of the wagon where he'd been tending the blond-haired working girl. He darted toward the stretcher being carried out of what was left of Goldie's.

It didn't take long for the doctor to shake his head and draw a sheet over the victim's face.

But it was long enough for Cass to recognize Sterling Sutton.

CHAPTER 2

Have mercy upon me, O God, according to thy lovingkindness:
according unto the multitude of thy tender mercies
blot out my transgressions.
PSALM 51:1

Ludwig Meyer's house was so small it barely deserved to be called a house. Yet as Margaret followed Sadie and Mr. Meyer inside, the aromas of soup and pipe tobacco, along with the warmth of a tiny coal-burning stove in the miniscule parlor, transformed her first impressions. The house might be tiny, but it was also cozy. It felt like a home.

Divided down the middle, it boasted a combination parlor and kitchen on the left and what Margaret assumed to be two bedrooms on the right, both of them opening directly into the living area. In the parlor portion of the house, two rockers sat atop a large rag rug. Between the chairs, a revolving table crowded with colorful, leather-bound books supported a lovely oil lamp, its shade adorned with painted roses.

Curtains served as doors to the other two rooms. Meyer pulled aside the one obscuring the view of the nearest room. "The bed is not so large," he said, "but I have many comforters and quilts. We can make a pallet on the floor for one of you."

"The bed's fine," Sadie said, patting him on the chest as she nestled close and looked at Margaret. "Ma loves it, don't you?" Meyer's face turned red. When he cleared his throat, Sadie laughed and patted his shoulder. "It's all right, sweetie. I was just teasing." She stepped into the little room and perched on the edge of the only piece of furniture beside the iron bed—a low trunk shoved against a wall. "We'll do just fine."

"Whatever you're cooking," Margaret said, "it smells wonderful."

Sadie smiled at Mr. Meyer. "That's a real compliment. Mama's a wonderful cook. Wait till you taste her biscuits. They melt in your mouth. The girls practically fight over them."

Mr. Meyer nodded before disappearing into the other room at the back, returning with a piece of paper and a pencil in hand. He offered it to Margaret. "If you will make a list, I'll see that you have whatever provisions you might need." His face flushed again. "I am hoping you will stay. We have some ready-to-wear at the store where I work, although nothing quite so fine as what you are"—he glanced at Sadie—"what you are accustomed to."

Sadie pointed at the list in Margaret's hand. "Put down what you need to make biscuits." She smiled at Mr. Meyer. "Goldie said she'd send someone around tomorrow. She'll loan us enough money to last until she has a new place."

"But—" Meyer frowned. "I thought all was lost in the fire."

Margaret explained. "Goldie keeps cash sewn into the lining of that dressing gown she had on tonight. She doesn't trust banks. You can bet there's even more cash hidden somewhere else." She looked at Sadie. "But I don't think we should take much from Goldie. Maybe just enough for some proper clothes so we can look for work."

Sadie laughed. She held her hands out, palms up. "Do you really think the good people of Lincoln will give Simone LaBelle a job? Can't you just see me behind the counter where Ludwig works?" The robe threatened to fall open.

Mr. Meyer crossed the room to stand at the small cookstove. Lifting the soup pot lid, he busied himself stirring, tasting, and adding spices.

"No," Margaret said, "but they might be very willing to give a lovely girl like Sadie Gregory a chance."

Sadie rolled her eyes.

Mr. Meyer turned around. "Sadie?" he said. "You are not Simone?"

Sadie glowered at Margaret. "I needed something exotic."

Mr. Meyer smiled and repeated the name. "Sadie Gregory." He nodded. "That's a nice name. For a nice lady." He ladled soup into a bowl and set it on the table. "A nice lady who is also hungry, perhaps?"

Sadie sashayed over to the table and sat down on one of the two chairs.

Mr. Meyer pulled out the other for Margaret. "Please. You are my guest."

Margaret sat down, and Mr. Meyer retreated to the back door, stepping out onto a covered porch. When he came back, he had a battered stool in hand. He served himself and Margaret, then perched on the stool at one end of the small table. He bowed his head.

"Blessed God in heaven, thank You for saving the lives of Goldie and the others. Thank You for Your kindness and Your love to us, and for allowing me to share my home. Thank You for the promise of new life in Christ. Let us live to accept it. Amen."

Margaret dared not look up at Sadie after such a prayer. She did, however, dare to say *amen* along with Mr. Meyer. She wanted to believe in a new life for herself and Sadie, even though she wasn't sure she had a right to ask for it.

—⁂—

As Juliana headed the buggy toward home, Juliana took her nervous mare in hand and tried to calm Aunt Theodora. "Fancy's in a hurry, but she won't bolt. It's the scent of the fire making her so flighty. You don't have to be afraid."

"I believe you," the older woman muttered. But when Juliana glanced down, Aunt Theodora was still braced against the buggy seat as if at any moment she might be pitched onto the prairie.

Finally, Juliana pulled back on the reins harder than she really wanted to, and Fancy slowed to a dancing walk, all the while snorting and tossing her head.

With a visible sigh of relief, Aunt Theodora reached up to adjust her bonnet. "Thank heavens." She settled back. Presently, she said, "I know that any fire is a tragedy, but I cannot regret the destruction of that particular edifice." She sighed. "I suppose Sterling will think us foolish to have worried. He'll probably be seated at the kitchen table having cocoa with Lydia when we walk in. We must have just missed him."

Not knowing what to say, Juliana kept silent. Alfred and his wife, Martha, must have been watching for them, because they were both waiting by the back door as Juliana drove up. Aunt Theodora reported that Sterling had apparently already left the office. Sutton Builders was safe. The fire had eradicated a building no worthy citizen would miss.

Martha offered to help her inside, but Aunt Theodora waved her away. "I realize that I look as brittle as a dried twig, but I am still quite capable of carrying myself up three shallow steps."

Juliana glanced Martha's way and gave a little shrug. Martha smiled and headed off to the barn—undoubtedly to help Alfred unhitch the buggy and tend to Fancy. Part of her wished she could go with them instead of heading inside. If Sterling had come home, Martha would have said so, and Juliana was far too angry to murmur either excuses or concern. By the time she stepped into the kitchen, Aunt Theodora had already removed her bonnet and taken a seat at the table. Aunt Lydia was pouring hot chocolate into three of the four cups and saucers sitting atop the kitchen table. Juliana sat down, murmuring her appreciation for the rich, dark chocolate.

Finally, Aunt Theodora spoke up. "Could there have been a lodge meeting?"

"I suppose so," Aunt Lydia said. "He belongs to so many, one loses track." She smiled. "Do you remember that time back in Chicago? He had an unfortunate meal—fish, I think. It didn't agree with him, and he stayed over at a hotel instead of driving home."

"And you scolded him within an inch of his life for worrying us." Aunt Theodora glanced at Juliana. "I know it's hard to imagine Lydia scolding anyone, but she did."

18

"And I will again. My goodness, there's simply no excuse for it. Why have a telephone installed if he doesn't use it for things like this? Wherever he is, he had to have heard the fire alarm. He must know we're concerned." Aunt Lydia reached over to pat Juliana's hand. "Don't worry, dear. I won't be too hard on him."

After another sip of cocoa, Juliana rose to go. Both aunts decided they would finish their hot cocoa in their respective rooms, and so the ladies filed up the back stairs to worry, to pray, to ponder, and, in Juliana's case, to simmer.

The brisk April morning brought the sound of someone knocking at the front door. Juliana tried to ignore it, but whoever it was seemed determined not to be turned away. Because it was Monday, Martha and Alfred's day off, no one but Juliana or the aunts could answer the door.

With a sigh, Juliana stepped out onto the upstairs porch to see if she recognized the offender's rig. There was no rig, and she didn't recognize the rangy buckskin tied to the hitching post. Finally, she went to the edge of the porch. She was just about to call down and tell whoever it was to come back at a decent hour, when she heard the front door open and—Lydia? Yes. Aunt Lydia. Inviting the person in!

She stepped back inside, lingering in the upstairs hall. As expected, Aunt Lydia came up. First, she knocked on her sister's door, but she didn't wait for an answer before opening it and leaning in to say something. When she turned around and Juliana saw how pale she was—how her eyes had filled with tears—dread washed over her.

"It's Marshal Hastings, dear. We'll wait for you in the library."

It took Juliana twice as long as usual to get her waist-length, dark hair wrapped up. She kept dropping hairpins. It seemed to take half a lifetime to manage the row of tiny buttons marching up the front of the white waist she pulled out of her wardrobe. Thank goodness she'd just bought lace-up shoes. The way she was shaking, if she'd

19

had to wield a buttonhook, she'd probably have given up and gone downstairs in her stocking feet.

Her emotions a jumble, Juliana finally joined the aunts in the library where they waited, already seated, their hands clasped in their laps. She crossed the room to stand behind them, feeling like a sleepwalker in one of those dreams where things moved in slow motion.

"With all due respect, ma'am," the marshal said, nodding at an empty chair. "You might want to sit down."

"Thank you. I'll be fine." She wasn't at all certain of that, but the truth was she felt safer here, with the aunts between her and whatever the marshal was about to say.

He gave an almost imperceptible nod. Cleared his throat. "I imagine you heard the fire alarm last night."

Juliana nodded.

Aunt Theodora spoke up. It wasn't like her to ramble, but now she did, like a woman trying to fend off the inevitable. "We tried to call Sterling at the office. He was working late. When he didn't answer, we drove down to the office. But he wasn't there, so we drove back. We saw. . ." Her voice trailed off. Her sister reached over and took her hand.

"We saw the fire," Juliana said. She gripped the chair harder in a vain attempt to stay her trembling. "Of course we cross that street on our way to the office. By the time we headed home—it was a terrible scene." *Just say it. Don't make us wait any longer. Just say it.*

The marshal nodded. He took a deep breath. "I am very sorry to have to tell you that Mr. Sutton was a victim of that fire."

Aunt Theodora covered her mouth with both hands while Aunt Lydia rose and guided Juliana to sit in her chair, then sat on the other side of her sister. Juliana couldn't speak. All she could think of was the locket upstairs. Dry eyed, she looked down at her hands. At her wedding ring.

Anguish sounded in Aunt Theodora's voice as she wailed, "But— how? *Why?*"

"You said Mr. Sutton was working late. He must have run to help as soon as he heard the alarm. He was found—inside. There was a woman in his— He must have dashed in with no thought of his own safety. Tragically, he and the woman he was trying to rescue perished together."

Aunt Lydia closed her eyes. Her lips moved in what Juliana assumed to be a prayer.

Still, Juliana could not bring herself to speak. A ray of morning sunlight streaked across her green silk skirt. Sterling had died *in a brothel*. Marshal Hastings might have couched what happened in terms of heroism, but in light of that locket upstairs. . .Juliana knew. And just as she had last night, she pushed back hurt and betrayal and summoned anger to help her cope.

"Who was she?"

The marshal frowned. Tilted his head like a man who was hard of hearing. "Ma'am?"

"The woman who died with my husband. You must know her name."

Aunt Theodora let out a soft grunt of protest.

Juliana ignored it.

"Well, ma'am. . .I. . .uh. . ." The marshal fiddled with the brim of the hat he was still holding. "Nell," he finally said. "Nell Parker."

Juliana blinked. *Nell Parker? Not "P. L."?* Not the woman in the locket. *There was more than one?* She closed her eyes. Angry tears gathered. *How could you? How dared you?*

Aunt Lydia began to weep softly.

Juliana gazed at iron-willed Aunt Theodora. She was maintaining her composure but, Juliana thought, just barely.

You can do this. You can. Think of the aunts. They need you to stay calm. Help them bear it. You can deal with the rest later. You'll have all the time you need. Later.

She took a deep breath "Where is he?"

"At Lindermann's Funeral Parlor."

"Is there anything else we need to know?"

"Not from me. Of course Mr. Lindermann will be fully prepared to assist you with everything."

When Juliana rose from her chair, the marshal sprang to his feet like a trapped animal being set free. He put his hat back on, tugging on the brim as he nodded good-bye, first to Aunt Lydia. "Miss Sutton." Then to Aunt Theodora. "Miss Sutton." And finally, to Juliana. "I am so sorry, Mrs. Sutton."

With a nod, Juliana opened the door to dismiss the marshal, just as Reverend Burnham's carriage pulled up to the house.

"I took the liberty of asking him to come out," Hastings explained. "I hope you don't mind."

"You're very thoughtful." Juliana smiled.

But she did mind.

CHAPTER 3

A friend loveth at all times, and a brother is born for adversity.
PROVERBS 17:17

Dawn had barely tinged the eastern sky when Cass Gregory closed the door to his room and descended to the street. It was too early to expect the hotel dining room to be serving. He didn't have much of an appetite anyway. Not today. He couldn't get his mind off the fire and what it would mean for Ma, for Sadie, for Mrs. Sutton, for Mr. Sutton's elderly aunts. . .and for him. What would happen to Sutton Builders?

Goldie's ruined building stood between his rooming house and work. Instead of walking past, he stopped in front of it to think. The city would be buzzing with the news of the boss's death, and he shuddered to think what some people would have to say about that. How would the Sutton ladies manage the news? What would the coming weeks mean for the two dozen men working for Sutton Builders? He'd spent half the night bouncing from one thought to the next and run the gamut of emotions from shock, to grief, to disgust, to sadness. . .to hope.

Looking at the remains of the place where two people had lost their lives just hours ago, he felt fresh guilt. Hope seemed wrong. So did concern over his own future, but he couldn't seem to help that, either. He would be in charge of the company, at least until wills were read and questions answered. The crew would have questions,

23

too, likely first thing this morning. They most certainly would have heard about the boss. News like that traveled fast. For all Cass knew, some of them had been at the scene last night. He'd been too worried about Ma and Sadie to notice.

Ma and Sadie. He thought back to the last fight he'd had with Ma in the kitchen that was little more than a pile of rubble now. He'd been trying to talk her into leaving Goldie's employ, whether Sadie would or not. She refused.

"If I'm here," she'd said, "maybe I can keep her safe." Tears had sprung to her eyes. "I didn't keep you safe. I have to try with Sadie."

Cass touched her arm. "There's plenty of guilt over the past on both of us, Ma. I'm just glad I finally found you both."

Ma had smiled and swiped at her tears. "I'm very proud of you. Don't ever forget that." And then she'd given him all kinds of directives about how and when to visit her. Always by the back door, never in the day. If he saw them on the street, he must never show that he knew them. "You've the beginnings of a fine life here in Lincoln," Ma had said. "Why, who knows but what one day you'll be asked to be a deacon at that church you're attending. I won't have you risking your reputation, and I won't listen to any arguments. You will do this my way, or I won't see you at all."

And so it had been. Ma in the back at Goldie's, cooking and mending. Sadie upstairs as Simone LaBelle. And Cass, holding on to his faith, working hard for Sterling Sutton, saving every penny, investing with the boss's help, hoping to lure Sadie away from the life she'd taken on after Cass had run away from home and she and Ma had faced hard times.

His culpability in it all haunted him. He'd lost track of them after running off, and that was entirely his fault. He hadn't written home. Not once. He was too afraid of being found out and hauled back to more abuse at the hands of his stepfather.

He'd told the Union Army he was eighteen and gotten away with it, thanks to his height and the years of hard labor that had roughened his large hands. Then, just weeks after he left, his stepfather had died at the hands of Quantrill's raiders. Ma took Sadie and moved to Kansas City, and when Cass came home, no one knew where they'd gone.

Fate brought them together again in Nebraska. At least that's what he'd called it at first. Now he knew God had a hand in it.

He glanced toward the Russian Bottoms and thought about Ludwig Meyer's "little house," and the way the man looked at Sadie. What did it mean?

A train whistle broke the quiet. Cass started. Shoving his hands in his pockets, he headed on into the warehouse district, to the sprawling combination office-warehouse-lumberyard that belonged to Sterling Sutton. He tried to pray while he walked. He asked comfort for the Sutton women. He prayed about the girl who'd died in the fire and asked God to give Pastor Taylor and Reverend Burnham wisdom, for they would both likely be called on today to visit the boss's house. Miss Lydia Sutton attended St. John's, where she was so beloved that everyone, including Cass, called her *Aunt Lydia.* The rest of the Suttons were at First Church with Reverend Burnham. As he finished his prayer, Cass asked for help to do a good job for Mrs. Sutton. Starting right now.

Half-a-dozen men were already waiting outside the office, smoking and talking. At first sight of Cass, they squelched their cigars and began asking questions. He answered what he could as he unlocked the door. Yes, the boss was dead. No, he didn't know what would happen to the company—whether Mrs. Sutton would keep it or sell it.

"Does she even own it?" one of the men asked. "Did he have a will?"

"I have no idea, but until someone with the authority to do it tells us to stop, we'll keep working." He led the way through the front office and toward the back lot, pausing to grab the day's work order off the nail by the door. Once in the lumberyard, he waited for the men to gather around again, calling out who would hitch up the teams while the others loaded materials.

25

The assignments given, Cass turned to go, but one of the men asked, "That's an awful big place we're building. You think she'll move into it all by herself? Just her and those two old ladies?"

It was a fair question. Cass had already wondered about that himself. The new Sutton mansion was the talk of Lincoln—not all of it admiring. The boss had bragged that it would be one of the finest houses west of the Missouri. Cass had thought he might be exaggerating—until he saw the plans. What would a new widow and two maiden aunts do with all those rooms?

"As I said before, all I know is that we have work to do, and we'll go about doing it until someone in authority tells us to stop or we run out of materials."

Jessup folded his arms across his broad chest. "No disrespect intended, but if I'm to be out of a job in the near future, I'd like to know so I can be looking for something else. I've a family to feed."

A chorus of new questions rose in the wake of Jessup's comment. Cass hesitated only a moment before inspiration struck. He held up his hand for quiet. "I'll tell you what. You men load the wagons and head out to the job site just like any other day, and I'll check in with the boss's banker." He nodded at Jessup. "Think you can keep things going out there for an entire morning without me looking over your shoulder?"

"Reckon I can," Jessup said, then grinned. "Although if I'm to be foreman, I'll be needing a raise."

The others laughed and offered themselves to take over if there was a raise in the works.

If felt strange to be joking. Cass nodded at the waiting wagons. "Just get to work. Anything comes up, take it to Jessup. I don't imagine they'll tell me much over at First Nebraska, but maybe I can at least find out if there's any problem making payroll in light of last night. Soon as I know anything, you'll know. Is that fair?"

Four men headed for the long, low shelter at the back of the lot, intent on getting the draft horses hitched up, while others loaded lumber and tools.

Cass had just stepped back into the office when Christopher Finney, the office clerk, arrived for work. "It's terrible," he said. "Just terrible." He hung his hat by the door and made his way to the massive desk where he spent most of every day, handling the business books, writing letters, keeping up with inventory, placing orders, and generally keeping Sutton Builders running. Cass didn't think the lanky father of five was really aware of how important he was to the operation.

Cass nodded. "I'm going to have a talk with Mr. Duncan over at First Nebraska. The men are worried about payroll."

"This company is beyond solvent," Finney snapped. "Mr. Sutton was an excellent businessman. An excellent man. No matter what people may be saying."

Already? Cass had heard the fire chief's interpretation of events with his own ears last night. Hastings had wasted no time praising Sutton's bravery at charging into a burning building and trying to save lives. He'd said it more than once. With conviction. Perhaps that was the problem. Too much conviction.

His meandering thoughts came to an abrupt halt when Finney cleared his throat pointedly and raised his voice.

"I *said*," he repeated, "Mr. Sutton doesn't deserve to be the brunt of such outrageous commentary." He waxed on about the "spurious remarks" and "knowing looks" he'd endured on his way to work. "I wish we could do something to squelch it. What if Mrs. Sutton were to hear?" Finney reached for a pile of correspondence on his desk. "And what am I to do about all this? Most of these are inquiries about building projects."

"Put them in order while I talk to the bank," Cass said. "Most urgent first. We'll come up with a plan when I get back."

"What constitutes urgency?"

Cass thought for a moment. "Highest potential for profit."

Finney nodded. When Cass opened the door, he called after him. "Do you think we should hang a mourning wreath?"

Cass shrugged. "I suppose. But I've no idea where to—"

"I'll do it when I go to lunch." Finney paused. "And armbands. We should wear armbands."

"Good thinking. Get enough for all the men. We'll plan on walking together behind the hearse out to Wyuka."

"An honor guard," Finney said, nodding his approval.

"I expect that'll be taken care of by one of his lodges. But we can still walk together and show our respect."

Finney said he'd take care of everything. Cass thanked him and headed off to First Nebraska, hoping that bank president George Duncan would give him the reassurance the men needed to keep them working. Hoping that Mrs. Sutton's personal disaster wouldn't mean disaster for the crew building her mansion. And wondering how she was coping with the news. Hopefully, she would find comfort in the heroic version of events.

Hopefully, she would never know the truth.

—⁓—

Cass stepped into the bank president's office, hat in hand, surprised when Mr. Duncan stood up to greet him and then suggested they conduct their business over breakfast at the Commercial Hotel. It wasn't the kind of greeting Cass expected, and instead of making him feel relaxed, it made him wary. Duncan's conversation as the two walked to the hotel didn't help. By the time he and Cass were seated at a table in a remote corner of the dining room, Cass felt like he was on the witness stand in a trial.

"Sterling was impressed with you" had been followed by seemingly innocent questions, but Cass couldn't shake the impression that Duncan was checking what he heard today against what the boss might have said at another time. Duncan even brought up the war. "Sterling said you were in the thick of it. I was surprised. You don't seem nearly old enough to have served."

The tone was affable, but the unspoken question set Cass's nerves on edge. Why was a man who hadn't so much as bothered to talk to him when the boss brought him out to the job site suddenly so interested in Cass Gregory? While the waiter poured coffee, Cass pondered what to say about his war service. He didn't want to admit to running away from home and lying. Not to a man who would probably wield a significant amount of power over the company, at least until the estate was settled.

"I wasn't old enough," he admitted. "But I've always been big for my age, and I grew up fast. I was working long days on the farm by the time I was ten. I've always acted older than my age."

"Which is?"

"I'm thirty-four." *Not that it's any of your business.*

Duncan frowned. "It's a pity you have so little schooling."

Was the man going down a mental list? *War record.* Pass. *Education.* Fail. Cass shrugged. "My stepfather thought school a luxury for the rich. He didn't see a need for anything beyond the basics."

Duncan's bushy eyebrows rose with surprise. "And you haven't wished for more?"

"I have," Cass said, "and I've found ways to get it over the years. Lincoln has a good library, and I've attended more than my share of lectures and lyceums." He paused. "What I do suits me. There's great satisfaction in being able to say, 'I built that.'"

The waiter came to take their order. Cass asked for a stack of flapjacks and a refill on the coffee. Duncan wanted poached eggs and dry toast. Cass wondered if the man had a nervous stomach—and if that was the case, what was making him nervous.

After Duncan had asked a few more pointed questions, including if Cass had family, Cass said, "I don't mean to be rude, but I wasn't expecting to be interviewed this morning. I came on behalf of the crew. We just need to know if payroll will be on schedule—or if there's to be a delay while lawyers divide the spoils." He leaned forward a bit to emphasize his point. "They're good men, and the boss always did right by them. I'd appreciate your letting me know if you think the company's in danger of folding—or if the house isn't going to be finished. The men deserve fair warning."

Duncan made a show of spreading his napkin on his lap while

the waiter settled their food before them. Once the waiter was out of earshot, he said, "Surely Mr. Finney knows that the company can make payroll."

"Mr. Finney doesn't sign the checks."

Duncan poked at one of his eggs with a fork and muttered, "I said soft poached." With a sigh of displeasure, he laid his fork down. "I can sign the bank drafts. In fact, I am mandated to act on Sterling's behalf in the matter of day-to-day business, should the unforeseen occur. Which it has. That is why I thought it might be good for you and me to become better acquainted."

So, Cass thought, *this doesn't just* feel *like an interview. It* is *an interview. Duncan's in charge now.*

Cass thought of Mrs. Sutton. Did a woman have property rights in Nebraska? He hoped so. He might not know her well, but he associated her name with elegance and style. And he'd never felt like she was looking down her nose at him. He hoped the boss had provided for his wife. Duncan cleared his throat. Loudly. Cass started and looked across the table at him.

"Am I boring you, Mr. Gregory?"

"No, sir. I was just—" Cass took a gulp of coffee and forced his attention back to the conversation at hand.

"I was talking about the house," Duncan said. "Of course people's foremost concern when they hear of last night's tragedy will be for Juliana and Sterling's aunts." He set his fork down and, picking up a knife, cut his toast in half. "That is as it should be. But people being what they are, their *second* thought will be of what's to happen to the business—and that house. Everyone knows a ship without a captain is destined to wander off course."

Cass frowned. *He doesn't think I'm up to the task without the boss to oversee things.* "I realize there's no reason you would know my professional qualifications, but finishing that house on schedule won't be a problem. If you need references, I can get them. I worked for Mr. Eads on the bridge at St. Louis and Mr. Wilson on the one connecting Council Bluffs and Omaha before Mr. Sutton hired me."

He sat back. "I can handle building a house."

Duncan took a bite of toast and washed it down with coffee. "You misunderstand me. Your qualifications are not in question." He set the piece of toast down and leaned back in his chair. "I shall get to the point. Mrs. Duncan is on more than one board with Mrs. Sutton. It has been her impression all along that the mansion was Sterling's dream—not his wife's. In fact, Mrs. Duncan has heard Juliana refer to the house as 'that monstrosity.'"

He cleared his throat. "Only a handful of people in Lincoln have the means to sustain the opulence represented by that new house." He paused. "Slowing things down a bit would keep the price down so that, when Juliana decides to sell it—which I fully expect she will—a buyer can be found quickly."

Cass frowned. "Who'd want an unfinished house?"

Duncan looked out the window for a moment. Finally, he said, "Mrs. Duncan relishes the idea of a home on the outskirts of the city." He sat back. "And the property boasts mature trees—a rare thing in our part of the country. However, not all of my assets are as liquid as I would like. I need a little time. A few weeks. Perhaps two months."

Cass's mind raced. Duncan wanted him to delay Mrs. Sutton's house to give him time to gather enough money to buy it—at a reduced rate because it wouldn't be finished. "But it won't be finished until late November, anyway."

Duncan pressed the point. "Every bit of progress adds to the value." He shrugged. "I recall Sterling talking about imported hardwoods for the upstairs bedrooms. 'A showcase of exotica,' he once said. And marble for the entryway floor. Once those things are installed—" He broke off. Cleared his throat. "See it as an opportunity. A new property owner would likely offer a bonus to the foreman who showed the right amount of enthusiasm for realizing his vision."

Cass took a renewed interest in breakfast, washing down a mouthful of flapjacks with coffee while he tried to think things through. What a snake, offering a bribe and coloring it as concern for Mrs. Sutton and opportunity for Cass. He forced a smile. "I expect Mrs. Sutton will be grateful to hear of your interest in the property and to know that she has options." Duncan's expression soured. "Of course you'll want to give her the news yourself, you being a trusted friend and all. In the meantime, the best way I know to prove myself worthy of the boss's trust is to keep things on schedule. Until I hear from Mrs. Sutton."

"She never wanted that house," Duncan snapped. "Mrs. Duncan is certain of it. And the truth is, Juliana could give *both* her houses away and hardly notice the loss—beyond the need to move. No one is proposing anything that will harm her financially. She has just become a very wealthy woman."

Cass wiped his mouth with his napkin and laid it alongside his plate. "Well, then. That answers the question for my crew—which is why I wanted to talk to you this morning. There won't be a problem making payroll. They'll be really glad to hear it. So am I. We all need the work."

Duncan snatched his napkin off his lap and plopped it atop his plate. "Your loyalty is admirable." His tone made *admirable* sound more like a curse than a compliment.

Cass ignored the tone. "Thank you." Duncan rose and hurried off—without shaking hands. Cass finished his flapjacks. His appetite had returned. Apparently, loyalty agreed with him.

CHAPTER 4

Miserable comforters are ye all.
JOB 16:2

J uliana didn't wait for Reverend Burnham to make his way up the path from the drive. Instead, she followed Marshal Hastings out the front door and onto the porch to greet him, even more dismayed when she saw that he'd brought his wife along. She'd never really cared for the Burnhams, but Sterling had been adamant: *"Where a man goes to church is just as important as where he banks. All the right people fill the pews of that church every Sunday morning, and we will be among them."*

At sight of Juliana standing on the porch, Mrs. Burnham launched herself up the gravel path ahead of her husband and, once on the porch, engulfed Juliana in a hug that nearly squeezed every bit of air out of her lungs.

"You poor, poor dear," Mrs. Burnham clucked, then turned her attention to Lydia and Theodora lingering just inside the open front door. "You poor dears." She snapped at her husband to "take Mrs. Sutton's arm" and led the way inside.

Juliana and Reverend Burnham followed, just in time to see Mrs. Burnham hesitate at the door to the formal parlor.

"We'll be in the library," Aunt Lydia said. "We've been using the parlor to finish our fund-raising quilt in time for the bazaar in June."

33

"Bazaar?"

"St. John's is hosting one to benefit the Society of the Home for the Friendless."

"Oh, yes." Mrs. Burnham remained in the doorway to the parlor, peering into the room. "You must let me invite my circle to join you one day. They'd love to help." She sighed. "What an exquisite room."

"Francis!" The reverend's tone was firm. Almost scolding. When Mrs. Burnham whirled about, he handed her his hat and gloves. She placed them on the hall tree and then removed her own mantle, bonnet, and gloves.

Juliana watched with dismay. Were they planning a long visit? Anger could only fuel a person for so long. She was beginning to feel weary. She led the way into the library. This time, she sat down right away. When she shivered, Lydia pulled the paisley scarf off the Steinway in the corner and draped it about her shoulders.

The aunts exchanged glances. "I believe tea is in order," Aunt Lydia said. "If you'll excuse me, Alfred and Martha have Mondays off. I'll just be a few moments."

"You must let me help," Mrs. Burnham said and followed Aunt Lydia out of the room.

Reverend Burnham selected the most substantial chair in the room. As he lowered his bulk into it, the chair creaked. He cleared his throat and opened his Bible, into which he had inserted a few sheets of blank paper. Lifting the sheets of paper away, he said, "Before we address the grievous but necessary details, I should like to offer a few words of comfort."

Juliana didn't particularly want to be comforted at the moment. She did, however, have a strong urge to march upstairs and empty the rest of Sterling's drawers. Into the pit behind the carriage house where Alfred burned the household trash. She said nothing.

Aunt Theodora thanked the reverend for his thoughtfulness.

He waited a moment, obviously hoping that the other ladies would return from the kitchen, but when they did not, he cleared his throat and began to recite the Twenty-third Psalm. After reaching the end of the psalm, he continued on to other less familiar—at least to Juliana—scriptures until, at last, he concluded with, " 'The Lord gave, and the Lord hath taken away; blessed be the name of the Lord.' "

He closed his Bible and, balancing it on one knee, put the blank sheets of paper atop it. "It is my hope that you will find comfort in your faith and in the knowledge that your loved one is with God. Now. Shall we designate Thursday morning for the service?"

The abrupt segue caught Juliana off guard. Aunt Theodora was looking down at her hands, a slight frown on her face, her left thumb making small circles on the surface of the large garnet set into a ring Sterling had given her years ago.

Did Nell Parker have a garnet ring? A locket?

The other ladies finally returned with the tea tray. While Aunt Lydia poured tea, Mrs. Burnham popped one of the pastries Aunt Lydia had put on a small plate into her mouth. After eyeing the available chairs doubtfully, she pulled out the piano bench and sat down. When she leaned in to take tea, a crumb that had dropped on her bosom fell to the floor.

"We are simply devastated by your loss," she said. "It's always been a joy to see such a handsome couple occupying the same pew every Sabbath." She gazed over at Juliana. "Herbert and I were just saying last month how fortunate we are to have a future governor as a member of our congregation." She sighed. "*Governor* Sutton. A bright star has been extinguished."

While Mrs. Burnham waxed poetic, Juliana's mind wandered. She ran her finger along the rim of her teacup, thinking back to the day all those years ago when Mama opened the barrel of dishes Papa had ordered from England to celebrate their fortieth wedding anniversary. Somewhere in his professorial mind, Papa had remembered Mama admiring Spode's "Greek" in a store window, when it was actually Staffordshire's "Palestine" Mama loved so. Papa was mortified when he realized his mistake, but Mama laughed, and for the rest of their married lives, Mama and Papa enjoyed "afternoon tea with the Greeks."

Why did remembering how much her parents had enjoyed afternoon tea make her want to cry?

Silence called Juliana back to the present. Everyone was staring at her, clearly waiting for her to say something. She couldn't think what.

Aunt Lydia spoke up. "The reverend has asked if Thursday morning would be all right for the service, dear."

Mrs. Burnham chimed in. "And the Ladies' Aid will serve a nice lunch at the church after the graveside service." Her eyes wandered toward the formal parlor again. "Unless you'd prefer to have luncheon here."

A nice lunch. Juliana blinked. *Nice.* What an odd thing to say. "I don't. . .know." She looked to the aunts. "We haven't had a chance to talk about it."

Reverend Burnham cleared his throat. "Of course. We do understand. The entire city has had a shock." He tapped the still-blank paper on his knee with the pencil. "The difficulty is that there's to be a conference at First Church the latter part of the week. The session planned it more than a year ago, and the first gathering is to be Thursday afternoon. So you see, if your service could be Thursday morning. . ."

Mrs. Burnham chimed in. "What Herbert means to say is that of *course* our parishioners come first. But Thursday morning would be best for all concerned. If you don't mind."

Aunt Theodora spoke up. "We mind very much."

The reverend and his wife looked her way with surprise.

"We mind being hurried to decide something because it is convenient for you." Her voice wavered. "We cannot possibly be expected to answer such questions barely an hour after we've learned that our dear boy is—" Her voice wavered. She turned to her sister. Shook her head.

"It is most unfortunate," the reverend said.

Juliana wondered what the man meant. Unfortunate? Was he referring to Sterling's death or the fact that his personal schedule was being inconvenienced? She glanced at Mrs. Burnham and noticed two things. There was another bit of tea cake on her expansive bosom. And she was discreetly checking for the maker's mark on the bottom of her saucer.

Anger flared again. At Reverend Burnham for caring more about his schedule than his parishioners. At Sterling for caring more that they attend "the right church" than that their souls be fed. At Mrs. Burnham for behaving like she was on a social call. At herself. At life. "I am afraid," she said, as she shrugged out of the shawl, "that you are going to have to excuse me." She held her hand up to stay Aunt Lydia, who was already coming to her side. She paused in the doorway and, turning around, said to Mrs. Burnham, "Spode. 'Greek'."

And she fled the room.

Tears began to flow as Juliana ascended the stairs. She walked past her own bedroom door to stand at the doorway and look north. How she'd hated the prairie when they first moved here for Papa to be professor of classics at the fledgling University of Nebraska. For weeks after their arrival, Juliana had longed for the wooded vistas of home and the splendor of Lake Michigan. She'd been miserable. And then she met Sterling Sutton at a literary society meeting.

Mama had liked him right away and invited him to supper. After an evening spent learning how Sterling's original plan to make a fortune in the salt business wasn't panning out and how he planned to make up for it, Papa had liked him, too. "That's a young man who will make something of himself," he'd said.

And Sterling did, working dawn to dusk, investing every dime he made, buying and building and selling and buying again, even as he swept Juliana up in a whirlwind of romance that left her breathless.

Breathless. She felt that way again. Only this time, it wasn't passion making her catch her breath. Turning her back on the prairie, she went into the bedroom to retrieve a clean handkerchief, then went back out to the upstairs sitting area and sank into one of the chairs. As tears flowed, she tried to remember just when their trouble had started.

They'd grown apart. Never fighting, never obviously unhappy, yet—she hadn't been able to give him children. That had to be the reason. Her failure had driven him away. But if that was the reason, why the other night? She thought of the locket. Had guilt fueled his passion?

She leaned her head back and closed her eyes. She would never know.

Voices sounded below. The Burnhams were leaving. Finally. Juliana sat listening to their murmured platitudes. Mrs. Burnham telling Aunt Theodora to be certain to let her know if there was anything the Ladies' Aid could do. Reverend Burnham expressing a desire to "make everything work out for all concerned." The door closing. The carriage leaving. The silence descending.

Juliana rose and went to the banister, calling softly, "I'm going to lie down for just a little while."

"Take all the time you need, dear," Aunt Lydia said.

Aunt Theodora agreed. "It will do us all good to have a little rest. We'll talk later."

Stifling a sob, Juliana headed into the bedroom. She closed the door behind her and leaned against it, her eyes closed, more tears streaming down her cheeks. Bombarded by memory, heartbroken by doubt, haunted by the photograph in the locket, she slid to the floor. At some point she crept into bed, where she could muffle her wails with a pillow. Sterling's pillow, scented by the pomade he had specially mixed at an old-time apothecary not all that far from Goldie's.

Goldie's. Would it haunt her for the rest of her days?

―✺―

In the dream, fire ate up the ground as it flowed toward the buggy. Juliana lost control of Fancy. Terrified by the scent of the fire, the mare bolted, charging into the boisterous crowd gathered near the building. But this wasn't the usual curious crowd. This group was dancing. Drinking. Celebrating. Cheering the flames.

Then Sterling charged out of the building. But he wasn't alone. Several women followed him, each one dressed in a gown Juliana recognized. The pale green silk she'd worn to the governor's for dinner last fall. The dark blue velvet made for the Christmas ball. The shimmering gold gown she'd worn on her wedding day. And then...the last woman...in a simple calico frock...with a baby in her arms. A boy. Juliana didn't know how she knew that, but she knew. It was a boy.

The scene changed, and she was standing on the front porch here at home. As she watched, Sterling brought the other woman up the path to the house. The front door was flung open from the inside, and Aunts Lydia and Theodora came out, exclaiming over the baby. They all went inside, but when Juliana tried to follow, Sterling closed the door in her face. She began to weep.

I need to wake up. It isn't real.

Slowly, she clawed her way out of the dreamworld and back to consciousness. Her pillow was damp with the tears she'd shed. Then she remembered something new from last night. Something she hadn't consciously thought about.

Last night at the lumberyard, she and Aunt Theodora hadn't even bothered to get down from the buggy. It was obvious no one was there. Juliana had negotiated a tight turn and headed the buggy back the way they'd come. They were just crossing the street when a loud crash from the scene of the fire was followed by a shower of sparks and smoke. When the wind blew the smoke their way, Fancy nearly bolted.

In the struggle to keep control, Juliana had barely caught a glimpse of the fire itself. But she'd recognized Sterling's foreman, his arm about a red-haired girl wearing—something that meant she "worked" at Goldie's.

Juliana opened her eyes and stared up at the ceiling. What was Sterling's most trusted employee doing with his arm around that girl? Did he know of his employer's private life? If so, he must think Juliana a complete fool. The idea that at some point she was going to have to speak to Cass Gregory about the half-finished house filled her with dread. How could she face him, knowing what he must think of her?

That infernal house. She'd never wanted it, but Sterling had insisted. He would run for the governor's seat one day, and the house would make everyone sit up and take notice. Two and a half stories of brick and stone. Ten fireplaces. Half-a-dozen porches and a two-story turret to the right of the front entrance. A ballroom on the top floor. A slate roof and a plan to panel each of the upstairs rooms in hardwood from a different country. What would she do with it now? What of the entire business? What would become of Sutton Builders?

What's to become of us all?

She closed her eyes again and wished for sleep.

CHAPTER 5

Let the wicked fall into their own nets,
whilst that I withal escape.
PSALM 141:10

Juliana woke to the sound of Theodora playing the piano. She lay quietly for a moment, listening to the beautiful music. And then she noticed the minor key and the ponderous tempo, and she remembered. *Sterling.* The sun might be shining, but everything was different. As Theodora played on, the weight of her grief seemed to ascend to the second floor and slide beneath Juliana's bedroom door, wrapping her in a thick cloud of sadness.

Slipping out of bed, she began to dress, all the while listening to—Chopin, she thought. Music meant a lot to Theodora. She played beautifully. So beautifully, in fact, that the ladies on the society committee had once tried to cajole her into playing a benefit concert for the Home for the Friendless.

"Don't be absurd," Aunt Theodora had said. "I shall do nothing of the kind."

"But it's for a good cause," Aunt Lydia had ventured.

Aunt Theodora had glowered at her sister. "There is no cause worthy of a lady being dragged up on stage and displayed as if she were a—commodity."

No one had ever suggested Miss Theodora Sutton's gift be used to raise funds again. Even for a good cause.

41

Juliana had protested when Sterling first ordered the piano. She hadn't known his aunt played at all. She thought it just one more way for Sterling to be conspicuous about his success. But when Juliana first heard the older woman play, when she saw Aunt Theodora's face as she caressed the ebony finish and touched the ivory keys, she realized that the piano wasn't just about showing off. It was about Sterling's love for his elderly aunt. And now, thanks to that, she would have her music as she grieved his death.

Aunt Lydia would find comfort in the worn pages of her Bible and, perhaps, in her church friends. She had visited First Church on occasion, but for reasons Juliana was never quite clear about, Aunt Lydia favored what Sterling called a "less sophisticated" form of worship. He didn't seem to mind, but he hadn't shown any interest in his younger aunt's brand of faith. At times, Juliana had envied Aunt Lydia her church friends. There seemed to be something different about their connection to one another.

So. Aunt Lydia had her faith and her friends, Aunt Theodora had her music, and she—Juliana glanced out the window at the blue sky touching the horizon. She had Tecumseh, the fleet, chestnut saddle horse she doted on to the point of what Sterling called "absurdity." Neither the aunts nor Sterling understood it, but for Juliana, there was something spiritual about her connection with that horse. He could be counted on to do exactly as she wished. Sometimes he seemed to sense her thoughts. And today, streaking off toward the horizon held a special allure. If Mr. Lindermann wasn't expecting them at the funeral parlor, she'd don her riding habit and head out to the barn this instant.

There was something strange about being expected to make plans for a funeral right away. She hadn't really grasped the reality of Sterling's death yet. Still, she was expected to have him buried by Friday.

She looked around the room she'd shared with him for all these years, and once again she longed to go for a ride. Was it possible to outrun grief? Her gaze landed on the dresser drawer where the locket waited. Could a woman leave betrayal behind?

She had just slipped back into her green silk dress when a light knock sounded at the door. Hairbrush in hand, Juliana went to open it to *Martha*? Tears gathered. "But it's your day off."

Martha pulled her into her arms. "And I'm spending it here. I am so sorry Alfred and I weren't here for you. So very sorry. Alfred had an early breakfast with the deacons or we'd have been here when Marshal Hastings rode out. Deacon Hill suggested the men pray for you. That's how we found out." Her voice wavered. "We hurried home, but you were all resting when we got back." She leaned away. Stared into Juliana's eyes. "But I can see you weren't really resting."

Juliana shuddered. "I dreamed of fire." She choked back a sob. "I couldn't seem to cry at first. Now I can't seem to stop."

"There's a psalm that says the Lord stores our tears in a bottle. Whatever else that means, it means tears are important. You let them out." She opened one of the dressing table drawers and handed Juliana a kerchief. Then she reached for the hairbrush in Juliana's hand and guided her to sit down at her dressing table.

"I look frightful."

"You look like a grieving woman." Martha worked quickly to let Juliana's hair down. "I don't know that there's a thing anyone can say to truly comfort you right now. But you remember that Alfred and I will help in any way we can."

Juliana reached up and caught the woman's work-worn hand. She gave it a squeeze and met Martha's gaze in the mirror. "You have already helped," she said. "You came." She closed her eyes as Martha drew the brush through her thick brown hair.

"I saw Miss Lydia down in the kitchen," Martha said as she worked. "She said Marshal Hastings had the Burnhams come out."

Juliana allowed a grunt. "Did she tell you he had the nerve to *tell* us when the funeral should be scheduled so that he isn't inconvenienced?"

Martha paused before adding. "It takes a lot to make Miss Lydia angry."

So. Aunt Lydia was upset, too. Somehow that was a comfort.

Juliana opened her eyes and looked at Martha in the mirror. "Can you imagine? After all the money Sterling has poured into that church." She paused. "I know it's not supposed to be about the money, but—honestly. It seems like they would at least make the effort."

"Did the reverend say he wouldn't?"

"No. But he whined. I *hate* whining. What does he expect us to do?"

"Miss Theodora said you're not having Mr. Sutton brought here at all." Laying the brush down, Martha began the process of braiding Juliana's dark, waist-length hair.

"I suppose she's upset with me about that."

Martha shook her head. "Just surprised. You know Miss Theodora. She does like to abide by the rules."

I've lived by the rules, too. It doesn't seem to have done me much good. "I don't want to hurt her, but—I can't. Not here." Martha looked up, still holding a braid in her hand. Their eyes met. "You know how things were between Sterling and me these past few months." Martha barely moved, but the slight nod was enough.

"There's something I—I need you to see." Juliana got up and retrieved the locket and handed it to Martha. "Open it."

Martha gasped. "Lord, have mercy."

Juliana's eyes burned with still more tears. She sniffed. "I want to protect the aunts, and heaven knows I don't want to cause still more gossip. But a wake in my parlor? No." She reached for another handkerchief. Somehow, she managed to choke out the story of how she'd found the locket. And when.

"Dear child." Martha closed the locket and put it back before returning to braiding Juliana's hair. Finally, she said, "I know it's hard for you to believe right now, but in time you'll be able to remember the good, too." She reached for a hairpin and tucked it into place.

"I—am—so—angry." The words came out in measured bursts.

"Nothing wrong with a little righteous anger. Seems to me you have a right to it."

"You should have seen Francis Burnham looking over this house.

For a moment I thought she might ask for a tour." Juliana shook her head. "I will *not* have people like her using Sterling's death as an excuse to see my home."

Martha nodded. "I know you feel like you're standing in front of a big, yawning hole, just about to fall in. But that's not going to happen. You're going to be fine. You're a strong woman."

Juliana closed her eyes. "I don't feel strong."

"And still, having just learned what you learned, having lost the chance to do a thing about it—you're headed to the funeral parlor to make plans. You are protecting the aunts. You are doing your duty by a man who didn't do his. Lots of women would just call for the doctor and go to bed."

"Last night when I found that locket, I wished I could be the kind of woman who faints in a crisis," Juliana said. "But I'm not."

"That's what I mean. Strong."

"Yet I fled the room earlier today and left Sterling's aunts to deal with the Burnhams."

"To hear Miss Lydia tell it, they were happy to do so."

"Perhaps, but it wasn't really fair."

"Could be they liked you trusting them. Could be that was a comfort to them. Knowing that even though they're *Mr.* Sutton's blood, they have a strong bond with you, too."

Juliana forced a smile. "I can't imagine life without the aunts."

Martha nodded. "That's good. You all need each other right now." She handed Juliana a hand mirror so that she could check her hair.

Juliana waved it away. "I'm sure it's fine." Taking a deep breath, she rose and followed Martha toward the upstairs hall. At the door, she reached for Martha's hand. "Thank you." She glanced back toward Sterling's dresser. "I think it helps, having someone know."

Martha headed on down the back stairs to the kitchen. Juliana lingered on the upstairs landing for a moment, trying to collect her thoughts. Meeting with Mr. Lindermann about the funeral was only the beginning. Beyond deciding about the new house, she would need to speak with Mr. Duncan at the bank. And Mr. Graham, Sterling's attorney. Her throat constricted. Did Sterling have a will? Surely he wouldn't leave her unprotected. Would he?

She thought of the woman and the child in the photograph. *To my P. L.* Whoever it was, would she even know that Sterling was gone? If she wasn't in Lincoln—if she lived somewhere far away—she would think Sterling had abandoned her.

Maybe the two of them weren't all that different.

—∽—

Jenny
Monday, April 16

Footsteps on the porch.

Her eyes flew open. From beneath the pile of blankets, Jenny listened. It wasn't the right day, was it? She thought hard. No. It was Monday. He never came on Monday.

Someone knocked on the door. She wasn't supposed to answer the door when strangers came knocking. Which was fine with her, anyway. It wouldn't be long before they were moving away. They'd have a nice house and a new life where Johnny would be accepted as the son of a rich man. Soon, the loneliness and this farmhouse would be a bad memory. If only she could hold on. She hunkered beneath the blankets and waited for them to leave.

"Jenny. It's George Duncan." He pounded on the door. "Open up. We need to talk."

Maybe this was it. Maybe the plan had come together. And her looking such a mess. "Just a minute. I'll be there in a minute." When she stood up, she felt dizzy. And chilled. She hurried to the bedroom and pulled on a wrapper. No time for anything else. No time to do her hair, either. What would that matter, anyway? It was only George Duncan.

She crossed the hall and checked in on the sleeping baby. Such a beautiful boy. The white-blond hair was beginning to darken. He was going to be a handsome boy. George knocked again. Buttoning her robe, Jenny went to the window and peered out before opening the door.

Mr. Duncan glanced behind him like a robber making sure there were no witnesses. Finally, he stepped inside and pulled the door closed. Jenny backed away from him, frowning. George Duncan had never been particularly nice to her. Oh, he'd been polite. He had to. Sterling would never have put up with anything less. But the manners were exaggerated just enough that Jenny knew what he really thought. Today, he wasn't hiding his dislike for her. His disdain.

She was tired of pretending. Tired of waiting, too. On everything. Johnny was six months old. He'd started to recognize his daddy and smile at him, and it was time Sterling made good on his promises.

"I'm afraid I have bad news."

"What kind of bad news?" She swallowed. If Sterling was going to go back on his promises, he would find out something new about her. She was not going to go away quietly. She'd given him a son. This wasn't just a little fun under a moonlit sky anymore. There was a life at stake. An important one.

Mr. Duncan pointed at the sofa. "You should probably sit down."

Jenny sat. She'd taken another chill. Perspiration broke out on her forehead. She suppressed a cough.

"Don't tell me you're sick."

"Don't you worry about me," Jenny said. "Just tell me what you came to say."

"Sterling's dead."

"Wh–what?" She felt woozy. She couldn't have heard that right.

"You heard me. Sterling's dead."

"But—how? Why?" Fear clawed at her.

"There was a fire. He went in to save—" Mr. Duncan broke off. "That's the official version. The fire was at Goldie's. He didn't make it out."

Jenny blinked. "But Goldie's is a. . .". She wiped her brow with a trembling hand. "No. He would never—" She began to cry. "We were going away. We were going to start a new life together. You know that. He. . .he was going to—" Sobs smothered the words.

Johnny began to wail. The cries carried down the hall. Jenny got up and went to him. Pulled him close and carried him back into the parlor.

Mr. Duncan avoided looking at the baby.

"Wh—what's to happen to us?" She could barely speak. How could Sterling be gone?

"You won't be named in the will, if that's what you're wondering. You need to be thinking about what you're going to do." He frowned. "You might think about contacting your uncle."

"He doesn't care about me. He sent me packing as soon as he found out. If it hadn't been for Sterling, I'd have been out on the street." A cold chill crawled up her spine. She shivered and pulled Johnny closer. He'd fallen back to sleep as soon as he was in her arms. She looked down at the precious round face, the silky eyelashes, the pink cheeks.

"If it hadn't been for Sterling," Mr. Duncan said, "you wouldn't be in this mess."

"He loved me."

"Fine. Have it your way. He loved you. But that's not going to do you any good now, is it?" Duncan took a deep breath. "I'll see what I can do. You think about what you want to do. Where you want to go. I'll make discreet inquiries. I'll get back out here as soon as I can. Do you need supplies?"

Jenny shook her head. She'd been feeling poorly for a few days, but it was nothing to worry about. She'd always been the picture of health. And now she had to be. For Johnny. She stroked the sleeping baby's cheek. "We'll be fine."

"All right, then." Mr. Duncan turned to go. "I guess I should say I'm sorry for your loss. I am sorry for"—he gestured around them—"all this." He looked at the baby. Shook his head. And he was gone.

—∞—

Margaret had just scrambled three eggs and toasted a piece of bread for her lunch when Mr. Meyer stumbled in the back door carrying a stack of boxes so tall it was a wonder he could see to walk.

"Good afternoon," he huffed as he plopped the boxes on the

table. "I hope that you slept well."

"I did," Margaret said, then answered Meyer's unspoken question. "Sadie's still asleep."

Meyer nodded. He laid an open hand atop the stack of boxes. "I have brought things for you both. Dresses. Bonnets. Shoes. And—" He blushed as he tapped the bottom box. "Other things."

Margaret smiled at the man's inability to say the word *unmentionables*.

He motioned to Margaret's plate. "But please. Don't let me interrupt your lunch." He sat down abruptly. "May I speak with you while you eat?" He blushed as he glanced over his shoulder at the room where Sadie lay sleeping.

"Of course. What is it?"

"I wish to ask for Sadie's hand in marriage. And I will also ask Mr. Gregory's permission this evening. I should. Is that correct? It seemed correct, but yet—" He stopped. Reached up to adjust his spectacles. "Please forgive me. I am nervous and ignorant of the custom here. Perhaps this is not the correct way to do this?"

Margaret stared at him. "You truly want to *marry* Sadie." It wasn't so much a question as an amazed statement. It wasn't unheard of for men to blather about such things at Goldie's. But no one ever took them seriously.

Meyer fidgeted. "It is not often that we Germans speak of what we feel," he said. "But ever since that first night—when she was so kind—and ever since— She is so beautiful." He nodded. "Yes. If she will have me, I want to marry." His expression changed. "Do you think she will have me?"

"I don't have any idea." Margaret had given up understanding Sadie a long time ago. It was impossible to read the girl's mind and doubtful she would trust a man enough to marry him. She didn't trust her own brother, even though he'd proven himself over and over in recent years. Margaret swallowed. "It's difficult for Sadie to trust," she said. "Life hasn't been easy."

"For either of you."

Meyer's expression was so kind. Could God be answering her prayers for Sadie after all this time? "You are correct, Mr. Meyer, that in most circles in America, it is the custom that a man asks permission of the father before proposing marriage to his daughter."

Mr. Meyer nodded. "And Mr. Gregory is gone, as is Mr. Nash, Sadie's stepfather. May God rest their souls. Which is why I ask you."

Margaret smiled at him. "Neither my opinion nor her brother's will matter to Sadie."

"That may be true," Mr. Meyer said, "but it matters to me."

Tears sprang to Margaret's eyes. What a generous soul. He treated her as if she were just a mother with a daughter of marriageable age. An honorable woman. She blinked and looked away.

"I've upset you," Meyer said. "I am so sorry."

Margaret shook her head. "You haven't upset me. You've amazed me." She paused. "I haven't been respected in a very long time by anyone other than my son."

Meyer shrugged. "We are all the same in God's eyes, yes?"

"If you really believe that," Margaret said, "you are a rare man."

Meyer blushed. "You haven't answered my question."

"If Sadie will have you," Margaret said, "I will be tempted to believe that God answers prayers—even for people like me."

CHAPTER 6

*Surely every man walketh in a vain shew. . .he heapeth up riches,
and knoweth not who shall gather them.*

PSALM 39:6

Alfred drove the Sutton women to Lincoln in the town coach. All
the way in, Juliana replayed the argument she and Sterling had had
when he ordered it.

"It's too ostentatious," she'd protested.

"It's practical. It will keep my aunts out of the weather. And
Alfred will feel like a king up on the driver's seat."

"You're the one who wants to play at king."

Remembering it made Juliana wince. That argument had gotten
entirely out of hand. She gazed off toward the north, wishing she'd
taken that ride today. It would have done her good to get the fresh
air and to get her blood moving. Would she always feel like she was
wading through mud?

When Aunt Theodora sniffed, Juliana looked over at her. "I'm
seventy years old." She choked out the words. "*I* was supposed to be
next. Not—not the dear boy. It isn't right."

"Of course it isn't right," Aunt Lydia said, and took her sister's
hand. "Death is our enemy. An outrage against those God created in
His image."

"Why couldn't God take me? I've had my time. He should have
taken me and left Sterling." Aunt Theodora shook her head. "What

51

was he *thinking* running into a burning building?" Tears flowed down her cheeks. "And Reverend Burnham." She shook her head. "Was there ever a man so devoid of tact."

Aunt Lydia squeezed her hand. "I am so sorry."

"You?" The older woman glared at her. "What do you have to be sorry for? He's *my* minister." She sighed. "Job's comforters. I suppose each generation has a few."

The coach had just reached the outskirts of Lincoln when Aunt Theodora said crisply, "We must contact your committee as soon as possible to move that quilt."

"That won't be necessary," Juliana said. "Aunt Lydia's friends will be a comfort to her. I have a feeling to us all, if we'll let them. I want them to come and work on the quilt as planned." She paused, almost afraid to say it. "I do *not* want to transform our home into a crepe-draped mausoleum." She'd known Aunt Lydia would approve of the way she wanted to do things, and the woman's expression proved her right.

She spoke up. "I know you don't particularly enjoy needlework, Theodora, but it can be very soothing."

"Soothing? It's drudgery made lighter by the opportunity to gossip. And gossip has no place in a house of mourning."

"We do not gossip," Aunt Lydia said firmly. She nodded at Juliana. "The worse the heartache, the more one needs the company of friends. And when it comes down to it, I've always believed that some of our mourning customs are too severe."

"You didn't think that when Teddy died," Aunt Theodora said. "You wore mourning for a full year. And the two of you were only engaged."

Aunt Lydia had been engaged once? Juliana watched the sisters' exchange with renewed interest.

"Invoking the name of the love of my life will not make me change my mind. When Teddy died, I was little more than a child. I didn't *think* at all. I did what was expected." Aunt Lydia shuddered. "I *despise* crepe. The best tribute I could have paid my Teddy was to celebrate his memory among the living." She turned to look out the coach window. "And that is what I shall do with my quilting friends.

I shall celebrate Sterling's life."

Juliana gazed out the window. Had Sterling been the love of her life? She would have said yes before last night. Even with recent difficulties, she would have said yes. *It doesn't matter. I wasn't the love of his life.* She looked back at Aunt Lydia. There didn't seem to be one bitter bone in that woman's body, even though she'd lost much. Somehow, it gave Juliana hope. Maybe she could get past this and be happy again.

Aunt Theodora glared at her sister. "The older you get, Lydia Johanna Sutton, the less I know you. 'Celebrate Sterling' indeed. It's positively *common*."

Aunt Lydia smiled as if she'd just been complimented. "Think what you will; I already have an idea for a memorial. Would you like to hear it?"

"I cannot imagine anything more delightful." Aunt Theodora's voice dripped with sarcasm.

"We should establish the Sutton Foundation to provide education for the children in the society's care. At last count we were responsible for two dozen. I propose we begin with a day school. Perhaps, in time, we can add evening classes for adults wishing to better themselves." She paused. "And we should announce it at the June bazaar. In memory of Sterling."

Aunt Theodora stared at her in disbelief. "You aren't planning on *attending* the bazaar?" She counted on her fingers. "That's only ten weeks away. Keeping our promise to your committee regarding that quilt is one thing. *They* will come to *us*. But we absolutely cannot be attending *social* events only ten weeks after the funeral."

"It isn't exactly socializing. We'll be announcing something wonderful. In Sterling's memory. I think he'd approve." Aunt Lydia appealed to Juliana, although a bit of doubt sounded in her tone. "Don't you think?"

Juliana nodded. "As far as I'm concerned, it's settled."

Aunt Theodora pursed her lips. "I never thought I would live to see the day that women I have loved and admired would toss good manners and custom to the wind."

Did she just say she loves me? She admires *me?* Juliana glanced at Aunt Lydia, who merely smiled and shrugged. As they descended from the coach just outside the funeral parlor, Aunt Lydia leaned close. "Give her time. She'll come around."

—᠅—

Aunt Lydia's pastor was waiting for them in the reception area at Lindermann's Funeral Parlor. The moment they entered, he smiled warmly at Juliana and said, "I hope you'll forgive my intrusion. I was actually on my way to call at the house when I saw your town coach headed this way." He bowed to the aunts. "I am so sorry for your loss. At times like these, one can be tempted to wonder if the Almighty has taken His eye off things."

Aunt Theodora glowered. "At times like these, one would be well served to refrain from questioning the Almighty, lest He take offense."

Pastor Taylor smiled. "I rest on the promise that 'He remembereth that we are dust.'" Without waiting for a response, he turned to Juliana. Something in the man's kind, gray eyes drew her in. She offered her hand. He took it and repeated, "I am so very sorry."

Juliana swallowed. How could those simple words evoke emotion, when Reverend Burnham's visit had succeeded only in making her angry? Her voice wobbled when she thanked him.

"Mr. Lindermann said he'd be out in a moment." The pastor gestured toward a circle of chairs arranged around a low table adorned with a floral spray. "Perhaps you'd like to be seated while you wait?" As soon as Juliana was settled, he reached into his vest pocket and took out a card, which he offered to her. "In time, you may wish for someone to yell at. If so, please remember that I am at your service. Of course God can handle yelling, too, but I have found that sometimes it helps to have a more visible target."

He shook Aunt Theodora's hand briefly, but when Aunt Lydia reached for him, he held both her aged hands in his and said, "Don't forget, Aunt Lydia. *God knows. God allows. God plans. God permits.* And someday, we will know, too—even as we are known." He released her hands. "I'm praying. For you all."

Just as Pastor Taylor exited by the front door, Mr. Lindermann entered through a door in the back wall. Thinking of what was behind that door, Juliana looked away to concentrate on the flowers and the elegant card on the brass easel at the base of the arrangement. *Provided by R. S. Frey. Mourning wreaths and bereavement our specialty.* It was odd to think of people "specializing" in bereavement. Yet she supposed they did. Reverends and pastors, undertakers and florists. Mr. Lindermann bowed a greeting and took a seat in one of the empty chairs. His next words swept her into a foreign landscape.

"You will of course want memorial cards printed." He had written a preliminary newspaper announcement that he wanted Juliana to approve prior to publication. Had she decided who would read the eulogy? Had she selected pallbearers? Mr. Duncan would expect to be asked, as would Mr. Graham. Which suit would the deceased wear? He had done his best, but they might wish to forgo the window in the casket lid. As to flowers, Frey's would be the best. Mr. Lindermann dared to suggest a large casket spray. It was customary to provide long-stemmed roses at the graveside service so that mourners could file by and offer a gesture. They could meet another time regarding a monument, but there was definitely something stately about an obelisk. Had they selected a lot yet?

Juliana frowned at the word. "Lot?"

Aunt Lydia answered for her. "We'll have Alfred drive us home by way of the cemetery. We'll let you know."

A grave. The man who had owned so much still needed one last bit of land.

What had Pastor Taylor said when he gave her his card? *"In time, you may wish for someone to yell at."* She wanted to yell now. Not at God, but at Sterling. Brave or betrayer, either way he'd left—left her alone to deal with the absurdity of all these questions. With Aunt Theodora's disapproval. With that half-finished monstrosity south of town. And with questions that would never be answered. The unanswered questions were the worst of it.

Mr. Lindermann's voice faded. Memories Juliana had been avoiding all day finally found their way to the forefront. Young Sterling's handsome face, smiling at her through the small crowd that had attended that first literary club debate where she'd defended— something. She couldn't remember the topic. She only remembered being drawn to the tall man with the thick, wavy hair, an air of self-confidence, and strong hands calloused from hard labor. He'd apologized for those calluses the first time he'd caressed her face.

As Mr. Lindermann talked on, Juliana lost the battle to keep doubt and anger at bay. Emotions swirled. Her pulse quickened. Her stomach clenched. Tears threatened. Again. She must not let them come. Not here. Aunt Theodora would be embarrassed. Aunt Lydia would reach out with compassion, and that would surely break the last thread of Juliana's weakening resolve to cope.

When Mr. Lindermann suggested they might wish to follow him into the viewing room to select a casket, Juliana stood up. Mr. Lindermann broke off midsentence and sprang to his feet.

"Please," she said and gestured for him to be seated. She looked over at the aunts. "I'm sorry. I know I've already run away once today, but I can't—" *Not without screaming, anyway.* "I—I need some fresh air." She glanced over at Mr. Lindermann. "Whatever my aunts decide about things will be fine with me." She took a step toward the door.

Mr. Lindermann called after her. "There is one thing you should know before you take your leave. It will affect everything else."

Reluctantly, Juliana turned back around. But she stayed by the door.

"Pastor Taylor asked that I offer St. John's for the service, if it would help you. They won't be impacted by the conference demanding so much of Reverend Burnham's attention this week." Mr. Lindermann smiled. "He didn't tell you himself because he didn't want to seem to be pressing the matter."

Juliana frowned. "I don't understand."

"He wants the funeral," Aunt Theodora snapped. "Although he's been clever enough to couch it in decorum and dignity." She shot a look at her sister. "There is a sizeable honorarium involved in holding a service for a leading citizen. And St. John's is desperately in need of improvements. Anyone can see that just driving by."

"Theodora." Aunt Lydia shook her head sadly.

Mr. Lindermann cleared his throat. "Pastor Taylor assumed that Reverend Burnham would conduct the service. He also said that St. John's would neither expect nor accept remuneration for the use of the facilities, should you decide to have the service there."

Aunt Theodora sniffed. "I don't suppose he'd return a new organ if one were to suddenly show up, though, now would he?"

Aunt Lydia's tone sharpened. "Theodora."

Juliana thought back to Mrs. Burnham discreetly admiring the parlor. And not so discreetly examining the china. She thought back to the way Reverend Burnham kept tapping that infernal piece of paper with his pencil, pressing for a commitment to a service time.

She thought about Pastor Taylor's promise to pray for them. Reverend Burnham's scripture reading had been delivered in the manner of a field marshal firing off orders. Feel this way. Think that. Believe this. Pastor Taylor hadn't quoted one Bible verse at them. He'd offered to let Juliana yell at him.

She needed to think. She turned to go.

Aunt Theodora called after her. "What of the music?"

"Who better to select it than you?"

"Reverend Burnham will want to consult regarding the order of service."

Juliana took a deep breath. "That will have to wait until I speak with Pastor Taylor tomorrow."

"Whatever for?"

"Because I'm going to accept Pastor Taylor's offer to have the funeral at St. John's." She didn't dare look at Aunt Theodora when she said it. "I'll have Alfred wait for you two. I'm going to take a walk. I'll meet you at the dresser's." She exited quickly.

Outside, she put her hand on the coach to steady herself as she looked up to where Alfred sat on the driver's seat. "Please wait here for the aunts. When they're finished inside, they'll want you to bring them to Miss Thornhill's. Then I'd like you to carry a message to Pastor Taylor of St. John's, asking him to call tomorrow. Mid-morning, if he can manage it."

Alfred looked toward O Street. "You sure you're up to walking all that way?"

"I'm sure." She headed off up the street, hoping that she looked more determined than she felt. What a jumble of emotions she was: one moment nearly consumed with anger, the next drowning in hurt and regret. One minute unable to decide which shoes to wear, the next making a monumental decision to leave First Church. For she was. Leaving. Reverend Burnham could have Sterling's funeral. She would do that for Aunt Theodora. But the next time she attended a religious service, it would be with Aunt Lydia. It was unfortunate that Cass Gregory also attended St. John's—Aunt Lydia mentioned him from time to time—but Juliana supposed every church had its hypocrites in the pews. At least there wasn't one in the pulpit at St. John's.

As she walked, she looked in shop windows but had no interest in the merchandise. She nodded at passersby but didn't really look them in the eye. Thankfully, no one imposed themselves on her. She walked, head down, her thoughts swirling. And then. . .she was there, staring at a roped-off, ruined building, trying to grasp the truth of Sterling in this place. She looked at the curved brick archway over the door. The narrow steps. The streaks of soot accenting each of the windows, like painted eyelashes on a broken doll. And again, she wept.

"Mrs. Sutton?"

A deep voice sounded from just over her left shoulder. She turned to see who it was, just as Cass Gregory dismounted from a muscled bay. The minute Gregory's feet touched the earth, he swept his black hat off his head and then, reins in one hand and the hat in the other, he said, "You shouldn't be here." He glanced about them. "How did you get here, anyway?"

"I walked." Juliana nodded toward the east. "From Lindermann's." She took in a deep breath. "We were making. . .arrangements. And suddenly I just. . .couldn't." She looked back at the building. "I meant to walk to the dresser's. My feet brought me here."

A wagon trundled past. When Gregory's horse snorted and skittered away, he grabbed the bridle throatlatch. "Steady, boy." The horse snorted again then settled and snuffled Gregory's shoulder.

"Handsome animal," Juliana said, grateful for the chance to shift attention off herself.

"He's not mean-spirited. Just headstrong."

"I can see that," Juliana said. And she could. Something in the creature's dark eyes. The way he held his head. Now that Mr. Gregory had hold of the throatlatch, the horse had settled. Trusting.

"Allow me to offer my condolences," Gregory said.

Juliana nodded. She thought about seeing him talking to that woman last night. Had he known Nell Parker? She wanted to ask about it. But that would be unthinkable. A lady didn't even acknowledge the existence of. . .*those* females. She looked north, toward O Street. "I should be going. If the aunts get to Miss Thornhill's and I'm not there—"

"I'll walk you." He offered his arm.

Juliana hesitated, rebelling against the idea of accepting Mr. Gregory as a gentleman when, based on his associations, he clearly was not. "That's not necessary. You were on your way somewhere." She took a step back, newly aware of the rope behind her and the pile of rubble behind it.

"A few minutes' delay won't make any difference. I'd already be at the job site, but I needed to speak with Mr. Duncan."

"Is something wrong?" *What a stupid thing to say.* "I meant—besides the obvious."

"No, ma'am. It'll be fine. Although I imagine that sounds like an empty promise at the moment."

Juliana nodded. How strange that the rest of the world simply went on as if nothing had happened. It seemed that creation should at least pause while the world reoriented itself around the empty place Sterling used to occupy. She looked up at Mr. Gregory. For some reason she noticed his eyes. Hazel, flecked with green. Shining with compassion and, perhaps, just a hint of worry. What was wrong with her, that she would notice a man's eyes at a moment like this?

"We'll carry on with the original plan," Gregory said. "You can count on us."

Juliana blinked. The original plan? The original plan was to live happily ever after. To give Sterling children. To grow old together. The original plan was out of reach. Lost forever.

"Mrs. Sutton? May I walk you to Miss Thornhill's?"

Juliana took his arm and let herself be led away. Goldie's was just out of sight when she stopped and looked back. "You were there last night. I saw you." *With one of those women.*

"I heard the fire bell. My rooming house isn't all that far away."

So perhaps he was just being. . .gallant when it came to the redhead. "The fire bell carried all the way to the house. When I came out on the porch and saw the flames, it seemed like it could have been the lumberyard."

"You must have been terrified."

She took a deep breath and barely managed not to say it aloud. *Actually, I think I was disappointed. I thought maybe—if he lost everything—maybe he'd come back to me. Of course I didn't realize. . . . I didn't know I'd lost him to more than the business.*

Later that afternoon, Cass stood in what would, by fall, be the impressive entry hall to the Sutton mansion. He gazed through the doorway as the last of the supply wagons trundled past, headed back into town. Jessup raised a beefy arm in salute. Cass returned the gesture, then turned in a slow circle, imagining polished finials, gleaming marble floors, and crystal chandeliers reflecting candlelight onto the massive dining table that, at this very moment, sat beneath a heavy tarp in the warehouse in town.

"Don't tell my wife," the boss had said, when he sent Cass with Jessup and three other men to hoist the table off the freight car and deliver it to the lumberyard. "I want to surprise her."

Cass went to the arched doorway leading into the dining room. And he worried about Mrs. Sutton. He'd thought of little else since leaving her with "the aunts" at Miss Thornhill's. She'd been calm enough, but a couple of times there'd been an edge to the things she said. Like when she said that she'd seen him at the fire. Had she seen him with Ma and Sadie? He could just imagine the assumptions a woman like Mrs. Sutton would make about that. And if she suspected her husband, what might she think of him, now? The idea made him uncomfortable.

Cass wanted her to trust him. Especially after his meeting with Mr. Duncan this morning. She might need a friend in coming days, and he was in a unique place to help her. At least he thought so. He understood more about the business than anyone else. That might prove fortunate at some point. When it came right down to it, George Duncan reminded him of a vulture circling until the time was right to dive in and savor the spoils of death.

The minute he thought of the analogy, he could almost hear Sadie teasing him. *Aren't you the dramatic one?* Sadie. What would become of her, now?

Climbing down from the entryway—Jessup would begin the steps up to the front door in a couple of days—Cass whistled for Baron. An answering whinny led him to the other side of the stone cottage they'd built first on the site. At the moment, the house served as an office and center of business for the massive undertaking that would result in the biggest house in Lincoln. Someday it would house a groundskeeper. A hobbled Baron was grazing contentedly beneath one of the mature cottonwoods growing near the house. Before long, Cass was headed back toward town and supper with Ma, Sadie, and Ludwig Meyer.

At the far edge of the Sutton property, he pulled Baron up and looked back at the house. The tops of the chimneys glowed red, reflecting the last of the day's sunshine. From this distance, he might be looking at all that was left of a once fine home gone to ruin, or at progress toward the realization of a dream. As he nudged Baron into an easy lope, Cass wondered which version of the site would prove to be true.

CHAPTER 7

Above all things have fervent charity among yourselves:
for charity shall cover the multitude of sins.
1 Peter 4:8

Have I sprouted horns?" Sadie took Cass's hat and placed it on the shelf just inside Mr. Meyer's front door.

Cass shook his head and teased, "Horns wouldn't be as big a change." He inspected the striped calico skirt, the white waist with the brooch pinned in place at the high neckline.

"You could be a schoolmarm."

Sadie reached up to smooth her hair. "There's no need to be unkind." She laughed.

Cass protested. "It's a good change. You look *sweet.*"

"Did you hear what he just said?" Sadie called to Ma, who was standing at the stove dipping a ladle into the juices surrounding a roasted bird and pouring them over the browned carcass.

"I did." Ma nodded and looked up with a smile. "And I agree."

Sadie rolled her eyes. "Sweet? I am not sweet." She nudged Cass's arm. "I'm. . .saucy." She looked down at her skirt and gave a dramatic sigh. "It's really a shame that Ludwig has such horrific taste. I detest this shade of green. But I couldn't exactly do my own shopping today dressed in a blue silk dressing gown." She motioned toward the table. "I hope you don't mind sitting in a rocker. There's only two proper

62

chairs. Ludwig sits on that stool."

"And where is Ludwig?"

"Here." Meyer stepped in the back door. "We were out of coffee."

Sadie leaned close and murmured, "Be nice. He's nervous about officially meeting you."

Meyer handed Ma a small paper bag and then stood, hat in hand, gazing at Sadie with an expression that made Cass feel like an intruder. Instead of settling in the rocker, he offered to grind the coffee beans and joined Ma near the stove. In moments, the four of them were seated around Meyer's small table, exclaiming over the delicious meal.

"You were right," Meyer said to Sadie as he took a bite of a biscuit. "The best I've ever eaten."

"And you," Sadie said, leaning toward Cass, "got your wish. I'm not going back to Goldie's." She grinned. "Put your eyes back in your head, Brother." She nodded at Meyer. "Tell him."

Meyer gulped. "I've finally saved enough to open my own store. I have asked Sadie and Mrs. Nash to join me in that endeavor."

Cass glanced at Ma. He'd been dreaming of them all living together as a family again for a long time. It didn't look like that was going to happen.

"I haven't given him my answer," Ma said, smiling at Mr. Meyer. "But I very much appreciate being included in the invitation."

Meyer glanced at Sadie. "Sadie says that I should ask if Sutton Builders might take on the building."

"New construction?"

Meyer nodded. "In Roca, to the south of Lincoln. It's a growing place, thanks to the—"

"Stone quarries," Cass said. "I know."

"Of course." Meyer nodded. "You would."

Sadie spoke up. "Ma said we should look for work. As it happens, work came looking for us. In Ludwig's store."

Meyer cleared his throat. "There is something else, Mr. Gregory."

His face reddened. "I mean to marry your sister if she will have me." He gazed across the table at her.

"But we aren't rushing into it," Sadie said quickly.

From the look on Meyer's face, Cass gathered that waiting was Sadie's idea. She seemed to realize she'd hurt him. "Although Ludwig has many fine qualities." She smiled at him. "He's kind."

Meyer shrugged. "And too shy."

"Hardworking," Sadie countered.

"Only a storekeeper and likely never to be more. Not handsome. Not rich."

"Thank God." When Meyer looked confused, Sadie reached across the table and took his hand. "I've known plenty of handsome, rich men, Ludwig. None of them ever actually saw *me*. You do. You know I'm afraid of—"

"Spiders."

"And my favorite color is—"

"Red."

"And I grew up in—"

"Kansas."

"And my mother is—"

"The kind of woman you hope to be."

Ma looked at Sadie, who nodded. "Exactly."

Meyer looked at Cass. "I know all of these things about her, but still she will not marry me. Yet."

Sadie changed the subject. "So what do you say, Brother? Will you build Meyer's Mercantile? Ludwig wants a stone building. I told him you're an expert."

Cass sat back. "I've supervised jobs, but I'm no stonemason, and the job I'm working on will take the rest of the summer and into the fall."

"Mrs. Sutton's mansion," Meyer said.

"You know about it."

"All of Lincoln knows about it." Meyer shook his head. "Today is a sad day for her." He looked up at Cass. "And for you. And for poor Nell Parker's friends."

Sadie got up—Cass thought abruptly—and refilled everyone's coffee cups.

"Was she a friend?" Cass asked.

Sadie shrugged.

Ma spoke up. "Nell was—difficult. Unhappy."

"Let us hope she has found peace," Meyer said.

Sadie sat back down. "You should take Ludwig's job, Cass. If you get booted when the smoke clears—no pun intended—you'll still have a job. It never hurts to have a backup plan."

She didn't want to talk about the fire. So be it. Cass nodded. "It couldn't hurt." He looked at Meyer. "I'll tell you what. We've got a great stonemason. I could mention your job to him. See if he's interested."

"I would appreciate that."

Sadie grinned. "Meyer's Mercantile is on its way." She leaned over and kissed Meyer's cheek before serving up another helping of potatoes. "But you are going to have to agree to let me order the ready-to-wear." She glanced over at Cass. "My brother thinks I look like a sweet schoolmarm. That is *not* acceptable."

—⁌—

Infernal rooster. Juliana had just managed to fall into a deep sleep when Martha's prized rooster announced dawn. With a weary groan, she grabbed a pillow and put it over her head, willing herself to sleep more. But the rooster crowed again. And again. So Juliana threw the pillow off and lay, counting the roses on the bedroom wallpaper and trying to stave off conscious thought. It didn't work.

Sliding out of bed, she reached for her wrapper and headed into the hall. Intending to go out onto the balcony for a moment, she paused just outside, savoring the aromas of fresh coffee and warm bread wafting up from the kitchen. She was hungry. Instead of heading out onto the balcony, she padded downstairs.

Martha was setting up a breakfast tray, obviously intending to take it upstairs. She glanced up. "Thought I'd offer breakfast in bed to anyone who wanted it." She frowned. "Guess I don't have to ask if you slept well."

"Do I look that bad?" Juliana sat down at the kitchen table.

Martha poured coffee and set it before her, then put a hand on her shoulder. "When Alfred drives into town today, you should have him stop at Dr. Gilbert's for something to help you sleep."

"Not necessary," Juliana said. "Just kill the rooster." But Martha had raised the current king of the henhouse, and the attempt at levity fell flat. "You know I don't mean that."

Martha hefted the tray and headed for the back stairs. "Lots of fresh air and sunshine out there this morning. If a person was so inclined, they might think it a good morning to take a ride."

"Are you kicking me out of the house?" Juliana reached for the stack of paper they'd left on the table after getting back from Lindermann's yesterday. "I've run off on the aunts twice now. If I do it again, they may not be so understanding."

"Pastor isn't expected until midmorning. There's plenty of time." Martha headed on upstairs. Juliana glanced through the kitchen windows to where Tecumseh was prancing around his small pasture, tossing his head, half rearing, spinning about, reveling in the beautiful spring morning.

Juliana looked down at the paper in her hand. *Pallbearers*. She wrote *George Duncan* and *Harry Graham*. Both men would probably call sometime today. Bankers and lawyers never wasted time circling the wreckage—at least that's what Sterling always said. She filled out the rest of the list with friends from the Odd Fellows and the G.A.R. encampment. She would ask Aunt Theodora to look it over. She could be counted on to know what was what when it came to who might be offended if not included. Juliana set the list aside and reached for the piece of paper Miss Thornhill had given them at the shop yesterday.

RECOMMENDED FOR LADIES
FULL MOURNING
FIRST YEAR

DRESSES
One best dress of bombazine, trimmed entirely with crape
One dress trimmed with rainproof crape

MANTLES & JACKETS
One mantle lined with silk and deeply trimmed with crape
One warmer jacket, trimmed with crape

BONNETS
One bonnet of best silk crape, with long veil
One bonnet of rainproof crape, with crape veil

ACCESSORIES
Twelve collars and cuffs of muslin or lawn, with deep hems
One black, stiff petticoat
Four pair black hose
Two dozen handkerchiefs with black borders:
Twelve cambric for ordinary use
Twelve of finer cambric for better occasions

Mourning was an expensive endeavor. Miss Thornhill thought she might be able to remake the bonnet Juliana had worn when mourning Mama and Papa a few years ago, but with the need for a widow's veil, she'd have to see it to be sure. And the line had changed in recent years. The black petticoat Juliana already owned might not work, either. Alfred was to take everything that needed to be refashioned into town for them later today. But first, Juliana had to collect it all. Thinking about it made her head hurt.

Martha came back downstairs. "The aunts are taking tea up in their sitting room," she said. "You're to come up if you'd like."

"Are they all right?"

Martha nodded. "Just taking it a little slower this morning. Gathering what they need to send to Miss Thornhill. Reminiscing about when Mr. Sutton was a boy."

Juliana took a deep breath. "Last night I thought I heard him coming upstairs. I actually sat up in bed and looked at the door, waiting for him to enter. That's insane."

"From what I know about it, most people experience things like that." Martha ducked into the pantry and returned, dust cloth in hand. "As long as you know it isn't real, you aren't insane. You start having conversations with an empty chair; we'll start to worry."

Juliana laid the notice from Miss Thornhill's aside. She really should go upstairs and sort through the wardrobe. She might even have to check the attic. "What time did you say you're expecting Pastor Taylor?"

"Around ten o'clock. Thought I'd head into the library and freshen things up a bit. Open the windows, let the morning breeze blow through."

Juliana glanced upstairs. "Do you think Aunt Theodora will come down to meet with him? She has to be furious with me over what I've done."

"Don't you worry. Miss Lydia will smooth her ruffled feathers. And furious or not, Miss Theodora would never snub a minister."

Juliana rose to follow Martha up the hall. "I think I'll open the windows in the parlor, too."

The memory of Francis Burnham lingering in the parlor doorway set her teeth on edge. Drawing the drapes, she drew back the inner shutters and raised the windows. Fresh air wafted into the room, rustling the fronds of the potted fern on the plant stand in the corner.

She hadn't paid very much attention to Aunt Lydia's quilt project, other than to pay the requisite fifty cents to put her name on it. Now, she took a minute to look it over, remembering the committee meeting that had taken place right here in the parlor last fall. She'd breezed through on her way to a board meeting in town, but even in that short moment of greeting and wishing them well, she'd envied Aunt Lydia and her quilting friends their enthusiasm for the project and the obvious camaraderie among them as they selected patterns and planned colors so that the colors on the quilt would be balanced.

They'd recruited women to piece sixty quilt blocks. A few weeks later, when they'd gathered up the finished blocks, they met again to decide how to arrange them, laying the finished blocks out on the parlor floor. Home that day with a slight cold, Juliana had lingered only long enough to make certain the women knew they were welcome. She'd kept her opinion to herself, but she thought the potpourri of blocks a hopeless hodgepodge. Now that she took time to look at the finished top in the frame, she realized that Aunt Lydia had an eye for design. She'd set the blocks on point with a narrow stripe as the sashing, and the result was really quite lovely.

Juliana sat down at the quilt. Piecing the individual blocks had only been the beginning of the project. Next came the gathering of signatures, with each person donating fifty cents for signing the quilt. Sterling's name was on it somewhere. So was Juliana's, although not on the same block as his. *How apropos.*

Sterling had offered to gather signatures and tucked a block in his coat pocket one day on his way out the door. When he returned it, he'd charged the signers ten times what the committee had. Lydia had protested when he handed her fifty dollars for the ten signatures, but Sterling just smiled and said it was for a good cause and he'd only had to break one arm to get them to pay up.

President Arthur's signature was on the center block. Aunt Lydia had been thrilled when it arrived in the post one day, a strong signature on a square of muslin, the ink so dark brown it was almost black. Most of the signatures had been applied with a pencil and then embroidered over. But no one was going to embroider over the name

Chester A. Arthur. Aunt Lydia had spent hours piecing a special block with the president's signature in the center of a sunburst.

Juliana leaned down, reading some of the names. *George Duncan. Mrs. G. C. Duncan. Harold Graham. Mrs. H. C. Graham. James W. Dawes.* Sterling really had gone all out to get the governor's signature. And then, *Sterling Sutton.* She traced the letters with her index finger then read more names. *Marvin Lindermann. Pamelia Lindermann.*

Juliana caught her breath. Mr. Lindermann was a widower. Who was Pamelia Lindermann?

She frowned. "Martha."

Martha came to the door.

"The Lindermanns didn't have a daughter, did they?"

"Not that I know of. I believe a niece was here for a while last year, keeping house for Mr. Lindermann."

"But she's not here now."

"I don't think so." Martha came to the door. "Maybe the funeral business bothered her. I recall that Alfred overheard an argument. Mr. Lindermann had asked him to come by to finalize some plans for Deacon Hobart's service last summer. He said the young lady came out of the back room and scurried upstairs without paying him any mind. She was very distraught, but when Alfred expressed concern, Mr. Lindermann said that the matter had been resolved and Miss P—" Martha swallowed. She covered her mouth.

"Miss Pamelia."

Martha nodded. "Yes. Miss Pamelia had decided that she should make her home elsewhere." She closed her eyes. "Oh, missus." She took a step into the parlor, but Juliana waved her away.

"Just—give me a moment. I'll be. . .all right." She sat staring at the name. *Pamelia Lindermann. P. L.* Perhaps she should give the locket upstairs to Mr. Lindermann. Wouldn't that be something?

She looked down at the names on the quilt. Had it really only been moments ago when she'd been tracing Sterling's signature, remembering happy times and longing for another chance? Here it was again. The anger. *Use it.*

Aunt Lydia's workbasket stood beside the quilt. Opening it, she took out the silver sewing scissors. She paused, her hand poised over the quilt. And then she slipped the silver sheath off the blades and began to snip threads. In less than a moment, the name *Pamelia Lindermann* was little more than a shadow on the quilt.

Returning the scissors to Aunt Lydia's workbasket, Juliana plucked the loose threads into the palm of her hand. Opening the front door, she let the spring breeze blow them away. Having heard the front door open, Martha came into the hall. Poor Martha. The look on her face.

"I'll be all right. It's done." Juliana nodded toward the quilt. "If there's a way to get rid of the shadow of that name, I'd appreciate your doing it. You'll see what I mean if you take a look."

And then she went upstairs to change.

—⁓—

"Hello, old man." Juliana reached up to tug on Tecumseh's forelock. The horse nuzzled her arm. "I know. I've neglected you. But I'm here now." She slipped a hackamore over his head and led him out of the small pasture and into the barn. Hitching him to one of the iron rings placed at intervals along the row of stalls, she went to work brushing him down, happy for the diversion, trying to forget the name on the quilt and knowing that she never would.

Glancing at the other horses who'd thrust their heads across their stall doors and were looking her way, Juliana spoke to Tecumseh. "You wouldn't go off with some other woman, now would you?"

The horse looked back at her as if pondering the question. He shook his head.

It was only a game, but when Tecumseh shook his head, tears sprung up. Juliana sniffed. "I know. You never would." She cried through the rest of the process of saddling and bridling, but once she'd mounted, she felt better. And when Tecumseh moved into an easy lope, she forgot everything but the ride.

A few miles away at the entrance to Wyuka Cemetery, she pulled Tecumseh up, gazing toward the place they'd selected for the family

71

plot when Alfred drove them here late yesterday afternoon. The sight of it made her want to tear off across the prairie again; but instead, she put Tecumseh through his paces along the winding lanes of the park-like setting. They practiced flying lead changes and a series of gaits until both horse and rider were breathing hard. Finally, Juliana pulled up to walk. There was a new grave dug in the far back corner, as far from the road as one could get and still be inside the cemetery proper.

I'm not the only one burying someone they loved. She gazed about her at the rows of gravestones. *I'm not the only one. I'm probably not even the only one to bury an unfaithful husband. Or wife. Not the only one to find evidence. Not the only one to be hurt. Not the only one.*

Somehow, the idea gave her comfort. Generations of people had had to do exactly what she did yesterday. Buy a lot. Select a place. Say good-bye. All the way back to Abraham himself, who'd had to buy a place to lay Sarah to rest. *Ashes to ashes, dust to dust.* It was part of life.

She wished that Mama's and Papa's graves where here, but Sterling had paid to have them taken back to the family plot near Chicago. It had cost him dearly, but he hadn't complained. He'd said it was his duty and he was glad to do it. *He did a lot of very nice things for people.*

She didn't want to think about them, though. So she slid out of the saddle and led Tecumseh down to the creek that wound its way through the property. She'd just gathered up the reins to leave when a small procession turned in at the gate. The deceased was being transported in a farm wagon decorated with swags and floral wreaths. The team of horses pulling the wagon wore black fly nets. The wagon driver looked like. . .it was. *Pastor Taylor.*

A second wagon followed the first, this one bearing mourners. This one driven by Cass Gregory. The woman sitting next to him on the wagon seat was obviously the woman from the fire. Even with a hat perched atop her head, the red hair shone like a beacon in the morning sun. Was the older woman the infamous Goldie? This must be Nell Parker's service.

To reach the grave in the far corner, the procession turned away from where Juliana stood watching. Taking up the reins, she strode up the hill toward the caretaker's house just inside the gate, where a carriage block would enable her to mount Tecumseh without help. She'd just done so when the caretaker stuck his head out the door. He expressed his condolences.

Juliana thanked him, then nodded in the direction of the wagons trundling away from them. "I imagine they'd prefer not to have someone meandering about when they're trying to have a service for their friend."

"Friend." The caretaker snorted. "Sorry you had to see that. I told 'em we didn't want it. This is a resting place for respectable people. But the old woman got it done anyway. Went over my head. I told 'em they had to get it done before Friday. At least they listened to that. Can you imagine Pastor Taylor agreeing to this?" He shook his head. "Bet his deacons have a thing or two to say about that when they find out."

All the way home, Juliana pondered the strangeness of a world where Sterling Sutton was honored with ceremony and Nell Parker's friends had to fight for a place to bury her. She wondered if the caretaker was right. Would Pastor Taylor be in trouble for praying over a harlot's grave? She supposed he might be. People had scolded Jesus Christ Himself for being kind to a harlot.

She wished she hadn't remembered that. She didn't want to feel sorry for that woman. Or for Pamelia Lindermann. She didn't have the strength for anything right now but simmering anger. At least at Sterling and his *P. L.* She would leave compassion and forgiveness to Pastor Taylor. It was, after all, a minister's job. Which didn't explain Reverend Burnham, but then who could?

73

CHAPTER 8

*Beareth all things, believeth all things, hopeth all things,
endureth all things. Charity never faileth.*
1 Corinthians 13:7–8

Daily State Democrat
April 15, 1883

Mr. Sterling Sutton, 42, died unexpect-edly in a heroic
effort to save the life of an unfortunate soul caught in
the wicked embrace of a fire that completely destroyed a
building in the western part of the city.

Mr. Sutton was born in Cook County, Illinois, February
17, 1841. He came to Nebraska about thirteen years ago,
intent on getting in on the ground floor of the salt business
once touted as a promising industry of the fledgling state.
Together with his widowed father, Mr. Sutton helped a
friend haul an engine and a pump and several railroad cars
full of lumber for vats to evaporate brine from Nebraska City,
the end of the railroad at that time, to Lincoln. When the
promise of the salt business did not meet with expectations,
Mr. Sutton stayed on and was eventually rewarded by those
habits of self-reliance and industry that made him just such
a man as this country most needs—active, energetic, self-
reliant and of uncompromising integrity.

Perhaps no man in this community has done more

to build our city than Sterling Sutton. The fruits of his labor are to be seen in the numerous buildings which dot our fair city in every direction, enduring monuments of his industry and skill. He has left his "footprints on the sands of time." When the demon of war broke loose, he stood firm and loyal by the old flag, serving with honor as part of Company D, 12th Regiment from Cook County, Illinois.

Mr. Sterling united with the First Church of Lincoln at the age of 30 and was an honored member at the time of his death. He was united in holy matrimony with Miss Juliana Masters in 1873, who mourns his loss along with his aunts, Theodora Humana Sutton and Lydia Johanna Sutton, and a large circle of friends.

The funeral services were held on Thursday afternoon, April 19, the Reverend Mr. Herbert Burnham preaching from Job, the fourteenth chapter. Many were unable to gain admission to the service, which was held at St. John's. A large crowd, among them an honor guard from the various lodges in the city and a second guard consisting of the loyal employees of Sutton Builders, formed a long procession which made its way on foot to Wyuka Cemetery, where Mr. Sutton's earthly remains were laid to rest with all the dignity due a man of his stature in the community. The Reverend James Taylor offered a prayer at the graveside and led the company in a closing hymn, which created a most fitting opportunity for friends to bid the deceased farewell.

As angry as Juliana was in the days that followed Sterling's funeral, she was surprised at how much she missed him. When he was alive, she'd learned to cope with his absences by immersing herself in charity work. She'd filled her days with meetings and, on occasion, a stint at one of the homes throughout the city where the Society for the Friendless housed orphans. She'd served on committees and boards and participated in endless rounds of fund-raising and plans. Keeping busy salved the wound of her troubled marriage. But now that Sterling was truly gone forever, Juliana found that not an hour went by but that she didn't find herself listening for his footsteps, wishing to hear his voice calling hello, longing to hear him breathing next to her in the night.

She didn't expect the sense of loss to be such a threat to her peace of mind, but anger could only sustain a woman for so long. At some point she had to face the notion of permanent loss. There would be no opportunity to find each other again. No confrontation. No accusation. No admission. No chance to reconcile. That inescapable reality deepened Juliana's sense of loss in a way that no one could understand—no one save Martha, who had seen the locket and succeeded in reducing the shadow on the quilt to something only she and Juliana would ever notice.

Sometimes at night, Juliana opened the locket and stared at the faces, wondering how it could be real. One afternoon she walked back and forth, back and forth in the yard, looking for the locket she'd thrown off the upstairs porch. Wherever it had landed, she couldn't find it. The prairie was green and the grass lush.

Tecumseh saved her sanity. She didn't have a black riding habit, but Aunt Theodora didn't make note of it. Apparently, since she knew that Juliana usually ended up at the cemetery, she saw the riding as a wife mourning a beloved husband. Juliana did nothing to dissuade her. In some ways, maybe that's what she was doing. She rode there every day and dismounted and sat, staring at the grave and trying to understand. More than once she walked up to Nell Parker's grave, too. At some point she realized she didn't hate Nell Parker. She felt sorry for her. Whatever circumstances landed a girl in that place, Juliana couldn't imagine. But one thing was certain. If it weren't for men like Sterling Sutton, "fallen women" wouldn't exist. It might not be the kind of reasoning the Ladies' Aid at First Church would approve, but it helped retain Juliana's sanity. As did the words to the hymn Pastor Taylor had had them sing at the graveside:

> *While life's dark maze I tread,*
> *And griefs around me spread,*
> *Be Thou my Guide;*
> *Bid darkness turn to day,*
> *Wipe sorrow's tears away*
> *Blest Savior...*
> *Fear and distrust remove....*

The words were something of a jumble, and Juliana supposed she wasn't thinking of them in the pious way they were intended. Yet they spoke to her. She was treading a dark maze. She did need help to find her way through the darkness. The hymn talked about sorrow's tears being wiped away. She was tired of crying.

—⁂—

Jenny
Friday, April 20

She was so tired of coughing. It just wouldn't let up. Tired of coughing and crying and being afraid. Lonely, too. It hadn't been so bad when she could spend the days cooking and cleaning the house and getting dressed up for Sterling. She sometimes spent the better part of a day just on her hair. She liked to rinse it in the rainwater from the barrel out back. Sterling never failed to say something about her soft, silky hair.

That's over now. Forever. You have to face it and decide what you're going to do.

And she would face it, as soon as she got over this spring ague that kept hounding her. Just when she thought she was over it, she started coughing again. If she didn't feel better soon, she might see if George Duncan would bring her a bottle of remedy. At least for the cough.

More than anything, she worried about Johnny. He seemed so

hungry all the time. But she couldn't imagine discussing such private matters with any man, let alone one like George Duncan.

Maybe she should just hitch up the pony and head into town on her own. If she didn't feel better in a few days, she would. Surely Dr. Gilbert would help her. He might even know about a wet nurse if he thought Johnny needed help.

How much did a doctor charge these days?

—⁂—

Margaret and Sadie stepped into the spring sunshine. Margaret pulled the door closed, and together they set off for Ernie Krapp's saloon.

"I wish you'd just let me write her a note," Sadie said. "She's not gonna be happy to hear what we've got to say." She looked over at Margaret. "You've never been at the other end of Goldie's temper. I have." She shuddered.

"I'm not looking forward to it, either," Margaret said. "But she deserves more than a note, and it's been over a week since the fire."

"I still don't like the idea of sashaying in there in broad daylight and telling her I'm not coming back."

They crossed the street and made their way past half-a-dozen houses, each one small, each one well tended. Daffodils bloomed in a row along the front of one, tulips at another. Margaret paused before the one with the pink tulips in bloom. "Tell me right now if you're going to change your mind. Right now. I mean it."

Sadie rolled her eyes. "Ma. I'm not gonna change my mind. It's just...a big change, is all. I know you've hated every minute of it for—"

"Seven years. Since that day I got well enough to realize what you'd done." Margaret shook her head. "I'll never forgive myself."

"For what? Sticking with me when I was too bullheaded to listen?" Sadie shook her head. "You were sick. We were gonna end up out on the street. I did what had to be done. And then I just kept at it—I don't know why. But I'm finished with it now." Sadie took her mother's hand and smiled. "Who would have thought a bespectacled German would come along and win Simone LaBelle's heart?"

"Has he? Has Mr. Meyer won your heart?"

Sadie didn't answer the question. "I still have trouble believing he wants a future with me."

"Sadie." Margaret chucked her daughter beneath the chin. "Look at me. Ludwig Meyer does not deserve to have his heart broken."

Sadie pulled away and strode on up the street, with Margaret hurrying to keep up. "Don't you think I know that? I've got no plans to break his heart. It's just—this is all so new." She pointed back at the little house. "I don't even know how to *talk* to regular women."

"You know how to talk to me," Margaret said. "I'm as regular as they come."

"You don't count. You're my ma. You have to put up with me and pretend to like it."

Margaret put her arm around her daughter's waist. "I bet you love Roca when you see it."

"What if Roca doesn't love me?"

"The wife of the owner of their new store? The woman who sells them calico and lace? Why wouldn't they like you?"

"Because I'm loud and I say what I think." Sadie took a deep breath. "Don't you dare tell Ludwig or Cass, but the truth is I'm scared. Scared to death I'll say or do something wrong. And people will punish Ludwig for taking up with me. And he'll be sorry he ever met me."

"He isn't taking up with you. He's marrying you."

"What if he changes his mind?"

"I've had two weeks to watch the two of you. Mr. Meyer loves you. Very much. And if you doubt it, explain his moving over to Cass's rooming house to protect your reputation."

Sadie rolled her eyes. "And if that isn't a sign that he's lost his mind, I don't know what is. Next thing I know, he'll be expecting me to go to church with him and Cass." She gave a nervous laugh. "Can you imagine Simone LaBelle at church? Don't say it. The answer is no, but maybe Sadie Gregory could fit in. Someday."

"He's a good man."

Sadie's eyes filled with tears. "I know it. I know he is." She looked away. "And I can't see why he'd settle for the likes of me."

"Do you remember what you said that first day when Cass came to supper? That Mr. Meyer sees *you*?"

Sadie nodded.

"That's the answer. He doesn't see Simone LaBelle when he looks at you. He sees the young woman who will do anything to protect the people she loves. Who makes hot tea for her friends when they're feeling low. Who's always willing to listen. And who has a way of making people smile."

"Don't forget the part about being kind to wounded animals and orphaned children," Sadie muttered. "Might as well spread it thick if we're gonna make me over."

They neared the burned-out building, and Margaret gestured toward the rubble. "That fire destroyed two lives. We can keep it from destroying ours. In fact, we can use it for good. We can claim the new life God's offering us. Just like Ludwig says in his prayer every evening before supper."

Sadie looked at her mother. "You have to know that I'm not real big on the idea of God. Not since—a very long time."

"I know," Margaret said. "I've wondered where He was, too. Ever since Quantrill's raiders did what they did to us. But I love you with all of my battered heart, Sadie. And somewhere in the Good Book it talks about love hoping all things. I guess I'm hoping that you and me and God can all get reacquainted."

Sadie gazed across the road at the saloon. "Well, Lord knows we're going to need some new friends in about ten minutes." She glanced up at the sky. "You listening? This would be a good time to step in, if Ma's right and You do care, after all."

Taking a deep breath, Sadie led the way in search of Goldie.

———

Tuesday morning, nearly a week after Sterling's funeral, Juliana lay in bed, listening to the steady rhythm of rain in the predawn light. When she finally got out of bed and went to the window to look outside, the sodden landscape only darkened her mood. She and the aunts were supposed to meet with Mr. Graham today for the inevitable "reading of the will." Perhaps she could call and postpone it. Aunt Lydia never complained, but Juliana had noticed her massaging her arthritic hands in recent days. Heading out into damp weather would do nothing to ease her aching joints.

Pulling on a dressing gown, she descended to the kitchen, surprised to find the aunts already dressed and seated at the table, toast and tea before them.

"Here you are," Aunt Theodora said. "We were just talking about you."

Oh, no. What have I done now? The past few days had been hard on them all, and Aunt Theodora especially seemed to have an extra portion of vinegar in her attitude.

"We're proud of you," she said.

Rendered speechless, Juliana put her hand on the back of a chair and glanced over at Aunt Lydia, who only smiled. "You. . .are?"

"We are. I am." Aunt Theodora nodded at her sister. "My sister has reminded me that I can be less than accepting when my strong opinions are not validated." She took a deep breath. "I was, of course, disappointed in some of the details of the service, but Lydia is right. My own minister caused the difficulty, and I should not put blame where blame does not lie." She took a sip of tea. "I don't always express myself as clearly as I should," she said. "So I wish to make it clear that, while the details of Sterling's memorial service may not have been to my preference, in the end I feel that we all did a very nice job of honoring his memory. And—" Her voice wavered, and she blinked. Unable to stay the tears, she let them flow. "And I hope you will forgive me if I made things more difficult for you." She broke off. "I am very fond of you, Juliana. You have no idea how fond."

Juliana sat down next to her and reached for her hand. "It's been horrible for us all."

"But worse for you," Aunt Theodora said. "And I think perhaps I was too caught up in my own sorrow to realize that."

"Sterling was more your son than your nephew. Mothers aren't supposed to outlive their children. It's all wrong." Juliana swallowed. "I'm sorry if my. . .fighting you. . .on the rituals has made it harder for you."

Aunt Theodora shook her head. "No. Don't apologize. You are an intelligent woman, and you are most certainly entitled to your opinions." She glanced at Aunt Lydia. "I have no right to dictate to you. It is particularly egregious of me to do so when you have so graciously deigned to share your home with us all these years."

Juliana didn't know what to say. Were they feeling insecure about their situation now that Sterling was gone? She spoke to that. "Aunt Theodora. Aunt Lydia. This is your *home*. You aren't guests; you're all the family I have. I cannot imagine life without either of you. Forgive me for not making that clear. I need you."

Aunt Theodora shook her head. "I cannot imagine what for. I'm an outspoken old woman." She glanced at Aunt Lydia. "At least my sister is a peacemaker."

"I need you both," Juliana said. "And don't either of you ever forget it." She took a deep breath. "And now I need to get dressed so that we can get this infernal meeting over with." She paused. "I don't suppose you'd support me in calling and canceling? It's a dreadful day out there."

"You'll feel such relief once it's over with," Aunt Lydia said. "We don't mind the rain."

"And a lady does not say *infernal*, dear," Aunt Theodora said, although she was smiling as she said it.

CHAPTER 9

Thou art my hiding place and my shield.
PSALM 119:114

The offices of Amasa J. Graham, attorney at law, occupied an impressive street-level suite in what was known as the Richards Block on the northeast corner of Eleventh and O Streets. By the time Juliana and the aunts alighted on the boardwalk just outside, the town coach had driven through a downpour that made them all worry about poor Alfred huddled beneath a mackintosh on the driver's seat above them. But "poor Alfred" gave no sign of discomfort as he opened a huge umbrella and escorted each of the women in turn across the boardwalk.

When it was Juliana's turn, she lingered at the door to press a coin into Alfred's hand. "I will not have you waiting out here in the rain. Find something hot to drink where you can get warm and dry. I'll send someone to find you when this is done."

"But the team—"

"If they didn't bolt on the way in, they aren't going to do so now," Juliana said. She pointed up at the parting clouds. "The storm has passed. Please, Alfred." She lingered inside the door watching as Alfred closed up the umbrella and slid it beneath the driver's seat. He made sure the team was securely hitched to the iron post at the edge of the boardwalk, then ambled off in the direction of the only place in town that would serve a black man. He would have to walk several blocks in what was now a light drizzle.

Taking a deep breath, Juliana headed for the conference room. Aunts Lydia and Theodora had chosen chairs on either side of an empty chair at the head of a polished mahogany table. Mr. Graham took a seat at the opposite end. He had just opened the folder before him when a soft rap on the door announced George Duncan's arrival.

Mr. Graham explained. "I thought it in your best interest if your husband's banker—and of course he is now your banker—joined us. There are trust funds to be discussed, and Mr. Duncan has been named the administrator of those accounts."

Juliana's heart sank at the phrase *trust funds*. She folded her hands in her lap and waited. If Sterling had established trust funds, he didn't trust her. At least that's how it felt.

"Are we ready?" Mr. Graham looked around the table then began to read.

As it turned out, the trust funds were for the aunts. Everything else—Sutton Builders, the railroad stock, the bank interests, the homes, the land—Sterling had left it all to "my beloved wife, Juliana Regina Masters Sutton." Mr. Graham made a joke about the largest estate he'd ever represented resulting in the shortest will he'd ever read. The enormity of the estate left Juliana reeling.

"The dear boy," Aunt Theodora said, her voice warm with emotion.

Aunt Lydia chimed in with a low laugh. "The blessed child."

Then Mr. Duncan spoke up. "Mr. Graham and I have conferred," he said. "It is most unusual for a man of Mr. Sutton's status to burden his wife with this amount of responsibility. The tragic circumstances of Sterling's death can only make that responsibility more challenging." He looked at Mr. Graham.

Mr. Graham cleared his throat and pulled a lone piece of paper from beneath the file containing the will and, Juliana assumed, real estate deeds. "Mr. Duncan and I have prioritized some of the more pressing matters that should be addressed as soon as possible." He adjusted his spectacles. "You will, of course, want to sell the farm."

"The farm?" Juliana frowned.

Mr. Graham nodded. "Several hundred acres just to the west of the penitentiary."

Juliana glanced at the aunts. "Did you know Sterling owned a farm?" They shook their heads.

"I daresay that Sterling owned a great many things you wouldn't necessarily be directly aware of," Mr. Graham said.

"I daresay," Juliana agreed. "But I don't think I'll be inclined to sell any of it until I've had a thorough look at whatever you have in that file."

Graham nodded. "Of course." He glanced at Mr. Duncan. Something passed between them.

"There is the matter of the new house," Duncan said. "That could very quickly become a liability and a drain on your circumstances."

"In what way?"

He leaned back in his chair and tented his hands across his midsection. "There's not much of a market for anything so grand, for one thing. It might be wise to put a stop to the construction while you decide what to do."

Aunt Lydia spoke up. "And put all those men out of work?" She looked at Juliana. "I'm sorry, dear. I know it's not my place to speak, but—surely we have some responsibility to the workforce."

Juliana nodded. "My aunt makes a good point."

"It would only be a delay," Mr. Duncan said. "And a temporary one, at that. Whoever bought the property would of course continue the project. But stopping it now would increase the likelihood of selling it in a timely fashion. You could price it reasonably and move it quickly. And be done with it." He paused. "It's not exactly uncommon knowledge that the house was Sterling's idea and that you had. . .reservations. There's no need to burden yourself with it any longer. If the workers are a concern, we could prepare a generous severance package and promise the best of recommendations would be forwarded to the new owner."

Something didn't seem right about this. Duncan was pressing the point too strongly. And he was nervous. Dots of perspiration had broken out across his brow. Juliana looked over at Mr. Graham, who had taken a sudden interest in the piece of paper lying on the table before him.

"What else, Mr. Graham? You said you had a list. What else must I decide today?"

"The monument. And the charitable donations for the year."

Juliana held out her hand. "I'll look the donations list over right now."

Mr. Graham slid the list across the table to where Aunt Lydia could reach it. She, in turn, placed it before Juliana.

"Do I understand my situation correctly?" She looked at Mr. Duncan. "I have nothing to worry about when it comes to personal finances."

"Absolutely nothing. In fact, you could *give* the unfinished house away and never miss the money."

Juliana nodded. "Very well." She looked at the aunts. "Would you look at the list and tell me if you agree that these are all still worthy causes?"

Aunt Lydia looked the list over while Aunt Theodora reached into her bag for her spectacles. When it was the older woman's turn, she took her time, tracing her progress down the list of a dozen different charities with a gloved hand as she read. Finally, she sat back and nodded. "We agree. Very worthy causes, all."

Juliana smiled. She looked to Mr. Duncan. "Please triple these figures. And we might have a few things to add in due time." She glanced at Aunt Theodora. "St. John's really does need an organ." She'd never heard the old woman laugh out loud, but that did it, although it was more of a snort that was very quickly swallowed.

"I suppose you do have a point," Aunt Theodora countered. "I simply cannot join a church that does not provide the appropriate atmosphere for worship."

Aunt Lydia spoke up. "Sister! Does that mean you will join us at worship?"

"These gentlemen have neither the interest in nor the need

to participate in our private affairs. We shall discuss it later." Aunt Theodora's silk mourning gown rustled as she repositioned herself in the leather chair.

The scolding only made Aunt Lydia's smile brighter. "I told you so," she said to Juliana in a low voice.

Mr. Duncan cleared his throat. "Back to the subject at hand," he said. "Shall I make inquiries as to whether there is interest in the property as it stands?"

"As long as you make it clear that nothing is officially for sale," Juliana said.

Duncan nodded. "Of course. I shall be clear."

Juliana spoke to Mr. Graham as she rose from her chair. "I'll take the folder with me and study the documents at home."

"Are you certain you wouldn't rather do that here, where they can be kept secure?"

Juliana smiled. "I appreciate your concern, but I think, between the three of us, my aunts and I can manage to keep track of it." She looked to Mr. Duncan. "I'd appreciate another meeting next week. That should give you and your clerks time to prepare a detailed list of the cash assets. I'm assuming Sterling had funds in a variety of accounts." She paused. "And I would also appreciate it if both of you gentlemen would stop looking so surprised. I am a woman, not an ignoramus. The two terms are not necessarily synonymous."

Happily, Alfred had returned and was waiting for them. The clouds had cleared. Other than the sound of the coach wheels hissing their way through the muck, the drive home was pleasant. Aunt Theodora congratulated Juliana on her parting request, and Aunt Lydia rejoiced openly at the increase in charitable donations.

"I didn't forget your idea regarding an education fund as a memorial," Juliana said. "The thing is, knowing that Sterling left us in such a healthy financial state, I thought we might want to do more." She smiled. "And won't it be fun to think what that might be?"

"The dear boy," Aunt Theodora said. "He left nothing to chance." She smiled at Juliana. "What better declaration of love could he have given than to entrust it all to you?" She nodded. "He knew you well, my dear. And respect for your intelligence was part of his devotion. That should comfort you."

It was a comfort, but it did nothing to heal the pain of betrayal. Even if Marshal Hastings's version of what had happened the night of the fire was right, Juliana would be haunted by the locket for the rest of her life. *He may have trusted me. He may have respected me in his own way. But I wasn't enough. I was never enough.*

—⁓—

Jenny
Wednesday, April 25

Where was George Duncan? Why didn't he come? He said he would come. She lay on the bed, a wailing baby next to her. How long had it been? She thought it was Wednesday, but she wasn't sure. Johnny. . .for Johnny she had to try. She was so sick. So weak.

Dragging herself out of bed, Jenny stumbled to the door. She felt her way down the hall to the kitchen. Once there, she slumped into a chair, trying to gather strength. There was a little wood left by the stove. If she could just get a fire started, she could heat some water. Have a cup of tea. Eat something. Anything.

Water. That would make her feel better. She rested her head on her arms. *Come on, Jenny. The pump's just outside the back door. You can do it. You have to do it.*

Johnny's cries fueled the impossible. She made her way to the pump, used what little reserved strength she had to fill a bucket with water. Too heavy. It was just too heavy. She knelt down by the bucket and, cupping her hand, sucked the water into her mouth. Her hair fell forward. When she lifted her face to the sun, the wet curls dampened her nightgown.

Shivering, she began to scoot the bucket of water back toward the house. It took most of her strength, but finally, she shoved the bucket in the back door. Exhausted from the effort, she curled up on the kitchen floor and slept.

Pounding on the door. Johnny wailing.

Jenny opened her eyes. The sun. . .what had happened to the sun? She raised her head to look toward the front of the house just as George Duncan stepped into the hall. Swearing, he hurried to her side.

—⁂—

Jenny
Friday, April 27

Someone was in her kitchen. No. . .*she'd* been in her kitchen. On the floor, trying to get a drink of water. *Johnny.* She sat up. The baby was gone. Her heart pounded.

Who was in her kitchen?

Humming. Was that *humming*?

The sour smell was gone. Her bedding was clean. The window was open. A fresh spring breeze rustled the lace curtains. She pushed back the blankets and wobbled her way to the door. She could just see the tip of Johnny's head cradled in the arms of the dark-skinned woman sitting in a rocker by the back door. The woman was singing while she rocked him.

> *Bye-o-baby,*
> *Go sleepy,*
> *Bye-o-baby,*
> *Go sleepy,*
> *What a big alligator*
> *Coming to catch the one boy.*
> *Diss here the Sutton boy child,*
> *Bye-o-baby,*
> *Go sleepy,*
> *What a big alligator,*
> *Coming to catch this one boy.*

As Jenny drew near, the woman looked up and nodded. "And look-a here, Johnny. Here's Mama now." She leaned over and laid

Johnny in the cradle at her feet then rose to settle Jenny in the rocker.

"Got some soup on the stove. You need to get your strength back."

Jenny sat watching as the woman ladled soup into a mug and handed it over.

"You sip that slowly. Make sure it's going to stay down. I only filled it half full. Doctor said to be real careful at first."

"Doctor?" Jenny frowned as she lifted the mug to her cracked lips with a trembling hand.

"Dr. Gilbert. Mr. Duncan found you. Put you in bed and hightailed it after the doctor." She sat down on one of the kitchen chairs. "You were not long for this world to hear the doctor tell it." She glanced down at the sleeping baby. "Baby, neither." The woman lowered the gaze of her clear blue eyes to Jenny's bosom. "Poor thing wasn't getting hardly anything."

Jenny moistened her lips. The salt in the soup stung. She took another sip. "We were doing just fine until I got the ague." She looked toward the front door. "Mr. Duncan was supposed to come back. It was a whole week before he did."

The woman nodded. "You be glad he came when he did. Glad he went for Dr. Gilbert." She lowered her gaze. "Guess you can be glad the doctor knew about me just losing my own child." She ran her palms over the tight amber curls cut close to her head. Tears spilled down her cheeks.

"I'm sorry," Jenny said. She couldn't imagine losing Johnny. Life wouldn't mean a thing without him.

"Name's Susannah. Mr. Duncan is payin' me to take care of you and the baby until you're better and can handle things yourself."

When Susannah reached for the mug of soup, Jenny said, "I'd like some more." She put her hand to her stomach. "I feel hollow."

"You lay down a bit and see how your stomach does. If it keeps that little bit down, you can have some more. That's what the doctor said to do."

Jenny bent down to stroke Johnny's cheek. When she rose to

return to bed, the room swam. For a minute she thought she might faint. But Susannah steadied her and helped her back to bed.

—⁓—

"No one can tell you what to do, dear. You must decide." Aunt Theodora took up her spectacles and bent to the task at hand. Both aunts had taken to working on the signature quilt for an hour or so each morning. Apparently Aunt Theodora's aversion to needlework was weakening. Juliana's had not. Even though Martha had eradicated the shadow of "that name" and rolled it out of sight, Juliana couldn't bring herself to work on the quilt.

This morning, she'd brought the folder from Mr. Graham and taken a seat at the drop-front desk tucked into one corner of the room, reading through the deeds and documents, trying to understand all that was hers. Mr. Duncan had called just a few moments ago. He had someone interested in the property south of town. Would she be open to an offer?

Juliana had come back from talking with him on the phone in the kitchen and told the aunts about the call. "He says I'm at an advantage with this buyer because the house isn't finished. Whoever it is would want to change some things, and that's less costly at this stage."

"What stage is that?" Aunt Theodora asked.

"I don't know, exactly. I haven't been out there in weeks."

"We can go with you," Aunt Lydia said. "If you can wait until this afternoon. I'm expecting Edith Pritchart and Lutie Gleason to stop by." She glanced at her sister. "I see what you're thinking. It isn't a social call. We need to have a preliminary meeting to plan the bazaar. It's only a few weeks away."

"You still plan on attending?"

"You need to ask?" Aunt Lydia didn't so much as look up from the quilt. "You should stay downstairs and meet Edith and Lutie. You'd like them." She glanced up. "Edith has tried unsuccessfully to get an organ campaign going more than once in recent years. The two of you are kindred spirits in that regard. You should hear her play the piano."

Aunt Theodora pursed her lips. "Perhaps I shall one day." She rose from the quilt. "But it will not be a mere eleven days after our dear boy's funeral." She paused in the doorway to look back at Juliana. "As to your 'monstrosity,'" she said, "you must decide. And I, for one, think that you should decide without either of us imposing our views on the decision. It's a lovely day. Why not ride south instead of north today?"

"Ask Mr. Gregory what he thinks," Aunt Lydia said. "He's a good man."

Aunt Theodora sighed. "The willingness to set up tables at an ice-cream social hardly qualifies a common worker to advise in matters of finance, Sister."

"It doesn't automatically disqualify him, either," Aunt Lydia retorted. "Everyone at St. John's thinks very highly of Mr. Gregory."

Juliana closed the folder with a sigh. It was all well and good for Aunt Lydia to sing Mr. Gregory's praises because she knew him from church. Aunt Lydia hadn't seen him at the fire. *Maybe it didn't mean anything.* Of course that didn't explain his involvement in Nell Parker's funeral. *You don't suspect Pastor Taylor. He was driving the other wagon.* Yes, but Pastor Taylor was sitting *alone* on the wagon seat. He didn't have a woman snuggled up to him.

Would she ever learn to trust again?

CHAPTER 10

Be not hasty in thy spirit to be angry.
ECCLESIASTES 7:9

It was one thing to see Sterling's drawings of the mansion he planned and hear him describe the progress, and quite another to see the brick and stone walls rising out of the prairie. Juliana pulled Tecumseh up and sat, taking it all in with a combination of delight and dismay. This was no monstrosity. It was going to be spectacular.

A newly fenced pasture lay to the east of the caretaker's house. Inside the barbed wire enclosure, Mr. Gregory's bay grazed alongside a team of draft horses. Mr. Gregory was nowhere in sight. She walked Tecumseh closer in, up to what would be the back door of the manse, and called up to a worker nailing subflooring down in the back hall. "Where would I find Mr. Gregory?"

The man snatched his cap off his head. "My condolences, Mrs. Sutton." Juliana thanked him, and then he nodded toward the stone cottage. "Boss is in the office."

Riding up to the cottage, Juliana slid off Tecumseh and peered through the open door. Mr. Gregory was bent over a drawing laid out on some planks spanning a pair of sawhorses to form a makeshift table.

"Good morning," she called.

"Mrs. Sutton." He grabbed a rumpled brown coat and pulled it on, then raked a hand through his unruly hair before stepping outside.

93

"I thought it was time I rode out and saw things for myself."

"I'm glad you did." He nodded toward the pasture. "Would you like to turn your horse in with the others? Baron's fairly peaceable. The draft horses won't pay him any mind at all."

"I was surprised to see a fenced pasture. That's new."

"The boss wanted us to do it, but we just got it finished the other day. He was hoping you'd start riding out more often."

While Juliana held Tecumseh's bridle, Mr. Gregory unsaddled him and set the saddle and blanket against a tree. Next, he opened the gate. Juliana walked through, unbuckled the throatlatch, and let Tecumseh go. He and the big bay snorted and danced about for a few minutes, but before long they gave up posturing and settled down to graze.

She gazed up at the cottonwood trees towering above the stone cottage, then at the carpet of deep pink wildflowers blooming off to the south. "I'd forgotten how beautiful it is out here." She glanced to the north. "I don't suppose it will be long before Lincoln grows out this far."

"Hard to imagine, but of course you're right."

She motioned toward the open windows across the face of the cottage. "I see you're taking advantage of the warm spring air."

"Yes, ma'am."

She went inside and looked about the room. "This place was little more than an empty shell the last time I was here. Do you mind if I see what's been done?" She crossed the room to peer into the kitchen, admiring the tile work on the wall above the sink.

"I've had the inevitable meeting with attorney and banker. They've encouraged me to think about selling. Mr. Duncan offered to make what he calls 'discreet inquiries' to gauge interest in the property. He called this morning. He has someone interested." She glanced back at the kitchen. "I didn't remember we were having tile work."

"The boss had Mrs. Gaines choose it. Said that if they were going to live in it, they should have a say. He had me order the stove she wanted, too. It's already been delivered, but we're keeping it in town.

I thought we should wait to install anything like that until someone was on the premises permanently." He paused. "We noticed buggy tracks in the grass around the house last Wednesday morning after that rain. It made me think we were beginning to attract unwanted visitors. Now I wonder if it might have been Mr. Duncan." He paused again. "I wish he'd let me know he was showing the place."

Juliana shared Mr. Gregory's displeasure at the idea of George Duncan hauling people out here without her knowledge. It felt presumptuous. She walked over to the mantle, admiring the carving that made the edge look like a twisted rope. "Beautiful work."

"Yes, ma'am. We've a first-rate carpenter. He's already started on the finials for the staircase in the big house. Says it's the most fun he's had in a decade."

"Fun?"

"It's a joy to work on something that uses all your skills." He nodded at the main house, just visible through the open front door. "To say you had a hand in building something that fine? Plenty of craftsmen never get the chance." He paused. "I hope you won't let Mr. Duncan rush you into a decision. Things have to be overwhelming right now."

She tried to keep bitterness out of her voice. "You have no idea."

"Would you like a tour?" He offered his arm, and together they crossed the prairie to the building site, pausing first near the front entrance. Juliana stared up at the massive house. The sound of hammers and saws and the faint scent of sawdust wafted on the breeze.

"I'm curious about something," she said. "Mr. Duncan warned me about what he called 'inevitable delays' that would occur without my husband overseeing things out here." She looked around them. "This doesn't look like 'delay.'"

Frustration sounded in Mr. Gregory's voice. "I did my best to assure Mr. Duncan there would be no delays. Apparently I failed to gain his confidence."

"When did you talk to him?"

"When I came to work the morning after the fire, about a dozen of the crew were waiting for me. You can imagine they had questions. The only one I couldn't answer had to do with payday. I offered to talk to Mr. Duncan for them. I assumed the boss's banker would know if there was going to be a delay. I'm sorry if that sounds callous."

"You don't have to apologize. They're working men with families to feed. I don't blame them for wondering, and I don't blame you for acting quickly. In fact, I'm glad you did."

"If I'd known Mr. Duncan could sign the checks, I wouldn't have bothered him. Finney knows the business is in good shape financially."

George Duncan can sign Sutton Builders checks. Why hadn't he mentioned that at their meeting? She would need to think about that. "You said the meeting didn't go well?"

"It didn't stay. . .simple. He asked me to breakfast. And he brought up the idea of 'delays' with me, too. At first I thought he was just reassuring me. The payroll would be on time, and people would be understanding while everyone adjusted."

"That's not what he meant?"

He shook his head. "No, ma'am. He kept talking around it, but I'm not used to reading behind people's words. Finally, he came out and told me that Mrs. Duncan has her eye on this place, but he needs time to liquidate some assets before he has the money to purchase it. Even at that, he would need the place to be unfinished."

"He told you to slow things down?"

"Not directly, no. He was. . .careful. But it was apparent that he anticipates having an important say in the business with the boss gone."

Vultures circling. Just as Sterling always said. "But you're not slowing down."

He shook his head. "Mr. Duncan isn't my boss, ma'am. You are."

He seemed sincere. Aunt Lydia said he had a good reputation. But still. . .he'd been with those women. As to George Duncan's machinations, she was disappointed but not surprised. Helen Duncan had always seemed to take an inordinate interest in what other people possessed. Let one of the women at a function wear a new fur, and Helen had one the next time you saw her. Let someone redo a room, and Helen redecorated two. She had made no secret of her opinion of what she called "conspicuous excess" on the part of the Suttons. *I guess it's only excessive if it's someone else's.*

Mr. Gregory cleared his throat. "It isn't my place to sway your decision one way or another, ma'am. But I do feel that I should tell you that if you sell to Duncan, I'll be giving my notice. I won't work for him."

They had been standing near the house. A worker appeared in one of the turret windows. " 'Scuse me, Cass," he called down. "Did I just hear right?" He glanced at Juliana. "Ma'am? You sold to Duncan?" He looked back at Cass. "We can look for work together." He bobbed back out of sight.

"I want to talk to him," Juliana said.

Cass called. "Klein. Elmo Klein." When Klein reappeared in the window, Cass motioned for him to join the two of them.

As soon as he hopped down and came near, Juliana asked, "Why would you give up a good job, just because the owner changes?"

"Mr. Duncan was my landlord last year. I missed a payment. The baby got sick. I could either pay Dr. Gilbert or pay the rent. Well, Dr. Gilbert sat up for three nights with my Betsy. Said not to worry about the money, the baby was the thing. So when I had to choose, I paid Dr. Gilbert. Figured Mr. Duncan would understand. I'd rented from him for two years, and it was the first time I'd missed. He understood, all right. Understood that he wasn't getting paid, and he didn't care why. He put me and my wife and our new baby out on the street."

Juliana frowned. "I can't imagine George Duncan doing something like that."

The worker's voice trembled with barely contained rage. "Oh, he didn't do it himself. He didn't have the gumption. He sent someone else to do it." He glanced at Cass. "Mr. Gregory, here, offered to help pay the rent, but I'd had enough of that landlord. The Friend's Society took us in. They didn't really have room, but one of the ladies let us camp out in her parlor until I could find something new."

"You mean the Society for the Friendless?"

The man shrugged. "The other name fits better, doesn't it?" His gray eyes glittered with rage. "We had a month-old baby, and Duncan didn't care a bit. I'd move to gol-durned Indian Territory before I'd work for that man." He apologized for swearing.

One of the stonemasons waved for Mr. Gregory to come and answer a question, and he stepped away. Juliana smiled at Mr. Kline. "If any rumors get started about what's going to happen out here, would you do your part to squelch them? I'm not saying I will never sell this place, but as of today, *nothing* I own is for sale, and I own everything that belonged to my husband. I hope no one objects to working for a woman."

Mr. Klein grinned. "Don't imagine anyone will care a bit. As long as the lady in question is smart enough to keep her foreman on." Klein nodded at Cass. "You've got a good one there, ma'am."

Juliana thanked Klein, and he returned to work. She caught up with Mr. Gregory, who was standing by the broad stone stairs that would lead guests up to the massive double doors tucked beneath an arched overhang rimmed with stone. "I've never seen this kind of work done before," she said.

"You've Jessup to thank for it." Mr. Gregory pointed to a big man dressed in overalls. "He did the work on the stone cottage, too. And he's done a fair amount of work south of here around Roca. In fact, there's someone driving out from town this afternoon to talk with him about a project down there. They wanted me to bid it. I told them I have a job."

"So does Mr. Jessup."

"It isn't unusual for the men take on side jobs. Don't worry. They all know your house comes first. Weekends only for second jobs."

"Tell me about the progress here."

Mr. Gregory pointed up to the roofline. "The slate for the roof is due in next week. We'll be ready when it comes. I've talked to the factory manufacturing the windows. We should have them set in place by the first of June. Once we've got the windows in and the roof on then the interior work will begin." He paused. "Mr. Sutton said you'd likely have a lot to say about that."

That was so like Sterling. Determined to go his own way and equally convinced that she would, eventually, see things his way. Maybe she would have. Mr. Gregory's voice brought her back to the moment. "Would you like to go inside? It takes a little imagination, but the framework is in place. I think you'll be able to see it."

Juliana shook her head. She didn't know why, but she didn't feel ready. Instead, she led the way around the corner turret to the side of the house, staring up at the brickwork and then ending up at the back corner of the house, peering up at a doorway on the second floor.

"That's the master suite," Mr. Gregory said. "There's to be a large porch off that doorway. A good view of the eastern horizon. Mr. Sutton said you like to watch the sunrise."

She didn't want to think about that, and so she headed around the other side of the house and walked up to what would be the rear entrance and peered inside. "Are there really ten fireplaces?"

"Yes, ma'am."

"I remember something about paneling for the upstairs bedrooms."

"A different wood in every room—English brown oak, chestnut, cherry, teak, French walnut, padauk. None of it's arrived yet."

"Is it too late to cancel?"

"I can check. I don't know."

"If you can, cancel it."

"Yes, ma'am."

"All that wood. . .it's too dreary. Too dark."

He nodded. "I'll do my best."

She met his gaze. Those hazel eyes. That square jaw. *And a red-headed paramour.* She looked away. "Thank you, Mr. Gregory."

"For what?"

"For telling me about George Duncan." She took a deep breath. "Maybe I'm behaving like a child with a toy she doesn't want to share, but the idea of Helen Duncan crowing about 'her George' landing the biggest house in town at a bargain price—and she would crow—just makes me want to dig in my heels." She paused. Looked through to the front door. "I want you to build it. I'll decide what to do with it later."

"All right."

"I would like to know more about the detailed plans, but I need to get back home now." She headed for the pasture. "Aunt Lydia has a meeting with a couple of friends about the bazaar in June, and I want to make certain they know I'm glad to have them. It's more than a little unusual for a house in mourning to invite people to call."

"It's for a good cause."

"Yes. It is. We're hoping to fund a couple of new residences so that 'camping in the parlor' like Mr. Klein and his family experienced is never necessary." She paused. "Sometimes I think I should just buy the properties and save everyone all the hours of baking and stitching."

"Pastor Taylor is big on people working together, each one contributing their 'widow's mite.' It's a nice feeling, working together with like-minded people toward something everyone cares about." He unlatched the pasture gate. "And now I'm joining the ranks of people telling you what to do." He smiled down at her. "Trust yourself. You'll find your way." He reached for the bridle draped on the fence post by the gate. "And now to catch your horse."

Juliana chuckled. "Tecumseh and I have an understanding. And I see that look. Watch and learn, Mr. Gregory." She took the bridle from him and whistled. Tecumseh lifted his head. She whistled again, and he came trotting to her.

Mr. Gregory's jaw dropped. "Is that a horse or a dog?"

"More like a spoiled child." Tecumseh lowered his head. She tugged on his forelock and offered the bit. He tossed his head and stomped. "I know. I'm a wretched human being. But I'll get your carrot as soon as we get home. I promise. So please, take the bit and don't be a brat." Tecumseh took the bit. She slipped the bridle over his ears, buckled the throatlatch, and led him back out of the pasture to be saddled.

When she was ready to mount up, she asked for a hand up. Gregory laced his fingers together and bent down. She put her foot into the makeshift step and he boosted her into the saddle. She smiled down at him. "Perhaps a mounting block would be in order."

"There'll be one by the end of the day."

She touched the brim of her hat with her riding crop. "We may just get along, Mr. Gregory."

—⁓—

Juliana was nearing the edge of Lincoln when she caught sight of a buggy headed across the prairie. As it came closer and she caught sight of the occupants, she frowned. The driver raised a hand in greeting. Juliana pretended not to see and kicked Tecumseh into a canter. In a moment, though, she reined about to look after the buggy. It was definitely headed for the building site.

Mr. Gregory had said someone was coming out today to speak with the stonemason about a side job. A new business, he'd said. And here they were. No wonder he hadn't said much about it. She'd recognize that red hair anywhere. The older woman had to be Goldie. And Juliana knew just what kind of "business" they wanted built.

Just when she'd decided to give Mr. Gregory the benefit of the doubt about the night of the fire and that day at Wyuka. Just when she'd decided Aunt Lydia was right about him.

He was a "good man," all right. Good at playacting. Good at fooling naive pastors and old ladies.

Good for nothing.

CHAPTER 11

Wherefore, my beloved brethren, let every man be swift to hear,
slow to speak, slow to wrath.
JAMES 1:19

Cass introduced Ludwig Meyer to Jessup, and while the two men talked about Meyer's proposed building, Cass gave Ma and Sadie a tour of both the houses. They were standing in the kitchen at the stone cottage when Sadie pointed out the window and said, "I'd put a flower bed right out there. It'd be so nice to look out and see blossoms when you were cooking or washing dishes." She glanced at Cass. "What? I like flowers. And I can grow 'em, too, if you will recall."

"Of course I recall," Cass said. "You resurrected half-dead things I thought didn't have a chance. And you begged seeds off half the county."

"And it turned out real nice, didn't it."

"It did."

"Until—" She glanced Ma's way and shook her head.

"You don't have to protect me," Ma said. She gazed out the window and sighed. "I am so sorry for everything that man did. For him smashing flowers because he said we needed that strip for more vegetables." She looked at Cass. "And for the way he treated you." Her voice wavered. "I didn't know it was that bad. I didn't know."

Cass hugged her. "We've got to put that all behind us now. God's given us a chance at a fresh start. A new life."

Sadie spoke up. "And I'm going to plant flowers again. Lots of them."

As Cass showed Ma and Sadie through the mansion, Sadie grew increasingly quiet. He told them about the massive dining room table waiting beneath a tarpaulin in town and the plans for bringing in enough wood to fuel the ten fireplaces—not a small feat in a county where surveyors actually noted mature trees on their surveys because they were so rare. He described the stairway and the design that would be inlaid to create the library floor. Finally, they stood at the front of the house while Cass described the porches that would extend out from this doorway or that. Sadie stepped back and looked the place over. She sighed audibly. "What's she like?"

"Mrs. Sutton?"

"Yeah."

"I haven't spent much time with her."

"But she was here earlier. That was her we saw riding away when we drove in?"

Ma spoke up. "A tall red horse."

"That was her. The horse is Tecumseh." Cass smiled. "He comes when called. Like a dog. And she talks to him like he's human."

Sadie frowned. "She's touched in the head?"

Cass laughed. "No. She's. . ." He tried to remember what he'd learned about her over the years. "Educated. Her father was a professor at the university. The boss met her at a literary meeting. She was giving a speech."

"So she talks fancy."

"Not the way you mean. Not like she thinks she's better than everyone else." He paused. "She does a lot of charity work. And it isn't just giving money. The boss used to complain about it a little. About her off visiting this homeless family or that, taking the doctor to see this baby or spending time reading to the children."

Sadie tilted her head as she looked up at him. "You like her. Is she pretty?"

"I don't see what that has to do with anything." Of course she was pretty, and who wouldn't have noticed that? Flashing dark eyes. A man could get lost in those eyes if he didn't remember his place in the scheme of things. She sat a horse like royalty. The sweep of her riding habit emphasized a tiny waist.

Sadie shrugged. "Just wondering. I never gave much thought to the wives." Shading her eyes with a gloved hand, she looked back up at the house. "Never would have thought one of Nell's customers would be building something like this for his *wife*."

Cass thought about that for a moment. "I don't think he was building it for her. I think this place was all about the boss and where he was headed. He wanted to make a statement."

"Well this sure would have done that." Sadie lowered her voice as she rumbled, 'I'm richer than you, and don't you forget it. Make me mad, and you'll get what's coming to you'."

Cass shrugged. The boss had never been anything but fair with him, but Cass had worked for him long enough to have heard stories. Sterling Sutton was not a man to cross. Mrs. Sutton, on the other hand, was something of an enigma. "She rarely came out here," he said. "The boss made excuses for her, but the truth is I don't think she was all that interested. Just now? She didn't even go inside. Just walked the perimeter and asked a few questions."

Sadie frowned. "Now I'm back to thinking she's touched in the head. A woman's got to be crazy not to like something this fine."

"You haven't seen the house in town. She doesn't exactly live in a hovel." He grinned at Sadie. "Now that I think about it, Mrs. Sutton reminds me a little of you."

Sadie rolled her eyes. "Why? Because we both have heads and hair?"

Cass laughed. "First, because I got the impression today that she's smarter than she lets on. Mostly, though, because I don't think Mrs. Sutton appreciates being told what to do."

"Goodness," Ma teased, "why on earth would *that* make you think of Sadie? She's so malleable."

Sadie glowered at Ma. "A girl's own mother shouldn't call names."

She gestured around them. "She's got all this money. Who'd dare try to push her around?"

Her husband's banker. In cahoots with the lawyer. Cass thought it, but he couldn't say it. Instead, he said, "Money lures varmints as surely as a worm lures a fish to a barbed hook."

Sadie grimaced. "You taking up philosophy now?"

Cass chuckled. "Some varmints wearing suits and calling themselves friends are trying to arrange things so that Mrs. Sutton sells this place. It seems to me a real friend would give her time to get over the shock before expecting her to make big decisions like that. But these people—I think they'd force the sale if they could. They can't, and so they've taken to some less—forthright ways."

"Underhanded ways," Sadie said.

Cass nodded. "She's standing her ground, though. Which is where I got the idea she doesn't appreciate being told what to do."

"Of course you can't say who the varmints are, you being a gentleman and all that." Sadie paused. Presently, she smiled up at him. "I hope she knows she's got herself a good man for a foreman. Someone she can trust."

"I hope *you* know," Cass said, "what it means for me to hear you say that."

Sadie glanced at Ma. "When Ludwig prays, he says that we got to take the new life that's offered. He keeps telling me I got to forget all the mess." She looked from Cass to Ma and back again. "Seems like maybe Ludwig is right. Let's stop rolling around in it. Let's all just say we're sorry and I forgive you and you forgive me and Ma forgives us both and we forgive her and everybody ends up all forgiven and that's that. What d'ya say?"

"If only it were that easy."

"Well of course it isn't that easy," Sadie said. "You've got to be stubborn about it." She tapped her temple with her finger. "When it gets in there"—she swiped her palm across her forehead—"we erase it. And we say a prayer or think about bluebirds or something nice. However many times it takes." She drew in a deep breath.

"I'm gonna go find Ludwig."

Ma spoke up after Sadie was out of earshot. "Do you think it's truly possible to be finished with the past?"

Cass bent down and kissed her on the cheek. "I certainly hope so." He offered his arm and nodded to where Sadie stood next to Ludwig, listening in on his conversation with Jessup. "Is she going to marry him?"

"I hope so. I was worried she'd change her mind. But she—we—talked to Goldie."

"How did that go?"

Ma didn't answer for a moment. Finally she said, "There were words, but no blows. I suppose it went as well as could be expected." She paused. "I'm reluctant to look for work until I know what Sadie's going to do."

"I thought Mr. Meyer was counting on you living with them."

"Mr. Meyer is a gracious man, but the last thing they need is Sadie's mother hovering. There's no reason I won't be able to find work, and I mean to do it. I just hope Sadie practices what she just preached about taking the new life that's being offered. She needs to marry the man."

Ludwig and Jessup shook hands just as Cass and Ma walked up.

"Everything's set, then?" Cass said.

Ludwig nodded. "Mr. Jessup and I will take the train down to Roca on Saturday so he can see the building site."

"And I get a flower garden." Sadie nudged Meyer's arm. "Right?"

He beamed at her. "As big as you want, mein Schatz. I forgot to tell you that I spoke with Mrs. Cranford at the store just yesterday. She is one of our regular customers and is always speaking of gardens and flowers. When I told her that my Sadie is a great admirer of flowers, she insisted that we come to her home and see her garden. She wants to give us seeds and cuttings to get us started."

"You thought of that? To ask about flower seeds for me?"

"Of course. It's important to you. And I have told Mr. Jessup that we will want flower boxes at the windows of our new store." He glanced at Ma. "You two ladies will have to get really serious now about planning the upstairs." He put his hand over Sadie's. "And we will order stone to border a flower bed. As big as you want."

Sadie nodded. Swallowed. "Ludwig."

"Yes, dear Sadie?"

"Will you marry me?"

Meyer stared at her in disbelief. He looked at Ma and Cass, then back at her.

She nudged his arm. "Did you hear me?"

"I. . .I—of course I did, but. . .you said you wished to wait."

Sadie nodded. "I did. I have. You've been asking me to marry you for a long time."

"Yes. Last Christmas Day. And again on New Year's. And again on my birthday. And—"

"Don't rub it in," Sadie muttered.

"What has changed?"

Sadie smiled. "You're giving me *flowers*." She kissed his cheek. "And I love you."

Juliana seethed all the way back home. The idea that Cass Gregory—the man Sterling had hired and, for all Juliana knew, the man who'd introduced Sterling to Nell Parker—the idea that he had the gall to invite a madam and one of her. . .employees onto her property. And all the while he was talking to her about "Pastor Taylor this" and "good causes that." How could he? How dared he?

The longer she thought about it, the angrier she got. Men. Were they ever honest? Sterling. Cass Gregory. George Duncan. Amasa Graham. Not a single one of them worth—much. Even the ones who were moral could be so completely inept. She thought back to Reverend Burnham. Come to think of it, who knew if he was morally upright? If Sterling could fool her, wives everywhere beware. What was wrong with people, anyway? Was anyone ever honest about who they really were? How could they sit in church on Sunday and then. . . do the things they did?

Her mind whirled from one lie to the next, one disingenuous smile to the next. George Duncan, so solicitous, all the while planning to get his hands on her half-finished house. Amasa Graham, so organized and all the while helping Duncan manipulate her. Reverend Burnham, so pious, as long as Sterling's funeral didn't disrupt his conference. And Cass Gregory. Handsome and earnest and with such an air of *concern* about him. Advising her to trust herself.

Trust herself, indeed, and all the while he was inviting that Goldie person onto her land to talk to her stonemason about rebuilding a brothel. She could just imagine how Gregory would justify it, too. *It's only business. A man's got to make a living.* And all the while making it easy for that *woman* to destroy more marriages.

She should go back there and let Cass Gregory know what she thought of him. Maybe she'd fire him. Maybe that would let everyone know that she was not to be toyed with. They'd laughed behind her back and taken advantage for the very last time. Ladies weren't supposed to know about such things, but thanks to Sterling, she knew. And she had had enough. She would talk about it, all right. And Cass Gregory would never forget it.

Planning to reverse direction and do just that, Juliana jerked on the reins. Tecumseh responded so quickly he nearly sat on his haunches. For a moment, Juliana thought she would manage to keep her seat. She failed. Sailing headlong over Tecumseh's head, she landed hard. The wind went out of her, and the world faded. But not before she heard an odd crack. And then pain. . .and the world went dark.

—⁂—

"What do you mean you aren't moving to Roca with us?!" From her seat next to Margaret in the buggy, Sadie reached up to tap Ludwig on the arm. "Tell her, Ludwig. Tell her we want her. We need her."

Ludwig glanced back at Margaret. "Of course we want you. And we will need help. You must come." He smiled at Sadie. "We insist."

"That's very kind, Ludwig, and I believe you mean it." Margaret glanced at Sadie. "But it's time you had a life of your own. And time I thought about a new life, too." She smiled. "Didn't we just agree to that a few minutes ago?"

"I wasn't agreeing to losing my ma."

"And you never will," Margaret said. "At least not without a fight."

"What will you do?"

"What I've always done. I'll cook. Lincoln is growing, and I'm a good cook. It won't be difficult to find a place."

"Where? In some dreary rooming house?"

Ludwig pulled the buggy up and turned about. "If you are truly set on staying in Lincoln, I wonder, Mrs. Nash, if perhaps you would wish to buy my house."

Own her own home? What a thrilling idea. Not remotely possible, of course. "That's very kind, but—"

"You don't like my house?"

"Of course I do. But I've no way to buy a house."

Ludwig smiled. "Unless you negotiate favorable terms with the present owner."

Sadie spoke up. "You could take in a boarder. I bet Cass would love to get out of that rooming house."

"That I know is true," Ludwig said, but then he looked off into the distance and frowned. "Do you see? What is—?" And then he shouted something in German, grabbed the buggy whip, and urged the rented horse into a trot.

"Isn't that Mrs. Sutton's horse?" Sadie clutched the edge of her seat as the buggy clattered across the prairie.

The tall red horse lifted its head and trotted away, its reins dangling. When the buggy stopped, so did the horse.

Margaret clambered down out of the buggy and went to where Ludwig knelt over the crumpled form of a woman.

Sadie hurried up. "Is she—?"

"*Nein*," Ludwig said. "She breathes."

"Thank God." Margaret knelt beside Mrs. Sutton. "Sadie," she said, as she pulled her gloves off, "see if you can catch the horse." When she put her hand to the woman's forehead, she stirred. "It's all right, Mrs. Sutton. You're going to be all right." *Dear God, let that be true.*

First, Margaret felt her way up each of Mrs. Sutton's booted legs. "It doesn't seem that anything is broken." But when she took the left hand and began to examine that arm, the unconscious woman groaned. "Help me get her riding jacket off." When they'd managed that, Margaret unbuttoned the cuff and rolled up the right sleeve.

"Thank the Lord," she said. "It may be fractured, but at least the skin isn't broken. There's very little swelling. Perhaps it's just a strain. But I don't like it that she isn't waking up."

Sadie led the horse back. "Cass wasn't joking when he said this horse is more dog than horse. He came to me when I spoke to him. It's almost like he's relieved we came along." She hitched the animal to the buggy.

Ludwig carried the still-unconscious Mrs. Sutton to the buggy and laid her in the seat. Margaret perched in the floorboard to keep an eye on her. Sadie climbed up beside Ludwig, and they headed into town.

—⚬—

Had someone put her head in a vise? Wincing, Juliana reached—but then the pain in her head was overshadowed by other pain. What had she done to her arm? She groaned.

"Oh, thank heavens!"

"Thanks be to God."

She opened her eyes. The aunts? Looking extremely worried. The ceiling was. . .green. She didn't have green ceilings. She closed her eyes again. "What's happened? Where am I?"

"Don't you remember?"

"If she remembered," Aunt Theodora snapped, "she wouldn't be asking, now would she?" After a pause, she answered Juliana's question. "That infernal horse threw you. Some dear people found you unconscious, the horse grazing nearby. They brought you to Dr. Gilbert. He rang us up, and Alfred brought us right away." Her voice wavered. "You're going to be all right. It could have been so much worse."

"Tecumseh? I don't. . .remember."

110

Dr. Gilbert spoke up. "Don't let that worry you. It's normal to have a memory lapse after a trauma."

"My arm. . .hurts." And why couldn't she seem to draw a deep breath?

"You are very fortunate. I don't think the wrist joint itself is involved. It's not displaced. I'm recommending ice to keep the swelling down and a wrap to stabilize it while it heals." He paused. "You've also had a slight concussion from the fall. But you'll be fine in a few days. The arm will heal. A few weeks at the longest, and that's only if it's truly fractured. I'm not convinced it is."

A few weeks? But she needed to do things. Slowly, she opened her eyes again. *Green ceilings*. Of course. Dr. Gilbert's clinic. She blinked. Grimaced. And finally the world came clear. "Tecumseh. Did Tecumseh run off?"

"He was grazing near you when Mr. Meyer and the ladies found you."

Juliana smiled. Sweet horse. "It wasn't his fault. I did something stupid. He did exactly what he's been trained to do, but I wasn't prepared and went flying. It wasn't his fault." She looked to the doctor. "May I sit up?"

"Of course. But you may feel a little dizzy."

He helped her sit up, and for a moment she was sorry she'd asked. Her stomach roiled. She closed her eyes again. Presently, things stopped spinning. "When can I go home?"

"I wanted to keep you in the clinic overnight," Dr. Gilbert said, "but your aunts have convinced me they'll keep an eye on you. And call if there's a change."

"Alfred's coming back with the town coach, dear," Aunt Lydia said.

"He doesn't have to do that."

"He wants to do it. It will be so much more comfortable."

Juliana nodded. She smiled. "Aunt Theodora."

"Yes, dear?"

"A lady does not say *infernal*."

111

CHAPTER 12

Two are better than one;
because they have a good reward for their labour.
ECCLESIASTES 4:9

Cass had scaled the skeleton of boards forming the interior of the house and was checking the angle of a roof beam when he caught sight of a buggy headed in from the direction of town. When he saw who it was, he descended as quickly as he could and hurried to the back door of the manse, waving to get Ludwig's attention as he pulled up. Where were Ma and Sadie? What had happened? *Not now. Not when things have been going so well.*

Ludwig drove the buggy right up to the house. "It's Mrs. Sutton," he said, explaining that they'd found her unconscious on the prairie. "She's been thrown by her horse. She might have a broken arm. We knew that you would want to know—even though Dr. Gilbert said that he didn't see any need to worry. She will mend."

"But she wasn't awake yet when you left?"

Ludwig shook his head. "Dr. Gilbert called for the aunts to come. I took Sadie and Mrs. Nash home, but then we decided you would want to know—perhaps right away."

Cass hesitated. How could the doctor know she'd be all right? Plenty of people died after being thrown from a horse. And a broken arm? That wasn't exactly a minor injury. Aunt Lydia and her sister had to be terrified.

112

Pastor Taylor would want to know. And while Cass wasn't sure about Miss Theodora's spiritual bent, Aunt Lydia would surely be comforted to have her pastor call. He saddled Baron and headed into Lincoln alongside Ludwig Meyer's rented buggy. They parted ways at the livery, and Cass hurried to the parsonage.

"Will you let me know how she is?" Cass asked.

Pastor Taylor smiled. "Why don't you come along?"

"I don't want to overstep."

"It isn't overstepping to show concern. And surely your mother and sister would like to know. I take it they didn't linger at the doctor's office."

Cass shook his head. "They wouldn't." Ma and Sadie were shy about meeting what Sadie called "real people." They hadn't even braved going to church yet. Cass understood, although he hoped that would change soon. He'd been what people called a loner, too. The situation was just awkward. It was hard to know how to handle conversations that most people didn't give a second thought about. He couldn't exactly talk about his family when Ma and Sadie were at Goldie's. Most people at church probably thought he didn't have family. That would change now, but the idea of people asking questions still made him nervous, especially for Ma and Sadie's sake.

"Come with me." The pastor smiled. "It'll be fine."

Cass went, but he was relieved for more than one reason when they got to the doctor's. First because Dr. Gilbert's diagnosis hadn't changed and second because the aunts had already taken Mrs. Sutton home. He wouldn't have to explain his mother and sister "suddenly" appearing in Lincoln—to Aunt Lydia or to anyone else. Pastor Taylor knew the truth, but he could be trusted to give it all time to work itself out.

The pastor bid Cass good-bye just outside the doctor's office. "I'll call on Mrs. Sutton tomorrow and leave any news with Mr. Finney at the office." He paused. "Would you like to send a message either to Aunt Lydia or to Mrs. Sutton?"

Cass said no, but once he stopped by the office himself to go over the next day's work assignments, he decided it couldn't hurt to send a note to reassure Mrs. Sutton that there wasn't anything about the project that she needed to worry about.

Mr. Meyer rode out to inform me of your misfortune. I am so sorry. I went at once to inform Pastor Taylor, thinking that you all might welcome his concern. I hope that that was all right. The pastor encouraged me to accompany him to the doctor's office. I was greatly relieved to hear Dr. Gilbert say that he expects a full recovery, although the arm will take a few weeks to mend.

Please know that I am at your service and am happy to offer regular reports as to our progress on the house if you do not feel up to making the journey to the site. I can also bring the plans to you if you wish to see them or to offer further advice as to how things should proceed. If I can be of assistance in any way, please do not hesitate to send word. May God grant you a speedy recovery. I remain,

Respectfully yours,
Cass Gregory

He rewrote the thing over and over, checking for misspelled words, correcting the sentence structure, and hoping that the tone was the appropriate combination of respect and Christian concern. When he finally felt that he had it right, he tucked it into an envelope and placed it in the inside pocket of his jacket. He would take it to Mrs. Sutton's himself. At least he'd know he'd done what he could to allay any concerns she might have about Sutton Builders while she was on the mend. If there was one thing she didn't need, it was more worry about the business.

The sun had just dipped below the horizon when he rode up the drive and dismounted by the walkway that led up to the front porch. He hesitated. Front door or back door? He was a hired worker. *Back door.* Walking around to the back, he stepped up on the porch and knocked. When Martha Gaines opened the door, Cass could see

Aunt Lydia and Miss Theodora seated at the kitchen table. He reached inside his coat and withdrew the envelope, intending only to hand it to Martha and leave, but before he could say anything, Aunt Lydia called for him to step inside. He did so, hat and note in hand.

"Mr. Meyer rode out to the job site to tell me about Mrs. Sutton's accident. I wanted—"

Aunt Lydia rose and took the note. "Pastor Taylor told us. It was so kind of you to let him know about Juliana. I'm certain she'll be very touched by your concern." She took his arm. "Now you must join us and have a cup of tea." She glanced at her sister. "You remember Mr. Gregory from the funeral, Theodora. St. John's can always count on him to help set up for ice-cream socials and Ladies' Aid events." She winked at him. "And of course it never hurts when one's helpers are handsome."

Aunt Lydia was a dear, but she was making him blush, and it was clear that Miss Theodora was not amused by her banter. Cass declined the tea and prepared to make his escape. "Please tell Mrs. Sutton not to worry about anything but getting better. I'll see to the change she requested, and anything else can wait until she's fully recovered." With a nod to the ladies, he put his hat on and turned to go.

"Change?" Miss Theodora spoke up. "Why would changes be necessary? Mr. Duncan advised her to sell—and quickly."

Cass turned back. Took the hat off again. "Yes, ma'am. She told me as much today. But as I showed her around, it seemed that she wasn't certain about it."

"So you encouraged her to ignore her banker?"

"No, ma'am. But I did try to convince her to think it through on her own. To give herself some time and to trust her own judgment. Of course I was forthcoming about the fact that I want to finish the place. It's something any builder would be proud to say he created. I think all of us working out there feel that way. And then there's the fact that that project is supporting several men with families."

"You are a philanthropist, Mr. Gregory?"

115

Aunt Lydia spoke up. "You must excuse my sister, Cass. It's been a difficult time for us all, and she's more testy than usual."

Should he tell them about Duncan? Finally, he said, "I am not convinced that Mr. Duncan has Mrs. Sutton's best interests at heart. I told her so." He glanced at Miss Theodora. "If that results in a delay in her making a decision, then I suppose I must accept responsibility for that. But I stand by what I did. I don't think it's right for anyone to rush someone who has just endured a terrible loss to make a major decision. Especially if the decision maker doesn't have all the information."

"How fortunate for Juliana that you had *all* the information," Miss Theodora muttered.

Aunt Lydia glanced at her sister. "I'm certain Juliana appreciated Mr. Gregory's candor, Theodora. And he is correct. It is *her* right to decide for herself."

Miss Theodora snorted. "Must she always exercise every right to the nth degree?" She sounded weary.

Once again, Cass donned his hat. "I'll bid you both good evening now and look forward to hearing that Mrs. Sutton is recovered and ready to provide direction on the project."

Back in the saddle, Cass walked Baron out to the road before glancing back at the house. A faint, golden light illuminated an upstairs window. He said a quick prayer for Mrs. Sutton's healing. And another one regarding Mr. George Duncan that wasn't quite so kindly worded.

—⁕—

After bedding Baron down at the livery, Cass walked over to Ludwig Meyer's, pleased when a light in the window to the left of the front door indicated that Ma and Sadie were still up. When he knocked, Ma came to the door.

"I was just at Mrs. Sutton's," he said. "They're keeping a close watch on her, but everyone agrees that she's going to be all right."

"Thank God," Ma said. "I shudder to think what might have happened if we hadn't come along."

"I may suggest she drive a buggy out from now on. If that horse of hers is so flighty—"

"She said it wasn't Tecumseh's fault," Sadie said. "And I believe her. He's a sweet horse."

"*Sweet*," Cass said. "And you know this how?"

"He let me walk right up to him, and he seemed relieved someone was there to help. And as to telling her to bring a buggy next time, I thought you said she doesn't like being told what to do."

Cass relented. "You have a point." He noticed a pie atop the stove. "Is it too late to beg a piece of that?"

Ma smiled. "Never."

Once Cass was seated at the table, Ma sat down next to him. Folding her hands atop the table, she said, "I have something to discuss with you. Ludwig has made an interesting proposal. He's offered to sell me his house. Without a down payment and for very little monthly. Of course I'll also look for work as a cook," Ma said, "but I'm hoping that you might agree to board with me instead of over at that rooming house."

"Yes!"

He couldn't believe it. Sadie married to a good man, and Ma with her own house. What more could a man want? *A lot more.* A home. A family. A woman to love. An end to being the loner the old ladies at church loved and tried to pair off at every turn. An end to being alone. Did he dare let himself hope. . .even for that?

—⁂—

In the days following Mrs. Sutton's accident, Cass did his best to be a conscientious foreman. At first, he used the boss's phone in the office to call every day and report on progress out at the building site. Of course he didn't expect to talk to Mrs. Sutton every time he called, but as time wore on, he began to feel like she was avoiding him—especially the day that Martha went to get her, but then came back with the message that Mrs. Sutton didn't feel up to coming to the phone.

After a while, Cass couldn't help but think she didn't want to speak with him, and since he didn't have anything really important to say, he quit calling. Still, he couldn't shake the uneasy feeling that something was wrong. She'd been so easy to get along with that day out at the job site. Kind, interested, charming, even. Had he said something, done something to lose her trust? If so, he needed to know. Was George Duncan up to something? If so, Cass felt that he deserved a chance to defend himself. Why wouldn't she come to the phone?

Finally, after nearly two weeks had gone by, Cass was delayed in town checking on the request to cancel the order for the exotic woods the boss had planned to install in the upstairs bedrooms. While he wouldn't be able to show a lady the contents of the telegram that finally came, the supplier had agreed to a cancellation. Since Cass had promised to let Mrs. Sutton know if he managed it, he called right away to share the good news and was pleasantly surprised when she answered the phone.

"It's good to hear your voice. This is Cass Gregory."

There was a long silence. Finally, she said, "Is there something you need?"

"No, ma'am. I've been concerned, is all. Hoping you were on the mend."

"I am."

Silence. Again. "You said to cancel the shipment on the exotic woods if I could. There's an unhappy middleman in Chicago, but I managed to do it."

"Good."

"Is there anything else you'd like changed? Is there news?"

"I'll let you know."

She hung up. So abruptly, that for a moment Cass sat staring at the earpiece in his hand like an idiot.

Finney, who'd heard only Cass's part of the conversation, looked over at him. "Sounds like you didn't exactly get a warm reception."

Cass hung up. He didn't know what to say. He could not imagine what he might have done or said to offend her. Or was he right? Was

George Duncan up to something? The idea put a knot in the pit of his stomach.

—∾—

Juliana put the earpiece back in its cradle and stood looking out the kitchen window toward Tecumseh's pasture. She looked down at her arm, wishing Dr. Gilbert could be convinced to reconsider the six-week moratorium he'd declared against her riding. She might not want to hobnob with Mr. Gregory at the building site, but that didn't mean she was content to forgo riding.

From where she stood in the kitchen, she could hear murmuring voices floating down the hall from the parlor. Aunt Lydia's quilting friends were having their first meeting here since Sterling's death. It had taken a good deal of convincing on Aunt Lydia's part to assure the ladies that they were welcome—in spite of the custom which dictated no visitors for six months.

Good cause or not, Aunt Theodora had made no secret of her disdain for her sister's "flaunting convention." Juliana hesitated in the kitchen, torn between welcoming the ladies and checking on Aunt Theodora in her room upstairs. Finally, she opted for the latter. She'd just reached the landing off from which the aunts' rooms opened, when the older woman opened her door. She had changed into her best mourning attire and stood framed in the doorway, a look of uncertainty on her face.

"Perhaps I have been too severe," she said. Doubt clouded her features. "But I don't know. Now that I'm dressed and thinking of descending—" She paused. "I do wish God had granted me the self-assurance He seems to have given my sister." She looked at Juliana. "And you."

"Me?" Juliana almost laughed out loud. "Nearly everything I've done since Sterling died has shocked and irritated you."

"Nonsense." She gazed down the stairs. "They *are* doing a very good work. And the house has been so. . .quiet. . .since the dear boy. . ." She blinked back tears.

"Why don't we go down together? I'm useless with this arm, but perhaps we could offer to read to the ladies while they quilt. You do read so very well, Aunt Theodora." Juliana smiled. "I'd think you'd been on the stage if I didn't know better."

"And now you're making fun of me." A smile lingered behind the words.

"Just a little. It's inspired by affection, you know. Do you mind, terribly?"

"Not at all. I miss Sterling's teasing me."

"He used to call you the dowager countess." Juliana nodded. "I'd forgotten."

"And I always pretended to take offense."

"He knew you loved it." She smiled. "If you'll linger in the sitting area up here, I'll get changed, and we can go down together. I'm running late because of that phone call."

"I heard. Anything to be concerned about?"

Aunt Theodora considered telephone calls in the category of telegrams. They only arrived with dire news. "No." Juliana shook her head. "Mr. Gregory was able to make a change I'd requested in regards to the new house."

"How kind of him." The older woman paused. "He seems rather young for the amount of responsibility that's been thrust upon him. I do hope he's up to the task. Do you know what kind of experience he had before my nephew hired him on?"

Juliana shook her head. "Sterling always seemed pleased with his work ethic and skill. He trusted him. I do know that."

"Well, then. It would appear you have a good man on board. Intelligence, work ethic, honesty, and all of it in a very handsome package." She motioned up the hall. "Shall we, my dear? I'll wait for you."

As it always did, the specter of the locket lurking in that drawer across the room rose up the moment Juliana closed the bedroom door behind her. Today, it was joined by the memory of Mr. Gregory's redhead and the madam driving out to Juliana's property to talk about rebuilding.

Aunt Lydia would be crushed if she knew that her "good" Mr. Cass Gregory had such dealings. What if Pastor Taylor knew that one of his church members was helping someone build a brothel?

And what did it mean for her? Juliana sighed. She couldn't avoid him forever.

—⁂—

The moment Juliana and Aunt Theodora descended to the parlor, conversation around the quilt stopped. Juliana forced a smile. "I'm afraid I'll be of no help at all with the quilting, but I have convinced Aunt Theodora to grace us with a reading."

"How wonderful!" Aunt Lydia looked at the three other women seated at the quilt. "You are in for a delightful afternoon. No one has more refined elocution than my sister."

Clearly taken by surprise, Aunt Theodora bowed as she was introduced to Edith Pritchart, Lutie Gleason, and Medora Riley. Then she excused herself and fled into the library in search of "an appropriate offering."

When Juliana headed toward the sofa by the open windows, Mrs. Pritchart spoke up. "Now, dearie, don't be taking yourself all the way across the room from the conversation." She rose and pulled the desk chair out of the corner and plopped it at the quilting frame, then hesitated. "Unless of course, it pains your arm?"

At the mention of Juliana's arm, Lutie Gleason retrieved a needlepoint pillow from the sofa. "Here you are, my dear. Always keep it elevated. It will help keep the swelling down."

Medora Riley chimed in with a mention of an herbal tea known to promote healing of the bones. "I'll have my man bring you some first thing in the morning," she said. "Warm compresses help, as well."

"Indeed, they do," Mrs. Gleason countered, "but alternating between warm and cold is even more effective."

"Do you still suffer from headache, dear?" Mrs. Prichart asked. "Lydia said it's been frightful. Nothing is better for headache than Dr. Chase's drops. I'll write out the recipe and have it brought down. Catnip tea is good, too."

All in all, not half an hour after Juliana had joined the group, she felt literally wrapped in affection. She'd known that Aunt Lydia felt close to her church friends, but this was Juliana's first chance to be among them. She was so glad that she had not hidden away, that she and Aunt Theodora had joined them.

When Aunt Theodora concluded her first reading of Tennyson, the friends demanded an encore. Lutie Gleason spoke up. "Would you mind reading 'Crossing the Bar'? I find that such a comforting perspective, especially the closing line about seeing our Pilot face to face."

After the reading of "Crossing the Bar," it was time for lunch. When Martha served up gooseberry pie, the talk turned to the bazaar. Martha offered to make five pies and a batch of jelly for the silent auction. And before Juliana quite knew how it had happened, she had agreed to accompany the ladies on a gooseberry-picking outing.

"And I know just where to go," Aunt Lydia said. "There is a massive thicket of bushes on Juliana's land south of town."

CHAPTER 13

Mercy and truth are met together;
righteousness and peace have kissed each other.
PSALM 85:10

It had been weeks since Margaret had been awakened by the sound of crying. Thinking that she'd been dreaming, she adjusted her pillow and lay back down. But there it was again. *Sadie?* In the pre-dawn light, Margaret glanced over at the pallet on the floor. Sadie had insisted she be the one to sleep there. Neither one of them felt comfortable in Ludwig's room, even though he was living at Cass's rooming house.

Margaret went to the door. Sadie stood by the stove, her head in her hands.

"What's wrong?" Margaret hurried to her side.

"I c–can't d–do anything," Sadie sobbed. "I—I woke up and was going to make biscuits, but I don't remember how." She sniffed loud and long. "And I ground the coffee, but I don't know how much to put in to make it. She dropped her head in her hands again. "Ludwig won't w–want me. He'll st–starve w–with me as h–his w–wife."

Margaret pulled Sadie into her arms and let the girl weep. "Ludwig," she said quietly as she stroked Sadie's long red hair, "adores you. And I believe you know someone who can teach you to cook. All you have to do is ask."

Sadie calmed a bit. Margaret sat her down at the kitchen table.

123

"Wait here," she said, and went into Ludwig's room to retrieve paper and pencil from the small box on his desk. Back in the main room, she set the paper before Sadie. "What do you need to know how to make?"

"Everything," Sadie moaned.

"Not everything. You could make breakfast when you were only twelve years old."

"Anybody can fry up ham and eggs." Sadie shrugged. She looked up at Margaret. "Ludwig likes pie. He was down talking to Mr. Jessup last week, and when he came back, he said there's a big thicket of gooseberries down that way. He went on and on about how his *Mutti* used to make the best pie." She began to cry again. "And I don't know the first thing about making a pie." She looked at her mother. "He's going to hate being married to me."

"Sadie Gregory!" Margaret gave her a little shake. "Stop your blubbering." She tapped the paper with her finger. "Write down a whole week of meals. Think about what I cooked at Goldie's. What did you like? What do you know Ludwig likes? Make a list. We'll ask Cass about the gooseberries this evening."

Sadie wrote while Margaret made coffee. By the time she set a steaming mug in front of the girl, Sadie had a week's worth of meals written down. Margaret looked it over. As she read down the list, she nodded until she came to some words she didn't know. "What's this?" she set the paper down and pointed to the group of foreign words.

"I don't know how to spell them, but those are things Ludwig said his ma made." She pronounced the words as she went down the list. "Boarsht. Feffernoose. Plat-shinda. Kook-in. Flyshkookla."

"Well," Margaret sighed, "I haven't any idea what any of those are. We'll have to ask Ludwig."

"No! I want to surprise him! I don't want him to know I can't cook."

"Sadie." Margaret sat down again. She looked meaningfully into her daughter's blue eyes. "Ludwig knows you haven't spent your time cooking."

Sadie blinked. She looked away. "I still want to surprise him. And I want to be a good wife."

Margaret chuckled. "Daughter, I do believe you have fallen in love."

Sadie ducked her head. Shrugged. "I guess I have. I sure don't want him to starve because of me."

"All right, then." Margaret got up and, crossing to the hooks by the door, took down two aprons and handed Sadie one. "Biscuits," she said.

And the lessons began.

—⁓—

Just after sunrise early in May, Cass met Ma and Sadie at the livery. He rented a buggy and an ancient mare for them and led the way south of town, crisscrossing ahead of the buggy, keeping his eye out for the thicket of gooseberries he'd found after Ma had asked about them. It had to be near here—*there. Right there.* He urged Baron to a trot, and when he'd verified the find, he waved in the direction of Ma and Sadie's buggy.

As they drove up, Ma asked again. "You're sure Mrs. Sutton won't mind?"

"I asked Aunt Lydia at church yesterday. She said it would be fine. Her committee wants to come out this week, but she said they'll never use them all."

Ma climbed down from the buggy. "My goodness," she said. "I don't know when I've seen bushes so laden with fruit." She smiled up at him. "We only want enough for a pie-baking lesson. They won't even notice we've been here."

Cass dismounted, hitched Baron to the rented buggy, and began to pick gooseberries. Ma began to hum, and before long the three of them had filled the basket she'd brought along.

Sadie climbed back up to the buggy seat. "There's gooseberry pie tonight if you know anybody who might be interested."

"Is that an invitation to supper?"

"It's an invitation to dessert."

"Accepted. Pie for supper. I like it." Cass untied Baron's reins and stood watching as the buggy headed back into Lincoln. If he'd ever doubted Sadie's feelings for Ludwig Meyer, the fact that she wanted to learn to cook for him was proof. He lifted his face to the sky. "Thank You." *This is the day the Lord has made. I will rejoice and be glad in it.* He bent to pluck a wildflower and tucked it into his coat lapel. Baron whickered. Someone was headed this way. Riding a tall red horse.

Mrs. Sutton? She wasn't supposed to be riding until June sometime. He took his hat off and waited for her to come within earshot.

"Does Dr. Gilbert know you've disobeyed his orders?"

"Does my aunt know you've been purloining the berries she needs for her fundraiser?"

The look on her face—she was really angry. Over gooseberries? "I thought you knew. I asked at church yesterday. Aunt Lydia said it would be all right." Tecumseh had sensed her distress. Tossing his head, he began to prance about. "Doesn't that hurt your arm? Can I help you down?"

"Dr. Gilbert decided it's just a sprain. And please do not change the subject."

Cass nodded. "All right. I'm sorry if I misunderstood. It was only enough for a couple of pies." He looked at the thicket of bushes and then back up at her. "I doubt you'll even miss them."

She looked after the buggy. Back at him. "You said one pie. Now it's two?"

"Ma'am?"

She nodded toward the buggy disappearing in the distance. "I saw you with your arm around that—woman—the night of the fire."

All right. So she'd seen more than she'd let on before. "Yes, ma'am. I was thanking God they were all right."

Mrs. Sutton sucked in a breath. "I do not wish anyone ill, Mr. Gregory. But I object in the most intense way possible to your association with those—people."

"You object?"

"Yes." She nodded. "To your inviting them onto *my* land and offering a stonemason in *my* employ to help them rebuild. And"— she was picking up steam—"to my gooseberries being given away." She glowered at him. "Do you have any idea—"

She broke off. She must be in pain. She was trying not to cry and losing the battle. Or maybe this was just a bad day. People could act strange after losing someone. Half the men in Cass's regiment in the war had seemed crazy at one time or another. Back then, the best thing had seemed to be to let them have their feelings and avoid trying to talk them out of them. Trying to convince Mrs. Sutton that she was being ridiculous was probably the worst thing he could do. So he'd apologize. Over the gooseberries he had permission to pick.

"I'm sorry. Truly. Aunt Lydia said you wouldn't mind about the berries. I should have talked to you myself. But you haven't seemed to want to speak to me. I would never intentionally presume on your gooseberries." Did he really just say that? He pressed his lips together to keep from laughing. "And as to the building, I told you about Jessup taking that job, remember? The day you came out to the house. The day of the accident. You didn't seem to have a problem with it then. Jessup's kept his word, and so have I. You aren't being cheated out of a minute of his time. Or mine. But if you've changed your mind and you don't want him to—"

"It isn't that," she snapped. Tecumseh's ears shot back to take in what she was saying. It did nothing to calm him down. "It's the principle of the thing. The sneaking around. The hiding. The pretending that all is well." She glared at him. "How *can* you sit in Pastor Taylor's church on Sunday morning, pretend that you're helping him with some poor unfortunate's funeral, and then continue to *consort* with them? How can you?!" She drew in a ragged breath. "I suppose you think it doesn't matter. After all, my own husband. . ." Her voice wavered. "Well, I didn't. . .*know* about St–Sterling." She was losing the battle not to cry.

He wanted to reach over and take her hand. Help her down off that horse. Comfort her. Of course he didn't dare.

She recovered enough to continue. "I was stupid and naive. But I am no longer either one, and I *will not have any more of it*, do you hear me?" She spoke slowly, her voice clear, her tone cold, now that she'd conquered the tears. "I will not have men working for me who pretend to be gallant and go to church and then laugh behind my back all the way to the brothel."

His mouth dropped open. "You what?"

She drew herself up. "I am giving you notice, Mr. Gregory. I do, however, expect you to remain on task until I have found a qualified foreman. You're very good at playing the gentleman. It shouldn't inconvenience you to continue the charade while I seek your replacement."

Half of what the woman had just blathered didn't make a bit of sense. But he'd understood the last part, loud and clear. "You're *firing* me?" He looked toward the buggy disappearing into the distance. "Because I let my mother and sister pick gooseberries?"

She gazed after the buggy. Looked back at him. "Please, Mr. Gregory. I know who that was."

"Who do you think it was?"

"The madam they call Goldie. And one of her. . .girls." She swallowed. "As I said earlier, I saw you with them the night of the fire. And again at the cemetery. You were driving a wagon. And those same women were on the seat next to you."

"You were at the cemetery when we buried Nell Parker?"

"I was. I often ride there. I'd taken Tecumseh down the hill to the creek. But there was no question that it was you."

She'd seen him. He took a deep breath. "Of course it was me. But that's not Goldie." He sighed. There was no way around it. He had to tell her. Firing a prayer to heaven, he explained. "My mother's name is Margaret. And the redhead is Sadie. She's my little sister. And yes, they worked for Goldie. Mother was the cook, and Sadie was exactly what you think. But neither of them works for Goldie anymore—and neither of them ever will again. And if you'll just. . .calm down, I'll explain it. All of it. Anything you want to know."

He didn't know how to interpret the expression on her face. He glanced off toward the job site. "Are you up to riding all the way out to the place? The men will be wondering where I am. I had Jessup oversee loading things up this morning so that I could help Ma and Sadie." He looked up at her. "Truly, Mrs. Sutton. Aunt Lydia said it was all right. I wouldn't have presumed. Ever."

Her jaw was set. She didn't answer.

"Please. You can't fire me. I mean, of course you can—but please don't. Not until you've heard what I have to say."

She looked back from the direction she'd come. "Everyone will worry if I don't come right back. They didn't want me riding yet. Alfred had to help me mount up." She looked down at her gloved hands. Put one palm to her injured arm.

"I'll send someone to tell them you're all right. That you came out to the site. And once I get things going, once we've talked, I'll escort you back. If you're tired, I'll drive you back. Please, Mrs. Sutton. Just. . .let's talk."

She didn't look him in the eyes, but she nodded and gave a curt, "All right."

Cass mounted Baron, and they headed out.

———

By the time Cass Gregory and Juliana rode onto the job site, a few men had begun to work, but more were milling about, clearly waiting for Mr. Gregory. Before he went to speak with them, he helped her dismount. "I'll turn Tecumseh into the pasture. You look a little pale. I hope this wasn't a mistake."

"I look pale because I haven't been allowed out of doors by the aunts," Juliana snapped. "My arm hurts and I have a bit of a headache, but I'll be fine. I'll wait inside." She took a deep breath. "I wouldn't refuse a drink of water." She wouldn't refuse something a little stronger, either, but a lady didn't admit to such things.

Mr. Gregory nodded. "Jessup! Get Mrs. Sutton a drink of water while I turn her horse out." He called for Mr. Klein and handed him

Baron's reins. "You know Mrs. Sutton's house? Good. Ride in and tell them she decided to come out to the building site. I'll drive her back in shortly. Just make sure they know she's all right."

As Klein urged Baron into a lope and headed off, Mr. Gregory unlocked the door to the caretaker's house. It was cool and quiet inside. Juliana opened the windows in the main room. Wincing, she pulled her gloves off and flexed her fingers. Her right hand and arm throbbed. The part of her hand that was exposed seemed a little puffy. She shrugged out of her riding jacket. Rolling up the sleeve of her waist, she began to unwrap her arm. The cooling breeze felt good.

Mr. Jessup, tin mug in hand, knocked on the doorframe. "Your water, ma'am?"

Juliana sat down on the stairs and took the water with her left hand. "Thank you." He turned to go. "Tell me about the building you're doing—for those other people."

"You mean the general store in Roca?"

"General store?"

"Yes, ma'am. I told them right up that I can only work on the weekends. I hired a couple of men to keep things going during the week." He frowned. "Is that a problem? Because if it is, I'll tell Mr. Meyer he has to find someone else."

Juliana shook her head. "No. I was just—interested."

"It's pretty standard fare. Store on the first floor. Living quarters on the second." He smiled. "Mr. Meyer has himself a right pert fiancée. Almost as pretty as my Diana." He tugged on the brim of his hat and excused himself.

Mr. Gregory's voice sounded just outside, parceling out work, asking questions, answering others. Juliana took a sip of water and then sat, staring down at the floor, trying to remember everything she'd said in the heat of the moment.

Mr. Gregory came in. He removed his hat and set it on the makeshift table, then crossed to the three windows in the south wall and perched on one of the wide ledges. He folded his arms across his chest and met her gaze. "I have *never* lied to you. I have never deliberately misled you."

She set the mug of water next to her on the stair. "I want to believe that." She did. She wanted to be able to trust him. Heaven knew she needed someone she could trust in all of this.

He grimaced. Took a deep breath. "I thought you might have seen me that night, but I decided to hope that even if you had, you'd dismiss it as part of the chaos. There were a lot of people milling about, and more than just me trying to help the victims. I didn't say anything because I was trying to protect Ma and Sadie." He looked out the window. "And you, if you come right down to it."

"Me?"

He looked back at her. "Yes, ma'am. I decided that your knowing about my mother and sister would likely just stir up things best laid to rest. And not just for them. I was afraid you'd ask more questions about that night. About Goldie's and—"

"And my husband," Juliana murmured.

He nodded. "As I said earlier, both Ma and Sadie are finished with that life. Sadie's engaged to a good man, and Ma's going to look for other work. I didn't think anything but pain could come of your asking questions." He paused. His tone lost its defensive edge as he said, "And you've had enough of that."

Juliana looked away. How was it that sympathy and understanding made it difficult for her to control her tears? She wanted the anger back. Then again, lately she'd tended to shed tears when she was angry, too. Would there ever be an end to tears? Finally, she spoke up. "I told myself exactly that at first. That you were just in the crowd and what I saw didn't mean anything. But then I saw you again at the cemetery. And then those same two women came to the job site that day." She shrugged. "It all started to add up."

"They carried you to Dr. Gilbert's after you fell off Tecumseh."

"I know. I kept the doc from telling me very much about it. To be honest, I was glad they weren't there when I woke up. I didn't want to have to thank them." She paused. "It made me angry to think of owing thanks to the very people I blamed for my husband's—for our—" She couldn't say any more. She just shook her head.

Mr. Gregory nodded. "I understand." He took a deep breath. Raked his hand through his curly hair. "I'll tell you anything you want to know, or we don't have to talk about it at all. It's up to you."

Juliana reached for the cup of water and took a sip. "I'd like to be able to trust you, Mr. Gregory. Lord knows I need people I can trust. Sadly, I know you're right about George Duncan. And I have my doubts about Mr. Graham, as well." She forced a little smile. "Aunt Lydia has endorsed you, and that means a great deal. People tend to think she's gullible, but she isn't. She's just gentle hearted. She 'believes all things' and 'hopes all things' for the people she cares about. And for whatever reason, you are one she cares about."

"It's a great honor to hear you say that. Aunt Lydia is a treasure."

"They both are," Juliana said. "Aunt Theodora just hides it. I'm not sure why. She always has." She drew a deep breath. "I've never pried into her past, and it occurs to me that it isn't fair for me to pry into yours. You've explained enough. If you don't want to say any more, I understand."

"I offered, and now that I know what you've been seeing, what you've been thinking. . .I want to set things straight. The boss knew all about me. You might as well, too." He took a deep breath. "I was nine when my father died. Ma remarried fast. To a man named Ronald Nash. He was delighted when Ma got in the family way shortly after they married, but he didn't take to me." He shrugged. "For the most part, Nash did a good job of hiding his aversion. But one night when I was taking too much time mucking out a stall in the barn, he let his temper get the best of him." He grimaced.

Juliana wondered what he was remembering.

"I ran off that night. A few days later, I enlisted in the Union Army."

Juliana frowned. "But you would have been far too young."

He nodded. "I was only fourteen. But I've always been big for my age, and they didn't ask too many questions. I didn't write home.

I was afraid someone would discover the truth and send me back. After the war, I went back to see Ma and my baby sister." He stopped. Glanced back out the window. "You ever heard about Quantrill's raid on Lawrence, Kansas?"

Oh, no. Not that. "Yes."

"Well, they killed Nash and burned the house and barn. No one knew what had happened to Ma and Sadie." He shrugged. "So I spent the next few years looking. I went back to Ohio, first. That's where Ma grew up. But it was like they'd just disappeared. I drifted from job to job until Mr. Sutton visited the site of the bridge construction in Omaha. He kept at me to come to Lincoln. Finally, I did. Then one day I was in a lunchroom down by the warehouse, and three women walked by. It wasn't any secret what kind of women they were from the way they were dressed. But there was an older woman behind them. Sort of like a mother hen."

"Your mother."

He bit his lower lip. Blinked away tears. "Yes, ma'am. Turns out they'd drifted all around, too. Kansas City, first. Then Omaha. Finally, here with Goldie when she started a—" He cleared his throat. "A new business."

Juliana didn't know what to think. It was hard to believe a woman couldn't find honorable work. Couldn't she have been a seamstress or a nanny? Anything but what she did. When Mr. Gregory continued, it was as if he'd read her mind.

"I know what you're probably thinking. But Ma didn't start out in those places. She had a job cooking at a boardinghouse in return for a place for herself and Sadie. Then she got sick. She nearly died. And of course as the weeks went by and Ma wasn't cooking, they owed more and more money. They were about to get kicked out on the street. Sadie was fifteen. She'd been getting attention at the boardinghouse where they lived. And so—" His voice wavered. "Sadie took it on herself to earn the rent. When Ma got well enough to discover Sadie wasn't cooking to earn their way, she threw a fit. But Sadie wouldn't back down. Said she was tired of being poor."

He stood up. Thrusting his hands in his pockets, he stared out the window at the horizon. "So that's my tale of woe. If I hadn't run off, none of it would have happened."

"You were only a boy. What could you have done about Quantrill? They might have killed you, too."

Cass shrugged. "Ma had finally come to terms with my being lost to her. But she refused the idea of losing the only child left to her. So when Sadie took Goldie up on an offer to help open a new place in Lincoln, Ma came along as the cook."

"How are they faring now? Since the fire? You said your sister's engaged?"

He smiled. Nodded. "That's another long story. But he's a good man, and he's waited a long while for her. He took Ma and Sadie in the night of the fire. He has a little house in the Russian Bottoms. And he took a room in my rooming house to protect their reputation, if you can believe that." He started to laugh, but then tears began to spill down his face. He swiped them away, but they kept coming. "I guess that's a lot more than you needed to know."

Juliana didn't know what to say, so she waited.

Finally, he took a deep breath. "I'm sorry you've had even more trouble because of me." He turned to look at her. "I knew about him. I made excuses for myself. Told myself I couldn't risk it. I needed the job. After all, I had to be ready to take care of Ma and Sadie." He shook his head. "The truth is I was too much of a coward to face him, so I looked the other way." He glanced down at her. "I should have said something. Maybe he would have listened."

"He wouldn't have." Juliana hesitated, then decided to trust. "Nell Parker wasn't the only one. I found evidence of others." She allowed a bitter laugh. "The night he died. Right before the alarm rang."

After a long silence, he said, "I am so sorry."

"So am I. For so many things. Among them, throwing a fit over gooseberries." She took a last sip of water and rose. "You can open the door. I believe the hysterics are over for today." As she rewrapped her arm, she said, "If you're still willing to drive me back, I'd appreciate it.

134

Going riding today probably wasn't the wisest thing I've ever done. Although, I beg you not to tell the aunts I just said that."

"Your secret is safe with me, ma'am."

Juliana nodded. Yes. Somehow, Aunt Lydia's faith in him aside, Juliana knew that Cass Gregory was a man to be trusted. A man who had proven his capacity for great loyalty and the kind of love that lasted through the worst of circumstances.

She thought about it all the way back to town. About what Mr. Gregory's life must have been like all those years of searching for his family. The loneliness. And then the stubborn refusal to desert his mother and sister, even when there seemed no hope that things would ever change.

What would it be like to know that kind of love? The kind that survived in spite of circumstances? The kind that hoped all things and endured all things and never failed. *Even when a woman couldn't have children.*

Alfred came out of the house the moment the wagon drove up. "There was no small stir when Miss Theodora and Miss Lydia got your message," he said to Juliana as he took Tecumseh in hand.

"I've learned my lesson. It's too early to ride." After Mr. Gregory helped her down, she smiled up at him. "I've learned many lessons, today."

The foreman tipped his cap, climbed back up to the wagon seat, and headed south. Juliana stood watching until he disappeared from view. *Cass Gregory. Pastor Taylor. Sadie Gregory's fiancé. Alfred Gaines.* Maybe men of integrity weren't extinct, after all.

CHAPTER 14

Be ye therefore merciful, as your Father also is merciful.
LUKE 6:36

Jenny
Monday, May 7

Jenny sat in a chair on the front porch, a tattered quilt draped across her lap. She was trying not to feel sad, but it was hard. It didn't seem to matter how much she slept, she never felt rested. Susannah was a passable cook, but everything tasted the same, and nothing really tasted good. It had been a week of resting and eating soup, but she wasn't getting better, and she was scared.

Dr. Gilbert had called today, and all he would say was that she had been very sick and her lungs still weren't clear and she should rest. He hadn't heard from Mr. Duncan and he "couldn't speak to what that meant." He was kind enough. He just didn't know anything.

Susannah told her not to worry. She had all kinds of stories about sick women she had tended over the years, and she assured Jenny that she was on the mend and just had to wait. Johnny was doing fine. Maybe they could get Mr. Duncan to bring a goat out.

"Not that I mind tendin' the boy," she said, "but he'll do just fine on goats' milk, and then you won't need me."

Jenny couldn't imagine not needing Susannah. How would she keep up with washing diapers? She could barely pump a bucket of water and haul it into the house, let alone enough buckets for boiling diapers. Used to be that just sitting out here listening for the occasional birdcall and making plans for the future was enough to still her mind. But no more. Jenny was worried. Worried and afraid. Mr. Duncan had said she should make plans. How could she make plans when she was too tired to do her own hair?

Susannah stepped out on the porch, Johnny in her arms. "Now show your mama what you learned!" She plopped down on the edge of the porch and set the baby down beside her. At first, she held him upright, but then she said, "Just watch, Miss Jenny. You won't believe it." And she let go.

Johnny looked up at Susannah with a big smile on his face. Susannah clapped her hands. The baby followed suit, laughing for all he was worth. Laughing so hard it almost made him fall over.

"Isn't that somethin'?" Susannah said. "He's getting strong."

Jenny nodded. It was something. A good something. Except that it made her cry.

———

Cass patted his stomach even as he waved Sadie away. "I can't. It's delicious, but I'm going to turn into a gooseberry if I eat one more piece."

"You mean it? It's really good?"

"It's better than good," Ludwig Meyer chimed in. He winked at Ma. "It's almost as if you learned from a professional cook."

"Oh, you." Sadie smiled and plopped the pie plate down on the table. Then she invited herself into Ludwig's lap, wrapping an arm about his neck and leaning close to kiss his cheek. "It's only the beginning. Ma had me write down a week's worth of cooking. She's teaching me fried chicken and biscuits and gravy and roast beef and all kinds of things you like."

Ma spoke up. "There is a bit of a problem, though." She twisted about and pulled a piece of paper from beneath a bowl on the sideboard. "Sadie mentioned some things that I have no idea how to make."

Sadie nodded. "Kuchen?"

"A dessert pastry," Ludwig said. "With filling. It can be fruit, but my Mutti always made a custard filling."

"And borscht?"

"Soup," Ludwig said. "Mostly beets."

"Do you have recipes for these things?" Ma asked.

Ludwig shook his head. "I never saw it written down."

"I could ask Andreas Moser," Cass offered. "He's on the crew working on Mrs. Sutton's house, and he's always boasting about his wife's cooking. Or," he said, "you and Ludwig and Ma could come with me to church on Sunday and ask Mrs. Moser yourself. They go to St. John's."

Sadie shook her head. "She won't like me."

Ludwig leaned away to look at her. "Why would you say such a thing?"

"Because her husband—what if he. . .what if someone. . ." She shook her head. "They'll think I'm just pretending. Putting on airs."

Ma spoke up. "Are you pretending?"

"Of course not." Sadie looked at Ludwig, who had been strangely quiet. "Do you want me to go to church?"

Ludwig thought for a moment before answering. "Not for me. It should be for you."

She pondered that. "I won't fit in. They'll stare at me. And they'll know."

"What will they know, mein Schatz?"

"That I'm not like them. I'm not all hymn-sing-y and good."

Ludwig chuckled. "No one who goes to church is good without God's help."

"Well, you know what I mean." Sadie pointed at Ma. "You could go. You used to go all the time back home."

"And so did you."

Sadie shrugged. "I'm different now. You haven't really changed much. Only reason you worked at Goldie's was because of me."

Ma rose and began to clear the table. "We've put that all behind us, remember? Everyone forgave everyone, and we agreed to move forward."

Sadie rose and began to help clear the table. "And I meant it. I just—I'm not ready for church."

Ma smiled. "It's all right, sweetheart. I'll talk to Mrs. Moser about kuchen and borscht." She glanced at Cass. "If you'll introduce me."

"With pleasure."

After the women had cleared off the table, Ludwig brought out the checkerboard. Cass lost three games in a row. Finally, he sat back and said, "I give up, Meyer. I'm no match for you."

The men walked back to the rooming house together. As they passed the place where Goldie's had once stood, Cass thought back to that night and seeing Juliana Sutton driving her buggy home after finding her husband's office empty. *She knows.* What kind of pain did that cause a woman? How could she bear it? It was no wonder she'd been so angry with him when she thought he was keeping company with Goldie and one of her girls.

Once in his room, he lay on his back, looking up at the strip of night sky just visible through the small window above his bed. He replayed the day in his mind. He remembered the way Juliana's dark eyes flashed with anger and the way those same eyes had shimmered with tears. He remembered how, when he helped her down from the wagon, she smiled up at him. Sterling Sutton had been a fool to betray that woman's love. The worst kind of fool.

And he was a fool for lingering over dark eyes that might as well belong to the Queen of England.

—⁂—

"Dear me." From where she sat in the buggy with Juliana and Aunt Lydia, Aunt Theodora put a gloved hand to hold her hat in place as she craned her neck to look up at the house. "I had no idea." She looked at her sister. "Did you?"

Aunt Lydia shook her head. "It's one thing to see a drawing and quite another to see it realized."

Juliana nodded. "I know. And none of us had been out here in weeks when Sterling died." *Died.* Finally, she'd said the word. Sterling died. She looked about her. At the stone cottage, at the pasture. The

139

tall cottonwoods. All hers now. Saying that one word seemed to carve a new place for her in the physical space out here at the building site. It was hers to do with as she wished. Completely hers.

Aunt Theodora called up to Alfred. "And what do you think of the cottage, Mr. Gaines?"

He turned about on the driver's seat. "Can't quite think of it as home yet, but once Martha gets to nesting, I'm sure it'll be fine."

"Drive us around front if you don't mind, Alfred." Juliana looked at the aunts. "The stonemasons finished the front stairs this week. And I want you to see the interior."

Once inside, she pointed out the various rooms, still little more than framework. "Mr. Gregory said that the carpenter is already at work on the stairway. Apparently he's enjoying the challenge. I gather Sterling ordered something out of the ordinary."

"No doubt," Aunt Theodora said, looking up toward the second floor. "It's all quite out of the ordinary, isn't it?"

"There's a question about the entryway floor," Juliana said. "We have to decide if we want inlaid wood or marble."

"Marble? Really?" Aunt Lydia didn't seem to like that idea.

Juliana nodded. "Let's go upstairs." They all hugged the wall as she led the way up the sweeping staircase where more framing outlined the rooms. She named each one as they made their way up the hallway toward the back of the house.

"Goodness," Aunt Lydia remarked, looking over the temporary banister that framed the servant's stairs. "They're as wide as the front stairs at home."

Juliana nodded. She waved them into two rooms on the west side of the hall. "These are your rooms. Private dressing rooms off each bedroom and of course your own sitting room. Sterling told Mr. Gregory to put your suite toward the back of the house so that the comings and goings wouldn't disturb you. He expected we'd do a lot more entertaining once we moved out here." She pointed across the hall. "The master suite is over there. It's a mirror image of your suite except there's a porch." *Because I like to watch the sunrise.*

Together, they descended to the main floor and headed into the first room behind the stairs. "This would be the library," Juliana said and pointed at one corner. "Your piano will go there, Aunt Theodora." She crossed the room to the base of a spiral stairway leading up to a narrow walkway above. "Once the carpenter has installed the stairway—which of course has to wait until the windows are in— he'll begin building bookcases up there."

Aunt Theodora gazed around the room. "What library was Sterling going to purchase to fill them all?" She shook her head. "I know the dear boy has done well, but we aren't Vanderbilts." She paused. "I don't really recall Sterling being all that fond of reading. Unless you count the business page in the newspapers."

Aunt Lydia spoke up. "Martha cannot be expected to care for all of this."

"I know," Juliana said. "We didn't go up there, but the third-floor plan includes rooms for four servants off the ballroom."

"Four servants?" The aunts spoke in unison, but then Aunt Theodora finished the thought. "For three women? That's—"

"Absurd?" Juliana nodded. She finished the tour of the main floor, ending up in what would become the kitchen. Finally, she said, "George Duncan took Cass to breakfast the morning after the fire. And told him that he wants to buy this place."

"But. . ." Aunt Lydia frowned. "I don't understand. Didn't Mr. Duncan offer to make inquiries for you? He didn't say he was interested, did he?"

"No," Juliana said. "Even though he'd already mentioned it to Cass."

Aunt Theodora spoke up. "If George Duncan can afford a house like this, you might wish to request an audit of the bank books."

"Theodora," Aunt Lydia scolded.

"Well, it isn't even the largest bank in the city." She gestured about. "Where would George Duncan get the money for marble floors, servants, grand pianos, and libraries?"

"Apparently he wants to buy it as is," Juliana said.

"I see. A lower purchase price, and then Helen can finish it with inferior materials."

"There's no way to know what they'd do in the way of finishing, although I doubt marble flooring would remain on the list."

Aunt Theodora pursed her lips. "Do you remember the Duncans' parlor?" She shuddered. "Those abominable green draperies. And mauve walls. *Mauve*."

"Not everyone likes the same decor, Sister," Aunt Lydia said gently.

Aunt Theodora waved the comment away. "I can just hear the gossip now. 'What a shame the Suttons didn't have better taste. Can you *believe* the colors in that entryway?' When all the while it would be Helen Duncan's doing."

Juliana suppressed a smile. "Then you won't be upset to hear that I'm not going to sell to the Duncans."

"Thank heavens."

Aunt Lydia looked about her with an expression approaching dismay.

"What are you thinking, Aunt Lydia? I need your wisdom."

"That is very good of you, dear, but the fact remains that it isn't our decision to make."

"I'm not asking you to make the decision. I'm asking what you think. Honestly. Without worries about my feelings or desires. What do you think we should do?"

The older woman took a deep breath. "Well. . .of course it's stunning. But I just can't imagine rattling around in it. I'm picturing myself getting lost on the way to the water closet in the middle of the night and your having to send out a search party."

Juliana laughed. "All right, then. Let me raise a possibility. And while I hate to credit him after his underhanded ways, the fact is that the seed of this idea probably came from something Mr. Duncan said at that first meeting. Do you remember it? He said I could give this property away and never miss the money." The aunts nodded, and Juliana continued. "The first time I came out here after Sterling died, I met a man named Elmo Klein."

142

"I know Mr. Klein," Aunt Lydia said. "Lutie Gleason took him and his family in."

Juliana nodded. "Yes. When George Duncan, who apparently owns a number of rental properties, would have put them out on the street."

Aunt Theodora muttered, "How does that man sleep at night?"

"Obviously," Juliana continued, "we all agree that it's a travesty that good people like the Kleins should have nowhere to turn at times like that. That's part of the reason our society exists. But other people need help, too. People we tend to ignore. Girls like Nell Parker, for example. Did she turn to prostitution because it was her only alternative to hunger and homelessness?"

Aunt Theodora spoke up. "I applaud your concern and would also mention other girls who find themselves in a family way and cast out."

Juliana nodded. "Lincoln is growing, and as much as we all hate to admit it, when a city grows, problems multiply. Women like Lutie Gleason have been taking people into their homes for years now, and that's wonderful, but I think the society needs a building dedicated to helping even more people." She held out her hands, palms up. "And I have a building that I never wanted." She smiled at the aunts. "What would you think of giving it to the society?"

Aunt Lydia clasped her hands like an athlete celebrating a victory. "The Sterling Sutton Home for the Friendless. Yes!"

Aunt Theodora spoke up. "*Friendless* is such a bleak word. And the people who come to us won't be friendless, will they? I suggest we name it *Friendship Home*." She hesitated.

"But we must speak with Alfred and Martha. If we aren't moving out here..."

"We can't lose Alfred and Martha," Aunt Lydia agreed. She looked to Juliana. "If they want a stone cottage, can we build them one at home? We have an acre. There's plenty of room, isn't there?"

"There is." Juliana laughed. "And we'll give Alfred and Martha whatever they want."

But Alfred said that he and Martha wanted neither a move nor a stone cottage. "I won't say no to that stove Martha loves. But the fact is we like it right where we are." He smiled. "To tell you the truth, I have had some concern about living all the way out here in the country. A deacon should be close to home if he's to serve his flock. Martha and I will be more than happy to stay right where we are."

And so it was decided. They would announce the donation at the bazaar in June. The biggest challenge would be how to keep it a secret until then. There was much to do in the interim, and the three women chattered about it all the way back home. They would need a special meeting of the board to develop a new mission statement. A review of the house plans.

"We won't need a ballroom," Aunt Theodora said. "I was thinking perhaps a nursery, but it will be far too hot without cross ventilation in the summer. Do you suppose your Mr. Gregory would be able to add more windows to the third floor?"

Aunt Lydia chimed in. "And a full-time nurse can have one of the servants' rooms. There would be room for a large play area right there on the same floor." Her eyes sparkled with excitement. "We should have a toy drive in early December. People will be thinking about Christmas, and they can pass on their unwanted toys—the things their children have outgrown."

Aunt Theodora wondered if Mr. Gregory could manage a dumbwaiter to carry soiled linen from each floor to the basement. "Is there a basement? Because that would be a perfect location for a laundry room. And a pantry. We'll need a vast pantry. We should have him to supper. Or Sunday lunch. He can bring those plans in and tell us what he thinks."

Ideas blossomed all the way home. Ideas and joy. As the buggy drove into the yard behind the house, Juliana took it all in. *This* was where she wanted to live, sharing a home with the aunts, with Martha and Alfred in their apartment over the barn, the new capitol within view, the quilting group coming for the day on Thursdays, and all of them involved in a project that would transform the half-finished mansion she'd never wanted into a Friendship Home.

They were going to be all right. A cloud had lifted. And now, there was something Juliana had to do. She lingered outside, waiting until the aunts had gone in before asking Alfred to bring one of the empty trunks stored in the barn up to her room.

It was time.

—⁓—

Juliana sat at her dressing table for a long while that evening, letting down her hair, brushing through it, and thinking. When she knew that the aunts would probably be asleep, she went out onto the porch and looked up at the stars. She gazed off toward Lincoln, remembering that night when the life she'd known had crumbled.

I am going to be all right. I have the aunts and a new project to keep me busy. She might never get over what Sterling had done to her, but she would learn to get past it.

She retreated back to the bedroom and, opening the doors to Sterling's wardrobe, sat back down and stared at the things hanging there. Maybe it was her imagination, but it seemed that the scent of his cologne lingered in the air tonight. It didn't make her angry. He'd caused her great pain, but she had good memories, too. She would not allow their life together to be rendered meaningless by a curl of hair and a photograph.

Rising from the dressing-table bench, she retrieved the locket. Opening it, she stared down at the face. Was this Pamelia Lindermann? If so, where was she? *I hope she doesn't suffer.* Juliana frowned, surprised at her own thought. Could God's mercy cover over anger and hurt? Could it flow into the promise of a meaningful future? Could it enable her not to hate this woman? And the child. What of the child now that Sterling was dead?

Leaving the locket open on her dressing table, Juliana emptied the wardrobe, taking one piece at a time, folding it carefully, and laying it in the trunk. With trepidation, she checked the pockets. It wouldn't do for the aunts to find anything that would blemish their image of their "dear boy." She found nothing that would have done so. A program to a literary society meeting they'd attended together. Some loose change. A handwritten note about a meeting at the bank. And then a note that made her cry bittersweet tears. *Lilies. J's favorite.*

Had he written that reminder so that he wouldn't confuse her favorite flower with someone else's? She could choose to see it that way. Or she could choose to think Sterling loved her and cared to be mindful of her preferences. She would remember the good things. His whispers in the night. A lily on her pillow. The smile on his face when he surprised her with the rangy red colt that would become her beloved Tecumseh.

After the wardrobe came the dresser. The diamond studs, the gold money clip. She put it all in the trunk. And when the last shirt had been laid on top and she was ready to close the lid, she stood looking down at the contents and said quietly, "You weren't a bad man. You've hurt me, and I don't know if I'll ever forget that. But I won't hate you."

She hesitated about what to do with the locket. She might not hate Sterling, but she was far from finished with the emotions that swirled around what he'd done. Finally, she retrieved the diamond studs, added the locket to the box, and tucked it beneath the handkerchiefs in her dressing-table drawer.

Tomorrow she would ask Alfred to hire someone to help him haul Sterling's dresser and wardrobe out to the barn this next week. She didn't want them in her room any longer. He'd chosen to leave her for other women. She would let him go.

CHAPTER 15

*Now unto him that is able to do exceeding abundantly above all
that we ask or think, according to the power that worketh in us,
unto him be glory in the church by Christ Jesus throughout all ages,
world without end. Amen.*

EPHESIANS 3:20–21

A week after the decision to donate the house, Aunt Theodora
descended to breakfast dressed for church. Juliana and Aunt Lydia
exchanged amazed glances.

The older woman put her hand to the jet-black brooch at her
neck as she said, "You stare as if I had sprouted an additional nose.
Is there something I should know?"

An amazed Aunt Lydia could only say, "You're going to church
with us."

"I believe I asked if there was something I should know. This is
not new information." She lowered herself into a chair at the table,
head held high, back erect.

Juliana hurried to pour coffee and set it before her.

Aunt Theodora took a sip then eyed her sister and Juliana. "I may
be willing to bend the rules of mourning, but I am not yet willing
to give up on good manners. Let us relegate being late to Sabbath
services to the likes of Mr. and Mrs. Duncan." She sniffed.

Aunt Lydia patted Juliana's hand. "That means you and I need
to get dressed."

147

Aunt Theodora sent a frosty smile in Juliana's direction. "Have I not often said that my sister is brilliant? Her powers of deduction are unrivaled."

"Not so," Aunt Lydia said as she headed for the stairs. "Deducing the intended meaning is elementary, my dear Watson."

"There is no need to make vulgar reference to *popular* fiction."

Laughing, Juliana followed Aunt Lydia up the stairs. They paused on the landing, waiting to hear it. And finally, it came. Muffled laughter from down below.

—⁂—

Margaret finally gave up waiting for the sun to rise. Padding into the kitchen, she warmed up leftover coffee and got a piece of pie. Pie for breakfast was the least of the sins she had to worry over on this Sunday morning. It would be the first time she'd darkened the door of a church in more years than she cared to think. And now that she'd said she would go with Cass, here she sat, trembling with fear. Pastor Taylor had seemed nice enough that day at Nell's graveside. Would his kindness extend to the sanctuary of his church?

She was such a hypocrite. So certain when it came to telling Sadie that church was supposed to be a hospital for the sick, not a club for "good" people. And here she was in the predawn hours of a Sabbath, trembling with fear.

Sadie came to the door, yawning. "You all right, Ma?"

Margaret took a deep breath. "I'm nervous. Terrified, actually."

Sadie shuffled over to the table and sat down next to her. "You said church was—"

"I know what I said. And I believe it. I'm just not certain everyone attending St. John's has the same notion."

"Why are you going if you're so scared of it?"

"I promised to speak with Mrs. Moser about those recipes." Margaret was surprised when tears sprang to her eyes. "And I want to thank Him—formally."

"Thank who?"

"God."

"For what?"

"For this." Margaret gestured about them. "For Cass finding us. For Ludwig finding you. For a way out. A way forward."

Sadie was quiet for a while. "You really think God sent Ludwig after me?"

"I've been remembering things in recent days," Margaret said. "Things I used to know. Bible stories."

"I liked the one about David standing up to that giant," Sadie said. "And the lions not eating Daniel's friends."

"Those are good ones," Margaret agreed. "The one I've been remembering, though, is about a shepherd who goes after a lost sheep. I think Jesus told it. Something about an entire flock that was safe, but one sheep wandered off, and the shepherd went out in a storm to chase it down."

"Hmph," Sadie grunted. "Folks I know usually just say 'good riddance' to people who don't do right." She paused. "You didn't, though. You chased after me all these years. Cass chased after both of us until he didn't know where else to look. Then when he found us, he stayed close." She sat quietly, twirling a red curl around a finger. "Guess you and Cass and Ludwig have been like that shepherd, chasing me down. Trying to keep me from going off the cliff." She got up and poured herself a cup of coffee.

Margaret nodded. "I think the real point of that story, though, was about Jesus being the Shepherd who came to earth to chase us all down."

"You think church people see themselves as lost sheep?"

Margaret thought about that for a minute. She didn't imagine church people had changed all that much since she'd been a regular attender when the children were young. "I imagine Cass's church is made up of all kinds of people with hundreds of problems and just as many attitudes about God."

"Cass likes it, though."

"Yes, he does."

Sadie was quiet. Finally, she took a deep breath and said, "All right."

149

"All right. . .what?"

"I'll try it out." Sadie set her coffee mug down. "It'll be a nice surprise for Ludwig. Just don't you go leaving me to make small talk with church ladies." She got up from the table and headed for her room to get dressed.

—∾—

With every step closer to church, Cass expected Sadie to change her mind and run back to the familiarity of Ludwig's house. Once they were seated in a back pew, she was as nervous as a caged bird. Ma was little better until Pastor Taylor, God bless him, stopped at their pew and welcomed them. He asked Cass to introduce his "visitors," as if he'd never laid eyes on Ma and Sadie. Cass supposed there were people who might think that pretense a little too close to dishonesty. Cass saw it as a kindness. Beneath his smile and his greeting, it was as if the pastor was saying, "Who you were doesn't matter. God offers new lives, and so do we. You're welcome here."

As Pastor Taylor made his way to his place on the platform, Cass glanced around just in time to see the three Sutton women slip into the last row across the aisle in the middle section. It was a bit of a shock to see Mrs. Sutton in full mourning, her face obscured behind a long black veil. He caught Aunt Lydia's eye and nodded. She smiled at the sight of Ma and Sadie. Neither Mrs. Sutton nor Miss Theodora looked up.

When he glanced down at Ma and smiled, she tucked her hand beneath his arm then looked to the front of the church. As the congregation rose for the opening hymn, Ma and Sadie began to sing, and Cass realized that for all the time he'd spent trying to think of ways to rescue Sadie from Goldie's or trying to talk Ma into leaving whether Sadie would or not, he'd never simply asked God to make a way for the three of them to have a normal life and a normal Sunday morning together. Yet here they were. Together. Singing, "*My faith looks up to Thee, Thou Lamb of Calvary, Savior divine. . . .*"

When Pastor Taylor got up to give his sermon, Cass tensed. They'd been studying the Gospel of Luke, and Jesus said some harsh things to people. *You see Ma and Sadie here, Lord? Could You just please make things go all right for them? Please.*

Pastor Taylor laid his Bible on the podium and riffled through the pages. "Reading from the Gospel of Luke, chapter 15:

> Then drew near unto him all the publicans and sinners
> for to hear him. And the Pharisees and scribes murmured,
> saying, This man receiveth sinners, and eateth with them.
> And he spake this parable unto them, saying, What man of
> you, having an hundred sheep, if he lose one of them, doth
> not leave the ninety and nine in the wilderness, and go after
> that which is lost, until he find it? And when he hath found
> it, he layeth it on his shoulders, rejoicing. And when he
> cometh home, he calleth together his friends and neighbours,
> saying unto them, Rejoice with me; for I have found my
> sheep which was lost. I say unto you, that likewise joy shall
> be in heaven over one sinner that repenteth, more than over
> ninety and nine just persons, which need no repentance.

After reading from Luke, Pastor Taylor talked about how easy it was for people who'd been in church all their lives to think they were better than others. He mentioned logs and splinters in eyes and how Jesus had no patience with people who only pretended on Sunday.

"Our Lord Jesus," he said, "cares about the heart. He is the Good Shepherd who risks everything for lost sheep. Whether they know they need saving or not, lost sheep are dear to the Lord's heart, and we are all lost sheep. We may put on airs. We may like to pretend we are better than others. But the truth is each one of us owes everything to the Good Shepherd who came after us."

Toward the end of his sermon, Pastor Taylor smiled over the crowd. "Some of you have been unhappy with me of late because you disagree with some of the things I've done. You think I've stepped over the line in chasing after lost sheep in Jesus' name."

Cass sensed Sadie tensing up in the pew beside him, clutching at her "schoolmarm" skirt as the pastor drew dangerously close to mentioning Nell Parker's graveside service.

"Dearly beloved, if you don't want a pastor who will go anywhere it takes to share the love of Jesus, then you don't want this pastor in your pulpit. I love you all. You've been good to me, especially since Viola graduated to heaven last year. You've stood by me and been a great comfort. I hope with all of my heart that we can go on together, but I'm not going to change. I love lost sheep. And so should you.

"We are all sinners, folks. Our only hope is in the Christ who fiercely longs to rescue us and to have a relationship with us. Our only hope is in the Christ who has the power to transform us into new creations. Our only hope is in the Christ who went out in the darkness, where the night was cold and deep. And found the lost lamb.

"That lamb is you and me, folks. That's you and me. Christ chased after us all the way to the cross. Our hope is in Him. And we owe it to our Savior to chase lost sheep in His mighty, precious, holy, redemptive name."

—◦◦◦—

As Pastor Taylor delivered his lesson on lost sheep and kindness, Juliana sat, her gloved hands clenched in her lap, her head bowed. She wanted to listen, she really did. But she couldn't concentrate. Even here on the back row, she felt like she was on display. As if everyone in the congregation was thinking about that lost sheep Sterling Sutton and how he'd duped the poor thing seated behind that veil in the back pew. Poor woman. Poor thing. Poor fool.

Aunt Theodora had said that deep mourning was a protection. "It will encourage people to treat you gently, dear. They will know that you have had a grave loss. That you are fragile and deserve their tender care."

Juliana understood the point, but as she sat here shrouded in a widow's veil that reached to her knees, she didn't feel protected. Not only did she feel as if she were on display, she also felt trapped. She dipped her chin and looked to her right. All she could see was

Aunt Theodora's gloved hands clenched in her lap. At some point during the sermon, Aunt Lydia had reached over and handed Aunt Theodora a handkerchief. A moment later, the sisters were holding hands, and Aunt Theodora was dabbing at tears.

Meanwhile, it was all Juliana could do to sit still. Her mind wandered. She didn't dare look over, but she wondered how Cass's mother and sister were faring with all this talk of lost sheep. Maybe everyone in the congregation felt like Pastor Taylor was speaking to them. Juliana supposed that could happen when a sermon was particularly inspired. But her own thoughts were darting from one topic to another as quickly as a lamb skittering about a pasture in a moment of panic.

Why was Aunt Theodora crying?

She should thank Cass's mother and sister for rescuing her that day. Did they know she had deliberately shunned them? Should she apologize?

What would people think if a woman in full mourning paused to chat after a church service?

What would Aunt Theodora think?

She was supposed to stand apart. To settle into a pew, worship, and leave. But she didn't want to do that. She wanted to say hello to Lutie Gleason and the quilters who'd been in her home. She wanted to meet Cass's mother and sister and thank them for rescuing her. She wanted to tell Cass the exciting news about their plans for a Friendship Home. She wanted to ask him to bring the plans to the house so that they could all go over them together. Aunt Theodora had suggested it, but she would never speak up today. Especially not when she was apparently having her own problems with tears and emotions. Juliana wanted to move forward. Instead, here she was, hidden behind a veil.

Wasn't going to church supposed to make a person feel better? It wasn't working. She couldn't even hold her hymnal properly without getting all tangled in black net. All because of Sterling. It wasn't fair. It made her angry. Just when she thought she'd put the anger to rest and made peace with things after she'd emptied Sterling's wardrobe and packed his things away, here it was again in full force.

She felt hot. Short of breath. Like she might faint. Perspiration trickled down her back. Her chest hurt. She tried to calm down. What did Pastor Taylor mean about logs and splinters? She should listen. She couldn't. Something really was wrong. She was going to faint and make a scene right in the middle of her first service at St. John's. She had to get out of here. Now.

Juliana leaned close, murmured "I'm sorry" to Aunt Theodora, and slid out of the pew. Thank goodness the back door was only a few feet away. One of the ushers followed her out. Kind of him, but she held her hand up. "I'll be fine," she said and crossed the carpeted vestibule to the exterior doors.

Finally outside in the sunshine and fresh air, she tried to draw in a deep breath. She couldn't. She grasped the iron railing that offered a handhold for people climbing the stone steps up to the front doors while, with her free hand, she fought with the veil, finally managing to lift it up and over her head. Next she pulled her gloves off. Her heart began to slow. She took a deep breath. Another. And then she began to cry.

What was there to cry about? She couldn't be standing here when the doors opened and the congregation began to spill down the stairs. She couldn't just head up the street in this getup, either. Alfred had driven them to church in the town coach, but he and Martha had continued on to their church. They wouldn't be back until their service was over.

For once Juliana wanted the town coach. If only it were here, she could climb inside and be hidden from curious eyes. She could escape all this pretense. She wasn't a grieving widow. She was an angry woman who, at this moment, felt like shredding every bit of black in her wardrobe and doing—something. Something to escape.

She scurried around the side of the building. A narrow exterior stairway led down to what must be meeting rooms in the basement. With a glance behind her, she sat on the top stair, hunkered against the building, and let the tears roll.

A handkerchief seemed to float out of the sky. She glanced up and muttered, "You shouldn't be here."

"Aunt Lydia sent me," Cass said. "When I saw you leave, she caught my eye. She had hold of her sister's hand. Miss Theodora was mopping up tears." He gave a low laugh. "Poor Pastor Taylor. I don't think he's accustomed to his sermons having such an effect."

Juliana dabbed at her tears. "It wasn't the sermon—at least not for me." She drew another deep breath. "I'll be fine. You should go back inside. Your mother and sister will be worried."

"Lutie Gleason is sitting in the pew right in front of us. It's as if the good Lord put an entire welcoming committee on the spot in case I had to. . .check on my boss." He paused. "You said it wasn't the sermon. Do you want to talk about it?"

"First I couldn't concentrate. My mind bounced all over the place. Then I felt trapped. Like I couldn't breathe. For a moment I thought I was going to faint." Fresh tears threatened. "It's absurd. I just—I thought—" She gave up trying to speak. The congregation was singing the final hymn. And her in this state.

Cass held his hand out. "Keep the handkerchief. Take my hand and stand up."

When she obeyed, her gloves dropped out of her lap. He bent to pick them up and handed them over. Next, he reached behind her and lifted the veil back up and over her face. "Now. Take my arm and walk with me around back and over to the side street. We'll wait there for the town coach."

"What an introduction to a new church," Juliana muttered. "I'll be branded a madwoman."

He covered her hand with his. "You'll be branded a brave widow who wanted the comfort of her faith and was overcome with grief. Here come your aunts. You can all wait here together. I've got to find Ma and Sadie, but I'll try to watch for Alfred and the town coach and send him around the corner. Would you like me to send Pastor Taylor your way?"

Juliana shook her head. "I wouldn't know what to say." She paused. "I so wanted to meet your mother and sister and thank them for rescuing me."

"Another time. I'll let them know."

"And I have news. About the house. Aunt Theodora suggested we invite you to supper, but now—"

"Probably not the best time," he said and smiled. "You know where to find me. Feel better, Mrs. Sutton."

As he walked past Aunts Lydia and Theodora, Cass stopped and said something. Whatever it was, the aunts smiled and nodded. He turned back and bowed in her direction and then hurried off toward the crowd spilling down the stairs.

Juliana spoke to Aunt Theodora as soon as the aunts drew near. "Before you say 'I told you so,' I admit it. You were right. We should both probably stay home for a few more weeks."

"No," Aunt Theodora said. "I was wrong. We needed—*I* needed to hear those words today."

"But he made you cry."

Aunt Theodora was not one to show her emotions in public. Juliana had expected her to be mortified.

The woman smiled. "Not all tears are because of sadness, my dear." She took a deep breath. "I don't believe I have ever heard anyone say that God *furiously longs* for relationship with His creation. When the pastor said that, I thought, *How absurd.*" Her voice wavered. "But then I looked up at him, and all I could see was that cross hanging above the choir loft. And I realized if that terrible death wasn't about *furious longing* after humanity, what was it for?" She coughed. "I was quite overcome with the notion that the Lord of Heaven should care that much. I've been in church all my life. But today, it was as if I was hearing things for the first time." She dabbed at her eyes with the black-trimmed kerchief. "St. John's is a place of comfort. I look forward to returning. Often." Once again, she reached for her sister's hand.

"I'm sorry I couldn't come to you, dear," Aunt Lydia said. "Theodora needed me."

Juliana shook her head. "I wish I could say that spiritual enlightenment was the cause of my collapse. I just couldn't breathe." Cass reappeared around the corner of the church with his mother and sister and Mr. Meyer. He pointed behind them, and the town coach came into view. Juliana raised a hand. Cass's mother and sister returned the greeting.

Cass was right. They had time for meetings and for sharing news. And there was a better way to thank the people who had taken her to Dr. Gilbert's than speaking a few words from behind a black veil.

CHAPTER 16

Blessed is he that considereth the poor.

PSALM 41:1

The aunts fluttered over Juliana all afternoon, like mother birds tending a hatchling. They ensconced her on the sofa in the library and set a tea tray next to her.

Aunt Lydia worried aloud. "Are you sure we shouldn't call Dr. Gilbert out?"

Juliana shook her head. "It's nothing Dr. Gilbert can treat." She reached for a cup of tea.

As the afternoon went on, Aunt Lydia slipped into the parlor to work on the signature quilt. When she mentioned that she'd come to the block with Sterling's name on it, Juliana lay her head back against a pillow and closed her eyes. She tried to enjoy Aunt Theodora's playing the piano, all the while wondering if Martha had succeeded in getting the shadow of that other name off the quilt. Would it haunt her for the rest of her life? Eventually, Juliana dozed off.

When the telephone out in the kitchen rang three longs and one short, she started awake. Aunt Lydia hurried to answer it. Juliana kept her eyes closed, listening to murmured words until she sensed Aunt Lydia standing in the doorway. When Juliana opened her eyes, she said, "Pastor Taylor inquiring as to your health, dear."

Not long after Pastor Taylor called, Lutie Gleason and Medora Riley followed suit. And then, Cass Gregory. "I know he'd feel better

158

if he heard your voice," Aunt Lydia said. "He sounds so concerned." Juliana hurried to the kitchen to take the call.

"I suppose the fact that you came to the phone answers my question," he said. "You're all right?"

"I am. And I'm very sorry for causing such a stir this morning. I don't know what came over me. To tell you the truth, I'm embarrassed about the entire episode. The aunts have been treating me like a piece of cracked porcelain this afternoon—with the emphasis on the 'cracked' part of the image." She forced a laugh.

"No one thinks you're 'cracked,' least of all me. It's only been a month. Be kind to yourself."

"The aunts and I—we have something to discuss with you about the house. We've come up with an idea." Why couldn't the telephone exchange manage private lines? Knowing that people were probably listening in made things so awkward. "Would you be able to drop by tomorrow evening or Tuesday morning? Either one would suit."

"It's good news, I hope?"

"Very good news. And please bring the house plans with you."

"Now I really am intrigued. I'll see you tomorrow evening."

Juliana retreated to the library and told the aunts that Mr. Gregory would stop by Monday evening. "We'll tell him about Friendship Home then and get some preliminary ideas for what he'd advise in the way of changes." She glanced at Aunt Theodora. "You can ask him about windows on the third floor."

She sat down on the sofa. "I'm going to want it made clear that the current workforce will be kept on to finish the job." She paused. "And now that I think about it, we probably shouldn't just presume the board will be as delighted as we are. What if they don't want it?"

"Why wouldn't they?" Aunt Lydia said.

"I don't know. The location? Will they think it's too far out of town?"

"In a few years," Aunt Theodora said, "it will likely be in the middle of town."

Juliana nodded. "You're right about that. But I don't want to look like a queen pontificating 'in all her generous glory.'" She paused.

"Frankly, if it comes to a vote, you know Helen Duncan will be against it. Just for the sake of spite."

"I disagree," Aunt Theodora said. "She wouldn't dare refuse such a generous gift to a cause she's supported for years. Can you imagine what people would say if they knew about the Duncans' attempt to take advantage of a new widow? You needn't worry about Helen Duncan."

"Theodora's right," Aunt Lydia said. "It's all about what people think for Helen. She'll be all sweetness and light." She paused. "Although I wouldn't put it past her to find a way to be spiteful in the future—if she can do it without hurting her public reputation."

When Juliana raised the idea of calling the board together the next day, the aunts agreed. There was no need to delay. They weren't going to change their minds. And so Juliana returned to the kitchen to call the Duncans. Helen answered the phone.

"Hello, Helen. This is Juliana Sutton. I'm calling with three requests. First, I'd like to request a short society board meeting tomorrow. Second, I'm hoping George will let us use the conference room at the bank for the meeting. And lastly, I'd like to speak with him privately after the board meeting about some other matters."

"That's very short notice for a board meeting," Helen said. "Is there some emergency?"

"Not really. My aunts and I have something we'd like to discuss with everyone, and I'd rather not wait."

"Do you mind telling me the specifics?"

"I'd rather not via the telephone exchange. I'll call the others if you approve the meeting and if George grants permission to use the conference room."

After a pause, George Duncan came on the line. "Is there some problem looming, Juliana?"

"Is the conference room available tomorrow? Are you?"

"Is this about the house?"

"Please, George." She should never have done this over the telephone.

"All right. Of course. The conference room is at your service. As am I."

"Good. Thank you. I'll ask the board to meet us there at 10:30 in the morning. See you then. And George..."

"Yes?"

"You're welcome to sit in on the board meeting as long as your wife, the president, doesn't object."

Even though she was excited about everything that was about to happen, it rattled Juliana's nerves to think of facing Helen Duncan across the conference room table. The woman was going to be livid. And poor George. Juliana wasn't, however, so concerned for the Duncans' feelings that she was willing to speak with them privately. God would have to forgive her for that.

―∞―

As the sun set, the Sutton women gathered in the kitchen for a light supper. They set out a few cold cuts, slivers of cheese and bread, and a bowl of the wild strawberries Martha had picked on Friday. They talked about announcing the donation at the June bazaar.

At one point Aunt Theodora reached over and patted the back of Juliana's hand. "Sterling would be so proud of you, my dear."

Juliana nodded. She didn't know if Sterling would be proud or not. To be truthful, she rather doubted that he would like the idea of orphans and destitute families walking the halls of his mansion. She was pleased, though. And excited about the prospect of being swept up in something worthwhile instead of living quietly behind a black veil for the next year.

That confounded veil.

―∞―

Even being awakened by Martha's "infernal rooster" couldn't keep Juliana from smiling Monday morning. For the first few minutes of the day, she was happy. Then she slipped out of bed to get her wrapper, and there it was: the widow's veil hanging on the hook on the back of her bedroom door. The reminder of all the dark truths that hovered over her recent past. By the time Juliana had her long braid undone and was sitting at her dressing table, brushing her hair, the weight of memory had settled across her shoulders again.

With a sigh, she rebraided her hair and pinned it up. When she opened her wardrobe, the sight of all that black made her want to crawl back in bed and sleep for a year. Once dressed, she opened her jewelry box and retrieved the mourning brooch she'd had made when Mama died—an oval bit of faceted glass mounted above an intricately woven design created by an artisan back East who specialized in hair work. Aunts Theodora and Lydia had placed an order with the same artisan just last week. Soon, they would each own a similar piece made with a lock of Sterling's hair.

Crossing to her dressing mirror, Juliana pinned the mourning brooch in place. She reached for the widow's veil hanging on the door. Instead of putting it on, she retreated to the dressing table and sat down. She reached up to touch the brooch at her neck and thought of the lock of hair inside the locket in her drawer.

She looked down at the veil. She didn't want it. If she spent the next year behind a veil, she wouldn't be able to help with the school and the Friendship Home. Oh, she could throw more money at projects, but that wasn't what she wanted. It wasn't what she needed. She needed to wrest the good parts of the unfinished past and somehow piece it all together into something whole. Something good. Something that could dispel the shadow of that name on the quilt from her life, once and for all.

She lifted her head. Looked across the room at herself, seated, the long veil clutched in her arms. Opening a drawer, she took out a pair of scissors. Slowly, carefully, she snipped the threads attaching the veil to the black bonnet. The net fell to the floor. Rising, Juliana crossed to the dressing mirror and pinned the black hat in place. There. One step in the right direction. Out of the shadows.

Juliana headed down the back stairs, hesitating when she saw both aunts already seated at the table having breakfast. She forced herself to meet Aunt Theodora's gaze. "I'll dress simply and respectfully, but

I cannot bear that widow's veil. There is work to be done. I don't just want to throw money at our project. I want to *do* it."

Aunt Theodora glowered at her sister. "This is your fault. All that talk of Teddy and how you should have celebrated him instead of following tradition."

Aunt Lydia set her teacup down. "I see no reason for a young, beautiful woman to spend a full year of her life dragging about in weighted silk and black net. It's as if we're punishing her for surviving. It isn't fair." She studied her sister. "And now that I think about it, it seems to me that forgoing a widow's veil is a small thing compared to what a certain disciple of Miss Amelia Bloomer adopted for a few years in. . .let's see. . .about 1851."

"That," Aunt Theodora snapped, "has no place in this conversation." She turned her attention to Juliana. "Custom and tradition did not just spring up because old women take delight in making young people miserable. I do hope you realize that."

Juliana nodded. "I do. And I haven't forgotten what you said about the advantages of full mourning. But I didn't feel protected yesterday. I felt like a spectacle."

No one spoke for a moment. Finally, Aunt Theodora waved Juliana to the table. "Sit down and eat something. I may growl, but I never bite."

Juliana obeyed. She poured herself tea and buttered a biscuit.

Aunt Theodora reached over and plopped jelly onto the biscuit. "You cannot eat like a bird and expect to have energy to do the work, my dear." She allowed a little smile. "I do hope, however, that this is not a trend that will lead to bloomers. I have personal experience, and trust me. It is not an attractive look."

—⁂—

Juliana and the aunts arrived at First Nebraska ten minutes before the appointed time for their meeting. Still, when Mr. Duncan escorted them into the conference room, the five other members of the executive board were waiting. Mr. Duncan took a seat at the head of the table. Juliana sat to his right with the aunts next to her.

Helen Duncan sat on her husband's left across from them.

As soon as everyone was settled, Juliana thanked them for coming, and then she introduced the subject at hand. She made it a point to look away from Mr. Duncan as she mentioned meeting Elmo Klein and how grateful he and his family were to the society for meeting their needs "in a moment of crisis." She spoke of her own concern for the unfortunate victim of the fire and the desperate circumstances that often drew young women into "that life." She shared Aunt Theodora's wise observation about the dire circumstances that young women often found themselves in when "compromised" and abandoned by their families.

"We all know of similar instances," she said, "and we also know that, too often, only the women suffer the consequences of misfortune, while the men who share equally in their downfall continue on, unscathed.

"Lincoln is growing rapidly, and we welcome that growth. Each one of us has done our part to encourage it. However, we all know that, unfortunately, with civic growth comes a greater need for the kind of help we feel called to provide. In the past, we've depended on the June bazaar to provide most of our annual budget. We should congratulate ourselves on just how successful that has been over the years. But I think we need to be more forward thinking as we look to the future. I think we should be talking to the legislature about supporting our efforts. I have other ideas, as well, but that's not why I asked you to come here today."

She put her hand on Aunt Lydia's shoulder. "Aunt Lydia, Aunt Theodora, and I have two things we'd like to offer to the society. First, we want to establish an educational foundation in memory of my husband." She looked around the table at the women. "Our idea is to begin with a day school on-site. We've also discussed ways to fund the further education of promising students. We may want to pursue the idea of adult education someday. That will, of course, be up to the board. For now, we thought it important to present it here before we announce anything publicly." She looked around the table. "Do we have your support for this idea?"

Helen Duncan spoke first. "It's a wonderful idea, but we all know how overcrowded the current homes are. There isn't room for any kind of day school. I don't see how we can make it work. And we can't possibly afford to hire a teacher."

"The foundation would pay that salary," Juliana said.

Lutie Gleason spoke up. "In that case, I can't see any reason not to do it. I'll volunteer right now to organize a drive for school supplies."

"That doesn't solve the problem of space," Helen said.

Juliana glanced at her aunts. "We have an idea for solving that problem, too." She paused. "We want to donate a new facility. You all know my husband was building a new house—"

Helen Duncan audibly gasped. She whipped her head about to scowl at her husband.

Mr. Duncan spoke up immediately. "If I might interject a thought, here, Mrs. Sutton—we should discuss your situation before you commit to such a bold change of course." He glanced at his wife. "You will recall that I anticipated that you might wish to reconsider that particular plan, and I suggested—"

"Yes. I do recall," Juliana said. "We'll speak of that later."

Duncan glanced at his wife again, shrugged, and sat back.

Juliana continued. "My aunts and I propose that we donate the house and property south of Lincoln to the society. There's a stone cottage already complete that was to be the caretaker's house. We have ten acres and plenty of room for expansion. The house isn't finished, but that's to our advantage. It won't be that difficult to make changes."

Helen Duncan spoke up. "You're *giving* it—all of it—to the society?"

Juliana nodded. "Yes." She glanced around the table. "If you want it."

The women looked at each other, stunned.

Juliana filled the silence. "I know that we're asking you to do a prodigious amount of work. You'll want to look over the plans and see what changes need to be made. We'll need to hire staff. To be quite honest, it may overwhelm us." She smiled at each woman sitting at the table. "But you've each one proven over the years that you can handle just about any challenge that arises." She nodded at

Lutie Gleason. "Including sheltering desperate people in your own parlors." She paused. "You should probably drive out and see the place before you give us a final answer."

"We don't need to see it," Lutie said. "We just need to say yes. And thanks be to our God!" She laughed and sat back, her face glowing with a combination of joy and embarrassment over the outburst.

When the other members agreed, Juliana said, "We do have two stipulations."

"Here it comes," Helen Duncan muttered.

"First, that the current building crew be allowed to complete the project. And second, that we be allowed to name the house."

"Let me guess," Helen said. "The Sterling Sutton Home for the Friendless."

Aunt Theodora leaned forward. "If I may speak?"

"Sadly," Helen said, "the by-laws do not allow for input from non-board members without prior approval. I'm sure you can appreciate the need to maintain order."

"Madame President," Lutie Gleason said. "I move that Miss Theodora Sutton and Miss Lydia Sutton be extended invitations to join the board."

Before Helen could say another word, the motion had been seconded, approved, and a vote taken. Lutie nodded at Aunt Theodora. "Welcome to the board, ladies. Now, Miss Sutton, you were saying?"

"That we thought the word *friendless* rather bleak. We like the idea of calling it Friendship Home."

The board members agreed in chorus. In less than an hour, a formal vote had been taken to accept the donation and preliminary assignments doled out. Aunt Lydia would plan the drive for school supplies, and Lutie Gleason would initiate a toy drive. They would meet the next week to further discuss how best to proceed. The board would visit the building site on Friday and meet Mr. Cass Gregory, the project foreman.

They rose to leave. Promising to return right away, Mr. Duncan escorted his wife out.

"I don't envy him going home tonight," Aunt Theodora said.

Juliana sighed. "I don't, either, but he brought it down on himself. The sad thing is, if he'd been honest with me from the start, I might have agreed to whatever he wanted." She shook her head. "I'm going to have to interview some other bankers."

"We have Mr. Carter from First National at St John's," Aunt Lydia said.

"Good. I'll start with him."

———

Mr. Duncan returned to the conference room. He closed the door behind him. "Well. That was certainly one of the more. . .energetic events that's ever taken place in our conference room." He cleared his throat. "I do wish you would have consulted me before making the announcement."

Juliana nodded. "And *I* wish you would have consulted me before suggesting that Mr. Gregory arrange for a work slowdown so that you could buy the place at a bargain price."

Duncan's face turned red. "I was merely hoping to create a mutually beneficial situation. You had a half-finished house. My wife—"

"Yes. I know. And if you'd only been forthcoming about your interest, we might have been able to work something out."

"I apologize."

"I accept." When Juliana and the aunts stood, Duncan rose as well.

"I'll be interviewing other bankers in town about possibly taking over as my financial advisor," Juliana added. "I'm sure you can understand that my confidence has been shaken."

He gulped. "Is there anything I can do to change your mind?"

"No."

"Y–you'll want to speak with Graham about the property transfer. There are special rulings regarding such large donations."

Juliana nodded. "Yes. I imagined as much. Thank you." She paused. "I do have one question for you." She set the folder down and drew out a deed. "This farm. I didn't find an accounting for sale of any crops. Isn't the land being worked?"

"I don't know," Duncan said. "I'll have to look into it for you. I could drive down."

"I can do that for myself."

"You don't want to do that." He paused. "What I mean is, it's not an easy drive. With recent rains, it could be especially trying."

"Are there tenants? A house? Do you know why Sterling bought it? It was only last year. I'm assuming he discussed the investment with you."

Duncan shook his head. "I'm sorry, Juliana. I really can't say. I can look into it for you. As I said at our first meeting last month, it's a complicated estate, and Sutton Enterprises is only one of my accounts. I can't be expected to know about every aspect of every one of my accounts at the drop of a hat."

"Yet you know that the farm is remote and you don't recommend that I drive out to see it."

Duncan frowned. "I wouldn't advise that any woman take an excursion of any kind past the penitentiary and out into the country alone."

He had a point. But something bothered Juliana about the whole thing. Sutton Enterprises was about railroad stock and commercial construction. And one farm? It didn't make any sense.

—m—

Jenny
Monday, May 21

"I been sick for most of a month, Dr. Gilbert," Jenny said. "I don't know why I don't get better. Susannah cooks, and I eat, but it isn't helping."

The doctor, who had been listening to Jenny's breathing while she reclined on the sofa, bent down and returned the stethoscope to his black bag. He closed it and sat back. "You were very low when Mr. Duncan found you. Everything had been depleted as you tried to feed your child." He paused. "Am I right to think that you've never had a very strong constitution?"

Jenny shrugged.

"You have a delicate frame," the doctor said. "I didn't attend the baby's birth. Was it—difficult for you?"

"Isn't birthing a baby always difficult?"

"Do you know how much Johnny weighed?"

Jenny shook her head.

"And did the attending physician need. . .special tools? Forceps, perhaps?"

"Why's that matter? I had a healthy boy."

Dr. Gilbert nodded. "You did. But at what cost? I suspect you haven't felt yourself since. Am I right?"

Again, Jenny shrugged.

"You have all the reason in the world to feel melancholy. I'd like to recommend that you consider moving into town where I can keep a closer eye on you. Where you can have contact with other mothers. I think it would do you good."

She couldn't seem to keep the tears from flowing. They spilled down her cheeks and dripped off her chin. "I don't have any money for that kind of thing. I'm only able to stay here because Mr. Duncan was Sterling's friend."

"The place I'm thinking of won't require any money until you can afford to pay. But you would be able to make friends, and I could check on you more often." He glanced at the baby, playing nearby on a folded quilt. "Do you think it might be nice for Johnny as well? There would be other children to play with him."

"What about Susannah? Would she come, too?" Jenny put her hand to her bosom. "I still can't feed my own baby."

"She could if she wanted to, but the home I have in mind has access to goats. That would also provide excellent milk."

Jenny swiped at her tears. She didn't really care what happened to her. Johnny was the important one now.

"Will you at least think about it?"

Jenny nodded. "I guess." Mr. Duncan hadn't been out in over a week. It was looking more and more like she was on her own.

CHAPTER 17

Whatsoever thy hand findeth to do, do it with thy might.
ECCLESIASTES 9:10

On Monday morning, as Cass opened the office door, Finney held up an envelope. "Forgot to give you this on Friday."

Cass looked at the return address. *Denver.* He opened the envelope and read:

> *Dear Mr. Gregory,*
> *A small notice which appeared in the* Rocky Mountain News *a few weeks ago caught my eye in regards to the tragic death of a former business associate, Mr. Sterling Sutton. You and I have never met, but Sterling and I shared duty in the war and have stayed in contact through the years. I have applauded his success and I humbly acknowledge that he has been good enough to return congratulations when appropriate.*
> *One of the unfortunate results of situations such as these is that good men often find themselves the victim of unexpected changes. I have no idea what Sterling's arrangements may have been regarding the future of his business. If this letter finds you content, then you will of course disregard it. If, however, you should find yourself interested in a change, I encourage you to contact me. There is always room for a good man in a growing business, and happily, R. J. Greeley Company is growing.*

The letter was signed by R. J. Greeley himself.

"Good news?" Finney had looked up from his ledger.

Cass shrugged. "Strange news." He tucked the letter inside his coat pocket. He'd finished the work assignments for the day and had been out in the back lot looking over a stack of lumber and trying to estimate an order when Finney came to the door.

"You've got company." He grinned. "Of the attractive female variety." He stood aside to let Ma and Sadie pass.

"What's this?"

"This," Sadie said, holding up a huge basket, "is breakfast. I've been practicing those recipes Mrs. Moser wrote out for us after church yesterday."

"Practicing," Ma said, "as in nonstop baking until I made her quit around midnight."

"She said we'd never eat it all, so I thought maybe we'd share." She lifted the checkered cloth. "This one's the kuchen. Ma's got the *pfeffernuss.*"

Finney called from the doorway. "Did you say *pfeffernuss?*"

Sadie whirled about. "I did."

"I *love* pfeffernuss." Finney called to someone who'd apparently just come in. "It's Cass's ma and sister. They've made pfeffernuss."

Jessup hurried out into the yard.

"And kuchen," Sadie said.

The men looked Cass's way. He laughed and shook his head. "Gentlemen. It would appear that breakfast is served in the office." He squeezed past Ma and Sadie and cleared the long table just inside the door to make room for them to spread out their wares.

Jessup took a bite of pastry. "That—is the best d— Excuse me, ma'am." He took another bite. "What would you charge me for an entire one?"

Finney broke in. "And a dozen cookies?"

Sadie looked at Ma. "I don't know. I was just practicing. Ma's the real cook. You should taste her pie."

"Apple? I'd order an apple pie right now."

Cass crossed the office to a shelf of supplies and pulled down a sheet of paper and a pencil, then handed them to Ma. "Looks to me like you need to take some orders."

"I wouldn't know what to charge," Ma said.

"They charge fifty cents for a piece of pie at the hotel. That's three dollars for a whole pie."

"I could never ask that much."

"Two fifty then," Jessup said. "But let us know about the pastries and the cookies, too. If you're interested, that is."

Sadie nudged Ma. "Looks to me like you don't need to go looking for work. Work just found you, if you want it." She smiled at the men standing around the table. "She makes good roast beef, too. And soup. And bread. I bet she'd make lunches if you wanted. Bring them over all packed up. But you'd have to pay in advance."

"Sadie!" Ma was horrified and hurried to apologize to Cass.

"If you're really interested in doing that, ma'am," Jessup said, "some of these boys aren't married and what passes for meals at their boardinghouses—well. You should hear them complain."

"See? What'd I say?" Sadie nudged Ma. "Work just found you if you want it."

Cass herded the men out into the yard to begin the day, but then he retreated back inside.

"I'm sorry, Cass," Ma said. "I didn't mean to create a stir."

Finney complained aloud that he hadn't got but one bite of pastry. He spoke to Cass. "I hope you let her 'create a stir' again soon." He smiled and then, in a singsong voice said, "Remember: 'A happy crew is a hardworking crew.' Word gets out that Sutton Builders provides breakfast, and we'll have people lined up trying to get hired."

Cass laughed. "I think Mrs. Sutton would have to approve a regular repast." He smiled at Ma and Sadie. "If you're interested in selling on a more regular basis, though, I'd be happy to run it by her. She asked me to come to the house tonight."

"She did?" Finney's expression reminded Cass of a woman leaning in to gather the latest gossip.

"I suppose it wouldn't hurt," Ma said.

Sadie nodded. "Looks like it's your turn to make up a list, Ma. We could write up a menu of what you make, and the men could order and pay a day ahead. We come over and pick up their orders, and then their lunch or whatever is waiting when they get to work the next morning." She paused. "Means you'd be working half the night most nights, though."

"Not really," Ma said. "If I keep the choices simple."

Cass could see that she was already thinking about how to make it work.

"I'd need to shop carefully, or I'd never make any money at it."

"Ludwig knows all the stores in town. He'll help with that." Sadie grinned. "Might be he could even get you the best prices. Ludwig's smart at things like that."

———

Back in his room after a long day out at the job site, Cass washed up. He donned a clean shirt and did his best to get his too-curly hair to behave. He took down his Sunday coat and gave it a good brushing and polished his boots. Finally, he slung the leather tube holding the house plans over his shoulder and descended to the street.

Ludwig Meyer was just coming in from supper at Ma and Sadie's.

"Seems early for you to turn in," Cass said. "Everything all right?"

Meyer smiled. "Everything is fine. I was in the way of the work. I offered to help, but they shooed me out of the house." He patted the spot over his heart. "I have an entire list of ingredients for which they want costs. You would think they are starting a bakery."

"Maybe they are," Cass said. "Some of those men talked half the day about how good those pastries were this morning."

"As long as my Sadie doesn't get so interested that she decides she prefers baking to storekeeping with her husband."

"You don't have anything to worry about," Cass said.

Meyer smiled. "Well just in case, I already told Sadie that if she wants to sell baked goods in our new store, we will order a special display case."

"And she liked that idea?"

"She did. She thought we should offer coffee and tea and maybe a little table where people could have lunch."

"So it's going to be a combination general store and lunchroom?"

"If she wants it."

Cass bid Meyer good night and, mounting Baron, headed east toward Mrs. Sutton's.

This time he called by way of the front door. Still, he was relieved when Aunt Lydia was the one who answered the door. She waved him inside.

"We can't use the parlor because of that." Aunt Lydia pointed to a quilting frame in the middle of the enormous room. "So Juliana thought the library. Of course we'll move over to use the dining room table when it's time to see the plans." She smiled. "This is so exciting! Come this way!"

Before taking a step, Cass checked his boots for mud. It wouldn't do to mar the highly polished floor. As they passed the parlor, he noticed the oil portrait over the fireplace. Mrs. Sutton in a stunning ivory gown. She was seated in an elegant chair, her right elbow poised on the chair back, two fingers touching her chin. Her left hand held a bouquet of roses.

Aunt Lydia touched his elbow. "It's a beautiful portrait, isn't it?"

Cass started. Nodded. He glanced up the hall to where Mrs. Sutton stood waiting. *Yes. She is.* Feeling a little like a street urchin visiting a queen, Cass followed Aunt Lydia past the staircase. More oil paintings adorned the walls in the hallway. Landscapes and, tucked beneath the stairs, a still life.

"Do you fancy art, Mr. Gregory?" Miss Theodora was just now descending the stairs.

"I. . .yes, ma'am. I used to spend Saturday mornings on occasion at Washington University in St. Louis. The museum associated with the School of Fine Arts is housed there." The still life reminded him of a Cezanne he'd seen somewhere, but he decided it might be best not to say anything. Miss Theodora might think he was putting on

174

airs. He stepped into the library.

"Please. Sit." Mrs. Sutton motioned to the sofa, while she and the aunts each took their places in the chairs scattered about the cluttered room lined with barrister's bookcases.

Cass set the leather tube holding the house plans on the floor and sat down on the sofa, his palms on his thighs, his back erect. It was a feminine room, and that surprised him. Needlepoint pillows, figurines, a fancy photo album on a stand, doilies—even the grand piano was partially covered with a paisley shawl dripping with fringe. He couldn't imagine the boss in this room.

For a moment, the three women looked at one another, their expressions reminiscent of children waiting to reveal a secret. Finally Mrs. Sutton spoke. "We're giving it away."

Cass frowned. "Giving what away?"

"The house. The land. All of it. We met with the board for the Society—"

"—of the Home for the Friendless," Aunt Lydia broke in. "Only my sister decided that was a sad word, and so we're going to call it Friendship Home."

Mrs. Sutton nodded. "And Aunt Theodora had the idea of turning the ballroom into a nursery, but of course that would never work without cross ventilation, so we're hoping you can find a way to add windows. Do you think that's possible?"

"I. . .uh. . .ma'am?"

Miss Theodora spoke up. "Juliana has offered the house you are building to the society which oversees the current charities organized to help 'the friendless.' It's an unfortunate moniker. Since we intend to see that they no longer are friendless, we wish to call the house Friendship Home. The society accepted the offer this morning at a meeting at First Nebraska."

Cass glanced at Mrs. Sutton. "You met with Mr. Duncan?"

She nodded. "And Mrs. Duncan. She's the president of the board."

He suppressed a smile. How he would have liked to have seen

175

that. He cleared his throat. "I imagine that was quite a surprise."

"You should have seen it, Cass," Aunt Lydia said. "The committee went from dumbfounded to delighted in a split second. And then the ideas began to flow. It was wonderful."

"I can only imagine."

"We did make keeping the current work crew a condition of the donation," Mrs. Sutton said.

"Thank you. I appreciate that." Cass reached for the plans. "And you'd like to see the plans in order to discuss changes, now that it's to be Friendship Home and not a private residence."

"Exactly." Mrs. Sutton suggested they move to the dining room across the hall where Cass could spread out the plans. She sat at the head of the table with Aunt Lydia to her right and Miss Theodora to her left.

Cass presented the plans in order. First floor, second floor, third floor. As the daylight waned, Mrs. Sutton lit the massive chandelier. And still the ladies talked on. Cass sat back and looked about him at the polished wood, the crystal side lamps on the mantle, the Wedgwood tiles around the fireplace, the heavy draperies, the silver service on the sideboard. It was a gorgeous room, although small compared to the dining room at the new house. What would they do with that massive table sitting at the warehouse?

The voices had stopped. They were looking at him. "I'm sorry. What did you say?"

"How many do you think we can seat in the dining room?"

"On benches or individual chairs?"

"And how many beds in each room?"

"That depends on the size of the bed. A hired man's cot?"

"What on earth is a hired man's cot?" Miss Theodora asked.

"Long and narrow," Cass said. "It's what we have at the rooming house." He smiled. "I can measure mine when I get back. That would give you—but wait. What if I have Finney in the office do some preliminary shopping. He could measure various types of furniture. We could make a scale model of the house as it's planned now, and then you ladies could move in—with scale models of various types of furniture."

"It would be like playing with a dollhouse," Aunt Lydia enthused. "I loved that when I was a girl!"

"How long would it take to create something like that?" Mrs. Sutton asked.

Cass shook his head. "Hard to say. Where would you want it? I mean, it needs to be accessible to the entire board. Depending on what materials you want to use, it might not be very portable."

Mrs. Sutton turned and asked her aunts, "What if we had Mr. Gregory set it up right here in the dining room? I don't mind eating in the kitchen if you don't, and we have no plans to entertain company for quite some time."

"A scale model could end up saving later disappointments," Cass said. "It would undoubtedly enable you to use the space as efficiently as possible." He got up and went to the hallway, stretching his arms out. Next, he went to the front door and did the same. Back in the dining room, he explained. "It wouldn't do to arrive with a model that won't go through the front door, now would it? I'm just using my arm span as a measuring stick."

"You should measure the distance from the tabletop to the chandelier as well," Mrs. Sutton said, smiling. "I'd rather not have to cut the legs off the dining table."

Cass laughed as he held one of the plans up to span the space. "Duly noted, ma'am."

After taking the "measurement," he jotted down a few notes, then rolled up the plans and put them back in the leather tube.

"Now you must have a piece of Martha's gooseberry pie before we send you off into the night," Aunt Lydia said.

"I've had my share of sweets today," Cass said. "I'd better not."

"I insist," Aunt Lydia said. "Martha's taking five pies to the bazaar, and if you've tasted it, you can be counted on to raise the bid at the silent auction."

"I believe that is called 'fixing the bid,' Sister," Miss Theodora said.

"It is nothing of the kind," Aunt Lydia protested. "It's merely good planning."

"I promise to do my part," Cass said. "Mrs. Gaines's pie is well known. I'll make sure the crew knows about it, too. They've proven themselves to be more than willing to pay for sweets." He told them about what had happened earlier that day at the office. "Ma and Sadie were only trying to make sure nothing went to waste. And now it appears Ma may have a fledgling business." He glanced at Mrs. Sutton. "As long as the owner doesn't protest the idea. It would take a few minutes in the morning to handle orders and payment. They could eat on the way out to the site." He went on to describe Jessup's idea for Ma making up lunches, too.

"The bazaar would be a good place for her to advertise her wares," Aunt Lydia said. "Would she consider donating?"

"That's a superb idea. Thank you. I'll suggest it. Who would she need to let know?"

Mrs. Sutton spoke up. "We're all on the board now." She paused. "And I certainly don't object to her feeding my crew. You said she was going to be looking for work. It appears that work found her."

"That's exactly what Sadie said." Cass smiled. "Sadie's already talked Mr. Meyer into letting her do the same when they get their store open down in Roca."

"It would appear," Miss Theodora said, "that Gregory women have an entrepreneurial bent."

For a moment, Cass thought Miss Theodora might be making a veiled comment about the working class, but when he looked her way, she smiled. "I'm not criticizing. It has long been my belief that women who depend on men are more often than not, disappointed. I, for one, applaud your mother and sister. If more women were like them, there would be less of a need for Friendship Home."

"The poor we will always have with us," Aunt Lydia said gently. "Our Lord Himself said that, Sister." She led the way to the front door.

As they passed by the parlor, Cass glanced up at the portrait again.

"It is lovely, isn't it?" Aunt Lydia said. "And President Arthur signed a block for us. We're hoping it's fiercely contended for."

The quilt. She was talking about the quilt.

"I promise to bid," Cass said. And then he had an idea. "When did you say the bazaar is?"

"June 16."

"And it's at St. John's?"

"Yes. We're having a tent erected on that open lot next door. The Ladies' Aid will serve breakfast in the morning. Would your mother be willing to help? And items to be auctioned will be on display throughout the day. Some at silent auction, but the quilt and some other major donations at live auction that evening, right after supper. And then the announcement of the donation of the house. Followed by a hymn sing to celebrate the results."

"I'll ask Mother about helping," Cass said. He glanced at Mrs. Sutton. "What would you think of having the model on display at the bazaar—assuming we can get it finished in time?"

They called the idea *inspired*. Aunt Lydia even hugged him. "Now don't forget. We want Margaret's help with the food. You must warn her that I'll be seeking her out at church on Sunday to ask."

On his way back to the livery, Cass's mind swirled around building models and the possibilities for Ma to have a unique kind of business feeding construction workers. But the thoughts always swirled back to the portrait of Juliana Sutton and the idea that, however entrancing it was, it didn't hold a candle to the living, breathing, Juliana.

———

"You know what I bet you could use right now?"

It was late in the week after Cass's meeting with the Sutton women, and he'd spent most of every workday in the stone cottage, working and reworking the calculations for the model he'd promised to build in time for the fund-raising bazaar. He looked up and grimaced, then tilted his head from side to side and reached up to rub his neck. "I could use a back rub," he said to Jessup, slouched against the doorframe, his arms folded. "But I doubt that's what you were going to say."

Jessup laughed. "I was thinking you really need a big slice of your sister's kuchen." He held up his thumb and forefinger. "This deep in custard. Or maybe strawberry filling. I know where there's a great patch of wild strawberries."

"Are you offering to pick strawberries for my sister? What would Mrs. Jessup have to say about that?"

Jessup laughed. "Diana would say go right ahead. Just bring enough home for me to have a piece." He motioned for Cass to step outside. "I need to make sure we're headed in the right direction with those new windows."

Cass followed him out. Friendship Home was getting its roof this week. Next week they'd begin installing windows. Part of the crew was knocking out brick to make way for a few small windows in the east and west walls up on the third floor. Miss Theodora's nursery would have its cross ventilation.

After checking and approving what was going on, Cass returned to the table and went back to calculations and drafting. Finally, he tossed the pencil aside and headed back outside to stare up at the house. What had he been thinking to offer a scale model? It was a good idea, but he wasn't going to be able to make it work.

That evening he shared his frustration over supper at Ludwig Meyer's.

"You mean you can't do the computations?" Ma frowned. "Ask Mr. Finney. He works with numbers every day."

Cass shook his head. "It's not that. I want it to be as close to perfect as I can make it. The stone trim, the brick walls, the windows... everything." He held his hands up, fingertips touching, and moved them apart as if there was a hinge at his fingertips. "I want it to open like so, so people can see a cross section with the interior finished. Fireplaces, staircases, everything."

"You're making a dollhouse," Sadie said.

Cass nodded. "I suppose so. But my hands are just too big. I won't be able to get inside to paint a wall, let alone lay up a miniature fireplace."

"You were going to make miniature bricks?"

"Pfeffernuss," Cass said. "I thought you could roll it out and cut little pieces."

"Gingerbread would work better," Ma said. "Do you remember the little house the Knoerzers made when you were young? I could make a sheet of gingerbread and cut the bricks before we bake it. Although how you'll keep from attracting every mouse in the city, I don't know."

"Buy a cat?" Cass said.

"You'd need a cat." Ma held up her hands. "You got big hands from your father, not me. I'll help you."

And so it began. In a week's time, the carpenter had cut lumber to re-create the exterior walls, the interior partitions, and the roof. The model began to take shape on the table in the office. Cass stayed late nearly every night to work on it. Finney offered to scour his neighborhood for a cat and ended up bringing in littermates: one gray tabby that claimed a corner of Finney's desk as its personal property, and a calico that decided to annoy Cass. At least he called it an annoyance.

Ma and Sadie took on the interior, cutting fragments of cloth to make tiny draperies for windows and baking the gingerbread bricks. With them also working at baking and making lunches for the crew, Cass soon moved the model—and the calico cat he'd taken to calling Patch, home. Actually, they moved both cats home, but the gray tabby slipped out the door the first night and was found waiting at the office when Finney got there the next morning.

Patch soon proved herself a capable mouser at home. It wasn't long before the project took on a life of its own.

"You should move here," Sadie said, late one night when Cass was bemoaning the few hours he would have to sleep. "Use Ludwig's room. He won't. Someone might as well."

And so Cass moved out of the rooming house and, Ma and Sadie teased him, in with Mrs. Sutton's model.

One night Ludwig brought home a tobacco flannel printed to look like a rug. Sadie installed it in the miniature library and rewarded him with a kiss. Next, he brought a piece of striped calico. "I was thinking maybe wallpaper?"

They were spending a ridiculous amount of time on the model, but no one cared. Juliana was going to be so pleased. Maybe, Cass thought, just maybe he would finally see her smile. Not the polite smile, not the expected smile, but a real smile. One that included those dark eyes.

CHAPTER 18

A good man. . .hath given to the poor; his righteousness endureth
for ever; his horn shall be exalted with honour.
PSALM 112:5, 9

Gray light was spilling through the bedroom window when
Margaret woke Sadie. "I'm sorry to wake you, but this little business
of mine was your idea, and I need your help. If you can get the
lunches packed up, I'll get the kuchen in the oven."

Sadie groaned a protest. "This seemed like a much better idea
when the sun was shining."

The women dressed quickly, but the minute they'd pulled the
curtain aside and stepped into the main room, they stopped and
looked at Cass, sound asleep at the table in the parlor, the completed
model of Friendship Home before him.

Patch's head appeared from beneath one of Cass's flannel-clad
arms. Apparently she'd been curled up on Cass's lap. At sight of the
two women, she plopped to the floor and padded to the back door.
Sadie let her out while Margaret roused Cass with a gentle scolding.

"You didn't even go to bed?"

He started awake and sat up, bleary eyed. "I wanted to—finish
a few things."

Margaret inspected the model. It looked the same to her, but
she probably shouldn't say that to the man who had been up half the
night working on it.

183

He pointed at the model library. "Books," he said. "I painted books on the shelves. And the entryway floor. I didn't think it looked quite right. Just small things. But I want it to be. . . I want her to like it."

Margaret put one hand on his shoulder and leaned close. "It's stunning, but it was fine before, and you shouldn't have stayed up half the night. No one is expecting an exact replica. The measurements are what matters, so that when the committee goes to arrange the furniture—"

"Furniture!" Cass jumped to his feet. "Finney said he'd have a few model pieces ready. I have to get going. The board's driving out today. I want to set this up for them in the real dining room."

"You didn't say anything about needing to have it finished today."

"I thought of it at the last minute. As a nice surprise for Ju—for everyone." He glanced out the window. "And I've got to get over to the office and get a team hitched up so I can load this into a wagon and head out."

"Cass Gregory." Margaret pushed him back down. "You aren't going anywhere until you have a decent breakfast. And then you'll need to get cleaned up. You look a sight."

His hand went to his face. He scrubbed his whiskered cheek with the flat of his hand. "That bad, eh?"

"The last thing you want is for the women on that board to see you like this. The Suttons already know the man behind those whiskers, but I doubt you can expect the wife of a bank president to give you the benefit of the doubt."

"You're right." Bleary eyed, Cass stumbled into his room.

Sadie finished slicing a loaf of bread and retrieved the sliced ham from the icebox by the back door. She began to butter the bread and assemble sandwiches, wrapping each one in paper and tying them with string. "Did you know he was taking that thing out to the job site? I thought he was going to keep it here until the bazaar."

"He'll be careful with it," Margaret said.

Sadie shrugged. "Bet *you* won't miss walking around it every day."

"I've enjoyed helping him," Margaret said. "But the way this business you dreamed up has grown, it will be nice to have more time to cook."

Cass ducked out of his room and headed for the front door.

"You need to eat," Margaret protested.

"I will. Pack me up something. I'll eat on my way out to the job site." He didn't wait for a reply before leaving.

Sadie let Patch back in and poured herself a cup of coffee. "What next?"

"Let's try some biscuits today. I don't know if the men will want such plain fare after the way we've been spoiling them, but my biscuits are good."

Sadie began to mix the biscuits. She was rolling the dough out when she said, "You think he even knows that he's falling for a rich lady?"

Margaret frowned. "He's just—he's sympathetic. And who could blame him for admiring her? She's been through a lot. It's admirable the way she's rising above it."

"Sure it is," Sadie agreed. "But what Cass feels isn't sympathy." She dipped the biscuit cutter in flour and began to press it into the dough. "He's wearing his good shirt, Ma."

—⁂—

"Miss Juliana."

Martha knocked on the bedroom door, then opened it.

Juliana had already gotten out of bed and put on her wrapper. "I heard the phone. What is it?"

"Mrs. Duncan," Martha said. "And she wouldn't let me take a message."

What now? At least it wasn't Cass saying there was a problem with her bringing the board out to see Friendship Home today. She hurried downstairs. "Yes, Helen."

"I'm afraid I'm not going to be able to make it today. It's really little more than a sightseeing excursion, and I'm sure you know that I'm already quite familiar with the site."

"But unless you've been out there recently, you should see it. The windows are in, and the roof is on. The rooms are framed."

It was as if Juliana hadn't said a word. "You will have someone take good notes, won't you? It should be treated as a meeting, with a record created for posterity."

"I really wish you'd come." Juliana forced herself to sound truly disappointed. "We need our president."

"That's very kind of you, but George needs me today, as well. It's a private matter. You understand, don't you, dear?"

You could at least be more creative with your lies. Everyone knew that the Duncans barely spoke. It had been that way for years. Which, Juliana thought, with a sudden streak of unexpected compassion, was likely at the root of Helen's difficult personality.

"We'll miss you," Juliana said. She almost meant it.

—⁓—

Jenny
Tuesday, June 5

Jenny sat on the front porch, waiting. She'd worn herself out helping Susannah clean the place, ever since Dr. Gilbert had brought the news that Mr. Duncan had "made arrangements." Even if Mr. Duncan had been the kind of man who might let her stay, "the matter was out of his hands." Sterling's affairs were being handled by someone else now, and the farm was being sold.

No one had come to see it. For all Jenny knew, the new owners would let the house fall in. Still, it housed most of her life with Sterling. She would not have anyone saying the former tenant had been "that kind" of person. The kind that didn't take care of things.

Of course it wouldn't be long before the wind blew dust in through the loose windows and around the doors. Thinking of dust collecting on the things she and Sterling had shared made her want to cry. But then it seemed she was increasingly prone to tears.

Susannah and Dr. Gilbert had taken to nagging her about eating. They said she had to stop losing weight, that she had a child and to think of him. She tried. She really did. It was just so hard. It was depressing to think that her entire life fit into that small trunk waiting over there by the stairs.

Johnny would be crawling soon. When they put him on his belly, he flailed with his arms like he was a little turtle. Just yesterday he'd managed to scoot halfway across the floor. He could still make her smile. But he couldn't make her eat. Why was that?

Decoration Day had come and gone. She wished she could have at least gone and put flowers on Sterling's grave. They would have had a nice service at the cemetery. Last year she'd gone with her uncle. It was, after all, his business to honor the dead, and no one did that better. He didn't care for his living niece and great-nephew, though. Jenny was sure of that.

Here Mr. Duncan came to take her to town. Dr. Gilbert said that she might have to share a room with two other mothers with babies. By this fall there would be a grand new Friendship Home and things would be less crowded. Right now, people like her who needed special help stayed in private homes. Jenny was dreading that. She hoped the people would be nice to her and Johnny, but Susannah had told her to "be prepared." What that might mean made Jenny feel tired. And scared. Then she got tired of being scared and just felt tired again. Why did it have to take so much effort for every little thing?

Mr. Duncan climbed down from the buggy he'd driven out, cursing about the bad road.

He bent down to pick up the trunk. "Is this everything?"

Jenny nodded.

"Wait there," he said, while he loaded the trunk.

For some reason he seemed to think he should look the house over. He was inside when another buggy came bumping up the lane toward the house. Mr. Duncan's wife? Jenny remembered her from town. It seemed like half a lifetime ago, but she remembered. She and Susannah—who was holding on to Johnny—both stood up when Mrs. Duncan climbed down from her buggy. Without a word to either of them, she marched inside, the ostrich feather on her hat bobbing with every step.

"Helen!" Mr. Duncan said. "What on earth!"

"I had to see it for myself."

"You had to see what?" There was a long silence, and then Mr. Duncan swore again and said, "You think I'm that stupid?" Jenny could hear his footsteps as he stomped back out onto the porch with his wife in tow. "Tell her," he said, pointing at Mrs. Duncan. "Tell her who's child that is."

He called Johnny a name, of course. He didn't say *child*. It made Jenny angry. It wasn't supposed to be this way. She was trembling, but she did her best to glare at the formidable woman as she said, "I'm Jenny."

"I know who you are," Mrs. Duncan said. "And your name isn't Jenny."

Jenny nodded. "It is. It's Jenna Pamelia Lindermann." She nodded at Johnny. "And this is John Sutton Lindermann." She wanted to tell Mrs. Duncan about Sterling's promises and how it wasn't like that, but there didn't seem to be much point.

Mr. Duncan looked at his wife. "Yes. I'm cleaning up Sterling's mess, although why I bother, only God knows. At least it's the last one I'll ever have to deal with." He told Jenny and Susannah to get in the buggy.

Jenny ducked her head and followed Susannah. She held Johnny and then passed him up once Susannah was seated. Somehow, she managed to pull herself up without help. Mrs. Duncan stared after them. Then she turned away and spoke to her husband.

"Where are you taking them?"

"Dr. Gilbert made arrangements."

"But George. . .you can't. . ."

She lowered her voice, and Jenny couldn't hear the rest.

Mr. Duncan looked dumbfounded. "Why do you care? There is no love lost between the two of you."

"That may be true," Mrs. Duncan said. "But I wouldn't wish this—" She shook her head. "She's already survived the unspeakable. She doesn't deserve—you can't risk it."

More murmuring. Jenny stopped caring. It was true that she'd survived the unspeakable, but she didn't think Mrs. Duncan was talking about her. She concentrated on making Johnny smile, chucking him under the chin and playing patty-cake while the Duncans fought.

Finally, she spoke to Susannah. "You've been good to me. Thank you. You can come visit Johnny anytime. If you miss him."

"I already got another nursing job," Susannah said. "I'll be busy."

Jenny nodded. She blinked tears away and reached for Johnny. "All right, little man," she said in his ear. "It's just you and me now. We'll figure it out. We will."

—⁓—

Juliana hated the idea of anyone being shut up in the enclosed town coach on such a gorgeous day, but when Helen Duncan decided not to come, the coach made it possible for the committee to ride out to the construction site together. Making it work meant that Juliana and one other lady had to ride on the driver's seat with Alfred.

When Aunt Lydia volunteered, Aunt Theodora shook her head. "You are no longer thirty, Sister."

"Then I should do it now," Aunt Lydia retorted, "before I get too old." She scaled the steps leading up to the driver's seat like a twenty-year-old, albeit with a bit of ankle exposed on the way up.

The drive out along a trail that led through prairie bursting with color from spring wildflowers in bloom put everyone in high spirits. Cass Gregory stepped out of the front door of the stone cottage as soon as they drove up. Juliana glanced toward the pasture and wondered about Baron. Cass had driven a wagon out? While Alfred helped the committee down from the coach, she backed down from the heights, conscious of Cass's hands at her waist as he lifted her down.

"I hope Baron's all right."

"In fine fettle," Cass said. He offered no further explanation as he reached up to help Aunt Lydia.

"Promise me you will not peek at my ankles," she said, before turning about and planting her right foot on the first foothold.

"A lady doesn't have ankles, Aunt Lydia," Cass teased.

She landed safely, albeit with a blush on her cheeks and a little curtsy. Cass bowed. Aunt Lydia introduced him to the other ladies, ending with, "Mrs. Duncan sends her regrets."

Cass turned to Juliana. "I was hoping you'd lead the tour, Mrs. Sutton. I'll tag along to answer any questions that might come up, but you're in charge."

Juliana led everyone inside the stone cottage, first. "This was to be the caretaker's house. Shall we offer it to the matron?"

Everyone seemed to think that was a good idea. Lutie Gleason opened her bag and produced a notebook and a pencil and jotted down a note.

And off they went. The rest of the building crew drove up as they exited the stone cottage and headed toward the main house. Juliana asked everyone to wait to go in until Cass had a chance to speak to the crew. She pointed out the new windows up on the third floor and mentioned Aunt Theodora's idea that it be the nursery.

"Lutie, perhaps you'd give us an overview of how many people we expect to house here. It might help us all think more creatively as we walk through."

While Lutie talked, Juliana watched Cass. *He's wearing a good shirt.* That's what it was. She'd noticed something different but hadn't been able to place it. His hair was as unruly as ever and longer than the fashion. Charming, actually.

"Isn't that right, Juliana?"

Oh, dear.

"Excuse me?"

"There's to be a scale model ready soon. To facilitate the plans for furnishings."

Juliana nodded. "Yes. Mr. Gregory suggested it." Cass caught up with them, and she led the way inside. While everyone lingered in the entryway, Juliana motioned for the committee to consider the circular turret room for the office.

"And the parlor for a schoolroom?" someone said.

Aunt Theodora spoke up. "The library would be more suited to that."

"Show them, Aunt Theodora." The ladies moved on up the hall.

Cass fell in beside Juliana. "There's something of special interest in the dining room."

She followed him, gasping with delight as morning sun streaming through the high windows illuminated the model. "This is beyond belief," she said, as she bent down to peer into the rooms. "How did you ever—brick fireplaces?"

Cass grinned. "Gingerbread. And I'll have to take it back to town this evening so the cat can guard it from mice."

"We have—I mean, you have a cat?"

"Finney filled that order. Ma said if we were going to make it edible, we'd need a guard." He smiled. "Actually, though, I did end up taking it home to work on it. One of the cats refused to move, but the other didn't mind."

Juliana ran her hand along the roofline.

"More gingerbread," he said. "Ma cut it before baking to replicate the slate tiles. Of course we had to paint them to get the gray green. It isn't exact." He shrugged. "I was hoping we'd have some furniture set up inside, but my partner in the process hasn't made any yet."

"You're amazing," Juliana said. At just about the time she realized that the committee was standing in the hallway staring at the model. Or them. She motioned with both hands for them to come into the room. "Look what Cass has done for us!" She moved away from the model and walked to the windows. The warmth of the sun on her shoulders felt good.

Aunt Lydia spoke up. "Cass suggested we display it at the bazaar."

"That's a superb idea," Lutie agreed. "And we could have a formal 'unveiling' right before the live auction."

Aunt Theodora nodded. "It will encourage generous bids to support the cause." She smiled at Cass. "Well done, dear boy."

As the ladies continued on through the house, Juliana took

another look at the replica. She smiled at Cass. "Aunt Theodora called you 'dear boy.' I hope you realize that's rare praise."

He smiled. "She needs to be careful. Word will get out that there's a warm heart behind that imperious mask."

Juliana chuckled. "You're more discerning than I am. The aunts had lived with us for nearly a year before I realized it's mostly an act." Hearing footsteps echoing overhead, she headed to the back of the house and up the servant's stairs, catching up with the committee in what would have been the master suite.

"It's impossible to take it all in during one visit," Lutie Gleason said, as she scribbled notes. She shook her head. "Juliana, we are truly speechless. Such a generous gift."

"Hear, hear," the ladies all said, clapping with gloved hands to show their agreement.

Aunt Theodora spoke up. "It's magnificent," she said. "A magnificent gift, a magnificent legacy, just magnificent in every way. Untold good will be done within these walls, Juliana." Her voice wavered, and her gray eyes glimmered with unspilled tears. "Generations of children will rise up and call you blessed. Well done, dear girl. Well done."

CHAPTER 19

Neither as being lords over God's heritage,
but being examples to the flock. . . . Yea, all of you be subject one
to another, and be clothed with humility.
1 PETER 5:3, 5

Visiting the building site raised the society women's excitement to fever pitch and transformed Juliana's home from a quiet residence with a weekly quilting bee into a central meeting place. Buggies often lined the drive, and Martha was kept busy producing tea cakes and lunches.

One midmorning when Juliana stepped into the kitchen to apologize for the chaos, Martha said, "Don't you apologize. It's a joy to see you all smiling again. And I do mean *all.*" She nodded at Aunt Theodora, who was actually talking on the telephone to someone about a donation for the live auction.

Juliana shook her head. "I never would have believed it."

Helen Duncan made regular excuses for why she couldn't be at this meeting or take part in that project, but plans still went forward. In the days preceding the bazaar, the committee gave new meaning to the term "no stone unturned" in their determination to raise support. They divided the city into six sectors and assigned pairs of members to canvass for donations. While Aunt Theodora drew the line at "that kind of activity while I am in mourning," she continued to use the telephone and commandeered lists and kept records. When she wasn't organizing paperwork, she helped the quilters work on the signature quilt in the parlor.

When Aunt Lydia teased her about joining the gossip around the quilt, Aunt Theodora just shook her head. "Is it necessary that you point out my every mistaken assumption?"

The ladies convinced the largest printer in town to produce elegant invitations to the bazaar and hand delivered them to leading citizens. Medora Riley convinced R. S. Frey to donate floral arrangements to adorn the stage beneath the tent. Helen called one day to say that, for a small mention on the program, First Nebraska Bank would fund the printing. Aunt Theodora pressed for—and got—a promise that they would also pay for "nice thank-you cards." After all, she said, it would be out of the question to overlook formally thanking everyone for their support when the event was over.

When the editor of the *Daily State Journal* wondered in print about "the secret announcement" being promised to those who attended the June 16 bazaar at St. John's, the ladies congratulated themselves on "raising awareness" and planned for record attendance. The expectation launched a new search for more chairs. Alfred stepped in with the offer that he and the deacons from the A.M.E. church would handle the collecting, delivering, and return of chairs from residences and other churches.

Reverend Burnham of First Church sent his regrets. The elders felt that it would be poor stewardship of their resources to send chairs out the door for "a community event" where it was unlikely that a religious message would be given.

Aunt Theodora snorted with indignation when Alfred relayed the message. "He's upset that he hasn't been invited to speak."

"We could ask him to give the invocation," Aunt Lydia said. "Pastor Taylor wouldn't mind."

"I would," Aunt Theodora said. And that was the end of that.

On the Tuesday before the bazaar, Juliana was helping the quilters take the finished signature quilt out of the frames when someone knocked on the front door. Expecting Lutie Gleason, who'd taken a quick drive into town to deliver an article to the newspaper (Aunt Theodora had written about the signatures that would render the fundraising quilt an "important historical record"), Juliana called out, "Come in," and kept removing pins from along the edge of the quilt frame.

"Are you certain?" Helen Duncan called through the door she'd barely cracked open.

"Helen!" Juliana pricked herself with a pin. "You've been missed!" She went to the door and opened it wide. "Please. Do come in, and forgive me for treating you like a delivery boy."

"It's all right," Helen said, smiling at the quilters and offering praise for the completed quilt.

"Hopefully we'll get the binding on it yet today," Aunt Lydia said. "You're welcome to help."

"I just might do that." Helen turned back to Juliana. "After we have a word."

Juliana led her into the library, but not until she'd asked Martha to bring them tea and exchanged an "I-haven't-any-idea" glance with Aunt Theodora, who was in the dining room with two other committee members trying to finalize the order of the live auction.

As soon as the two women were alone in the library, Juliana said, "We've missed you."

Helen shrugged. "It's kind of you to say, but it appears you've all done quite well without me."

"Most of the plans were already made. We've just been trying to build on the foundation."

"I'm sure that seeing the property aroused new enthusiasm among all the committee members."

Martha brought a tea tray in, and Juliana motioned for Helen to sit down, pouring tea as soon as Martha had closed the door. "I hope you don't think I'm plotting to wrest any kind of authority out of your hands."

"I wouldn't blame you if you did."

"That's not what's going on. Keeping busy has been a great boon to both Sterling's aunts and to me. It's been healing. It isn't an attempt to undermine your position as president of the society. It's just our way of trying to cope."

"Well, I haven't been as involved as I might have, but at least I got George to offer the bank's support for the programs. And you should hear him grouse about it." Helen waved Juliana's apology away. "No, no. That's not necessary. George grouses. That's just his way." She paused. "It didn't used to be. . . ." Her voice trailed off. She reached for the sugar bowl. When she'd prepared her tea, she sat back. "I finally stopped by Sutton Builders this morning to see the model everyone has been raving about. I am amazed."

Poor Helen. This had to be so hard for her. "It was Cass Gregory's idea. A way to plan the furnishings to best advantage. I had no idea he would go to so much trouble. I can't imagine the time he spent on it. His mother and sister helped, too." She smiled. "Did he tell you the fireplaces are gingerbread?"

"Mr. Finney did." Helen paused. "Mr. Gregory's mother and sister delivered two baskets filled with baked goods and sandwiches while I was there. They seem very nice. Mrs. Nash has quite the fledgling business started. I suggested she donate samples for the breakfast we're all serving the morning of the bazaar. Apparently she's already promised to contribute."

Juliana nodded. There was an awkward silence. Finally, she blurted out, "It wasn't revenge." When Helen looked confused, she took a deep breath. "I didn't give the place away to spite you and George. I'm sorry if it seemed that way." She paused. "I should confess that I did take an unholy amount of satisfaction in announcing it the way I did. That was unkind, and I owe you an apology for that." She didn't quite know what to do when Helen's eyes filled with tears. So she sipped her tea. And waited.

"What George did was wrong," Helen finally said. "But if I hadn't nagged him—" She shook her head. "I didn't know he would try to take advantage that way. I truly didn't expect it. He told me about it later, and all I can say is that I am sorry." She took a deep breath. "It's going to be a wonderful place. A haven. You should be very proud.

I hope you'll accept *my* apology for my part in—everything."

"Of course."

Helen cleared her throat. "At some point later today you are going to wonder if this was a ploy to get you to give George another chance to manage your affairs. It isn't. A woman alone must have trustworthy counselors. Mr. Carter has an unblemished reputation, and I am sorry to say I know that my husband does not." She shook her head. "Husbands. They have no idea the heartbreak they cause us." After a moment, she forced a smile. "I predict that that model is going to result in a record-breaking fundraiser. The society will be the talk of the town for quite some time to come."

"I hope so," Juliana said, "because every once in a while when I really stop to think what we've taken on and what it's going to take to keep it running in coming years—" She shivered.

Helen nodded. "The second reason for my visit. I really meant what I said about this bazaar resulting in record donations. I believe we are at a point where we need to think about investing some of the funds that will come in—with the goal in mind that the operating budget self-perpetuate. Bazaars and silent auctions are all well and good, but we need more reliable, regular income if we're going to sustain Friendship Home and a staff to run it."

"I agree," Juliana said, "but I haven't any idea how to go about doing something like that."

"Mr. Carter would. I'm hoping you will agree to accompany me to speak with him about it."

Juliana frowned. "What will your husband think?"

Helen sighed. "George hasn't been happy with much of anything about me for a very long time." She repeated the question. "Will you set up a meeting with Mr. Carter sometime next week?"

"Of course."

"Thank you." Helen finished her tea. She returned her cup and saucer to the tray. Rising, she picked up the tray. "I'll take this to the kitchen if you'll open the door. And then, I believe I'll see if Lydia and the others really do need help finishing the quilt."

—✕—

Juliana spent a good part of the afternoon of the bazaar helping Cass's mother slice cake and serve kuchen and other delicacies to what seemed to be an infinite line of dessert lovers. The two women were so busy at first that their conversation took place in short bursts and half sentences.

"I still haven't thanked you for rescuing me," Juliana said.

"So glad we were there."

"I hope Tecumseh didn't give you any trouble."

"Tame as a puppy. Glad you're all right."

"The arm wasn't broken."

"Cass told me. Thank the Lord."

"I hope we don't run out of chocolate cake."

"I made five, but they seem to like it."

"Cass said you helped with the model?"

"He was whining about his big hands."

"Well, thank you. People are going to be amazed."

At one point, Mrs. Nash did the obligatory "I am so sorry for your loss," but by the time she said it, they'd talked about cake and kuchen, and Sadie and Ludwig Meyer had stopped and chatted, and it seemed the most natural thing in the world for Juliana to merely say *thank you* and move on to other topics.

When it was time for the buffet supper, Juliana helped haul fried chicken up out of the church basement and then returned to the replenished dessert table, where she worked alone for quite some time while the committee members tallied up silent auction items, closed down that part of the fund-raiser, and prepared for the evening's activities beneath the tent erected on the vacant lot next to the church. Lanterns were hung and lighted as daylight waned.

Finally, Cass walked up and said, "They're ready for you." He pointed her toward the front row, where the committee had already assembled.

Juliana put down the server in her hand and headed for the tent.

"Umm. . .Mrs. Sutton?"

She turned back.

"You might want to hand over the apron."

"Are you offering to take my station?" She untied the apron and handed it over.

"Sure thing." With a grin, Cass donned the apron and picked up the server.

"Charming," Juliana said, laughing as she ducked into the tent and took her seat on the end of the row next to Aunts Theodora and Lydia.

Helen Duncan went to the podium, but when she called out "Ladies and gentlemen," the conversation and laughter failed to dim. Jess Jessup and a couple of other men whistled everyone to attention. With laughter and good humor, the crowd settled.

Helen thanked everyone for coming and announced that she had been informed that the silent auction proceeds would set a new record for any society fund-raiser. When the cheers and applause died down, she glanced Juliana's way and said, "You've all been wondering about the promised surprise." She gestured at the model sitting on a table in front of the podium but still hidden beneath a sheet. "In a moment, we'll give you all a chance to get one more piece of fried chicken or cake while you take the opportunity to view what's beneath that sheet. But for now, I'd like to introduce the committee and thank everyone for making this day a success."

For the next few moments, it felt to Juliana like half the population in Lincoln had to be thanked for something. Just as the crowd began to grow restive, Helen said, "And now"—she motioned for Juliana and the aunts to stand up—"I have the honor to present Mrs. Sterling Sutton, Miss Theodora Sutton, and Miss Lydia Sutton." They all rose.

"You know these ladies. You know of the recent tragedy that has befallen them. What you do not know is that they have risen above that tragedy in a way that puts the Society of the Home for the Friendless—and the city of Lincoln—forever in their debt." She paused and cleared her throat.

"We have two wonderful announcements to make this evening. First of all, we announce the establishment of the Sterling Sutton Educational Foundation, which will be dedicated to providing an education to the children in the care of the Home for the Friendless."

As warm applause sounded, Juliana and the aunts exchanged glances and sat down.

Helen continued. "But that is only the beginning of the Sutton ladies' generosity." She indicated the model. "Many of us are aware of the lovely home that was rising to the south of Lincoln when Mr. Sutton's life was tragically cut short." Helen looked over at Juliana and the aunts, then back at the crowd. "It is my great honor to announce that that building has been donated to the society and is to be finished as a residence that will be opened to those less fortunate in our city." Motioning to Juliana to help her come and remove the sheet, Helen said, "Ladies and gentlemen, I give you Friendship Home."

Juliana and Helen removed the sheet. The crowd was silent for a moment, and then someone shouted, "Bravo!" and the applause began. And continued. Folding the sheet over her arm, Juliana hurried back to stand with the aunts. The applause continued. They swiped at tears. Still, the applause continued.

Finally, Helen called for quiet. "Now, we are going to give you that promised last chance to clear the tables of any remaining sustenance. We encourage you to please inspect this wonderful scale model of the future Friendship Home. Let it encourage your enthusiasm for the live auction, which will begin in ten minutes."

It was the longest ten minutes of Juliana's life. She really didn't want to be thanked by every single person in attendance, but as people filed by the model, they just naturally ended up coming to where she and the aunts were seated, and in no time there was an informal reception line. Finally, Juliana realized something. This was healing, too. Hearing Aunt Theodora praise "the dear boy," hearing people say nice things about Sterling was just that. It was nice. He had done nice things in the city. His sins didn't erase that, but as Juliana looked past the people in line to see the model, she felt the raw edge of her pain heal a bit.

Finally, everyone was back beneath the tent. She glanced over to where Cass still stood behind the dessert table, wielding a server and talking to Alfred and a couple of the deacons from the A.M.E. church as he piled their plates high with cake and pie. When the quilt came up for auction, Cass kept his promise to bid, although no one had a chance with Helen Duncan prodding George to go higher and higher all the way up to the unbelievable final bid of nearly two hundred dollars. It was the climax of the auction and one that earned a fresh round of applause from the crowd.

As soon as Pastor Taylor offered the benediction, Juliana and the committee went to work helping pack up the leftover food. Lutie Gleason's husband drove an exhausted Aunt Theodora and Aunt Lydia home. Eventually, the crowd thinned out, and the only people left were volunteers helping with cleanup.

Juliana finally took the last swipe at the last crumb-littered table and stood back. "All right, gentlemen, take it away." Cass Gregory and Jess Jessup turned the table on its side and headed down the narrow stairs into the church basement with it. Across the way, Alfred and his deacons loaded the last of the borrowed chairs into the back of a wagon and headed off.

Everyone was working in half-light, as the sun set and the moon rose. Juliana stooped to pick up a program someone had dropped on the grass, then headed back behind the church to add it to the burning barrel being tended by—

"Pastor Taylor?"

He peered around the column of smoke. "Don't act so surprised. I can tend a fire as well as the next man."

Juliana laughed. "Obviously. It's just not something one generally sees a minister doing."

"You must be exhausted," he said.

"I haven't let myself think about it. As long as I keep moving, I'll be fine." When she saw that Cass and Jessup were making their way toward the church steps to return the borrowed pulpit, Juliana excused herself and hurried ahead of the men and up the steps to hold the door open for them. Once they were inside, she retreated to the tent and stepped up on the stage to fetch the flower arrangement Frey's had donated for the event and take it inside. Helen had delivered the other one to First Church, since many of the committee attended there. Now, Juliana headed inside to put this one in position in front of the pulpit for the Sabbath service only hours away. Jessup and Cass were just descending the stairs as she headed inside.

"Can I carry that for you?" Cass asked.

"It isn't heavy," she said. "Just awkward."

"Then let me hold the door."

Juliana stepped inside. As she crossed the vestibule, she heard Cass tell Jessup to pull the wagon up alongside the tent so they could start taking the platform down. Then he hurried past her, just as she reached the inner doors.

"Don't let me be the reason you end up taking that platform apart in the dark."

"It won't take that long," he said and followed her up the aisle. "Let me situate it, and you stand back and make sure it's where you want it."

She handed the arrangement over and stood back while he put the flowers in place.

"To the left a little. There. That's perfect."

"Good." He nodded and they turned to go.

She touched his sleeve as he passed by. "Cass. I—" She allowed a nervous laugh. "First of all I should probably ask if you mind my calling you Cass."

He smiled down at her. "It's my name."

She blushed. "You know what I mean."

"Yes, Mrs. Sutton. I do. And no, ma'am. I don't mind. You're my boss. You can call me whatever you like." He laughed softly. "Although I'm counting on it not being anything profane."

"Well you're in luck. I only use profanity with Tecumseh. And he's promised not to tattle."

"Are you certain he can be trusted?"

She laughed. "Thank you for working so hard on that model. I can't imagine how many hours you must have spent on it."

"I had help."

"I heard." She smiled up at him. "From what people were saying today about your mother and sister's cooking, they're both going to be very busy in coming weeks."

"So are you and the others. Tonight was quite the success. Things are only getting started for Friendship Home."

Juliana nodded. "Don't I know it. It'll take a week just to write all the thank-you notes."

"Do you still want the model on your dining room table?"

"More than ever."

"Let me know when."

She thought for a moment. "How about tomorrow? If you come right after church, we'll pay you with lunch. Although I have to warn you that Martha doesn't cook on Sundays, and I'm no Margaret Nash. But you won't starve."

He smiled. "I'll eat a big breakfast just in case."

They descended the front steps together. Pastor Taylor had left the burning barrel to die out and was helping Jessup disassemble the platform. Cass turned back to Juliana. "Unless you intend to wield a wrench or a screwdriver, I'm thinking you can finally head home."

"I believe I'll put off learning carpentry until a day when I'm not so tired."

Cass walked with her to the buggy and offered his hand to help her climb up to the driver's seat. Was it her imagination or did he hold on for a fraction of a second longer than necessary?

She didn't mind. In fact, she took her time about pulling away. So much so that Fancy snorted with impatience. "You just hold your horses, young lady," Juliana said.

As she pulled on her driving gloves and tied her black bonnet in place, the phrase came back to haunt her. *Hold your horses.* Good advice for a widow.

Daily State Journal
June 18, 1883

The ladies of the Society of the Home for the Friendless are to be congratulated on the great success of one of the most well-organized and enjoyable events presented to the citizens of Lincoln in recent memory. Participants were treated to delectable baked goods throughout the day and a fine evening supper, which fueled great enthusiasm in the bidding for an impressive array of donated items made available through silent auction.

The committee will undoubtedly thank each of the donors in coming days, but this paper wishes to commend all who united to support such a worthy cause as what will soon be gathered together under one roof thanks to the generosity of Mrs. Sterling Sutton. Those present at the unveiling of the model of the proposed Friendship Home will likely never forget the admiring murmurs that flowed through the crowd as the donation of property just south of the city was announced.

Enthusiastic bidders made for a spirited live auction and took bids to heights that both astonished and delighted the crowd gathered beneath and around the tent. Congratulations are also in order to Mr. George Duncan, winner of the signature quilt, who generously bid over two hundred dollars for the privilege of owning the autographs of distinguished citizens including President Chester A. Arthur. The evening closed with a benediction offered by Pastor James Taylor.

Bravo, ladies. Well done. We applaud you.

CHAPTER 20

He that is faithful in that which is least is faithful also in much.

LUKE 16:10

Jenny
Friday, June 22

Jenny was changing Johnny's diaper when Mrs. Crutchfield appeared just outside the bedroom door that had been cut in half to allow people to see in, while still keeping the babies safely contained.

"Mrs. Duncan's in the parlor, asking to see you."

Jenny finished pinning the diaper. Johnny rolled over and pushed himself to a sitting position, smiling and clapping while he looked up at his mother. She didn't move to get up off the floor. "Do I have to see her?"

" 'Course not, Princess. I'll tell her Her Highness is busy." The older woman grimaced as she leaned across and hissed, "Get yourself up off that floor. She's the president of the board that pays for your keep. She asks to see you; you see her."

"But"—Jenny gestured around at the four babies that Mrs. Crutchfield had assigned to her care—"I can't just leave them."

"Of course you can. Where they gonna go? There's nothing in here to hurt 'em." She motioned for Jenny to get up. "And don't ask me to stay in here. You know I've got my report to finish before Mrs. Duncan leaves."

Bracing her palms on the cot she'd been leaning against, Jenny stood.

"You look a wreck," Crutchfield said. "Think maybe you could use a comb once in a while?" She opened the door and waved Jenny into the hall.

Johnny let out a protest and tried to follow.

"Mama will be right back, little man."

Johnny began to wail as Jenny hurried down the stairs and into the parlor where Mrs. Duncan was waiting.

"Is that Johnny crying?"

Jenny nodded.

"He's all right," Mrs. Crutchfield said. "There's nothing can hurt him and nothing he can hurt."

Mrs. Duncan smiled. "I don't doubt it, but from the sound of things, *he* doesn't think he's all right." She put her hand on the newel post at the base of the stairs and waved for Jenny to lead the way back up.

Jenny obeyed, already dreading the foul mood this would put Mrs. Crutchfield in. The dread faded a bit when she opened the door to the nursery and Johnny cackled with joy. Mrs. Duncan followed her in, looking about her at the cribs and the three other babies. "I thought Mr. Duncan said there would be two other young women your age in residence."

Jenny shrugged. "It's just me."

"Are you happy here?"

Was she making a joke? If Jenny complained, wouldn't they make her leave? Mrs. Crutchfield had hinted that they might. There were two Mrs. Crutchfields—the one who greeted the women who supported the society and gave her monthly report to the committee, and the one who lived here the rest of the time. Jenny wondered at the stupidity of the rich women who didn't realize that.

"I mean—I realize this isn't what you wanted. . . ." Her voice trailed off. Her face flushed as if she was embarrassed. She nodded at the other children in the room. "Tell me their names."

"That's Miller." Jenny pointed to the towheaded, blue-eyed child who had just pulled himself up to stand at the cot next to Mrs. Duncan. "The one under the bed there is Huldah. I used to pull her out, but she doesn't like it. She seems to like it under there. She had purple marks on her legs when she first came. I think maybe she's getting less afraid. She smiled at me yesterday." She wrapped one arm around the little boy who'd just toddled over to her. "This is Emil. I've been trying to get him to stop sucking his thumb. Mrs. Crutchfield put some nasty-tasting stuff on it to help with that, but it didn't work."

"You seem to know them pretty well."

Jenny shrugged. "Can't hardly help it. Been taking care of them nearly three weeks, now."

Mrs. Duncan drew in a deep breath. "I want to tell your uncle you're here."

"Why? He doesn't care. He made me leave. Sterling's the one who took care of me. We were going—" She broke off. In recent days it had occurred to her that maybe Sterling hadn't really planned to leave his wife. He'd never said anything bad about Mrs. Sutton. In fact, he'd never mentioned her except to say that they couldn't have children and that made Johnny even more special to him.

"What if I don't tell him where you are, but just tell him that you have a son? If he's inclined to help, then we would decide what to do next." She leaned forward. "People sometimes change their minds, Jenny. After the shock wears off."

Jenny studied the older woman's face for a moment before asking, "Why do you care?"

She frowned. "I don't know. But I can't seem to get you off my mind." She picked Miller up and set him on her knee. "Did you hear about the fund-raiser?"

"Mrs. Crutchfield told me about it. Sterling's wife is building a new place. They're calling it Friendship Home. Crutchfield's worried about it." She'd also been unusually ill-tempered since reading the article in the newspaper, but Jenny didn't think she should mention that to Mrs. Duncan. There was no point in complaining.

"My husband bought a beautiful quilt for me at the auction. It has the president's name on it." Mrs. Duncan cleared her throat. "I put it in the guest bedroom. One night when I couldn't sleep, I started reading the names."

"I signed that quilt. Did you find my name?"

Mrs. Duncan didn't answer. Instead, she said, "It reminds me of you and Johnny every time I see it." She took a deep breath. "It also reminds me of something I want to change about myself. I go to church every Sunday, but I've never really thought about how kind Jesus was to women in trouble. And that maybe He expected me to be His hands." Her voice wavered. "I really do want to help you if I can."

Jenny ducked her head to hide her tears. "I don't know what to do. Even if I was strong enough to work, there's no store going to hire a girl with a baby. And even if they did, I've no one to take care of Johnny while I work. I don't know how to sew well enough to take in mending, and I'm not strong enough to take in laundry. I don't like living on charity, but what else am I going to do?"

"Perhaps you could be a nanny for someone who would let you care for their child and Johnny at the same time."

"No one rich enough to pay for a nanny wants a girl who got in trouble around their husband."

"Let me talk to your uncle."

"I don't guess I can stop you, can I?" Part of her wanted to hope. Maybe if Mrs. Duncan talked to him, maybe things would be different.

Mrs. Duncan gave Miller a hug and set him back down as she stood up. "Don't give up hope, Jenny. Let me see what I can do." She said good-bye.

Jenny listened to her footsteps descending the stairs, chatting with the nice Mrs. Crutchfield. Then they were both gone.

―❦―

From the moment Cass delivered the model to Juliana's on the Sunday after the bazaar, she felt like a cloud had lifted. The committee continued to meet at her home on a weekly basis, reporting on new donations and writing thank-you notes to generous supporters.

On most days, her daily ride took her to the job site rather than the cemetery. Some days she dismounted only long enough to get a drink of water from the well behind the stone cottage, and yet, before long, she knew each of the two dozen workers by name.

As time went on, she began to take an interest in their families. The day Elmo Klein missed work and Cass said the Kleins' child was ill, Juliana asked Dr. Gilbert to make a call. When Jess Jessup mentioned that his daughter was hoping to apprentice as a seamstress, Juliana asked Miss Thornhill about what a girl had to know to interview for a beginning position at the dresser's.

The next week when she sought out Jessup to tell him what she'd learned, she caught Cass looking at her with an odd expression on his face. Thinking he was upset because she'd interrupted Jessup at work, she went into the stone cottage to talk with him. "I should have spoken with Mr. Jessup another time," she said. "I'm sorry I took him away from his work. It won't happen again."

"What are you talking about? I'm not upset about that."

"You had a look—"

"I had a look?" He grinned.

"I don't mean to make a nuisance of myself out here."

"You aren't a nuisance, Mrs. Sutton. A distraction, maybe, but a lovely distraction, and a most welcome one." He hurried to apologize. "I'm sorry, ma'am. That was inappropriate."

"I don't—care."

He sat back. "Ma'am?"

"I don't care if it was inappropriate. It's nice to know someone—" She shook her head.

"Someone?"

"It's nice to know someone thinks of me as a real person, not just 'a widow mourning her loss.' " She snorted. "You know the truth about all of that."

He nodded. "That may change the nature of the grief, but I don't imagine it erases it." He paused. "Some would even say it makes it harder. Not having people know the depths of it."

She swallowed. Looked out the windows. Reached up to clutch an invisible locket. When she realized what she'd done, she dropped her hand to her side. "I don't know if it's harder. It's surely different." She shook her head. "At first I thought it was a sham. The funeral. The foundation with his name on it. But then, that night at the bazaar, with everyone saying such nice things about him?"

She shrugged. "I told myself that it wasn't right to forget all the good things, just because. . ." Her voice wavered. She looked over at Cass and forced a nervous laugh. "Don't worry. I'm not about to subject you to more hysterics." And then she was mortified by unexpected tears. "I am so sorry."

He rose and pulled a handkerchief from the breast pocket of his jacket. As he handed it over, he said, "You've a right to your feelings, Mrs. Sutton."

She mopped up her tears, started to hand the kerchief back, then retracted it. Shook her head. "I'll return it after it's laundered."

"And I'll look forward to seeing you again."

That night she dreamed of widow's veils and weighted silk disappearing into the shadows while she chose a gown for some important event. Suddenly, she was dressed in a blue gown standing next to a bay horse in the middle of a field of wildflowers. A bay horse that looked exactly like Baron, Cass Gregory's gelding.

It didn't make a bit of sense.

—∙∙∙—

Cass swung down off Baron and tied the reins to the back porch railing at home. Ma was sitting beneath the overhang, stemming and snapping the green beans in a bowl in her lap.

"Fresh green beans for supper," she said. "Mrs. Howard, two doors down, is sharing her bounty."

"That's good, Ma. I'm glad you're getting to know the neighbors. But I won't be staying for supper. Finney got some more model furniture finished, and I want to take it to Juliana's." He bent to kiss her on the cheek as he passed by. "I won't mind a late supper though, if you don't mind leaving a plate in the oven."

"The aunts won't let you go hungry."

He crouched down in front of her. "You know I love your cooking. I just want to get these delivered so Juliana has them for her committee meeting tomorrow. They're going to have to start discussing rules and staff soon. If they can get the furniture decided, that'll just be one less thing they have to worry over."

Ma nodded. Then she did something strange. Dropping the green beans back in the bowl, she leaned forward and cradled his face in her hands. "She is a good woman, Cass, but you are from two very different worlds." Then she leaned forward and kissed his cheek. "I'll put a plate in the oven before I turn in. And I will take offense if you slight my pot roast and green beans."

"I won't, Ma, I promise." He stood up. "Where's Sadie?"

"Back any minute. She met Ludwig at work. He wanted her advice on some display cabinets for their new store." She smiled up at him. "*They* know better than to shun my pot roast." She winked.

Cass stood up and headed inside. He washed up and was about to exit by the back door when Sadie and Ludwig walked in the front.

"Where you going all gussied up? Oh, wait. Don't tell me." Sadie stuck her nose in the air and inhaled, then nudged Ludwig. "Smell that? That is the smell of a man out to attract a lady."

"And this is the sound of a man ignoring you," Cass said and kept going.

"You're wearing your best shirt," Sadie called after him. "You might as well get her name tattooed over your heart."

Cass whipped about to face her. He almost asked her how in the world she knew about tattoos. But then he thought better of it.

———

It wasn't until late in July that Juliana began to fully appreciate the enormity of the responsibilities the women had taken on themselves by agreeing to accept her donation. Prior to the bazaar, it had been all excitement and anticipation. Now the real work began. It took three meetings to agree on the "Rules Governing the Matron & Committees of the Friendship Home of Lincoln, Nebraska."

Once the basic organization was laid out, Helen Duncan and two other committee members traveled to Omaha to interview a superintendent of a Home for the Friendless there. They returned with a combination of good news and horror stories that alternately encouraged and intimidated the committee.

"We need far more staff than we anticipated," Helen said. "Once we gather the current residents into one place, we'll have more than two dozen in our care, and we know the number will grow quickly. We must prepare for that. The suggested list includes a matron, a physician, a teacher, three nurses, a cook, a laundress, a couple of general assistants, and a combination gardener/engineer. All those salaries add up to $255 a month." She nodded in Juliana's direction. "Thanks to Mr. Carter of First National, we are in a good financial position to support the first year, but I cannot stress enough that we must get the legislature to help us." She paused. "We'll table that for now, but please be thinking how we can impress the need on our state senators."

Lutie Gleason spoke up. "I propose we take the half-dozen babies into the chamber when it's in session. Preferably right before feeding time."

Helen laughed. "Let's remember that idea if more conventional means don't succeed."

When Aunt Theodora asked which staff member should be hired first, everyone seemed to agree that the matron was the most critical. According to the organizational rules the society had drafted, the matron was to "have full control of the family and household officers." That meant she would keep a record of all admissions and discharges and maintain individual files on each inmate. She would present a written monthly report "of important items of family interest."

Juliana suppressed a smile when Aunt Theodora said that it seemed to her they were looking for a living replica of Mary, the mother of Christ.

"Not quite," Helen said quietly. "We *are* willing to pay twenty-five dollars a month. The mother of our Lord would do a wonderful job without expecting a salary."

Someone mentioned Mrs. Crutchfield, currently in charge of one of the homes in town.

"Absolutely not," Helen said. She looked around the table and softened her tone. "I've stopped in a few times recently. The care is adequate, but we need someone more. . .patient. Warmhearted. The young women we will be helping need someone who can be firm, but they also need a friend and companion. That is not Mrs. Crutchfield."

They would also need more volunteers. A Placement Committee to oversee the process of finding homes for orphans, a Purchasing Committee to handle ordering supplies, and a Visiting Committee, "just to keep a friendly eye on things."

"They should arrive unannounced," Aunt Theodora said. "That will keep the staff on their toes."

"Are you volunteering?" Helen asked.

"You'd be wonderful at it," Aunt Lydia said. "Everyone in this room is frightened half to death of you."

"As it should be," Aunt Theodora said. She tried to maintain a stern face but couldn't quite manage it.

Finally, at the beginning of August, Helen brought a typewritten "Rules of Admission and Discharge."

RULES OF ADMISSION AND DISCHARGE

1. Applicants to the home may be received at the discretion of the matron for one week or until the Admissions Committee shall have an opportunity to decide upon the application.

2. An applicant who has property or friends able to pay an admissions fee shall do so, the amount to be discretionary with the committee.

3. Boarders may be received by special agreement with the committee, but never to the exclusion of those for whom Friendship Home was first created, and they shall be required to obey the rules of the home the same as other inmates.

4. Any person desiring to take a child from the home for adoption or to bring a child up to maturity must communicate in person or by writing with the matron, giving a full statement of all the circumstances into which the child will be placed, what position in the family such child will hold, what labor will be required, what advantages for education will be given, and what will be the religious privileges and training. These facts must always be accompanied with good and satisfactory recommendations or the request will receive no approval from the committee.

Aunt Theodora peered at her copy as if it might sprout wings. "Typewriter?"

"It isn't French, Sister," Aunt Lydia said. "It's the future."

The older woman sighed. "I see reference to the 'rules of the home.'" She peered over her spectacles. "What, pray tell, are those?"

Helen looked around the table. "Whatever we decide. Would someone care to volunteer to draft a list?"

"I don't suppose 'be good' is considered adequate?" Aunt Theodora said.

"If only it could be." Helen laughed. "Do I hear a motion to table that until the next meeting?"

"I'd rather make a motion that Miss Theodora be requested to draft something for us," Lutie Gleason said, glancing at Aunt Theodora. "You are so good with words."

When the motion was seconded and carried, Aunt Theodora promised to have "a few good words" as to rules of conduct prepared by the next meeting at the end of the month.

CHAPTER 21

Rejoice with them that do rejoice, and weep with them that weep.
ROMANS 12:15

Jenny
Thursday, July 26

On a blistering hot day in late July, when the shadow of Mrs. Crutchfield's house finally reached the well pump in the backyard, Jenny dragged a galvanized tub out of a shed and wore herself out pumping water into the tub. When it was half full, she talked one of the new residents into helping her carry the four babies downstairs. Jenny stripped them all down and removed their diapers and, one at a time, lowered them into the cold water. They shrieked with the shock at first, but it wasn't long before all four children realized how much better they felt and began to enjoy splashing the cool water on each other.

Jenny settled in the grass beside them and, dampening a clean rag, folded it and draped it across the back of her neck, closing her eyes with pleasure as cold water dripped down her back.

The nausea she'd been battling all day faded. She'd just reached for the dipper hanging on the pump head to get a drink when Mrs. Duncan came walking around the side of the house.

"You don't need to say a word," Jenny said. "I already see what happened. Thank you for trying." She hung the dipper back up. "I told you he wouldn't change his mind."

Helen reached in her bag. "Is Johnny teething yet?" She held out a rubber teething ring.

"He hasn't been sleeping well. You think that's it?"

"Could be. Has Dr. Gilbert been by this week?"

Jenny shook her head and reached over to tousle Huldah's blond hair.

"She's learned to trust you," Helen said. "She was still hiding under the bed when I was here last."

Jenny smiled. "She's better."

"I'm not giving up, Jenny. He'll change his mind."

She shook her head. "Even if he did, he'd be sorry."

"He wouldn't," Helen said. "Johnny's a lovely child, and you're a sweet girl." She came closer and bent down, smiling. "I'm going to bring him and the others some new clothes later in the week. Would you like a new dress?"

Jenny shook her head. "I'm all right."

"You'll like it at the new place. The construction is going along. It's out in the country, and there will be a new staff." She glanced back at the house and lowered her voice. "No more Mrs. Crutchfield. Better food. And the nursery! An entire floor for the babies. Plenty of room for them to crawl about and play. We're going to have a toy drive. It'll be so much nicer."

"It sounds like it," Jenny said, more because Mrs. Duncan seemed to need to hear it than anything. "When will you move people in?"

"Just after Thanksgiving." Mrs. Duncan smiled. "Johnny will be walking by then. Can you imagine?" She paused. "I don't want to upset you, but we've had someone apply to adopt a little girl. They'll be coming by in a few days to see Huldah."

Jenny blinked back tears. She nodded. "That's good. As long as they'll be good to her."

"We'll appoint someone to make unannounced home visits for the first six months, and if there's any question, we won't let her stay."

Jenny nodded. That night, when the babies were asleep, she crept downstairs to the kitchen where Mrs. Crutchfield kept her almanac. She had to check the newspaper to see what today's date was, but once she'd done that, she counted back to two days before Sterling died. Then she counted forward.

This one would be a Christmas baby.

———

"Of course you must go," Juliana said firmly. She laid the newspaper aside and looked across the breakfast table at the aunts. "You've spent August at the summer house for nearly ten years. I won't hear of you canceling your plans."

"We can't leave you alone. Not this summer." Aunt Lydia shook her head.

"I hope you aren't listening, Martha," Juliana said. "They're erasing you. And you standing over a hot stove to make them the chokecherry syrup they love so well."

"I didn't hear a thing," Martha said. "I'm not here, remember?"

Juliana looked back at the aunts. "I'll still have Martha and Alfred. And I promised Pastor Taylor I'd help with the homecoming picnic the first weekend in September. I need to be here to help make plans."

"Margaret Nash is on that committee," Aunt Lydia said, "and I imagine she'd blossom if only she had the chance. She's very capable. You don't need to be here."

Juliana smiled. "I'll let her blossom. She can head it up if she wants to, and I'll do her bidding. Even so, it isn't fair to dump the entire thing in her lap."

"There are other people who can plan a church picnic," Aunt Theodora said.

"Undoubtedly. But I want to help. And I don't want to spend a month playing backgammon with people I barely know. I'm sure your Lake Geneva friends are lovely, but they are *your* friends." Juliana paused. "And if you must know, I don't want to be 'the widow in residence.' People here are at least used to it by now. They are only minimally shocked when I smile and laugh."

She got up and took her plate to the sink and rinsed it. "Please. Aunt Lydia. Aunt Theodora. Go to Lake Geneva. Enjoy the cool breeze. There is no reason for you to stay here and melt with me. Beyond helping with the church picnic, I'm going to do very little but sit on the back porch, reading and drinking lemonade."

"She's trying to get rid of us," Aunt Theodora said, looking troubled.

"She is," Juliana agreed. "The truth comes out. I'm sick of you two. I need a break."

"I knew it. I am crushed." Aunt Theodora stood up. "Come, Lydia. We have packing to do." She hesitated at the bottom of the stairs. "Martha."

"Yes, Miss Theodora." Martha looked up from stirring the syrup cooking on the stove.

"You will telegram us if Juliana regrets kicking us out?"

Martha smiled. "The very instant."

"All right. Then I suppose one of you can tell Alfred that we'll be needing a ride to the train station on Monday."

—⁂—

When August heat began to take its toll, Cass had the crew load the wagons before dawn and head to the job site by moonlight. As soon as the sun came up, they went to work. By the time the heat was at its worst, they had put in almost a full day's work and Cass sent them back to town with a reminder not to push the teams and to cool them down carefully. He often stayed behind. It wasn't that bad if he took it slow, and he had grown to love having the place to himself.

Without the crew there, he could meander through the rooms and inspect the progress at his own pace. They were doing a fine job, but he still found little things on occasion that he could address. The plaster and lath would soon be finished. Things would go quickly after that. They shouldn't have any trouble being ready for the open house Juliana wanted the weekend before Thanksgiving.

Sadie and Ludwig were getting married the first Sunday in December. Their store was taking shape down in Roca. Ludwig had begun to order display cases, and Juliana had given permission for them to be stored in the warehouse behind the office. He still hadn't shown her the dining table the boss had had delivered all those months ago. There just hadn't been a right time.

He didn't expect to see Mrs. Sutton out at the job site much this month, and that was probably for the best. Sadie's teasing was getting old. Ma had only said that one thing on the back porch that day, but he could tell she was thinking about it. He couldn't understand what he did that made them worry. Of course he put on a clean shirt when he was going to see her. Wasn't that polite? And yes, he went out of his way to see that things were done in a way that pleased her. She was his boss. That didn't mean he was engaging in romantic flights of fancy.

If anyone knew how many worlds apart he and Juliana were, it was him. The woman had had her portrait painted by one of the premier portrait artists in America. She had a Cezanne hanging in the hallway. Every single thing in that house was a reminder that this was not a woman to be courted by a builder. The fact that she'd married one had nothing to do with it. Sterling and Juliana Sutton might have started out with very little, but that had changed quickly, thanks in part to the boss's skill, but mostly to an inheritance. The boss's father had died suddenly while the newly married Juliana and Sterling Sutton were on their wedding trip.

He shouldn't be thinking of her by her Christian name. She was Mrs. Sutton to him. And if he kept saying it enough, he would finally get it through his thick skull and stop wondering what it would be like to kiss those lips. . .to see passion glimmer in those dark eyes.

—⁂—

Juliana sat on the back porch, a glass of lemonade in her hand, praying for a breeze. With the advent of August, everything had seemed to slow down. The prairie shimmered as waves of heat rose from the earth. It wasn't unusual to see what appeared to be a lake on the distant horizon. The earth seemed to hold its breath. Tecumseh and Fancy and Sterling's prized bays stood side by side in the pasture, heads down, motionless except for their long tails swishing in an unending battle with flies. The shade in the barn offered little relief.

Alfred pumped fresh water into the stock tanks every morning. Even so, the water was lukewarm by noon.

Helen and George Duncan had departed for an excursion to the West Coast, and in Helen's absence, the committee decided to take a respite from weekly meetings. Lutie Gleason was dropping in on the home maintained by Mrs. Crutchfield in Helen's absence. She said visiting the children in person would help her be more familiar with the actual needs and help her plan a more successful toy drive.

Juliana had expected to enjoy the slower pace of life and some time to herself, but the aunts had only been gone a little over a week before she began to feel restless. She missed the constant activity around the opening of Friendship Home. Today, the quiet resulting from Alfred and Martha's second Monday off since the aunts had left was quickly becoming oppressive.

With a sigh, Juliana laid aside the copy of the *Ladies' Home Journal* she'd been trying to read. And she decided. She would only take a short ride, and she wouldn't demand much of anything past a brief trot from Tecumseh, but surely it would do them both good to get their blood moving.

She'd eschewed black since the aunts left. There was no reason to languish in mourning attire when she was home alone all day—save for the occasional visit from Cass, when he stopped to report on the building progress or ask a question. But Cass hadn't stopped by for a few days, and she missed hearing the news.

She'd started the day in white lawn. Instead of a black waist beneath her riding habit, she would opt for white voile. And it was ridiculous to wear a jacket in this heat. When she headed out to the barn to saddle Tecumseh, she was doubly glad she'd been sensible about that. She filled a flask with water and tucked it at her waist before heading out.

She hadn't consciously planned to ride that far, but she ended up at the construction site. She'd taken note of countless butterflies fluttering around the clusters of butterfly weed dotting the prairie and scared up a covey of quail that had given her the delightful sight of at least a dozen chicks.

As she rode up to Friendship Home, it appeared that she'd arrived at another empty house. Where was everyone? She dismounted and, pulling off her gloves, led Tecumseh to the well behind the stone cottage. "Don't you dare go anywhere," she said. "I'm getting us a drink." Tecumseh waited. She had lowered the bucket and hauled it halfway back up when the horse snuffled her shoulder. Startled, she let go of the windlass. Seconds later, she heard the splash far below, as the bucket hit the water.

"You are incorrigible." She led Tecumseh to the pasture fence and tied him up. "There. Now you'll have to behave."

"You sure he can't untie those reins?"

Juliana whirled about. *Cass?*

"Sorry if I frightened you. It's awfully hot for a lady to be out and about."

"It's awfully hot for a man to walk out here from town." She looked toward the pasture. "I don't see Baron. And where is everyone?"

"Baron's grazing east of the house today in the shade."

"Hobbles?"

He nodded.

"And everyone else?"

"I thought I mentioned that when I stopped in last week. We've been coming out early since it got so hot. Meeting at the lumberyard right before dawn, loading up by lantern light, and starting work out here as soon as the sun comes up. We still get in most of a good day's work, but we miss the worst of the heat."

"Don't *you* want to miss the worst of the heat?"

He shrugged. "I've gotten in the habit of lingering. It gives me a chance to check over things more carefully." He paused. "I didn't think you'd mind the change in schedule. I suppose I should have checked with you. As soon as it cools off even a little, we can put in extra hours if we need to."

"Of course I don't mind. You don't need to ask about things like that."

"Just making sure the boss doesn't think I'm slacking."

"I wish you'd stop calling me 'the boss.'" She began to haul the water back up. "I have a name. It's Juliana." She supposed it was rather. . .bold to suggest he use her given name, but why not? They'd become friends, hadn't they?

"Yes, ma'am." He came to her side. "Here. Let me do that." His hand grazed hers as he took over.

She went to Tecumseh and untied the reins from the fence. Cass set the bucket on the rim of the well and filled a dipper. He held it out to her. She took it and drank. He toasted her with the next dipperful and drank it himself, then set the bucket down for Tecumseh.

"I should probably carry a bucket over to Baron," Cass said. He nodded at the house. "The main-floor rooms are all plastered now, and we installed the stove in the cottage kitchen. I ordered a duplicate for Martha's kitchen in town."

"I thought you said you weren't going to install the one out here yet for fear of thieves."

He shrugged. "It wasn't thieves coming out here when no one was around." He lowered the bucket back down the well.

The Duncans. Juliana smiled. "The Duncans are taking the train all the way to San Francisco. I think George is trying to make up for the house."

Cass chuckled. "Then let us hope that no one tells Mrs. Duncan that the railroad often gives free tickets to stockholders." Setting the refilled bucket on the rim of the well, he untied it and headed toward Baron, just visible now grazing on the east side of the house.

Juliana followed him, still leading Tecumseh, who whickered when he saw Baron. Baron lifted his head and answered, then lowered his head to drink as Cass set the bucket down.

"Free tickets or not," Juliana said, "I hope the trip helps mend things between them."

Cass rested his hand on Baron's broad back. "You seem kindly intentioned toward the Duncans all of a sudden."

"Helen and I have made our peace." She told him about the day

Helen had come to the house to apologize. "We've done a lot of work together since that day. I almost dare to say we've become friends."

Cass pulled the bucket away from Baron and offered Tecumseh another drink, then emptied it and set it on the now-completed back steps leading up to the porch that spanned the rear of the house. "What would you think of screening this in?" he asked. "It would give children a fly-free place to play on hot days like this."

"Do it."

He laughed. "That was easy. Beware. If you're feeling inclined to say yes today, you never know what I might ask for." He looked away quickly. "I mean—I could ask for a raise."

"And I would give it." She looked up at the back of the house. "You don't happen to have an extra set of hobbles, do you? I think I'd like to go in."

"I don't. Why don't we turn both horses into the pasture? Then you can take your time walking through. They'd probably both rather drink muddy creek water anyway." When she nodded, he bent to remove Baron's hobbles and, grasping the horse's hackamore, led the way to the pasture.

A few minutes later, Juliana had been through the entire house and was standing in the first-floor turret room, wondering aloud if it was big enough for the matron's office. She told Cass about all the organizational details the committee had been dealing with and outlined the matron's record-keeping duties. "She's going to need at least one filing cabinet, and as the years go by, we're going to have to add on. Now that I think of it, wouldn't it be perfect to have a medical clinic on the grounds? Lutie Gleason has been visiting the babies since Helen left, and she says it's heartbreaking—the state of health when some of them arrive." She paused. "I should speak with Dr. Gilbert about that. Maybe we should be hiring our own full-time physician." She stopped abruptly and looked at Cass. He was leaning against the doorframe, his arms folded across his chest, smiling at her. "Did I say something amusing?"

"No, ma'am. I was smiling at you. At the way you think. The way you see it all finished and anticipate what's going to be needed in the future." He held up his hands. "You see the big picture. That's a gift. Simply put: you, Mrs. Sutton, are a wonder."

"Juliana." She could feel herself blushing.

He smiled. Nodded. "All right. You are a wonder, Juliana."

For some reason, the sight of a handsome man looking at her—that way—brought all the memories flooding back. Sterling had looked at her like that when they'd first met. A curious combination of longing and sadness made her turn away from him. She crossed to the windows, blinking away tears. *Wonders don't discover mistresses' photographs in dresser drawers. Wonders—*

"What did I say? Juliana? What's wrong?"

She shook her head. "Wonders' husbands don't die in brothels." Anger and sadness shoved the happiness she'd felt only moments ago back into the shadows.

Cass stepped close and put his hands on her shoulders.

She closed her eyes and leaned back against him. *Hold me.* She bent her head and rested her cheek against the hand gripping her shoulder. He traced her hairline with the forefinger of his free hand. Was he going to kiss her? Her heartbeat ratcheted up. Without letting go of his hand, she pivoted about and looked up at him. *Kiss me.* What did that expression in his hazel eyes mean? For a moment it seemed that passion flickered and then—it was gone.

He released her hand and stepped back. "I promised Ma I wouldn't be late for supper tonight. Let me take you home."

They saddled their horses and rode into town together, making small talk about nothing. Once they were back at the house, Cass pumped fresh water into the stock tank while Juliana unsaddled Tecumseh. Still, he stayed. He helped her rub the horse down and turn him out. When there was nothing left to do outside, he gathered Baron's reins and prepared to mount up.

She almost asked him to stay. *Have a glass of lemonade. Watch the sun go down. Talk about. . .anything. Just don't leave until we talk about whatever just happened.* But she didn't get the chance to ask.

"I appreciate what you said at the house," he finally said. "About calling you *Juliana*." He cleared his throat. "But I think it's best that things stay the way they've been between us. I don't want people thinking I'm taking liberties with my boss's widow."

It felt like he'd thrown cold water in her face. And all the while she'd thought—whatever she'd thought didn't matter. She took a step back.

He seemed to sense that he'd hurt her. "Don't misunderstand, Juliana, it's just—"

"You don't have to explain," she said quickly.

"You're wrong. I do need to explain." He took a deep breath. "You're an exquisite, desirable woman, and your world fell apart only four months ago. Wounds like that don't heal overnight." He tugged on the brim of his hat. Looked off toward the horizon. Finally, he met her gaze. "I know you're in need of a friend right now, and I'd like to be a friend, but the truth is, I don't think I'm strong enough to be just a friend." He paused. "Do you understand what I'm saying?"

He was saying *no*. She nodded.

"So. . .I need to go." He smiled. "For now."

"Good evening, then," she croaked and headed for the house, feeling foolish. Embarrassed. Like a child who'd reached for something and had her hand slapped. She hurried inside. But she couldn't keep herself from walking to the front of the house and watching him retreat toward town through the parlor window.

CHAPTER 22

Be ye all of one mind, having compassion one of another.
1 Peter 3:8

He didn't look back, even though he wanted to. Was she watching him ride away? Did she understand? *Please, Lord. Let her understand. I couldn't just come out and say it.* A man didn't blurt out his feelings to a widow of only a few months. But a man couldn't just stand a few feet away from a beautiful woman and let her cry without doing anything, either. At least he couldn't.

Did Juliana realize how close she'd been to getting herself kissed out at the house when she spun around and looked up at him? Did she have any idea what it did to him just now to have her look up at him in the fading light with sadness looming in those dark eyes? The power of the emotion that had roiled through him just now almost scared him. And recognizing it for what it was changed everything.

As he dismounted at the livery and went through the motions of unsaddling Baron and rubbing him down, Cass gave himself a good talking-to. It was true that his heartbeat ratcheted up a notch every time he saw Tecumseh loping across the prairie toward Friendship Home. More than once, he'd fabricated a reason to stop at the house to update Juliana or to ask a question he already knew the answer to. But it was also true that he and Juliana Sutton were worlds apart. Even if there was something between them beyond—even if there was, it couldn't happen right now. Juliana needed time, and he would be well served to remember that and to get on about the business of finishing Friendship Home and starting the next project.

The next project. What would it be? He and Finney had responded to a number of inquiries and put some bids out. A few decisions were also pending on bids the boss had handled before his death. Now that Cass thought about it, he should be giving more attention to the future of Sutton Builders and less to pondering sad brown eyes. Bids on new projects and visiting sites for new construction and poring over plans with potential customers wouldn't keep him awake at night. At least not in the same way thinking about Juliana did.

He thought his way back through what seemed to be her new vulnerability today. Why today? Maybe she'd spent more time with him since the aunts had gone on their summer retreat because she was unexpectedly lonely. She might have been surprised by new waves of memory and grief. Without the distraction of committee meetings and company, she was more vulnerable. All of that was very normal, and he shouldn't read more into what had just happened than that. He'd been a friend in a time when she needed a friend.

All the way home from the livery, Cass turned things over in his mind, and by the time he got home, he was thinking straight again. He would forget the warmth of her body leaning back against him. He would not dwell on the sweet scent of her clean hair or the fact that she'd asked him to call her Juliana. It would be one of the more difficult things he'd done in a while, but with God's help. . . *Please, Lord. Show me the way through this.*

Finally home, Cass made his way around the side of the house and to the backyard. He set his hat on the porch, then went to the pump and, ducking his head beneath the spigot, doused himself with cold water. He took a kerchief out of his pocket, soaked it, tied it around his neck, and headed inside. Not thinking about Juliana.

Sadie called out, even before he had closed the back door. "Don't believe I know you. You sure you got the right house?" When he didn't answer, but only bent to kiss Ma on the cheek and head into his room, Sadie called after him. "I remember now. I think we're related." She grinned. "That highfalutin boss lady didn't fire ya, did she? You look like you just lost your best friend."

Highfalutin? Juliana isn't anything of the kind. "She doesn't like being called 'the boss,'" he snapped. Snatching at the curtain across his bedroom door, he stepped inside. And of course, the first thing he noticed was the Bible on his night table. *Good work, Gregory. You ask God for help, and not a minute later you're lashing out at Sadie.* His anger dissolved just as quickly as it had flared up. With a sigh, he took his hat off and tossed it across the room, intending for it to land on his bed. It tumbled across the blanket and landed on the floor out of sight.

He turned around and stepped back out into the living area. Sadie was at the table, her head down, scratching Patch behind the ears.

"I'm sorry," Cass said. "I don't know what got into me."

Sadie shrugged. "It's all right. I shouldn't always be so full of sass." She sniffed and swiped at a tear.

"Please forgive me. You did nothing wrong. It's just this heat and—" He shook his head.

"'Course I forgive you. Whatever it is, though, I hope it gets mended."

He shrugged. *Not likely.* How could he stop thinking about Juliana when he had to see her several times a week? He avoided looking at Ma as he reached over and ran his palm across Patch's smooth coat. "I think I'm going to spend some time in my room. The heat's wrung me out. If I don't come to the table for supper, don't worry about me. I'm not really hungry, anyway."

Back on the other side of the curtain, he retrieved his hat from the floor and set it on the chair in the corner. Next, he raised the windows as far as they would go. Finally, he took his shirt off and sprawled across the bed, staring up at the ceiling. Not thinking about Juliana.

God, I'm gonna need some help here.

—⁂—

Jenny
Monday, August 20

It was getting harder to hide it. She hadn't really felt all that good since she came to Mrs. Crutchfield's, so the fact that she wasn't eating much didn't draw attention. Still, there were pains that Jenny didn't think were right. Sometimes they knocked the air right out of her. The heat wasn't helping. It made the babies fuss. Made them harder to take care of.

Johnny and little Huldah had raw bottoms. Dr. Gilbert said it was a heat rash. He had some ointment for it, but he said the best thing to do was to let them go without diapers, and that just wasn't possible.

Mrs. Crutchfield said that if Jenny would only train the babies, they wouldn't need diapers. That would save on laundry, too, and why didn't she just do that? Well, she just didn't have the energy. That's why.

Mrs. Duncan hadn't been by for a while. She'd gone off on a train excursion to the West Coast with her husband. Jenny wished that she could go somewhere. Anywhere. But of course her chance for that was past. Even if she were rich, she wouldn't be able to do it now. Not the way she felt. Not even with a full-time nurse for Johnny and a maid.

Her dresses had been so loose when she first came that it was easy to hide things, but as her body changed it was beginning to look like she had a rubber ball under her skin in front. Almost like a deformity. She supposed that was because she was thin. Maybe that was why the pains came, too. It wasn't going to be possible to hide it from Dr. Gilbert anymore. Of course he had to take care of her and be nice. But Mrs. Duncan was another matter entirely.

Jenny dreaded the next time Mrs. Duncan came to visit.

—⁂—

Just when Juliana thought that she had a friend in Cass Gregory, just when she'd asked him to call her Juliana, things changed. He stopped dropping by the house to tell her about the progress out at Friendship Home. She reminded herself that the summer heat would naturally make a working man eager to get home. She remembered what that had been like when Sterling was building his business. He used to come home on hot summer days and stick his head beneath the pump head and ask her to "soak me good" with cold well water. She couldn't fault Cass for not wanting to stop by her house as often.

But that didn't explain why he kept his distance at church. And it didn't explain the emphasis he seemed to put on calling her "Mrs. Sutton." She'd thought the two of them were past all of that awkwardness. She'd thought maybe. . . But apparently, she'd been wrong. Thankfully, with the planning for St. John's Founders' Day picnic, Juliana managed to stay busy. She began heading north to the cemetery when she went for a ride instead of south to Friendship Home.

Returned from her excursion west with her husband, Helen Duncan initiated more committee meetings. She seemed to have a renewed fervor when it came to providing for single women who found themselves "compromised" and took a new interest in the details of finishing Friendship Home, voicing a particularly strong opinion when it came to selecting which rooms would be available for single mothers. Helen wanted the former master suite with the private upstairs porch for them. And the rooms should be cheerful. She suggested yellow walls and white iron bedsteads. She brought in fabric swatches and wondered if the ladies might eventually make patchwork quilts "to give the rooms a homey feel."

Juliana decided that whatever had happened between the Duncans on their trip west, it had been very good for Helen. She offered her parlor for more quiltings and welcomed the opportunity to be drawn back into activities that kept her mind off pointless musings as to the nature of her friendship with Cass Gregory.

Still, at times, when she sat at her dressing table brushing her hair or when she reached past the white lawn waist in her wardrobe to retrieve something black, she thought back to that day when he'd held her, when he'd said "Juliana" in a way that seemed almost tender. Thinking on it caused a curious kind of longing to rise up alongside a deepening sense of what she'd lost and a helpless regret over the idea that what Sterling had done could never be made right. She couldn't confront it, because he was gone. If she forgave him, he would never know. She wanted him to know. To know that she had discovered his betrayal. And if she ever could forgive him, she wanted him to know that, too. It seemed important, although she didn't quite know why.

Sometimes when she thought back to those first hours when she'd truly thought about strangling him with that locket chain, those first days when she'd wanted to dump his clothing into the burning pit, she was grateful for the anger that had helped her survive. But that emotion had begun to mellow. Now when she thought about it all, more often than not she found herself wondering about that girl and the child and hoping they were all right.

Things were changing as blessedly cool, fall air floated in Juliana's windows at night to caress her skin. She was changing. And the words *Mrs. Sutton, ma'am* were beginning to grate on her nerves.

—⁂—

Juliana and the committee's efforts at staffing the Friendship Home took on new importance in the month of October. The committee had planned a celebratory open house for the weekend before Thanksgiving, and the ladies agreed that it was vital for the new matron to be in attendance at that event. The problem was, applicant after applicant for the position failed to impress.

They needed someone with a particular set of skills, and the more ladies the committee interviewed, the more they realized that Aunt Theodora's acerbic remark all those weeks ago about hoping to find a living, breathing woman like the biblical Mary wasn't all that far off the mark. However, if she did exist, it appeared that "Mary" either wasn't seeing the advertisements the society had placed in leading newspapers, or she wasn't looking for a position.

One particularly trying afternoon when the committee had spent yet another few hours interviewing three more unsuitable applicants and rejecting another half-dozen inquiries, Helen Duncan teased Aunt Theodora. "If only you were interested in the position. You'd be ideal."

The older woman sputtered disbelief. "Don't be ridiculous."

"You have all the requisite skills," Helen insisted. "You're detail oriented, you write beautifully, and there is no question you could maintain discipline."

"You are very kind not to take note of my advancing decrepitude." Aunt Theodora glanced around the table at the committee members. "Are we certain that Mrs. Crutchfield—?"

"We are," Helen said abruptly and handed over the recent batch of rejected applications, so that Aunt Theodora could send regrets.

In the end, the aunts would be credited with finding the perfect candidate. One crisp fall day, Aunt Theodora hurried into the parlor where Juliana and Aunt Lydia were at work on yet another quilt. Letter in hand, she enthused, "Listen to this! Mrs. Harrison has decided to visit! She's coming next week."

"We met her at Lake Geneva," Aunt Lydia explained.

"I remember." Juliana nodded. "A widowed schoolteacher?"

"Yes," Aunt Theodora nodded. "And a former minister's wife. She impressed us both. So much."

Aunt Lydia nodded. "She cared for her infirm parents until she married Reverend Harrison. Then once he was established in a ministry, they worked together, organizing a ministry to the needy poor. We couldn't ask for a better candidate."

Upon her arrival in Lincoln, Mrs. Harrison proved the aunts correct. Lovely, petite, and energetic, the young widow showed a particular tenderness toward the babies in Mrs. Crutchfield's home. She revealed in private conversation with Helen Duncan that she had lost her only child in infancy.

Caroline Harrison dressed modestly, exhibited excellent manners, and charmed everyone. Including, Juliana noted, Cass Gregory, who seemed to make it his personal duty to provide the lovely Mrs. Harrison a guided tour of every nook and cranny of the Friendship Home.

Offered the position by a delighted and enthusiastic committee three days after her arrival in Lincoln, Mrs. Harrison accepted. She stayed in Lincoln over two Sundays. On her first Sunday, she accompanied Helen Duncan to First Church. On her second Sunday, she accepted Aunt Lydia's invitation to come to St. John's and to have Sunday dinner at the Sutton home. Aunt Lydia also invited the Duncans to share Sunday dinner and, in her words, "our dear Mr. Gregory, who has been so vital to the project's success."

Cass had "sent his regrets" to at least two dinner invitations extended since the aunts had returned from Lake Geneva. Apparently, he'd caught up with whatever work he'd used as an excuse on those two occasions, for he quickly accepted Aunt Lydia's invitation. He seemed to enjoy himself, too, seated as he was at the opposite end of the table from Juliana, between his mother and the lovely Mrs. Harrison.

Oh, yes, everyone found Mrs. Harrison to be just perfect as the new matron. She took to the position like a woman born with the gift of administration. Of course, Juliana agreed when the topic came up. It was wonderful the way things had worked out. Just. Wonderful.

―∞―

Jenny
Friday, October 12

"You really should have said something earlier." Dr. Gilbert sighed as he took the stethoscope from around his neck and tucked it back into his black bag. He'd had Mrs. Crutchfield tend the babies in the other room so that he could examine Jenny in privacy. When Jenny said they shouldn't impose on Mrs. Crutchfield that way, Dr. Gilbert had gotten as close to angry as she'd ever seen him.

"Mrs. Crutchfield," he said, "will have to adjust."

Of course he probably didn't realize that Jenny would have to do most of the adjusting after he was gone—to the irascible woman's bad temper at being put upon. But now was not the time to worry over that. Jenny rolled onto her side, facing the doctor who was seated on the edge of the narrow cot. She felt better lying this way. It seemed that the baby didn't press on things that hurt quite so much.

"Do you know who the father is?"

She frowned. "Why are you asking me that? There's only been one man in my life. Ever."

The doctor nodded. "All right. I know the baby was conceived before the fire." He took a deep breath. "I was just hoping there might be someone who would take responsibility."

Fear clutched at her. Her throat constricted, and tears flooded her eyes. "Are they going to make me leave?"

"Of course not."

She sniffed. "There's rules. If they think I broke the rules, they'll make me leave."

"You didn't break any rules. I can affirm that." He put a gentle hand on her arm. "You'll be taken care of. I believe what you've said about who the father is, but this baby is too small. You have to do better at eating."

"Too small? I can't hardly walk some days."

"That's because Johnny was probably too large for a woman your size. A lot of damage was done. It can make it more difficult for future confinements." He stood up. "I'm going to tell Mrs. Crutchfield that you're going to need to rest a lot more. And she's going to have to help with the children. Or hire help."

"Please! Ask Mrs. Duncan to get someone. She'll get someone nice."

Two days later, Helen Duncan brought someone new to visit. "This is the new matron for Friendship Home, Jenny. Her name is Mrs. Harrison."

Mrs. Duncan sat down on the edge of Jenny's cot. She told Mrs. Harrison about each of the babies. And she remembered everything that Jenny had ever told her about each one.

Mrs. Harrison picked up each of the babies in turn. She even got little Huldah to smile. Huldah, who had been returned after only a week in her new home because the people said she cried too much.

After she met the babies, Mrs. Harrison spoke to Jenny. "Dr. Gilbert told me that you are going to have another baby?"

Jenny nodded. Here it came. She steeled herself for the expected scolding.

"He's very concerned that you aren't eating well. He's also concerned that caring for four babies is just too much to expect of you. Mrs. Duncan and I think we have a solution. But you do not have to agree to it if you don't want to. I want to make that clear."

"What is it?"

"We've arranged for Huldah and Emil and Miller to be moved to one of the other homes. Just temporarily, until Friendship Home is ready to open. I'm already living out there in a stone cottage on the grounds. It's a lovely place, and there are two bedrooms. I need only one. What would you say to moving there until the Friendship Home is ready? The thought is that, if you have a chance to rest, you'll begin to feel better. Your appetite will improve, and everything will go much better for you and the new baby."

Jenny frowned. "What about Johnny?"

"Why, he'll stay with us, of course." Mrs. Harrison smiled. "I love babies. I think between the two of us we can handle one Johnny, don't you?"

"He's a good boy," Jenny said. "He's hardly any trouble."

"So much the better."

"Won't Mrs. Crutchfield be mad?"

Mrs. Harrison and Mrs. Duncan exchanged knowing looks before Mrs. Duncan said, "I suspect she will, but that isn't any of your concern. *Your* concern is to take good care of yourself so that you can mother your children. We're going to help you, but only until you're well enough to do it yourself. How does that sound?"

Jenny began to cry. "I'm sorry. I cry too much. I know I do, but I can't seem to help it. I'm just so glad you came. And yes, please. I'd love to get Johnny away from here. As long as the others have a place to go, too."

Mrs. Harrison sat down on the bed next to Jenny and gently brushed the hair back out of her face. "It's all right, dear," she said. "Tears are precious to the Lord. You cry as many as you need to cry."

Long into the night, Jenny thought about Mrs. Harrison's gentle hand brushing her hair back out of her face. That must be what it was like to have a mother who loved you. She'd have to remember to pet Johnny like that. So he'd know he was loved.

CHAPTER 23

*I will be glad and rejoice in thy mercy: for thou hast considered my
trouble; thou has known my soul in adversities. . . . Blessed be the LORD:
for he hath shewed me his marvellous kindness in a strong city.*
PSALM 31:7, 21

Late in October, on the day when the committee would oversee
the furnishing of Friendship Home, Juliana rose before dawn. She
dressed quickly and descended to the kitchen, where she left a note
on the table for Martha and the aunts, then headed out to the barn
to saddle Tecumseh. A ring of thick fog surrounded the house, but
when she paused and looked up, Juliana could see the night sky and
a few glimmering stars. Her booted feet swishing through the dew-
laden grass sounded unnaturally loud in the predawn quiet. So did
the creaking of the barn door and the click of metal on metal as she
unlatched Tecumseh's stall door and led him out to be saddled.

She'd just tightened the girth strap when she heard footsteps on
the stairway leading down from Martha and Alfred's apartment above
the barn. Alfred appeared in the open doorway and teased, "Good to
know it isn't a horse thief rustling around down here." He stepped into
the barn and reached for the bucket sitting just to the left of the door.

"I should have known I couldn't sneak out on you."

Alfred smiled. "Truth is, I was already awake, sitting by the
window, reading my Bible. I saw you come out of the house." He
paused. "Everything all right?"

Juliana nodded. "The furnishings start to arrive today."

"I'm meeting Mr. Gregory with our wagon at the warehouse right after breakfast. Sounds like he's made arrangements for an entire wagon train. He said you're hoping to have everything set up by the end of the week."

"I'm not sure it'll even take that long—at least if all our playing with that model over the weeks bears fruit. We think we know where everything goes."

Alfred grinned. "I been married a long time, Miss Juliana. I know a thing or two about women and arranging furniture. Change is just part of things."

Juliana laughed. She gathered the reins and led Tecumseh out of the barn. "I left a note on the table, but it just says that I'll be back in plenty of time to hitch up the buggy so the four of us can head out to Friendship Home together." She paused. "Martha is still planning on going, I hope."

"She certainly is." Martha descended the stairs behind them. Alfred excused himself to fetch the team that had been turned into a field at the back of the property.

Juliana could just see the gate to that field in the distance. The rest was shrouded in fog.

"You all right?" Martha asked.

Juliana nodded. "I am. I just—" She looked off to the south. "I have a notion I'd like to see the house before it's once and for all changed into a home for the friendless." She shrugged. "A last walk-through."

"A last good-bye?"

Martha's gentle voice putting words to what Juliana had been thinking opened the floodgates. Tears clouded her vision. "I suppose that's silly. I never wanted it, and I haven't once regretted giving it away. I still don't. But—" She shook her head. "I can't explain it. I just need to say good-bye to everything. Again." She took a deep breath and glanced at the house. "Tell them not to worry. I really am fine. I just need to do this."

"The aunts have had enough of their own losses to understand," Martha said. "You think you'll be back in time for some breakfast?"

"I don't expect to be gone long."

"You remember the story of Joshua walking around the walls of Jericho?"

"*And the walls came-a-tumblin' down?*" Juliana quoted the last line of the spiritual.

"That's the one. While you're walking through and around that house, I'll be praying the Lord tears down all the walls."

"Walls?"

"This has been a hard year. You've had to face down a lot, and you've done it well. You keep marching, Miss Juliana. Right out of the shadows and into the sun." Martha paused. "I know it's not my place to say it, but someone needs to. I'm praying the good Lord gives you new love." She smiled. "I know. I know. You don't have room for that right now. But you will. And when you do, that'll be a good thing."

—◊—

Tecumseh's breath sent clouds into the brisk morning air as Juliana rode along what was now a fairly well-worn trail across the prairie. The first thing she noticed out at the site was the golden light shining in one of the upstairs windows over at the stone cottage. Mrs. Harrison must be up. Juliana guided Tecumseh to the opposite side of the main house and dismounted, hitching the horse to a fencepost where he wouldn't be visible from the stone cottage. She just didn't want to see anyone right now.

"I won't be long," she said, patting Tecumseh's neck and then scooting around the turret and onto the front porch. She paused to look off to the south. It was hard to imagine homes rising out of that prairie. Hard to visualize houses as far as the eye could see, but she supposed it would inevitably happen. She remembered Sterling saying the city planners had named the east-west trail that ran just on the other side of their property line South Street because they expected that would be the southernmost border of the city for some time to come. Sterling had called it shortsighted, and Juliana agreed. Before long, Friendship Home would have neighbors. *And if we want our own medical clinic, we'd better be building it before those neighbors have a chance to take issue with what we do.*

The thought made Juliana smile. Martha would be proud. She was looking to the future. *Would you be proud, Sterling?* Taking a deep breath, she opened the front door and stepped inside.

Even in the early morning light, the finished entryway fairly glowed with promise. The sweeping staircase seemed to reach out like a welcoming arm embracing visitors and drawing them in. Back in the library, warm red walls and polished wood created what Juliana hoped would be a sanctuary. The room still smelled of varnish and fresh paint. She opened the windows, then made her way past the dining room to the back of the house, pausing to peer into the gleaming kitchen, its black-and-white tile floor flowing about a marble-topped work island. By the end of the week, the floor-to-ceiling cupboards would hold mountains of practical, all-white dinnerware. The wire rack hanging from the ceiling above the island would sport all manner of cookware. They'd had to consult one of the hotel cooks about how to equip the kitchen. One could only hope they'd made the right decisions.

Back at the front of the house, Juliana ascended the stairs, pausing halfway up to look down upon the entryway, the heavy front doors, the leaded windows. Once upstairs, she circled the balcony to go into the second-floor turret room. There'd been many discussions as to what to use it for. They had finally agreed that at first it would simply be another sitting room, a small retreat where adult residents could enjoy the view of the distant horizon. Aunt Lydia was looking forward to supplying this room—which would contain rocking chairs and hand-crocheted afghans—with copies of various Sunday school publications. She'd also ordered subscriptions to the *Ladies' Home Journal, Cappers, The Delineator,* and *Godey's.*

After today, the wood floors in each of the bedrooms would boast fringed wool rugs. Helen Duncan had won the committee over to the idea of making the single mothers' rooms cheerful. Juliana stepped inside these rooms, originally intended to be hers and Sterling's.

Crossing the room, she stepped out onto the screened porch and looked down on Tecumseh.

The horse looked half-asleep, but as Juliana retreated back inside, the sun broke through the fog and began to stream in the windows, reflecting off the yellow walls. Envisioning the white iron bedsteads and the blue-and-white coverings the quilters had planned, Juliana realized that Helen would get her wish. These would be cheerful rooms—and God willing, a place where women could come instead of ending up like poor Nell Parker.

There were far too many Nell Parkers in the world. *Far too many P. L.s.* It was strange to be standing in this room thinking about those women—that particular woman—and feel concern instead of resentment. Compassion instead of bitterness. Did that mean she was doing what Martha said? Was she marching away from the shadows and into something new?

She thought of the day she'd been here alone with Cass. His hands on her shoulders. The way his presence had comforted her. He'd ridden home with her and lingered, but then he'd said she needed time. Since then, Juliana had done her best to keep her mind occupied with things other than smiles shared with Cass and those few moments alone. But Martha had just wished her new love. Was it all right to think of it now? Sterling had left her long before he died. She realized that now. And she was beginning to hope for new love. Maybe that's why she could stand in the very rooms originally built for her and Sterling and feel something besides anger. Heading out of the suite, she lingered in the doorway and allowed a faint smile. She did feel something new. Something akin to hope.

Upstairs on the third floor, Juliana tried to imagine a row of cribs, rocking chairs, and toys, but she was instead drawn to the eastern windows to look out over the landscape, to watch as the sun won over the fog and the prairie came into focus. It was going to be a beautiful fall day. *"This is the day which the Lord hath made; we will rejoice and be glad in it."* Juliana smiled. She *was* glad. Glad for the future promise this place held. Humbled by the fact that, while she'd endured pain and grief, her life had been blessed compared to many others. She'd had the love of Aunt Theodora and Aunt Lydia, the prayers of people like Martha and Alfred to help her through a terrible time. And she'd never had to worry about money. She had so much to be thankful for. *I'm sorry, God. I haven't been thankful enough.*

Back at the top of the front stairs, Juliana paused again, looking down on the foyer and thinking about all the pain and suffering people would carry with them through those doors. *Please bless what we're hoping to do. Make us wise in the decisions we still have to make. Thank You for showing me how to make something good out of this.*

She stopped praying, surprised by the tears that gathered. God really had done that. He'd taken a half-finished house, her ruined dreams, a failed marriage, and turned them all into a place where ruined dreams could find shelter. Hope. *Maybe we should have called it House of Hope.*

It had taken so many people to make it work. *Thank You for the committee. For Lutie and Medora, for Edith and Helen. For the successful bazaar. For the faithful workers. For Aunt Theodora's dry wit and affection and for letting me see that affection past the prickles. For Aunt Lydia's gentle ways and strong faith. For Martha's understanding and Alfred's kindness. For Pastor Taylor's love for lost sheep. For Margaret Nash's and Sadie Gregory's new lives. For Sterling's providing so well.* Once Juliana began to thank God for blessings, they seemed never ending. Words spilled out, and her heart swelled with joy. *Joy.*

Thank You for Cass. The man had worked so many long hours. He deserved a generous bonus. So did Mr. Finney, for that matter. All the model furniture he'd created. Some of it was little more than a block of unpainted wood with a word written on it to designate a desk or a bureau, but still. The scale was the thing that mattered. She would ask Mr. Carter to look back in the books and see what had been done in the past to reward special effort. Or perhaps she would simply make a decision and do what she thought best. *There's a thought. Trust yourself. Isn't that what Cass told you to do at the beginning?*

Finally, she descended the stairs. Her hand on the doorknob, Juliana looked up and chuckled as she said aloud, "Thank You, Father. Now if You could please just let the furniture fit."

241

—⁂—

Juliana heard voices as soon as she stepped out onto the front porch. Murmurs from the direction of the stone cottage. And a child giggling. After unhitching Tecumseh, she led him around the front of the house just as Cass Gregory reached out and took a child out of Mrs. Harrison's arms.

Ah, yes. The sickly young mother who'd been at Mrs. Crutchfield's. Together, Helen, Mrs. Harrison, and Lutie Gleason had enabled an early move. Juliana only knew that Mrs. Crutchfield had proven unsatisfactory in many ways, and the ladies who'd taken special interest in the situation were eager to sever ties. Mrs. Harrison had offered to share her home with the young mother—Juliana remembered the name *Jenny*. It was, now that Juliana thought about it, an exceedingly kind thing for Mrs. Harrison to do. The child was darling. While Cass held him, Mrs. Harrison pantomimed patty-cake. The baby cackled with joy. Mrs. Harrison looked up at Cass and said something. The two of them laughed.

Juliana's elation and thankful heart seemed to recede into the fog. Using the stone steps to boost herself, she mounted Tecumseh, half-tempted to retreat around the far side of the house again and head home without interrupting whatever might be going on. But then the child saw Tecumseh and squealed.

"Mrs. Sutton! What are you doing here?" Cass handed the child back to Mrs. Harrison, who waved at Juliana and retreated inside. He hurried over. "I thought you were coming out with the aunts."

"I am." She gathered the reins.

"You've been inside." It wasn't a question.

She nodded. "A final walk-through." She shrugged. "To say good-bye, actually. I suppose that's silly."

He shook his head. "Not one bit silly." He looked past her and up at the house. "You've done a grand thing here." He seemed just about to say more when Mrs. Harrison stepped out of the stone cottage and headed their way.

Juliana took a deep breath. "Well, I should let you get to—" She nodded in Mrs. Harrison's direction. "And I told Martha I'd be back in time for breakfast."

He stepped back. "Yes. Well. See you later, then?"

She nodded and nudged Tecumseh into a walk.

He called her name. "Mrs. Sutton." She swiveled in the saddle to look back at him.

"Are you all right? Really?"

Goodness. Was everyone she saw today going to ask that question?

"Perfectly, Mr. Gregory." She raised a hand in greeting to Mrs. Harrison and urged Tecumseh into a lope.

All the way home, Juliana told herself that it was none of her business if Cass rode out to see Mrs. Harrison. As long as he was back at the office in time to organize things for the day's work, it was none of her business. Mrs. Harrison was a lovely woman. And when it came right down to it, Juliana should have thanked God for her, too, when she prayed just now. She forced herself to say it aloud. "Thank You for Mrs. Harrison. She really does seem perfect for the position."

"This is the day which the Lord hath made; we will rejoice and be glad in it."

Was that how true faith worked? A person talked to God, and He talked back by bringing scripture to mind? *I want true faith, Lord. Or at least a truer version of it than I've had. I think You're giving it, and I'm grateful. And Mrs. Harrison really is a good woman. I know that. I just. . .* Finally, Juliana said it aloud. "I want Cass to wait. For *me.*"

Not a single Bible verse came to mind.

————

Alfred had already left with the wagon and the team by the time Juliana got back to the house, but he'd hitched Fancy to the buggy before leaving, so all Juliana had to do was see to Tecumseh, which she did in record time. Hurrying in the back door, she bounded up the kitchen stairs, nearly colliding with the aunts on their way down to breakfast.

"Good heavens!" Aunt Theodora said. "Have you already been out for a ride this morning?"

Juliana nodded as she rounded the corner and headed off up

the hall to change. "Be down in a minute." Back in her room, she changed out of her riding habit as quickly as possible. She and the aunts had already agreed that today was not a day for silks and velvets. This was a workday, and they would dress simply in black cotton day dresses. Juliana repaired her simple chignon, then stepped into black unmentionables. Even the corset was black. She did feel rather smart in the day dress, though, with its white pinstripe.

Once she'd fastened the last of the jet buttons marching up the front of the waist, she tucked it into the tailored skirt and took a turn before the dressing mirror. Not bad. Not as lovely as the rich indigo Mrs. Harrison was wearing today, but once Juliana donned an apron, she wouldn't look quite so gloomy. She forced a bright smile and headed downstairs, taking a moment to linger over the four pies sitting on the kitchen counter while Martha poured coffee.

"Blackberry?" she asked.

Martha nodded.

"I'm ready for lunch now."

"I'll save a piece back for you," Martha promised.

Aunt Theodora spoke up. "You are to be commended for recruiting Mrs. Nash to plan lunches for the workers this week," she said. "When I spoke with her at church on Sunday, she already had menus sorted out and half the baking for the entire week finished. And she had made arrangements to transport everything. Something about a new wagon." She plopped jelly onto a piece of toast and handed it to Juliana, then slid a poached egg off the serving dish and onto her plate. "We will all need our wits about us today. You must eat a good breakfast, dear."

Juliana smiled at Aunt Lydia, who rolled her eyes and shook her head. "I haven't seen my sister this excited in years. She's quite beside herself now that she's been given so much authority."

Theodora sputtered. "I am merely going to direct traffic so that things are done as efficiently as possible. Someone needed to be stationed at the front door to tell the gentlemen where to put what."

"And there's no one better at telling people where to put what than you." Aunt Lydia laughed; then she leaned over and patted her sister's arm. "Relax, Sister. I'm only teasing." She held up her coffee cup. "I salute you."

Jenny
Monday, October 22

Mrs. Harrison had taken Johnny downstairs as soon as he woke.

"If I could, I would order you to spend the day in bed," she'd said. "As it is, I'm begging you to please sleep a little more."

Mrs. Harrison was good with Johnny. He'd had a big smile on his face when he'd waved 'bye as she carried him out of the room. Thinking about the matron's kindness, Jenny put her hand to her belly and smiled. Things were better now. She felt better. Stronger. Part of her wished she could just stay here instead of moving across the way to the big house. But Mrs. Harrison had shown her the room where she and Johnny would be, and Jenny could see that it was going to be a nice place to live. Emil and Huldah and Miller and a new baby that had been left on someone's doorstep just last week would be moving out here the first of December. It would be nice to have them close again. Johnny would have someone to play with.

Jenny was beginning to hope. She hadn't said anything to Mrs. Harrison, but if she could get stronger, if she showed herself willing to work, maybe she and Johnny and the baby could even stay here. Earn their keep. For today, though, Jenny would watch the comings and goings from her bedroom window.

By noon, half-a-dozen wagonloads of furniture had been carried inside the house. People were having lunch now. A woman had driven in just a little while ago. As Jenny watched, she climbed up into the back of her wagon and began arranging things. Then she climbed down and lowered the *side* of the wagon, revealing platters of food lined up along the edge of the exposed wagon bed. People could pick up a plate from the stack near the driver's seat and make their way down the line. Two large watercoolers at the back of the wagon bed allowed people to stick a graniteware mug under the spigot and get a drink.

That was a smart woman. Jenny wondered if she was on the committee with the rich women, but she didn't think so. She was dressed plainer. And she didn't seem to be friends with any of the others. Except Mr. Gregory. He'd lifted her down from the wagon and was eating lunch with her and Mrs. Harrison.

Other workers were sitting on the ground under one of the trees at the back of the house or on the steps. Still others ate while standing in small groups and chatting. Everyone down there seemed happy. There were smiles and nods and gestures as they ate and talked. As Jenny watched, Mrs. Harrison stepped up to the wagon and loaded a plate of food and headed toward the cottage with Mr. Gregory.

Jenny glanced over at herself in the mirror. Sweeping her hands over her hair, she bent to pick up Johnny and head downstairs. Pain shot through her, and with a gasp, she plopped the baby on the floor and sat down. He began to fuss.

She heard the front door open and murmurs and then Mrs. Harrison's footsteps on the stairs. Johnny heard them, too. He stopped crying and crawled to the doorway. When he reached up, Mrs. Harrison bent and hoisted him into her arms as she said to Jenny, "We've brought you some lunch."

Jenny forced a smile. "That's nice of you. I'll come down when Johnny takes his nap. I'm not very hungry right now. But I'll eat. A lot. In just a little while. I promise."

Mrs. Harrison nodded. "As long as you promise." She smoothed Johnny's rumpled hair and asked, "Do you mind if I take him to meet everyone?" She paused. "I'd love for them to meet you, too. But I don't want you to feel like you're being put on display. It's up to you."

Jenny shook her head. "Not today." That was one of the differences between Mrs. Harrison and Mrs. Crutchfield. Mrs. Harrison thought about a person's feelings. Jenny smiled. "But I don't mind you showing Johnny off one bit."

Mrs. Harrison left with the baby. Jenny took a few deep breaths. There. That didn't feel so bad now. She peered back out the window, reveling in the smiles as people admired her boy.

CHAPTER 24

A man that hath friends must shew himself friendly:
and there is a friend that sticketh closer than a brother.
PROVERBS 18:24

Juliana had said that she didn't think it would take the entire week to prepare Friendship Home for residents, and as the day wore on, she became more convinced than ever that she was right. She even began to wonder if they really needed to delay until December to move people in.

Throughout the day, Theodora reigned from just inside the front door, guiding each piece of furniture to the correct room, where another member of the committee waited, drawing in hand, to oversee that room's arrangement. Boxes of kitchenwares were stacked on the back porch to be attended to another day. Once the long, narrow tables were brought in and positioned in the dining room, bed linens and towels were stacked atop the tables to be taken up to the appropriate rooms later.

By the time Cass's mother arrived with her newly outfitted wagon, the library where Juliana was stationed boasted two game tables with four chairs each set before the tall windows and two reading circles atop plush rugs in opposite corners of the room. The bookshelves that encircled the room would likely remain free of books until there was time to conduct a book drive. Juliana and the aunts would look into that after the first of the year.

They'd begun to jot down names of books they hoped to acquire. Even Aunt Theodora approved of Jane Austen and Charles Dickens, Martha Finley's ongoing Elsie Dinsmore series, and Sir Walter Scott. She was not quite so sure about Mr. Stevenson's new release, *Robinson Crusoe*.

"But," she sighed when they discussed it over dinner one evening, "I don't suppose it's fair for my tastes to dictate." And she'd pointed at Aunt Lydia. "Don't say it. I hear you. Just don't."

When it came time for lunch, Helen Duncan asked Cass Gregory to offer a blessing. Juliana had never heard him pray aloud. She stood on the back porch between Aunt Lydia and Aunt Theodora, her head bowed, her eyes closed. When Cass thanked God for what He'd done through the Suttons, she felt heat rise to her cheeks. When he asked God's guidance in all the details of the Friendship Home, she heard Aunt Lydia murmur an amen. He closed by asking God to bless the staff and Mrs. Harrison as they took on their responsibilities and to enable everyone involved in Friendship Home to bring the hope of Christ to future residents "by showing them the love of God."

When he said "Amen," a hearty chorus of amens answered.

Juliana and the aunts joined the long line of workers filing by the ingenious wagon Margaret had apparently just had built to enable her to cater to more such events. Cass chatted with Mrs. Harrison and ended up eating with her and his mother. Juliana could not seem to rid herself of the awareness of where he was—especially when he and Mrs. Harrison gathered up a plate of food and headed into the stone cottage together.

When they came back outside with the child she'd seen that morning in Mrs. Harrison's arms, Juliana finally admitted it to herself. She was jealous. She finished her own lunch quickly and then busied herself helping Margaret clean up while everyone else admired the child. Everyone, Juliana noted with amazement, including Aunt Theodora, who ended up sitting down on the back steps and asking Mrs. Harrison to let her hold the "little nubbin'."

"I never imagined Miss Theodora to be fond of babies."

Juliana started at the sound of Cass's voice just behind her. He'd apparently been gathering up people's tin mugs and was beginning to pile them into the cracker box that Margaret used to store them.

Juliana glanced at Aunt Theodora smiling down at the little boy like a woman who'd just discovered buried treasure. "Neither did I."

Martha approached with a piece of blackberry pie on a plate. "Promised I'd save you a piece."

"That's not fair," Cass teased. "You said it was all gone when I came to get a piece."

"It was all gone," Martha explained. "Just because it hadn't been swallowed yet didn't mean it wasn't all gone."

When Juliana passed the pie to Cass, Martha just shook her head. "You better appreciate that," she said to Cass. "She's been lookin' forward to that since before the sun rose this morning. It's her favorite."

Cass reached for a knife and cut the pie in half on the plate, then handed Juliana a fork and took one up himself. "Share?"

"You two go on over there in the shade and enjoy that," Margaret said. "I can finish up here."

Cass offered his arm, and together he and Juliana walked around the wagon and into a spot of shade. "The morning's gone well," he said as he took the first bite of pie.

Juliana nodded. "I don't think it's really going to take all week."

"You might be surprised. All the big furniture is likely the easy part. Now there's beds to make and that kitchen—that's going to take some time. You really are going to wash all those new dishes before they go in the cupboards?"

Juliana nodded. "And you're right. It's going to take a long time. Martha is friends with Mrs. Kennedy, the woman who's been hired to be the head cook. Mrs. Kennedy's coming out this afternoon so that she and Martha can look things over and try to plan what goes where. Apparently there's almost a science to setting up an efficient kitchen."

"You haven't eaten one bit of that pie. I thought you said it was your favorite."

Juliana looked down at the plate. Cass was finished. When she reached up to hold the plate and cut a bite with the side of her fork, their hands touched. He didn't let go. She felt herself blushing like a schoolgirl. Quickly, she took a second bite.

"Here you are." Aunt Lydia stepped up. Cass let go of the plate. "Dear boy," she said, "after hearing that prayer, I am more convinced than ever that your name should be submitted to Pastor Taylor as a candidate for deacon."

Cass seemed embarrassed. "That's one of the nicest things anyone has ever said about me, Aunt Lydia, and it would be a great honor—someday. But not yet."

"All right. But I have my eye on you."

Cass grinned. "I'll keep that in mind, ma'am."

Just then the child who'd been laughing on Theodora's knee let out a squeal and began to cry. Everyone looked over. Mrs. Harrison had the boy in her arms and was heading back to the house. He was reaching with both arms for Theodora.

Cass glanced at Aunt Lydia. "I was just telling Mrs. Sutton that I wouldn't have thought Miss Theodora one to be fond of babies."

Lydia shrugged. "First bloomers and now this. My sister is just full of surprises."

Cass looked at Juliana. "Do I dare ask about the bloomers?"

Juliana laughed. "You can ask, but when I did, they both just looked at each with a secretive smile."

"It was part of a conversation about widows' weeds and how tradition and custom don't always fit every situation," Aunt Lydia explained. She put her hand on Juliana's shoulder. "And you see the lovely evidence of that discussion before you, *sans* veil, *sans* crepe— although the younger generation doesn't always pay attention to such things. You probably haven't even noticed the difference."

"I've noticed," Cass said. After a brief silence, he pointed to the pie plate. "If you don't eat that soon, I won't be responsible for what happens. And future deacons should not be guilty of pie thievery."

—⁓—

The week sailed by. Finally, on Thursday evening, with all the heavy moving finished, Cass dismissed the building crew and told them to take Friday off and then report early Monday ready to tackle the next project. Sutton Builders had won the bid to erect a new church at Twelfth and M Streets in town. After poring over the plans the church had approved by a Mr. Wilcox in Minneapolis, Cass was already more than a little concerned that the $25,000 bid the boss had prepared might prove to be on the low side. He'd already met with Reverend McKaig about it. The reverend assured Cass that his people would be more than willing to solicit subscriptions to cover any increase in costs.

He was thinking of the Friendship Home with more than a little nostalgia. It was hard to imagine any other project would provide the kind of satisfaction this one had. *Unless I get to build something for my bride one day.* He put that thought away and headed back inside to see if he could help the kitchen crew by hauling boxes out of the back hall.

"Mr. Gregory, could I bother you for just a moment?" Mrs. Harrison stood in the doorway to her office. "I think I underestimated the amount of space there would be in here." She stepped back from the doorway to let him in. "I have a bookcase—a small one—in the house that I brought from Wisconsin. Do you remember it?" When Cass nodded, she chuckled. "Indeed, how could you forget it. I hovered like a mother over a newborn when you hauled it into the cottage." She paused. "The thing is, now that I'm moved in here, I think there's room for it." She pointed at an open space beneath one of the windows. "If I put it there, it would form a wing off the desk." Cass nodded. "Very functional."

"It was my husband's. I like the idea of having part of him here where I'll be spending so much time. I know you've sent the crew home, and I don't want you to make a special trip back out here. Do you think the two of us could manage it? I'm stronger than I look."

Cass hesitated.

"Can we at least try?"

Reluctantly, he agreed. There was no way this birdlike little woman was going to be able to haul an oak bookcase this far.

"Excellent!" She smiled. "If Johnny's still napping, I'll ask Jenny to hold the door open for us."

Much to Cass's amazement, the little birdlike woman was, as she said, stronger than she looked. They carried the bookcase out of the house and over to the steps, and then into Friendship Home and her office without a hitch.

When they had it settled into place, Mrs. Harrison clasped her hands together and stood, beaming down at it. "It's perfect." She stood on tiptoe and gave Cass a hug. "Thank you so much." She swept her hand across the smooth top. "I'm going to get one of my antimacassars and set Reggie's Bible atop it. Right here." Her voice wavered. "I like to think he'd be proud of my striking out this way."

"I'm sure he is," Cass said. He turned about at the sound of someone clearing her throat. Aunt Theodora stood in the doorway.

"I believe we have concluded for the day," she said. "I wanted to leave Mrs. Harrison with my notes. For her files."

"Thank you." Mrs. Harrison stepped forward and took the stack of papers in Miss Theodora's hand. She opened the top drawer of the oak filing cabinet that stood between the two windows just behind her desk and said something about "my first official filing." She turned about. "I've been meaning to speak with you about something, Miss Theodora."

"Indeed." She looked at Cass.

He reached up to wipe his mouth, thinking maybe he still had food on his chin from lunch. Ma had served the most amazing berry pie for dessert today. He was already looking forward to a second piece after supper tonight.

Mrs. Harrison seemed oblivious. She went on to ask Miss Theodora if she'd consider helping her organize the files that would be coming in when the residents began to arrive. "I've seen how gifted you are at organization. I don't want to impose on your good graces, but I wondered if you would be able to spare a little time that first week."

Miss Theodora didn't hesitate. "I'd be delighted."

"That's wonderful! Thank you!" Mrs. Harrison beamed.

"If there's nothing else, I'll excuse myself," Cass said. He retreated, very nearly shivering under Miss Theodora's icy stare. What had he done?

—⁀∽—

Juliana pulled the last pillowcase onto the last pillow in the upstairs room that would have been Aunt Theodora's and settled the pillow on the bed. She and Lutie Gleason had had a pleasant afternoon together as they made up beds and chatted about toy drives and book drives and whether or not they should have green plants in every room in the house or only in the rooms downstairs and what kind of framed art they should put on the walls. Lutie thought they should have something inspirational in each room, and Juliana agreed.

"Although I suppose there will be varying opinions as to what is and is not inspirational." Juliana smiled. "We do have several members on the committee who have somewhat strong opinions."

"Really?" Lutie forced surprise into her voice. "I hadn't noticed."

The two women shared a laugh, and then Lutie said, "Are you familiar with the hymn 'What a Friend We Have in Jesus'?"

Juliana nodded. "Enough to know it's perfect, and I wish I'd thought of it."

"I thought I would stop at the stationer's next week and see how much it would cost to have the lyrics printed up. Something attractive that we could frame and hang in each room."

Juliana took a deep breath. "It doesn't seem that we'll ever be truly finished."

"I think," Lutie said, "that for those of us who care to do it, Friendship Home can be a lifelong project. But for today, I think we say we're finished."

—⁀∽—

Juliana was on her way out the front door with the aunts when Mrs. Harrison called to her from the doorway to her office. "If I might have a word alone, Mrs. Sutton?"

Juliana stepped into the office. "It looks like you're ready to go to work today," she said. "We were concerned this room wouldn't be large enough."

"It's perfect. I love it. I love the view, and all this light? It's spectacular." She glanced pointedly into the entryway. The house was silent. She took a deep breath. "I can't help but sense, Mrs. Sutton, that I've done something to offend you. If so, I apologize. But I need to know what it is, so that I don't repeat the offense."

"I don't know why you'd think that."

"You've always seemed in rather a hurry to get away from me. At church. This past Monday morning. And most of this week, to be quite honest."

Juliana glanced out the window. Aunt Theodora was talking to Cass. What was that about? "Monday was. . ." She shook her head.

"It was probably very difficult for you." Mrs. Harrison's voice was gentle. "You've only been a widow for a few months. It's been two years for me. It may be hard to believe, but it will get easier." She rested her hand atop a Bible sitting on the bookshelf beside her desk. "Not a day goes by that I don't miss Reggie terribly. Of course nothing can ever fill the space in our lives they leave. But you learn to live around it. The raw edges heal with time."

Juliana could only nod. After all, the woman meant well. "I didn't mean to be rude on Monday," she said. "I'd ridden out here to be alone in the house for a few minutes before everything changed for good. And you clearly had plans with Mr. Gregory." She swallowed. "As for Sundays, every time I've intended to say good morning, you've been deep in conversation with Mr. Gregory. I didn't want to interrupt."

Mrs. Harrison stood transfixed, and then she smiled. Nodded. "I see." She glanced out the windows. "I am hoping that, in time, you and I will be friends." She smiled. "I suppose I am at an advantage, since I've heard so much about you. I feel like I know you, thanks to the time I've spent with Theodora and Lydia. They speak so highly of you. And then of course there's Cass. We've been rather 'thrown together' these past few weeks, what with all the plans for this place."

Juliana knew. Yes. She knew how that was, being thrown together with Cass because of the project.

Mrs. Harrison seemed to be studying her. Finally she smiled. "You really don't know, do you?"

"Know what?"

"About Cass."

Juliana's heart thumped. She didn't want to hear this. Not today. "He's in love with you."

She gasped. "What? But he hasn't. . . I thought you. . ."

Mrs. Harrison laughed. "Just as I thought. You didn't know."

"How could I? He hasn't said anything."

She crossed the office and looked out the window. "I think they're waiting for you." She nodded toward the Bible atop her bookcase. "Everyone is different, Mrs. Sutton. I don't think I'll ever remarry, but if I'm not mistaken, you will." She smiled. "He's a very good man. I hope you'll give him a chance when the time comes." She paused. "And I hope you'll reconsider my bid for friendship."

"I don't know what to say."

"Say yes," Mrs. Harrison said. "And call me Caroline."

CHAPTER 25

There be three things which are too wonderful for me,
yea, four which I know not:
The way of an eagle in the air; the way of a serpent upon a rock;
the way of a ship in the midst of the sea;
and the way of a man with a maid.
PROVERBS 30:18–19

On Saturday, Lutie Gleason came to the front door in a dither to show Juliana and her aunts what she'd found at the printer's. "Just look!" she said and opened the folder in her hand. "You won't believe where the printer sent me." She chattered as she followed Juliana into the library where she and the aunts had been taking their morning tea.

"To Lindermann's!" She nodded at the aunts. "He has all kinds of connections to various types of cards and greetings—for comfort, you know. And—" She held up a beautifully engraved sheet of paper, a poem in the center, a garland of forget-me-nots around it. "Or we can have dogwood, or even poppies. It's up to us. I suppose we could get some of each, depending on the room it's going in. But Mr. Lindermann said that he would be happy to provide them. As many as we want!" She broke off, breathless, and waved at Juliana. "You tell the rest of our idea."

"Lutie came up with the idea of framing the words to 'What a Friend We Have in Jesus' in each room." She glanced at Aunt

Theodora. "Do you remember the words? I don't know that we ever sang it at First Church. Lutie recited the words for me."

Aunt Theodora shook her head. "I don't recall. Read them."

Juliana read:

"What a Friend we have in Jesus, all our sins and griefs to bear!
What a privilege to carry everything to God in prayer!
O what peace we often forfeit, O what needless pain we bear,
All because we do not carry everything to God in prayer."

She swallowed. Cleared her throat, and managed to get through the next two verses:

"Have we trials and temptations? Is there trouble anywhere?
We should never be discouraged; take it to the Lord in prayer.
Can we find a friend so faithful who will all our sorrows share?
Jesus knows our every weakness; take it to the Lord in prayer.

Are we weak and heavy laden, cumbered with a load of care?
Precious Savior, still our refuge, take it to the Lord in prayer.
Do your friends despise, forsake you? Take it to the Lord in prayer!
In His arms He'll take and shield you; you will find a solace there."

When she had to stop reading again, she looked at the aunts and Lutie. All of them had tears in their eyes. Juliana laughed. "Well, it seems we've hit a nerve."

Aunt Theodora nodded. "It's perfect for a place called Friendship Home."

Juliana managed to read the last verse through tears:

"Blessed Savior, Thou hast promised Thou wilt all our burdens bear.
May we ever, Lord, be bringing all to Thee in earnest prayer.
Soon in glory bright unclouded there will be no need for prayer.
Rapture, praise, and endless worship will be our sweet portion there."

Together, the ladies removed to the dining room and spread out the samples Mr. Lindermann had provided.

"Now, what about frames?"

"Cabinet frames," Aunt Theodora said. "From Miss Stein's studio over on P Street."

Aunt Lydia chimed in. "Or Herpolsheimers?"

"You wouldn't want to go now and see?" Lutie asked. "I'd love to have these up when we have the open house."

And so the ladies set out on an impromptu Saturday afternoon shopping trip. The Sutton women offered to stop at Lindermann's and place the order for the prints on their way home. Mr. Lindermann, gracious as always, reassured them that it was his privilege to provide the prints at no cost to a good cause and promised that he would forgo the "courtesy of Lindermann's Funeral Parlor" insignia that he usually put at the bottom of such things.

"And now," he said as he set their order aside, "I wanted to tell you that the Sutton monument has arrived. The cemetery will set it in place on Monday."

It was good news in a way, but Juliana noted that the aunts were uncharacteristically quiet on the ride home. For her part, Juliana just felt. . .tired. She couldn't seem to stop thinking about Caroline Harrison's proclamation that Cass was in love with her. She couldn't seem to stop waiting for him to appear at the door, or to show. . . something. Some indication. But he was buried in work related to the new church Sutton Builders had taken on, and neither his family nor Ludwig Meyer had been in church on Sunday. Juliana didn't know what that was about, and she didn't dare ask. It would be rude to appear to be monitoring church attendance. Once again, a cloud hovered overhead. The ladies picked over their supper with little enthusiasm, and when Martha expressed concern, Juliana told her about Mr. Lindermann's news.

"I suppose it's good news in a way, but I feel as if someone has pulled a plug and drained all the joy right out of the day."

The aunts retired early. Juliana followed suit, but when she couldn't sleep, she grabbed her dressing gown and slipped out onto the balcony to look up at the stars. A line from the hymn came to mind. *Take it to the Lord in prayer.* She wanted to. She just didn't know what to say.

—⁂—

STERLING THEODORE SUTTON
FEBRUARY 17, 1841 – APRIL 15, 1883

WE'LL EVER HOLD THY MEMORY DEAR,
AS THROUGH THIS VALE WE TREAD,
AND BOW SUBMISSIVE TO THAT POWER,
THAT LAID THEE WITH THE DEAD.

Juliana stood dry-eyed at Sterling's grave while the aunts cried.

"It's a lovely tribute," Aunt Lydia murmured.

"It is," Juliana agreed. "Thank you for providing the epitaph, Aunt Theodora."

"We used it on my father's monument. I've never forgotten those words." She cried quietly for a moment before saying, "And it is no easier to 'bow submissive' today than it was then." She shook her head. "I'll never understand why he ran in to *that place.*"

As the ladies made their way back to the buggy, Juliana gazed across the cemetery to Nell Parker's grave. There would be no granite obelisk there. Between Nell Parker and Sterling lay the lots set aside for the Home for the Friendless. The society planted flowers every year in a crescent-shaped bed near a simple obelisk that marked the place, but individual graves remained unmarked. That was wrong.

As Juliana climbed into the buggy and took up the reins, then guided Fancy through the gates and out onto the road that connected with O Street in town, she began to make plans to do something about it.

Jenny
Wednesday, October 31

Jenny watched out her bedroom window as the shadows lengthened and Mrs. Harrison didn't leave the big house. She'd thought of taking Johnny with her and just going over there and getting it over with, but it was all she could do to carry Johnny downstairs these days. It scared her the way it hurt her. She'd just have to wait.

By the time Mrs. Harrison finally came out onto the porch and headed this way, Jenny had fed Johnny his supper and put him to bed. She supposed that was for the best. If Mrs. Harrison got too angry, if Jenny couldn't keep from crying. . .at least Johnny wouldn't have to see it. He was so sweet that way. He didn't like it when people got upset. When Jenny cried, even if she was quiet about it, he always knew. He'd toddle over and pat her cheeks and snuggle close, like he was trying to make her feel better.

Jenny got up and crossed the bedroom to where he lay sleeping. At times when she looked at her boy, she thought her heart might break wide open because it just couldn't hold all her love. Tonight was one of those nights. Tucking the baby's blanket close around him, Jenny smoothed the hair back off his face. "I love you," she whispered and then headed downstairs. She made tea, and when Mrs. Harrison came in the door, Jenny called to her from the kitchen doorway.

"I'm making you some tea."

Mrs. Harrison smiled. "That's very kind of you." She hung the key to the big house on the hook by the door and came into the kitchen. Sitting at the table, she chatted about all the exciting things happening across the way. About how efficient the kitchen was going to be and how pretty the library looked with the new plants lined up across the big windows, and all manner of things that Jenny pretended to be interested in until, finally, the tea was ready.

After the first sip, Mrs. Harrison closed her eyes and sighed with pleasure. "I do believe you make the best cup of tea I've ever tasted."

The compliment made it even harder. Jenny sat down. She blurted it out. "I can't move into that house. I'll pack my things tomorrow and you can send me and Johnny back to Crutchfield's, I guess. But I can't move over there."

Mrs. Harrison's brows drew together. "Calm down. Why don't you want to move over there? Aren't you tired of being alone all day? I thought you liked the idea of Johnny being able to play with the other children."

"I do, but it won't work. I didn't think— I thought she'd just give money. But she's been here nearly every day, working and helping and—if she sees me—" She shook her head. "Maybe she doesn't know, but I can't stay over there. I can't face it."

Mrs. Harrison rose and poured a second cup of tea for herself and one for Jenny. "Who are you talking about?"

"Mrs. Sutton."

"Juliana Sutton is one of the nicest women I've ever met. You'll like her. And she'll like you."

Jenny shook her head. "You don't understand. I can't—I can't face her." She'd done her best to keep the tears back, but they began to fall. "I didn't know she was so nice. I thought— I just didn't think about her. And then I thought it wouldn't matter because rich people just give money. They don't do the work. And it seemed all right because of Johnny. Sterling should take care of Johnny, even if it's only his money. But then I saw her." She was sobbing now. "I'll pack up. Whenever you say. But I can't face her. I just can't." She moved to get up, but Mrs. Harrison reached over and put a hand on her arm.

"Wait."

Jenny stilled.

"Take a deep breath. That's good. Another. Calm down." She took a clean handkerchief from her pocket and handed it over. "Now tell me—in words I can understand—what the problem is. Why are you afraid of meeting Juliana?"

Jenny couldn't look at her. She stared down at the handkerchief in her lap, twisting and untwisting it while she spoke. "Her husband. Sterling. He and I—he said—" She shook her head. "It doesn't matter what he said. When I found out I was going to have our baby, he took me out to his farm." She told Mrs. Harrison everything. "I shouldn't have even come here, but I didn't think Sterling's wife would be here. She was giving the house away. I didn't think she'd come here. But she's nice. She cares about people." Jenny shook her head. "I can't face her. Ever." She put her hand on her distended belly. "I'm feeling better now. We'll be all right somewhere else."

Mrs. Harrison was quiet for a long while. Finally, she said, "I wish you would have told me this sooner."

"I'm sorry. I needed the help. Until I could take care of Johnny, anyway."

"That's not what I mean."

Jenny looked up.

"What I mean is I've been dreading coming over here to an empty house every evening. Not hearing Johnny laughing." She took a sip of tea. "Not having hot tea waiting when I come in the door." She smiled. "Now it appears I didn't need to dread it. Because I won't be living alone, after all."

—⁓—

Margaret took Cass's arm Sunday morning as they descended from the train and walked the short distance up Roca's main street to where a new stone building boasted dark green shutters, flower boxes, and a sign that read, MEYER'S MERCANTILE. OPENING MONDAY, NOVEMBER 19.

Ludwig handed Sadie the key with a smile. "Do the honors, mein Schatz."

Sadie spoke to Margaret and Cass. "You're the first people to see it since we cleaned up from the construction. So if you see anything that doesn't seem quite right, you have to promise to let us know. And the upstairs isn't ready, but—" Church bells rang out. "Guess we'd better hurry if we're going to make it to church on time." She opened the door and stepped inside.

Margaret looked around the neatly arranged store. Empty

display cases lined the broad center aisle that spanned the length of the store. Both walls behind the display cases boasted floor-to-ceiling cabinets with drawers below and open shelving above.

Sadie hurried ahead of them, recounting what merchandise they planned on displaying where. When she reached the back corner, she rested her hand on one of the four ladder-back chairs crowded around a small square table. "This is for anyone who wants to rest a spell." She pointed up at the chalkboard on the shelf behind her. "I'll write what we've got ready to serve up there every day." She stepped to the doorway at the back. "There's a stove back here and a little oven where I can keep things warm. I'll do most of the cooking upstairs, though." She smiled at Ludwig. "Ludwig got me the best stove we could afford. Wait till you see it, Ma. It's something."

The church bells rang again. "But we don't have time to go upstairs now." She led the way out the back door, locking it and pointing to the two large plots of fresh-turned earth surrounded by a rock border. "The one on the left is for flowers and the one on the right is my kitchen garden." She pointed into the distance. "But we've got all of this space all the way to that row of cedars." She glanced back at Ludwig. "Ludwig wants to build a barn. Maybe we'll have our own cow and some chickens." She shrugged. "I told him I forgot a lot about how to tend cows and chickens. But I'll learn it all over again if he wants me to."

She took Ludwig's arm and dropped the key into his coat pocket, then glanced back at Margaret. "I know you're busy with the lunch wagon," she said, "but I hope you can come out sometimes and lend a hand. I don't mind telling you I'm a little nervous about keeping a store."

Ludwig covered her hand with his. "It will be well, *Liebling*. You must have faith."

"I'm doing my best," Sadie muttered.

Together, they all walked to the small Methodist church on the north side of the street. The moment they stepped inside, a small woman with a large smile reached out to them, greeting Ludwig as

263

"Mr. Meyer" and beaming at Sadie. "This must be the lovely fiancée we've heard so much about."

Ludwig introduced Sadie to the woman. "This is Mrs. Sperling, the pastor's wife."

Mrs. Sperling invited Sadie to a circle meeting. "As soon as you're moved in," she said, "we'll have an appropriate welcome lunch." She smiled at Margaret. "And you would be most welcome to join us. I know how hard it can be to begin life in a new community. We are so pleased that Mr. and Mrs. Meyer will be among us. It's going to be grand not to have to take the train up to Lincoln for every little thing."

While they were talking, several other women came in the door, and the pastor's wife effectively detained her visitors so that, by the time the service began, the visitors had met everyone in attendance. During the service, the pastor had them all stand again and introduced them.

Later in the day, as the train chugged north to Lincoln, Sadie turned to Ludwig and said, "Why do we have to wait until next month? Why can't we just go ahead and get hitched before we open?"

Margaret smiled as surprise, delight, and then doubt crossed Ludwig's face. "We just put that sign up. November 19."

Sadie shrugged. "I know. So we get hitched the Sunday before."

"And spend the next week setting up a store?" His face turned red, and he leaned close. "What about a honeymoon?"

"I don't need a fancy honeymoon off somewhere around strangers." Sadie leaned close. "We can make all kinds of memories while we're setting up our store."

Margaret turned her head to look out the window, all the while doing her best to stifle her laughter.

"Now, Ma," Sadie said. "You don't have to look all embarrassed."

Margaret glanced back just in time to see her daughter take Ludwig's hand.

"We'll have time to take trips after we've been storekeeping for a while," Sadie said. "If you want a trip. But all I want is to finally be home. With you."

"If we open the store as promised on Monday the nineteenth," Ludwig began, "that means we have a wedding—"

"Next Sunday? How about right after morning church? Ma and I can make a lunch for everyone." She smiled over at Ma and Cass. "You think Pastor Taylor would allow it? We'd have to have the party inside. It's too cold to do a picnic."

"I don't know," Cass said. "You'll have to speak to Pastor Taylor."

"We can do that, can't we, Ludwig? We could walk right over there from the train." Sadie glanced at Margaret. "You'd help me with a lunch, wouldn't you? Bake some of those angel food cakes everybody likes so much?"

"It's perfect," Ludwig said. "Angel food cake for my angel."

Sadie shook her head. "Angel? Now you're calling me an angel? Don't you be going crazy on me just yet. I haven't promised for better or worse yet." She put her head on his shoulder and snuggled close.

CHAPTER 26

But if we hope for that we see not, then do we with patience wait for it.
ROMANS 8:25

Daily State Journal
Sunday, November 4, 1883

The Society of the Home for the Friendless, recently renamed Friendship Home, invites the community to visit Friendship Home on Sunday afternoon, November 11, between the hours of 1:00 p.m. and 5:00 p.m. The home is located on the corner of South and Eleventh Streets. The city has watched with anticipation as the edifice was raised and furnished, and many of our citizens have contributed to this fine home, which will open its doors to welcome residents on Monday, November 12. The ladies of the society are to be commended for their efforts, which have been so energetic as to enable them to celebrate the open house fully three weeks ahead of schedule. Would that the gentlemen of the city could be so efficient in the paving of the downtown streets and the ridding of the environs of hog pens and wandering livestock.

The first thing that woke Cass Monday morning was loud purring and a not-so-gentle nudge as Patch burrowed her way beneath Cass's comforters. The second thing was the sudden realization that apparently fall had given way to winter at some point in the night. He opened his eyes. Yep. He could see his breath. With a shiver, he climbed out of bed and hurried to stoke a fire in the kitchen and get coffee going. Next, he fired up the woodstove at the other end of the small house. He'd just closed the grate when Ma padded into the room and headed for the cookstove, her long russet braid dangling down her back, the collar to her flannel robe turned up.

"Goodness,"—she shivered—"it's as if winter landed on the roof. Someone needs to tell Jack Frost it's only the first week in November. His presence is not required yet."

"You draw a bead on Jack," Sadie called from beneath her covers, "see to it you don't miss. He should be shot for sneaking up on us like this."

Cass chuckled as he rubbed his hands together, then opened the door for Patch. He retreated back to the kitchen, murmuring thanks as Ma poured him a steaming mug of coffee. Sadie stumbled to the table while they were eating. She poured herself coffee, then retrieved a thick comforter from her room and burrowed into it while she ate.

"You're up early," Cass said. "And you aren't grumbling about it."

"Figured I'd best get in the habit if I'm gonna be a storekeeper's wife," Sadie said. "Besides, Ma and I have a lot of baking to do this week. I don't want us running out of cake and such at the party next Sunday."

Cass reached over and gave her hug.

"What's that for?"

"Does there have to be a 'what for'?"

Sadie shrugged. "Guess not." She hugged him back.

Cass had barely hung his hat and coat on the hook by the office front door when he caught a glimpse of the Sutton buggy pulling up outside. When he saw Alfred helping a stern-faced Miss Theodora alight from that buggy, he hurried outside to greet her.

"You didn't need to rush over," he said. "I meant it when I said there wasn't any particular hurry about—" But Miss Theodora didn't even give him time to offer a proper greeting.

"I also wish to speak with you about another matter," she said and brushed by him. Once inside, she glanced at Christopher Finney, who'd just settled at his desk. "I wish to speak with Mr. Gregory in private."

Finney rose without hesitation. He looked to Cass. "I'll mosey over to the telephone exchange and see what kind of progress they're making on the Friendship Home service."

Cass nodded.

Miss Theodora stepped back to let Finney pass. Cass invited her to sit down, but Miss Theodora ignored the invitation. "Show me the table you mentioned when we were talking at Friendship Home."

"Yes, ma'am." Cass led her out back and pulled the cover off the dining room table.

"Heavens," she said, as she circled it. "My nephew purchased this?"

Cass nodded. "From New York. Said he saw it in a warehouse down by the docks. Imported by a company that brings in pieces from Europe."

Miss Theodora sighed. "It's hideous."

"You'll get no argument from me on that score. The thing is, what to do with it? Should I show it to Mrs. Sutton?" He paused. "It doesn't seem right to open the wound, but I don't feel comfortable not saying anything at all. Jessup and four other men on the crew helped haul it here from the station. They haven't said anything, but I imagine they're wondering why we didn't use it at Friendship Home."

"It would nearly swallow up that dining room," Miss Theodora said. "We'd never be able to seat all the residents if we used it."

"My thinking exactly," Cass said. "I'm glad you agree."

The woman nodded then gazed back at the table, clucking her tongue and murmuring, "Sterling, Sterling, Sterling." She leaned down and peered at the carved creatures clinging to the table legs. "Are those gargoyles or griffins?"

"I don't know the difference," Cass said. "Whatever they are, they're fearsome looking."

"I can't imagine Sterling thinking Juliana would like this."

Cass bit his tongue. He didn't think the boss had really considered whether Juliana would like it or not. He envisioned a savvy dealer stroking Sutton's ego with a fanciful story about a great find in a ruined castle.

"Do you know how much he paid for it?"

Cass shook his head. "I've had Finney look, but I can't find a receipt. Do you think he could have paid cash?"

Miss Theodora shrugged. "I haven't any idea." She shuddered. "Cover it up. I feel like those creatures are about to attack."

"Should I show it to Mrs. Sutton?" Cass pulled the cover back on.

Miss Theodora sighed. "At some point we'll have to, but this isn't the best time." She sighed. "I suppose you know that Sterling's monument was set in place last week?"

Cass shook his head. "No, ma'am. I haven't seen Mrs. Sutton since we all left Friendship Home at the end of the day a week ago last Thursday."

"Ah, yes. And you missed church yesterday."

"Mother and I accompanied my sister and her fiancé to Roca on the early train. They invited us to attend church with them."

"Forgive me," she said. "I didn't mean to sound like a Sunday school teacher scolding an absent pupil." She sighed. "The point is, the monument's arrival seems to have cast something of a pall over us all." She nodded at the table. "Is it in the way? Can you just shove it into some back corner and let it be for a while?"

Cass nodded. "Happy to. I just didn't want to make the decision."

"Do you have difficulty making decisions, Mr. Gregory?"

Uh-oh. He met her gaze. "We aren't talking about the table anymore, are we?"

"We are not." She shivered and reached up to grasp her collar and pull it closer to her bare neck. "Let us continue this discussion back inside."

Cass followed Miss Theodora back to the office. He didn't imagine

Finney would show his face until the buggy out front was gone.

Miss Theodora crossed the office to stand near the small stove. She tucked both hands inside her fur muff as she said, "I don't suppose it's any secret to you, Mr. Gregory, that I am not known for my tact. When I asked you just now if you have difficulty making decisions, I was referring to a topic that has been weighing on me for quite some time now. I thought perhaps I could avoid addressing it, but in light of events just last week, I have decided to face it straight on. And so I shall get to the point." She took a deep breath. "Exactly what are your intentions in regards to my niece?"

Stunned by the question, Cass stammered, "M–ma'am?"

"In the weeks during which the two of you worked closely together in regards to the Friendship Home, it seemed to me that you were growing quite fond of Juliana. But then, suddenly, you began declining invitations to dinner and fluttering about Mrs. Harrison."

"I'm afraid I don't—"

She held up her hand. "Now, now. There is no need to protest. Mrs. Harrison is a fine woman. I have no objection to Mrs. Harrison. What I do have objections to, young man, is inconstancy."

"Inconstancy?"

Her voice dripped sarcasm. "Do tell me you know the meaning of the word."

This must be what it felt like to be skewered by a displeased parent when asking permission to court a girl. "Of course I know the meaning of the word. But I haven't been—"

"Really, Mr. Gregory. Do we have to play at this? You've played the hero in our little drama very well these past months. We've all appreciated your dedication to the project. Your assistance with the bazaar. Your building that stunning model. Your willingness to go 'above and beyond,' as they say. We've appreciated *you*. But then suddenly"—she backhanded the air—"suddenly you were nowhere to be found. All business. Quite content to sit at the far end of our dining room table and charm Mrs. Harrison. Until two weeks ago, when there you were again, flitting about my niece."

"I don't recall flitting about Mrs. Sutton that Monday."

"I will grant you that my eyesight isn't what it used to be. I admit that I was quite taken with little Johnny that day. But it didn't take keen eyesight to see you drawing Juliana aside and practically feeding her bits of pie off your plate." Miss Theodora drew herself up. "Juliana is very fragile right now, Mr. Gregory."

"Yes, ma'am. I realize that. And I've tried to respect it." He cleared his throat. "I don't deny that I've entertained. . .thoughts. She's a beautiful woman, inside and out. We share many of the same interests. I respect and admire her, and I enjoy spending time with her. But—"

Miss Theodora actually stomped her foot. "I absolutely forbid you to toy with her affections."

"I'm not!" The protest was more forceful than he intended, but Miss Theodora didn't seem to notice.

"Not what? Not interested? Not sincere?"

"I'm not toying!" Miss Theodora blinked. Other than that, Cass couldn't tell how she was reacting to his admission. He took a deep breath and repeated—in a calmer voice, "I'm not toying with Juliana. I respect and admire her. Of course I'm attracted to her. She's stunning. I love the way her eyes light up when she lets herself laugh. I love her generous spirit and the way she's taken tragedy and found a way to make good come from it. I love that she isn't bitter after everything that's happened to her." He had to be careful. Miss Theodora likely didn't know everything. "But somewhere in the middle of that is the fact my mother and sister have brought up: Juliana Sutton and I inhabit very different worlds. I'd be a fool. I have no right."

"Your own mother called you a fool?"

Cass shook his head. "No, ma'am. She was just warning me."

Miss Theodora nodded. "Which means that I am not the only mature woman to observe what is happening between the two of you." She paused. "Yet in spite of your own mother's warnings, you have persisted."

"I have persisted," Cass said, "in doing my best to be a good

271

friend and to give Juliana time. It's only been seven months." *And there's been enough gossip swirling about the Sutton name without my encouraging more by romancing a new widow.* Of course he couldn't say any of that. He wouldn't. There was no honor in breaking an old woman's heart.

Miss Theodora seemed to be thinking about what he'd just said. Finally, she spoke. "And so you have taken a step back." She looked up at him. "But if I'm not mistaken, you love."

From being skewered to being under a microscope. Neither place in this conversation felt one bit good. Cass took a deep breath. "Yes, ma'am. I do." He forced an embarrassed laugh. "Pathetic, isn't it?"

The old woman pursed her lips. "Oh come now, Mr. Gregory. Let us not play the role of the tragic hero in a melodrama. You know as well as I do that a desire for material possessions has never fueled Juliana's decisions in life. In fact, you have recently experienced proof that just the opposite is the case."

He studied her expression. "Are you telling me you don't object— when the time is right, of course?"

"Are you asking my permission?"

How to answer that. He looked away. Thought about it, and decided that in this case it was best to be brutally honest, even if it did make the domineering old woman angry with him. "With all due respect, Miss Theodora, I'm thirty-four years old. Juliana is but a few months younger. I don't believe either of us should be expected to ask permission."

For a moment, her face was a mask of displeasure. But then he saw it. A distinct twinkle in her eyes. A failure to maintain the scowl. And finally, a little smile. She nodded. "Well done, Mr. Gregory. Well done." She took a deep breath and looked about the office. "All right, then. I've said what I came to say. I shall look forward to your *accepting* the next invitation to dinner."

"You sound fairly certain there will be a next invitation. You can't have failed to notice a decided chill coming my way from the lady in question."

"Have you noticed the inevitability of the seasons, Mr. Gregory? Personally, I've always loved spring best. We are sometimes tempted to forget that beneath the covering of ice, the current still flows. But with spring, that rushing water always wins and breaks through the ice. Blossoms rise up out of earth that has seemed lifeless." She tucked her hands back inside the muff and took a step toward the door.

"May I ask you a question before you go?"

She turned back. "Out with it."

"I just want to make sure you realize the logical conclusion of what we're dancing around."

"That isn't a question, and I don't believe I've taken one dance step this morning."

"I have the impression that you've recently changed your mind about me. Do you mind telling me why?"

"Let us just say that my involvement in the Friendship Home and the arrival of my nephew's monument have combined to encourage me to reconsider that the victims of tragedy don't always have to give it power to ruin their lives." She paused. "Juliana deserves a 'happily ever after.' The only real question here is whether or not you think you can give her one."

Cass smiled. "I intend to try. If she'll let me."

Miss Theodora nodded. "Then we have an understanding." She extended her hand. "Now give me your arm and walk me to the buggy. Poor Alfred is probably half-frozen, and Mrs. Harrison will think I've fallen down a well. She's expecting me to help her set up a filing system."

Cass helped Miss Theodora into the buggy while Alfred gathered up the reins and waited for her to signal that she was ready to go. At the last minute, the old woman reached out and put her hand on Cass's shoulder. She didn't say a word, only looked into his eyes and smiled. "In the event that you don't know very much about gardening, perhaps I should tell you that one plants bulbs in the fall if one expects to enjoy blossoms in the spring. When the ice finally melts." She patted his shoulder, then sat back and called out to Alfred that she was ready to go.

—⁓—

On the Sunday morning of Friendship Home's public open house, Juliana woke with a familiar glimmer of anticipation that had little to do with the day's events. *He's in love with you.* She'd awakened to that thought nearly every morning since Caroline Harrison had said the words. As the days went by and Cass continued to be absent from her life, though, Juliana began to wonder if Caroline was merely a romantic who had jumped to a conclusion based on little more than a shared piece of blackberry pie. And yet. . .she dared to hope.

As she slipped out of bed and padded across the room to open the bedroom drapes, Juliana pushed thoughts of Cass from her mind and focused on the day at hand. *Please, Lord. Today of all days, we need sunshine.* With her first view of the autumn prairie, she looked to heaven and said, "Thank You. This is the day that You have made, and I rejoice and am glad in it." The words to the hymn that had come to mean so much to her in recent days came to mind. *"What a friend we have in Jesus, all our sins and griefs to bear."*

Humming to herself, Juliana dressed for the day. And what a day it would be. Welcoming citizens to see what the committee had done—with God's help. And seeing Cass. First at church and later at Friendship Home. She smiled at herself in the dressing mirror.

—⁓—

Juliana and the aunts had just slid into their pew at St. John's when Cass rose from his place beside his mother and headed their way. At least that's what Juliana thought was happening. But Cass only said a brief hello on his way to speak with Pastor Taylor, who had just stepped into the sanctuary from the vestibule. Chiding herself for thinking like a schoolgirl with a crush, Juliana ducked her head and didn't look up when Cass passed behind them on his way back to sit with his family.

At the close of his sermon, Pastor Taylor surprised everyone by inviting Cass up to the podium to make an announcement. Juliana glanced at the aunts. Both gave little shrugs. *I don't know.*

Cass stepped up on the stage and cleared his throat. "First, I have the honor of reminding you all that Friendship Home's doors open to the public for the first time this afternoon. Those of us who have been personally involved in the project hope that you will come and see what your generous support has created." He paused. "But before you depart for Friendship Home, it is my joyous task to invite you to linger and witness the marriage of my sister, Miss Sadie Gregory, to Mr. Ludwig Meyer." When he motioned for Sadie and Ludwig to stand, applause erupted.

Juliana saw Sadie blush and duck her head. But then she raised a hand and gave a little wave in her brother's direction.

"My mother and sister have prepared a light lunch, and we invite you to celebrate with us in the fellowship hall downstairs right after the ceremony. And I am reminded to emphasize that Mrs. Nash's famous angel food cake will be served."

Laughter rippled through the congregation as Pastor Taylor stepped back up to the podium. "We will reconvene after a short recess of ten minutes or so to give those who cannot remain a chance to depart. Now, brothers and sisters, shall we pray." He bowed his head, thanking God for what he called the "privilege of celebration." He mentioned the blessing of sunshine and the completed Friendship Home, and asked God's blessing on it. And then he praised God for creating love and for bringing Miss Gregory and Mr. Meyer together.

The moment the pastor said *amen*, the sanctuary was abuzz with conversation. Lutie Gleason, seated in her usual pew in front of Cass's family, leaned over and gave Sadie a hug. Juliana caught Cass's eye and smiled. During the ten-minute interlude, no one left.

When it came time for the ceremony, Pastor Taylor called everyone back to attention by leading them in a hymn as Cass and Mr. Meyer, Sadie and her mother filed up to stand before him. The ceremony took only a few minutes, and then Pastor Taylor had the couple turn and face the congregation so that he could introduce Mr. and Mrs. Ludwig Meyer.

There was more applause as the newlyweds exited the sanctuary, leading the way to the fellowship hall. It took more than a few minutes for everyone to make their way down the narrow stairs. True to her nature, Aunt Lydia wasn't content with a handshake. When the Suttons finally got their turn to congratulate everyone, she hugged Cass and Ludwig, Sadie, and Margaret, beaming with joy as she wished Sadie happiness.

"You know everyone here wishes only the best for you two," she said. "Everyone stayed. They all wanted to share in this happy occasion."

Sadie grinned. "More likely everyone wanted some of Ma's angel food cake."

They all shared a laugh, and then Cass excused himself from the receiving line and drew Juliana aside. "Wonderful as Ma's angel food cake is, I'm guessing you would like to be on your way out to Friendship Home to make preparations. I'd be honored to drive you out. We rented a buggy this morning, but Sadie and Ludwig are just walking over to the train station and heading home to Roca. They already have everything moved in. And Ma said she'd get a ride down to Friendship Home with Mrs. Gleason, who offered to help with cleanup here."

Juliana hesitated. She shouldn't be deserting her aunts. "We have to go back by the house to fetch some framed prints they want to hang before the doors open."

Aunt Theodora overheard. "How kind of you, Mr. Gregory. My sister and I can help with cleanup and bring both ladies out with us in the town coach. The two of you can stop by the house and pick up the mottoes." She smiled up at Cass. "You won't mind helping Juliana hang them, will you? I'll bring a plate of angel food cake for the two of you to share later."

Mortified by Aunt Theodora's reference to that day out at the Friendship Home, Juliana felt herself blushing. But Cass took it all in stride. "I'll hold you to that," he said, laughing.

In moments, the two of them had said farewell to the newlyweds and were on their way to Juliana's house to retrieve the framed prints.

Expecting to feel awkward once she was alone with the man who she felt had been making it a point to keep his distance for weeks now, Juliana was amazed by Cass's relaxed manner.

On their way to the house, he drove Juliana past the new construction site at Twelfth and M Streets, then talked about the project all the way to the house. By the time they drove up to Friendship Home, Juliana dared to hope that she man she'd known before Caroline arrived—the man who was so easy to talk to, who made her laugh—had stepped out of the shadows and back into her life. Caroline had said Cass was in love with her. Juliana didn't quite dare to believe that yet, but the idea of having Cass Gregory her friend back made her heart sing.

CHAPTER 27

Now faith is the substance of things hoped for,
the evidence of things not seen.
HEBREWS 11:1

Cass had pulled the buggy up alongside the pasture fence and was helping Juliana down when Caroline Harrison emerged from the cottage and headed for the well, bucket in hand. "Didn't the good Lord give us a fine day?" she called out, even as she tied the bucket to the rope and lowered it into the well.

Juliana grabbed the box holding the framed prints and headed over to show them to Caroline while Cass unhitched the rented mare and turned her into the pasture for the day.

"You missed a wedding after church today," Juliana said.

"Congratulations," Caroline teased.

Juliana ignored her. "Sadie Gregory and Mr. Meyer. Pastor Taylor announced it just before the closing prayer. You could have heard a pin drop."

"I can only imagine." Caroline began to haul the bucket back up. "I'd help you two hang those," she nodded at the frames, "but Jenny isn't feeling well, and I don't want to leave her alone."

Cass stepped in and took over the windlass. "Should I head back into town and fetch the doc?"

"No, there's nothing specific going on, just a general malaise. He'll be out for the open house. I suppose if you see him before I do,

278

you might let him know that I need to speak with him. I'd like him to check in on Jenny before he leaves for town."

"Would it be any help if we took Johnny off your hands for a while?" Juliana offered.

"Thank you, but he's a little under the weather, too. In fact, he was just about to fall back to sleep when I came after the water." Caroline reached into her pocket and handed Friendship Home's front-door key to Cass, waving him away when he went to hoist the bucket of water. "You two go on and get those prints hung up. They're the perfect finishing touch. I'm so glad Mrs. Gleason suggested it." As they headed off, she called after them, "And see to it you behave yourselves. Sparking is not allowed within the walls of Friendship Home."

Feeling herself blushing, Juliana hurried ahead of Cass to the front door while he fetched a small toolbox out of the buggy. As soon as he unlocked the door, she pointed to the space to the right of Caroline's office door. "Right there."

They proceeded through the house, hanging framed prints in the dining room, library, and kitchen, and then, taking the back stairs up to the second floor, working their way through each of those rooms back toward the front of the house, ending in the second-floor turret room.

"Just inside the door," Juliana said, feeling self-conscious as she remembered the last time they'd been in that room alone together.

"You were right to keep this for a small sitting room," Cass said, as he stepped in and looked around. "It's very inviting."

It was. Especially with him in it. "I think I'll go on down to the kitchen and see if there's anything I can do to help ready things there." Without waiting for Cass to reply, Juliana skittered down the stairs and into the kitchen just as Mrs. Kennedy's buggy came into view from the direction of town.

Cass came up behind her. "So much for sparking," he murmured.

He was close enough that she could feel the warm of his breath on the back of her neck. And then he put his hands on her shoulders. Just as he had that day. Just for a moment. Just long enough.

—∞—

As the last of the open house guests left late Sunday afternoon, Margaret Nash made a last tour through the rooms, gathering up errant dessert plates and coffee cups left here and there. The committee had done their best to keep the food and drink in the dining room, but at times the crush of visitors had been so great it was impossible to police everyone. Margaret had found cake plates in the cribs up on the third floor, coffee cups left on the bookshelves in the library, and even half a piece of cake tucked beneath a fern frond in the upstairs sitting room. That one made her smile. . .because it was Mehetabelle's cake, not the leftover angel food Margaret had brought with her after the wedding reception.

As she headed into the kitchen with what she hoped was the last of the dishes left scattered about, she heard Mrs. Kennedy scolding someone who "had no business" doing whatever it was they were doing.

It had been quite the learning experience, helping out this afternoon with the open house. When Margaret first offered her assistance, Mehetabelle protested that she didn't need help. She could manage cake and coffee for an entire stampede of skinny white people; just keep out of her way and let her work. But then she tasted Margaret's cake.

"Please let us serve it," Margaret said. "Sadie and I baked most of the week getting ready—more out of nervousness than necessity, I suppose. But there's so much here, and it's only Cass and me at home now. I don't want it to go to waste."

Mehetabelle took a pinch of cake between thumb and forefinger and popped it into her mouth. Finally, she swallowed. "Not too bad."

"I cooked for a boardinghouse in Kansas City years ago. The owner's son had been to San Francisco and brought back a cookbook by a Mrs. Fisher. It's her recipe."

"How'd you get it so light and fluffy?"

"Are you asking for my secret?"

"Ain't no secret if you got it from a book, now is it?"

Margaret smiled. "Do you ever follow a recipe exactly?"

Mehetabelle shrugged.

"Neither do I. I'll write it out for you before I leave today."

And she intended to do exactly that—as soon as she rescued whoever Mehetabelle was scolding. The woman defended her kitchen like a soldier guarding a fort from the enemy. And my, did her big voice carry.

"You got no business doin' that."

Just as Margaret stepped into the kitchen, Mehetabelle grabbed a dish out of Pastor Taylor's hand and waved him away from the sink, glancing over her shoulder at Margaret as she fussed. "You believe this man? Washing his own dishes like he belongs in my kitchen."

Pastor Taylor backed away, grinning. "I was only trying to help." He looked at Margaret. "Tell her, Mrs. Nash. I am allowed."

"Not in my kitchen you're not," Mehetabelle snapped. She backhanded the air like a woman trying to bat a bothersome insect away. "You go on up to the front of the house and help someone else. Mrs. Nash and I don't need no help. We doin' just fine."

Pastor Taylor exited the kitchen, and Margaret set the dirty dishes she'd collected next to the sink. "Do you want me to wash those dishes or wipe down the dining room tables?"

"I want you to write out that recipe for me before you forget you promised. Tell Mrs. Harrison you need some paper." Mehetabelle turned back to the sink and plunged her hands into the soapy water.

Margaret ducked into the back hall and headed for the front of the house.

A smiling Pastor Taylor came alongside. "That is a woman who knows her mind."

"Indeed she does." Margaret laughed as the two of them made their way to the front of the house where Cass stood, chatting with Mrs. Sutton and her aunts.

"Mother." He smiled. "I was just coming to see what I might do to help."

"Don't even think about it," Pastor Taylor said and glanced back at the kitchen. "I just washed a dish, and Mrs. Kennedy nearly took my head off."

"We have everything under control." Margaret smiled. She glanced at Mrs. Harrison. "As long as you'll agree to provide paper and pencil so I can write out the recipe for my cake."

Mrs. Harrison showed Margaret into her office. *Beat whites of one dozen eggs until very light. Rub one pound butter and one pound powdered sugar together until creamed very light. Fold in beaten egg whites and beat again until very light.*

Laughter sounded out in the foyer. Margaret glanced up as Miss Theodora took the guest book from the stand just outside the office and began to count names. Finally, she looked over at the group standing in the foyer. "Nearly three *hundred.*"

Cass ducked into the office. "We've been invited to celebrate over supper at Juliana's. If you're too tired, I can drop you at home."

Miss Theodora, who was standing just outside the office, interrupted. "Young man, if a gentleman truly desires a lady's company, he doesn't provide choices." She smiled at Margaret. "You will come, won't you?"

"Of course." Apparently Cass was once again dining with Mrs. Sutton. Apparently Miss Theodora approved. Interesting. Margaret returned to the recipe. *Sift two teaspoonfuls yeast powder into one pound flour. Add to eggs, sugar, and butter along with one-half teacupful sweet milk. Flavor with two teaspoonfuls extract of almond or peach when beating cake the last time.*

Bake in any well-greased pan. Have stove moderately hot so the cake will bake gradually, and arrange damper so as to send heat to bottom of cake first.

Mrs. Harrison appeared in the doorway. "I'm taking Pastor Taylor over to call on Jenny, but I wanted to thank you for braving Mehetabelle's kitchen today. That is not a duty for the faint of heart."

Margaret laughed as she rose to leave the office, recipe in hand. "I enjoyed it. There's a dear woman beneath all that bluster. She has a special tenderness for Jenny and her baby. You should have heard her bragging on the little boy. She was so disappointed when they didn't join us this afternoon."

"So was I," Mrs. Harrison said. "Unfortunately, Dr. Gilbert has ordered Jenny to bed until her confinement. Which is one of the reasons I've asked Pastor Taylor to visit. 'A word fitly spoken is like apples of gold in pictures of silver' and so on." She smiled at the pastor.

Margaret made her way back to the kitchen and laid the recipe on the counter. "And before you ask, yes. I included the secret ingredient. The original said to use extract of almond. I use extract of peach."

Mehetabelle nodded. "Next spring when you start running that lunch wagon again, you let me know. I got a secret of my own that makes folks crazy for my roast beef. Might sell a few more sandwiches if you try it."

—⁓—

Jenny
Monday, November 26

She lay awake, staring up at the night sky. A light snow had begun to fall in the early evening. Now, even with only a sliver of a moon to light the landscape, shadows seemed to dance on the pristine snow. From time to time, Jenny looked over at Friendship Home. Miller and Huldah and Emil were over there, asleep in their cribs up on the third floor. Happy. Cared for by a nurse who was fond of them. A nurse who'd won smiles even from little Huldah.

Turning over in bed, Jenny gazed across the room at Johnny's crib, smiling at the sound of an occasional snort. He had a runny nose, but Doc Gilbert had been here this afternoon and checked him out. Johnny's lungs were clear. The doc said not to worry. He was a good man. Jenny had grown to trust him since coming here to Mrs. Harrison's. She was doing everything he said. The day of the open house he'd seemed worried when he stopped in. But since then Jenny was feeling better. She was resting, hardly even getting out of bed. She and Johnny and the new baby were in a good place, now.

She missed Mehetabelle, though—missed helping in the kitchen at the big house. The first time Jenny had seen the dumpy, dark-skinned woman with the big voice, she'd wanted to run for cover. But then Mehetabelle decided that Jenny was a "sweet little gal."

"You just call me Mattie, little miss," she'd said one day late in October. "Let that little boy play awhile longer with them upstairs babies and you set yourself right there on that chair. You know how to peel taters?"

Jenny nodded, and that was that. Any time she felt like it, she was welcome in Mattie's kitchen. Which meant a lot, because Mattie didn't let just anyone in her kitchen.

What Jenny liked most about Mattie was her singing. The big, powerful voice that had been frightening at first made Jenny feel safe now. She loved to hear Mattie sing about chariots carrying people home and having a friend in Jesus. Her favorite, though, was the one that started with, *"How do I know my sin's forgiven? My Saviour tells me so; That now I am an heir of heaven? My Saviour tells me so."* That song carried promises about His sheep being secure and reigning in glory and *"the pardon's free in Jesus' name."*

One night when Mattie finished singing that song, she turned around and looked at Jenny and said, "There now, honey-lamb. What you cryin' about?"

Jenny shrugged. "I just wish it was true."

"You wish what was true?" Mattie lumbered across the kitchen and put her hand on Jenny's shoulder.

"That it was free and I could be an heir of heaven."

"Who told you you can't?"

Jenny shrugged.

"You listen to Mattie, honey-lamb. You know that song I like to sing about 'Jesus paid it all'?"

Jenny nodded.

"What you think *all* means? You think it means 'Jesus paid it all—except for what Jenny done'? You think it means 'Jesus paid it all—except for that Mehetabelle Kennedy—ain't no Savior dyin' for her'? No, child. That *all* means just what it says. It means everybody for all time no matter what. Ain't nobody calls on Jesus gets told to go away."

As Jenny lay in her bed thinking about what Mehetabelle had said, she looked back out the window at the moon and whispered, "Jesus. Is it true? You love me? Even after what I did? I feel so bad every time I see Mrs. Sutton. I wish I could just feel right again. I wish my uncle wouldn't hate me." She cried quietly for a while. Finally, she fell asleep.

At first when she woke, Jenny thought she just needed to visit the necessary. But when she tried to get out of bed, she realized that wasn't it. It was too soon, but the baby was coming. . .fast. She hated to wake Johnny, but she had no choice. She called for Mrs. Harrison.

Mrs. Harrison didn't waste a moment. "I'm taking Johnny over to Nurse Wilder, and I'll be right back." She scooped the baby out of bed. As Jenny peered out her bedroom window, she saw Mrs. Harrison cross to the big house with Johnny in her arms and moments later come running back, her long hair trailing out behind her in the moonlight. Jenny didn't need to wonder who Mrs. Harrison was bringing with her. There was no mistaking Mattie, even in the moonlight.

"Now here is what we are gonna do, honey-lamb," Mattie said. "Mrs. Harrison, she goin' for the doctor, and I'll stay here with you." She looked over her shoulder to Mrs. Harrison. "We'll be all right. You go on."

"Not in the snow," Jenny gasped. "It's too cold. I'll be all right."

Mattie smoothed Jenny's hair back from her face. "You just lay back." She began to hum.

"Sing the one about 'Jesus paid it.' "

"You want me to get you some water? A cloth for your head?"

"Just sing," she gasped. "Sing."

After a while, Mattie's singing faded away. Jenny didn't quite think she was sleeping. There was still pain, but it wasn't the kind she'd had with Johnny. It wasn't really all that bad. She thought she heard voices. Dr. Gilbert? How did Mrs. Harrison get the doctor so quickly?

Mattie let go of her hand, and Jenny opened her eyes. *Dr. Gilbert?* "Where's Mattie? Don't let her—"

"Mattie's right here, honey-lamb."

Jenny searched the room. In the lamplight she could see that Mattie's face was wet. Why was she crying? Dr. Gilbert looked sad, too. . .and Mrs. Harrison. Everyone looked so sad. After a while, the pain stopped. That was good. It was too early to have the baby anyway. It was going to be all right. Maybe she would write Mrs. Sutton a letter.

"What's that you sayin', honey-lamb?"

"Mrs. Sutton," Jenny said, but she didn't open her eyes. "I should write her a letter. Tell her I'm sorry. I didn't know she was so nice. Sterling lied to me. Tell her I'm sorry. I should tell her. Tell her Johnny. . .Johnny's a good boy."

She heard singing. More than Mattie. Oh, such beautiful music. Like a choir. She took a deep breath. *"What a friend we have in Jesus. All our sins to bear. . . How do I know my sin's forgiven? My Savior tells me so; That now I am an heir of heaven? My Savior"*—Savior! Jenny opened her eyes. And she knew. She knew it all. Because her Savior told her so. . .and He was here. . .right. . .here.

CHAPTER 28

Yea, mine own familiar friend, in whom I trusted,
which did eat of my bread,
hath lifted up his heel against me.
PSALM 41:9

When the phone in the kitchen rang early on the Tuesday before Thanksgiving, Juliana hurried downstairs to answer, expecting to hear Cass wishing her a good morning. He'd called every day since the open house.

Just this past Sunday, Aunt Theodora had complained about a draft where they usually sat at St. John's and led the way to Cass's pew, waving Juliana in to sit next to him. When Lutie Gleason turned around and whispered, "It's about time," Cass murmured "amen" and reached over to give Juliana's hand a squeeze. Life had definitely taken on a new glow.

As she reached for the phone, Juliana glanced out the kitchen windows to where Tecumseh stood, looking scruffy in his thick winter coat. It had snowed in the night. Cass was probably calling to cancel the ride they'd planned for today. She didn't mind. Soon they would be taking out the sleigh. Perhaps she would even retrieve the old ice skates from the attic. *Sleigh rides. . .ice skates. . .hot cocoa. . .* Goodness. She was turning into a romantic.

But it wasn't Cass on the phone. It was Helen Duncan, choking out terrible news. "I've just heard from Dr. Gilbert. He was called out to the stone cottage in the night. . . ." Her voice wavered. "That sweet girl went into premature labor." Helen sobbed. "And she. . .she didn't survive."

Juliana closed her eyes. *Oh, no. Poor Jenny.* "The baby?"

"No. Too soon."

"Oh, Helen. I am so sorry. I know you were very fond of her and the little boy."

She could hear Helen weeping quietly. "Would you like for me to contact Mr. Lindermann?"

There was such a long silence that Juliana wondered if they'd been disconnected. "Helen? Helen, are you there? He's helped us in the past. He'll know what to do."

"Y–yes. Of course he will. But you shouldn't—no, it's my responsibility as president of the board. I'll speak with him."

"All right. But we must have a service. A real service. At church with Pastor Taylor officiating. I–I've been thinking about this for a long while. Since the fire, actually. That poor Nell Parker with no marker at all and—our own Home for the Friendless plot. It's lovely, but—it simply isn't right that people are laid in unmarked graves just because they don't have anyone." She paused. "Jenny and her baby deserve our best. *All* the residents of a place called Friendship Home do."

"You're right," Helen said. "George and I will want to contribute, and I'll bring it up at the next board meeting. A Friendship Memorial Fund."

Juliana turned to see a pale Aunt Theodora poised in the doorway, clutching her sister's hand. "Helen, my aunts have just come down. I need to go. I'll call you later today—or stop by." She hung up the phone and looked at the aunts. "It's Jenny. And the baby."

"Both of them?" Aunt Lydia's eyes filled with tears.

"I'm afraid so."

"No!" Aunt Theodora staggered to a chair. Once seated, she buried her face in her hands.

"That poor child. Motherless. What's to become of him?" She looked up at Aunt Lydia. "It's Felix all over again." She leaned into her sister, racked by sobs.

Juliana busied herself making tea. *Felix? Who was Felix?* She set two cups on the table before the aunts and motioned to Aunt Lydia that she was going upstairs to dress. Half an hour later, when Juliana went back downstairs, Martha was making breakfast, and a red-eyed Aunt Theodora was alternately sipping tea and dabbing at tears.

"That poor girl." Martha shook her head.

"We can be thankful that Caroline took her in," Aunt Lydia said. "There's no one more understanding than Caroline."

That was true, and how grateful Juliana was to know it. In fact, the more Juliana had come to know about the petite widow, the more she admired her. Caroline had had her share of heartache and disappointment, but she possessed a marvelous depth of faith. Unlike the aunts and everyone else Juliana had met at St. John's, Caroline was unusually open to talking about how faith could—and should—translate into life. She spoke about God as if He were in the room with her. Which, Juliana realized, He was. But the idea was new to her.

Caroline. Strong faith didn't mean a person was exempt from grief. She'd said that just the other day when she was caught offguard by unexpected tears over her Reggie.

"We should go to her," Juliana said. "She shouldn't be alone."

Aunt Theodora nodded. "Yes. We must." She glanced at her sister. "I'll feel better after a few minutes with little Johnny. He—he seems to l–like me." Fresh tears spilled down her cheeks.

"He adores you," Aunt Lydia said. "It will do him good to have his Auntie-T there."

She crossed to the stove to have Martha replenish her tea.

Juliana waited for Aunt Theodora to be out of earshot before saying, " 'Auntie-T.' How did I miss that? *When* did I miss it? And who is Felix? It's not like Aunt Theodora to be so. . .overcome."

"Johnny said it the last time Theodora visited. Actually, there was a gingersnap in her hand and little Johnny was likely trying to say *cookie*, but my sister heard 'Auntie-T,' and the smile on her face?

Who could begrudge her a little intentional deafness if it brings her joy?" She paused. "As to the other matter, that is not my story to tell." She headed upstairs to change.

Juliana had just lifted the receiver from its mount and was about to turn the crank to call Cass, when Aunt Lydia padded back down the stairs.

"About Felix. . ."

She placed the receiver back on its mount.

Aunt Lydia lowered her voice. "It is a matter about which we do not speak. I was shocked to hear Theodora say the name." She paused. "Your life has been singularly blessed, dear. But others. . . others have things in the shadows that are best left there. I hope you understand. My only motive in speaking of it now is to protect my sister from undeserved pain." She sighed. Glanced up the stairs. "She has had enough of that these past fifty years."

Juliana reached out and put a hand on the old woman's arm. "I won't speak of it again. You have my word."

"Thank you, dear." Aunt Lydia gave her hand a gentle pat and retreated back up the stairs.

Juliana took a moment to calm herself, and then she called Cass to relay the sad news. He prayed with her over the phone. Another new experience for the two of them. Strange, and yet comforting.

"Is there anything else I can do to help?"

"Would you come by this evening? It's going to be a hard day." *And I'm worried about Aunt Theodora.* She couldn't say that, of course. She would keep her promise. "I'd just like the company. I think we all would."

"I'll get there as soon as I can." There was a pause, and then, "Juliana?"

"Yes?"

"Have Martha fill those foot warmers with hot water. Have the aunts put their feet on the warmers and then wrap them up with blankets. And do you still have those buffalo lap robes the boss brought back from that trip west?"

"I. . .think so."

"It didn't snow much, but it's bitterly cold out this morning." He paused, and then Juliana heard him smiling as he said, "I will love you anyway, but I'd prefer you didn't lose the tip of your nose to frostbite."

Did he just say he loves me? "I'll be sure to keep my nose," she said, "and to preserve the aunts' toes, as well."

As she hung up, she realized the two of them had just given the telephone exchange operators quite the scoop when it came to gossip. And she didn't care.

—⁂—

Bundled and blanketed, the Sutton ladies made their way to the Friendship Home. When the buggy got within sight of the house, Juliana saw Mehetabelle waving for them to drive up to the back door. "Praise the Lord," she said. "I been prayin' for someone to come so Miz Caroline wouldn't be alone. How did you hear?"

She stepped back from the door as the ladies clomped inside, stamping their feet to remove the snow and sighing with relief as they made their way into the warm kitchen.

"Mrs. Duncan called," Juliana said. "Dr. Gilbert informed her when he got back into town."

Mehetabelle nodded. "Miz Caroline is upstairs, rocking little Johnny. Nurse Wilder brought the others down to play in the library so that poor little lamb could sleep. He's had a hard time of it." She smiled at Aunt Theodora. "He'll be glad to see his favorite auntie."

"You two stay here and get warmed up," Juliana said. "I'll let Caroline know we're here." She padded up the back stairs to the third floor. Caroline was seated in a rocker, a sleeping Johnny in her arms. When she saw Juliana, she rose and settled the baby in a crib.

"The aunts came with me. Aunt Theodora was especially distraught for Johnny's sake."

Caroline smiled. "He does win hearts."

Back downstairs, the older women offered hugs and murmured sympathy. "You should have seen her face," Caroline said. "So peaceful. She was a beautiful girl. I'm thankful I was there. There's no moment in life when a person is more aware that they are standing on holy ground. One moment a life is here with you, and the next they've stepped into Jesus' arms."

"She didn't suffer, then," Aunt Lydia murmured.

Caroline shook her head. "I don't think so. She just stepped over. One breath here. . .the next there." She smiled at the cook. "Mehetabelle sang her into glory. Just think of it. Breathing in heaven's air. What that must be like." She paused. "Who called you? I'm so glad you came."

Juliana told her. "And Helen is making arrangements. She called Mr. Lindermann. I expect he'll be here soon."

Caroline took a deep breath and swiped at a tear. "The baby was a girl. I never thought to ask Jenny about a name."

"Deborah," Mehetabelle said. "After the prophetess. And Joshua if it was a boy. She wanted strong names. Asked me what Bible names were good for that. She was worried that things would be hard for them in the world, them not having a daddy and all."

"Deborah, then," Caroline said.

The front bell rang. "I'll get that." Juliana was pleased to find Pastor Taylor standing on the front steps.

"Cass called and told me," he said. "I just thought I'd drive out and see if there's anything I can do."

Juliana nodded. "There is. Help us plan a service."

They gathered in the parlor. Caroline smiled through her tears as she told Pastor Taylor everything she could remember about Jenny. "Something had happened in recent days. She seemed more settled. Happier. Like a burden had rolled away. Oh—and she loved Mrs. Kennedy's singing. She just soaked it in."

"Do you think Mrs. Kennedy would sing at the service?"

Caroline nodded. "Jenny would like that."

—⁂—

Aunt Theodora had gone upstairs to check on Johnny when Juliana saw Mr. Lindermann's rig pull up to the stone cottage. Caroline asked Aunt Lydia and Juliana if they would mind checking on Nurse Wilder and the other babies while she and Pastor Taylor handled "the sad business at the cottage."

She and Aunt Lydia were headed to the library when Juliana said, "I wonder if it might help Caroline more if I pull Jenny's file and work on a memorial." She paused. "And the board hasn't really discussed a situation like this, but it seems to me that if there is family listed in that file, wouldn't they want to know? Even if. . .even if they are estranged. There's a child's life to be considered. Shouldn't we do what we can to find Johnny a family? And if it could be part of his real family, so much the better."

"Absolutely." Aunt Lydia nodded agreement. "They may regret severing ties. We should definitely let them know. I'll see to the children—and my sister. You see what you can find."

Before opening the file drawer in Caroline's office, Juliana glanced out the window. She didn't recognize either of the men talking to Caroline and Pastor Taylor. It was odd that Mr. Lindermann had sent someone else. Juliana hoped it didn't mean that he counted residents of Friendship Home unworthy of his personal attention. The elongated wicker "basket" in the back of the wagon made her shudder. Turning away, she opened the file drawer, trying to imagine the day when it would be filled with the records of people they'd helped. Today, though, finding Jenny's record was easy.

The name on the file was simply *Jenny L.* Dear Caroline, so kindhearted. Undoubtedly concerned about guarding residents' privacy—especially in the case of the children. Laying the file on Caroline's desk, Juliana took a seat. Taking a piece of notepaper from the letter box that was part of an ornate desk set—another of Reggie's treasures—Juliana set it alongside the file. She took the lid off one of the crystal inkwells, dipped the pen in the ink, opened the file, and prepared to write.

And then she saw the name.

Her throat constricted. *Jenna Pamelia Lindermann.* With a sharp intake of air, she looked out the window to the wagon. A smudge of ink reminded her to lay the pen down before she ruined the nib.

She closed her eyes and sat back, trembling. *God help me. Help me. Help me.*

Finally, her heart pounding, she opened her eyes and read:

> Jenna Pamelia Lindermann
> Born: December 1, 1859, Xenia, Ohio.

She wasn't even twenty-five. If he were still alive, Sterling would be celebrating his forty-third birthday in a few months.

> Children: A son, John S. Lindermann
> born October 14, 1882, near Lincoln, Nebraska.

John S. John Sutton? John Sterling?

"Here you are." Caroline was standing in the doorway.

Juliana closed the file. "I thought I'd help—" She glanced out the window. "Aunt Lydia and I decided. . . . We thought—if there was family. They should know."

The men Mr. Lindermann had sent out were back up on the wagon seat, driving the team of black horses in a tight turn that would head them back into Lincoln.

Caroline nodded. "I agree. We should create a policy to that effect." She paused. Cleared her throat. "In this case. . .I would imagine Mrs. Duncan has taken care of that by now."

Lindermann. Jenny cast out. Ending up here. . .destitute. Dying. And all the while her uncle—it was too much to process right now.

How much did Caroline know?

Trembling, Juliana returned the fountain pen to the groove on the desk set. She looked down at the smudged paper then put her hand atop the closed file. "Th–there isn't much here. If I hadn't recognized the name—"

"I thought it best to err on the side of privacy," Caroline said.

"Jenny requested it." She took a deep breath. "I suppose that's something else the board should discuss in the near future. A policy regarding our residents' privacy. And that of their families."

She seemed about to say more, but then the sound of baby laughter echoed in the hall, and Aunt Theodora appeared in the doorway with Johnny Lindermann in her arms. "The nap did wonders," she said and gave the child a hug. "I haven't seen a prettier baby since Sterling was this age."

Juliana could only nod.

Caroline's voice was gentle as she reached over and took the file. "I'll take care of the obituary. I probably knew Jenny better than anyone."

Was there hidden meaning behind the words? Juliana couldn't tell. One thing was certain: the aunts must never know. The only thing to do was to. . .do the next thing. Let Caroline and Helen handle the issue with Mr. Lindermann. And keep the promise she'd made to herself that women without anyone to care should not leave the earth without someone taking note. Without a proper burial and a proper granite memorial.

God help me.

CHAPTER 29

Behold, I have refined thee, but not with silver;
I have chosen thee in the furnace of affliction.
ISAIAH 48:10

How was it possible for a person to climb aboard a buggy and drive home when she couldn't breathe? Somehow, Juliana managed. But once home, once the aunts had climbed down with a shiver, all Juliana could think of was that she had reached the end of her ability to pretend. She needed time. Time to think. Time away from the aunts struggling with regrets that had, apparently, crept out of their own past to overshadow Jenny Lindermann's tragic story.

She needed Cass. Where was he? The building site or the office? She spoke up. "I–I'm going to see if I can find Cass. He was going to come by this evening, but I—I need him now." She didn't wait for a response before driving off. When she glanced back as she drove out onto the road leading into town, the aunts were standing in the cold, watching her leave.

And here she was again, driving a buggy into Lincoln because of something Sterling had done. Just when she had begun to find happiness again. Just when she was preparing to buy Nell Parker a headstone. And now. . .yet another name. A name she thought she'd snipped out of her life. Oh, she'd kept the locket, but she hadn't looked at it in a long time. And didn't that mean she really had forgiven Sterling? But this. . .this reality brought everything roaring back.

The photograph. The locket. The curl of hair. *Johnny Lindermann's hair.* In the bedroom she'd shared with Sterling for nearly ten years.

Dear God. Help me.

Raw emotion broke through her reserves of strength. There wasn't enough anger to mount a defense against the realization that if she continued to be involved out at the Friendship Home, she was going to see Sterling's boy grow up. Watch a living, breathing reminder of the only thing she could have given Sterling that he couldn't buy. . .and the very thing she'd been unable to provide.

A rabbit skittered from behind a patch of brown grass in front of Fancy. The little mare snorted and would have bolted if Juliana hadn't been quick to respond. As it was, she nearly had to stand up to regain control. The distraction helped her stop blubbering. By the time she got to the building site, she was almost in her right mind again.

Cass was there, dressed in overalls and a flannel shirt, his face smeared with dirt, his hands caked with filth. He didn't see her at first. She pulled the lap robe closer and waited. Finally, someone— Jessup, she thought it was—nudged him and nodded in her direction. Cass took his cap off and waved.

That smile. That blessed smile.

And then the smile faded. He said something to Jessup and ran to her, nearly stumbling over the uneven ground. Once at the buggy, he scrambled up beside her. "What is it? What's happened?"

She shook her head. Gulped. "I needed—I needed—"

"Is it Miss Theodora? Aunt Lydia?"

She shook her head. "It's Sterling. Always—Sterling." She began to sob.

He pulled her close. "Here. Give me the reins." She handed them over.

Somehow, he managed to drive the buggy and still hold on to her. She didn't know where they were going, and she didn't care. Just. . . away. Anywhere. Until she could find a way to stop crying. She huddled against him. When the buggy stopped, she looked around. He'd pulled up at the rear of a small house. "Wh–where are we?"

"Somewhere safe. From prying eyes, from listening ears." He jumped down and hitched Fancy to one of the back porch uprights. "Sadie was worried about cooking her first Thanksgiving dinner. Ma's gone down to spend the week."

Thanksgiving. Day after tomorrow.

So this was Margaret's house. The house she was buying from Ludwig Meyer. Now that Cass wasn't holding her anymore, Juliana realized she was cold. . .so. . .cold. She began to shiver.

Coming to her side of the buggy, Cass shoved the lap robe off and pulled her into his arms. He fumbled with the door handle, then carried her inside and settled her in the rocker by the stove. For the next few minutes he scurried about, gathering up a worn quilt, building a fire, heating up the stove, heating water, and finally sitting down opposite her and reaching out to take her hands in his.

But then he noticed the mud on his clothes. "I'll be right back," he said. "Just let me get cleaned up."

"No." Juliana held on. "Don't. Leave." Tears threatened. "Please. Just. Don't leave me."

He leaned close. "Juliana. Look at me."

She met his gaze.

"I will never leave you. Do you hear me? *Never.* I will never betray you, and I will never leave."

That made her cry again because she believed him, and believing him terrified her. She'd believed Sterling, too. Once.

The kettle began to steam. Cass reached over and moved it off the burner, but still he held her hand. He didn't urge her to talk; he just waited. Finally, she drew in a ragged breath and told him about driving out and finding Caroline up in the nursery with Johnny. About how calm Caroline was and how, when she and Pastor Taylor went out to speak with the undertaker, Aunt Lydia went to check on all the children and Aunt Theodora.

"I thought I could spare Caroline some work writing an obituary. Aunt Lydia and I decided that if Jenny had family, they should know. E—even if they'd refused to help. So I went into her office and I pulled the file and...." Her voice wavered. She clenched her jaw. Cleared her throat. "Jenny's name was Jenna. Jenna Pamelia Lindermann. P. L."

Somehow she muddled through the rest. The letters on the locket, the place the baby was born. "I think that was the farm I wondered about in the pile of land deeds and paperwork after he died." She sobbed. "He bought a farm for her. And when I sold it—that's when she came to Mrs. Crutchfield's. Everything fits. Even Helen Duncan's sudden interest in the unwed mothers. Her change in attitude toward me, for that matter." She broke off. Swiped at her tears. "She found out about Jenny, and she felt sorry for me. Poor, naive, ignorant Juliana."

"Oh, sweetheart...oh, darling..." Cass bent down and kissed her hands. "I am so sorry."

"I just keep wondering. Who else knows? Does Caroline know? Am I even right about the Duncans? And now...now there's a little boy...and I wanted a little boy, Cass. I wanted a little boy so much—I don't know what to do. I managed until we got back to the house. But I can't—I couldn't—all I could think of was that I wanted—I needed—you."

She began to cry again, but this time the tears flowed gently. "The aunts...this would kill them. Aunt Theodora is so fond of Johnny. She's even said he reminds her of Sterling. It was all completely innocent, of course, but—I don't know what to do."

Cass squeezed her hands. "You will. You'll find your way. You always do."

"How will I face Caroline? What if she knows? What if Jenny told her?"

"Even if she knows, Caroline would protect everyone concerned."

"I've never seen Aunt Theodora so emotional. Something in all of this opened...something from the past. Aunt Lydia called it 'the thing of which we do not speak.'" Juliana shook her head. "I can't just remain silent and hope for the best." Bitterness leached out of her as she said, "He doesn't deserve it, but I have to protect Sterling's reputation—for the sake of his aunts."

Cass nodded. "All right. I'll drive you out there tomorrow. We'll see to it. Together. But not until you've had a chance to think—and pray."

He made her tea. And then he went to change. They drove back to the job site, where Cass talked to Jessup again, and then he stopped at the livery to get Baron so he'd have a way back to town later. He took her home.

As they drove past Lindermann's, Juliana wondered aloud about how Mr. Lindermann was doing, and that set her back on a course of thinking about Helen's phone call this morning. "She didn't want me calling Mr. Lindermann. If she knows about Jenny. . ." She paused.

"Then she didn't want you giving Mr. Lindermann the news, because she was afraid that he might blurt out something that would hurt you."

Juliana sighed. "It's all so convoluted. It makes me tired." She put her head on Cass's shoulder and closed her eyes.

—⁕—

Cass helped Alfred tend the horses, then headed inside where Juliana had set the kitchen table for four. When they had all settled around the table, she asked Cass to say grace.

He bowed his head. "Most gracious heavenly Father, we know that somehow, You are in what happened in the night, but right now the truth is we can't see it. Right now, all we see is pain and sadness. Please comfort the ladies at this table. Make Your presence known to Mrs. Harrison and everyone involved with the Friendship Home. Please shine a light on the path You wish them to walk and give them the strength to follow that path. We know that You cared a great deal about children when You walked this earth, and so we trust that You will care for Johnny. Thank You for the Friendship Home and for the generosity that created it. And for this meal and the hands that prepared it. Help us to be the people that You died for us to be. I ask these things in the mighty name of our Lord Jesus Christ. Amen."

Cass had just spread his napkin across his lap when Miss Theodora blurted out, "Who on earth taught you to pray like that?"

"Sister," Aunt Lydia sent a warning glance Miss Theodora's way.

"Don't look so disapproving. I merely asked a question. *You* don't pray like that, either."

Aunt Lydia sighed. "Please don't attack the dear boy over syntax. It was a lovely prayer."

Miss Theodora pursed her lips. "Do you feel under attack, Mr. Gregory?"

"A little." Cass suppressed a smile. "But I'm getting used to it."

Miss Theodora glanced at her sister. "Some people at this table think that I am merely exercising my right to be an ill-tempered old maid, but the truth is—I'm interested in this matter of how one relates to the Almighty." She paused. "So please. Enlighten me on the subject of prayer."

Cass set his soupspoon down. He took a sip of water and thought for a moment. Then he said, "The first man I ever met who brought his faith with him when church was over prayed that way. I was a terrified fourteen-year-old who'd run away from home to join the Union Army, and Arnie—I never learned his story. But he wasn't an educated man. He could barely read the Bible he kept tucked in his shirt pocket. Still, it seemed to me that Arnie knew God better than anyone I'd ever known. He talked to God about everything. The men in the regiment made fun of him at first, but it wasn't long before they were asking him to pray for them. Almost giving him lists of the things they wanted."

"And I suppose God gave Arnie everything he prayed for?"

"No, ma'am." Cass shook his head. "After a while it seemed to a lot of us that more often than not, God didn't answer at all."

"And yet you still pray in the same manner this Arnie did. With simplistic language."

Cass nodded. "Yes, ma'am. Arnie used to quote a verse that said that God sees the heart. He took that to mean there was no reason to dress things up. Unless of course, we were praying to impress people with fancy words. Which, Arnie said, isn't prayer at all."

"Does God answer you any more often than He did your friend?"

"I believe God always answers," Cass said. "He just doesn't always say yes."

Miss Theodora snorted. "Balderdash."

"Sister!" Aunt Lydia scolded.

Cass shrugged. "I told Arnie once that God wasn't answering me, and he asked me how I knew. When I said, 'Because nothing's changed,' Arnie just smiled and said, 'Son, sometimes the thing that needs changing is you.' "

—⁓—

After supper, Cass was surprised when Miss Theodora lingered in the kitchen, helping him and Juliana clear the table while Aunt Lydia went on into the library alone. When piano music sounded, he turned to Miss Theodora and said, "I didn't know Aunt Lydia played the piano."

"Hymns. She says they bring her comfort."

Cass smiled. "I'm relieved that you're still speaking to me. I didn't mean to offend at supper."

"*Not* speaking would make it difficult for you to apologize," the old woman said, as she picked up a knife and began to cut the pie Martha had left on the counter. "You are going to apologize, aren't you? You were rather impertinent." She began to serve up the pie while Juliana poured coffee and Cass wiped down the table.

"If you felt that I was being impertinent, then I do sincerely apologize. Although I would like to make the point that sometimes it only *seems* that a person is being impertinent, when what they are really doing is presenting a differing opinion."

"I see." Miss Theodora began to set the dessert plates on the tray Cass was holding. "You do realize that your 'differing opinion' suggests that my conversations with the Almighty seem to be one sided because I refuse to change."

Cass cleared his throat. "But I didn't *say* that."

"It was implied." Miss Theodora put the serving piece in the sink and shooed him ahead of her toward the library.

—⁓—

Juliana retired late that evening, bent on savoring the lingering sensation of Cass's kiss on her check, determined to ignore the locket she hadn't looked at in weeks. But after she'd stood at the bedroom window watching as Cass rode away, she lost the battle to ignore the day and sleep. . .just. . .sleep.

Before long, she was once again seated at her dressing table, looking down at the images by the light of a shaded kerosene lamp. She wondered if Caroline was sitting in the stone cottage at this very moment, poring over her husband's Bible, looking for comfort. It was easy to envision her doing so.

Was Johnny back at the stone cottage sleeping in his own crib? Juliana looked down at the locket. She supposed not. He would likely be on the third floor now with the other babies. *Eligible for adoption.*

Juliana peered down at the photograph with new eyes. Caroline had said that Jenny was beautiful. And the girl in the portrait was. She took a deep, wavering breath. "I worried about you," she said. "When Sterling died. . .after a while. . .when the first round of anger melted. . .I worried about you." She took a deep breath.

I don't know what to do.

Juliana woke to the sound of the piano. A hymn—but from the skill and the amount of embellishment, a hymn being played by Aunt Theodora:

What a friend we have in Jesus, all our sins and griefs to bear.
What a privilege to carry everything to God in prayer.
Oh what peace we often forfeit, oh what needless pain we bear.
All because we do not carry everything to God in prayer.

Could the answer be that simple? Just to talk to God about it? The way Cass did? The way his friend in the army had?

Have we trials and temptations? Is there trouble anywhere?
We should never be discouraged. Take it to the Lord in prayer.
Can we find a friend so faithful, who will all our sorrows share?
Jesus knows our every weakness. Take it to the Lord in prayer.

Sliding out of bed, Juliana knelt and bowed her head. She took it all to the Lord in prayer, pouring out her pain and anger. Her sense of betrayal. She talked through the joy of Friendship Home and wept through the hurt from reading Jenny's full name in her folder yesterday. Then she thanked God for Cass, and something happened. As she thanked God, the hurt and anger retreated into the shadows. She remembered the day last month when she'd gone out to Friendship Home alone to say good-bye. She'd ended up with such a stream of things to be thankful for that she'd wept with joy. She had even more to be thankful for now. She began to say them aloud. More healing. More joy. More love.

"What a Friend" ended, and Miss Theodora segued flawlessly into another hymn:

> *My faith looks up to Thee,*
> *Thou Lamb of Calvary,*
> *Savior divine.*
> *Now hear me while I pray,*
> *Take all my guilt away,*
> *O let me from this day*
> *Be wholly Thine.*

Dear Aunt Theodora. "Please take her guilt away," Juliana whispered. "I don't know what it's about except for the name Felix. But You know. Please, Lord. . .help her to let go of it. Let her know joy."

Let go.

"While life's dark maze I tread, and griefs around me spread, be Thou my Guide; Bid darkness turn to day, wipe sorrow's tears away, Nor let me ever stray from Thee aside."

The locket still lay on her dressing table. Rising from her knees, Juliana crossed the room and opened it once again. Tears gathered as she looked down at the faces.

And she knew what to do.

CHAPTER 30

Love ye your enemies, and do good, and lend,
hoping for nothing again; and your reward shall be great,
and ye shall be the children of the Highest.
LUKE 6:35

Juliana dressed in the half-light just as the sun rose above the barren horizon off to the east. The sky was clear. It would be another cold day. Her hands trembled as she did her hair. Still holding the comb, she paused to pray aloud. "If this isn't right, show me." Taking a few deep breaths, she finished her hair and descended the front stairs. For a while, she stood in the parlor, looking up at the portrait of herself hanging above the fireplace. She'd been so young. So breathless with love.

Leaving the parlor, she ventured into the library. The hymnal was still there. Still open to "My Faith Looks Up to Thee." She read the words aloud. " 'May Thy rich grace impart strength to my fainting heart.' " She smiled. Fancy words for *help me, help me, help me.*

She retreated to the kitchen to make tea and wait for Cass. When she saw him ride in, she rose and went to the window. She knew it wouldn't always be this way. She wouldn't always thrill at the very sight of him. Over time, the emotions would mellow into something less chaotic yet just as wondrous. But for now. . .for now this was good. It was good to see him take off his hat as he headed up the back steps and then, when he realized she was there, to see him smile. To have him reach for her hands and lean down to plant a gentle kiss on her lips. And then, when she stepped close, a not-so-gentle one on her lips. . .her neck. . .and then. . .to stop. For now.

She closed her eyes and reveled in his warmth for a moment before murmuring, "I love you for saying we'll do this together, but. . .I was up half the night thinking. . .praying. . .and I want to speak with Caroline on my own." She pulled away and looked up at him. "I need to."

He smiled. "Tell me."

And she did. She recounted praying on her knees and listening to Aunt Theodora playing hymns, and how everything seemed to fall into place. "I told you I didn't know what to do, but now. . .I think I do. And I love you for holding me and letting me cry, for being willing to go with me, for all of it. But this is about Sterling and me, and I have to make peace with it on my own."

He searched her eyes. Nodded. "All right. When you leave, I'll head home and change and go on to work."

They cooked eggs and ate breakfast together before Martha came in for the day, and then, when it was late enough that Juliana wouldn't be dragging Caroline out of bed to talk, Cass went out to hitch the buggy for her. When Juliana climbed aboard, he wrapped her feet with a blanket.

"Keep your feet—"

"On the foot warmer." Juliana smiled. "And my nose out of the cold wind. Although you would love me, even if I froze my nose off."

"Absolutely." He mounted Baron and rode alongside the buggy for fully half a mile, then blew her a kiss and split off toward town.

When Friendship Home came into view, Juliana whispered another prayer.

—⁂—

Caroline looked weary but, Juliana thought, not surprised to see her. She offered to make tea for them both, and Juliana followed her into the kitchen. "How is everyone up at the house taking the news?"

Caroline put the kettle on to boil. "Supper last evening was very subdued. Mehetabelle sent me home early. She said she'd lock up."

She shook her head. "I don't know how we're going to manage a Thanksgiving dinner tomorrow. No one feels up to it."

"Then don't do it," Juliana said. "It's too much to expect, especially with Jenny and the baby's service looming."

Caroline nodded. "You're right. But you didn't drive out here to excuse Thanksgiving at Friendship Home."

"No. I need to tell you something. And then beg you to keep the confidence."

"Of course." Caroline poured tea and sat down opposite Juliana.

"When you met my aunts this summer, did they tell you how Sterling died?"

Caroline nodded. "And they shared many cherished memories."

Juliana reached into her reticule for the locket. She opened it. The curl of white-blond hair fell onto the table as she passed it over to Caroline. "I found this in my husband's things."

One look at the photographs, and Caroline gasped and put her hand to her mouth. She closed her eyes. A tear slipped down her cheek. "I—I didn't think you knew." She shook her head. "What you must think of me."

"I didn't come here to accuse you of anything, Caroline. I came here to ask you to keep a confidence."

"All of our residents' information is confidential. The board made that very clear when they hired me. I hope you don't think—"

"Aunt Theodora is going to be helping you with those files," Juliana said. "Things slip out sometimes." She nodded at the locket. "And knowing that? That would break her heart."

"Nothing will slip out," Caroline said. "You have my word." She frowned. "Why did you even keep this?"

"At first it was a reminder. I thought if I ever stopped being angry, I would disintegrate—or disappear into a sea of hurt. Once I started to come to terms with it, I thought about packing it away with Sterling's things. But that didn't make any sense, either. And still, I couldn't make myself throw it away."

She took a deep breath. "Now I think maybe I was supposed

to keep it for Johnny. Yesterday Mehetabelle said something about Jenny wanting to pick a strong name for the new baby because of the way our world treats children who don't have a father." She paused. "Johnny had a father. He was far from perfect, but he wasn't evil. And that locket—" She cleared her throat. "That locket says that he cared for Johnny's mother." She swiped at a tear. Shrugged. "Maybe someday it will help him. I don't think it's right for me to destroy something that might help an innocent child, just because it's caused me pain. As much as possible, I've come to terms with what Sterling did. I've had to. But I want to protect his aunts."

"Of course." Caroline closed the locket and set it down. "I'll keep it safe. For someday."

"Thank you." Juliana rose to go. "You look exhausted. Be kind to yourself today."

"I was up half the night thinking about—praying about something." She looked down at the locket. "If you just can't bear the idea, I'll understand. I'll resign and thank God for the blessing it's been to be here for these few months."

"What on earth are you talking about? No one is going to ask for your resignation. You had no idea I knew about Jenny. And what you did for her and Johnny only proves that you are the ideal woman to be the matron of Friendship Home."

"Thank you. That means more than you know." She swallowed. "But you didn't let me finish. I lost a little boy, and Reggie—Reggie was my only one. I'll never have another chance."

Juliana sat back down. "You want to adopt Johnny."

Caroline nodded. "I'll fight Mr. Lindermann if necessary, but I won't fight you. If you can't bear the idea—" Whatever she was going to say was interrupted by a thump overhead and a wail.

Caroline excused herself to head upstairs, and Juliana sat, trying to make sense of things.

She could trust Caroline with the locket. She could confide in her and ask her to protect the aunts. She could feel sad for Jenny and wish Johnny well. But Juliana did not think that today she could face meeting Sterling's son. So she rose from Caroline's kitchen table and called a good-bye up the stairs and headed outside. But for some reason, when she was about to climb aboard the buggy, she didn't feel ready to drive back to town, either, to face the aunts or to tell Cass what had happened.

If this isn't right, show me.

Something drew her up the stairs to the Friendship Home and in the front door. It was early yet, and the house was still. She looked up the sweeping staircase toward the second floor, remembering back to that other day when she'd come in here alone to say good-bye to Sterling's mansion. The day when she'd stood in the yellow rooms upstairs and realized that she didn't hate P. L. She didn't hate Nell Parker, either. In fact, she felt compassion for them. She had come so far.

Please, Lord God. Show me.

She didn't have to know Aunt Theodora's secret to understand a little of how she felt. The sense of being lost, of being haunted by a name.

Let the walls come a-tumblin' down. Martha had said she was praying that for Juliana. And a lot of walls had come down in recent months. She'd done a lot of forgiving and refused a lot of bitterness. And God had given her such joy. Oh, the anger wasn't completely gone. She still had her moments.

But she also had joy.

And she wasn't going to let the shadow of a name destroy it.

Please, Lord God. Show me.

Taking a deep breath, Juliana headed back outside. She intended to head back to town. But something made her stop. Something helped her put one step in front of the other. Someone helped her head for the stone cottage to meet Johnny.

Who, if Juliana Sutton-someday-to-be-Gregory had anything to say about it, would soon be John Harrison.

CHAPTER 31

My beloved spake, and said unto me,
Rise up, my love, my fair one, and come away.
SONG OF SOLOMON 2:10

Juliana woke to the sound of. . .*hail?* Surely not. Hurrying across the bedroom to draw the drapes, she looked out on clear skies. And Cass in the yard below, hat in hand, a smile on his handsome face as he motioned for her to come out onto the balcony. Reaching for her dressing gown, she headed outside and to the edge of the upstairs porch. "Pebbles? You threw pebbles at my window."

"Actually," he said in a stage whisper, "they were seedpods of some kind. Hard to find pebbles on the prairie." He grinned. "Can you sneak out? There's something I want you to see."

She leaned down. "Why do I have to sneak?"

"Because it's more fun this way." He grinned. "The three of us will wait by the back door." At Juliana's questioning look, he tapped his own chest, pointed to Baron, and then nodded toward the barn.

Cass, Baron, Tecumseh. With a smile, Juliana nodded and headed inside to change.

She hurried through pinning up her hair and donning her riding habit, feeling like a schoolgirl sneaking out to meet a beau her parents didn't quite approve of. Of course everyone under this roof approved of Cass. Aunt Theodora clearly enjoyed their spirited theological debates. Aunt Lydia loved the quilt stand he'd designed that enabled her to adjust the height of her quilting frame. And Martha loved him for his enthusiasm over anything she cooked.

Cass had already saddled Tecumseh and was waiting as soon as she appeared at the back door, boots in hand. "What's this all about?" She sat down on the steps and pulled her boots on.

"Spring." Cass leaned close to kiss her on the cheek.

Wildflowers would soon dance above the greening prairie. Today, though, Juliana gloried in the warm air that would hopefully, once and for all, melt the remaining strips of snow still visible on the north side of clumps of grass and the persistent shelves of ice hovering over running creeks.

They rode south, and for a moment Juliana thought they might end up out at the Friendship Home, where ground had been broken for the construction of a new dormitory and a school. But they weren't headed to the Friendship Home. Instead, Cass led the way along the banks of Antelope Creek to a spot where Margaret's lunch wagon waited, the side lowered, a quilt spread in the bed, and a basket waiting to be unpacked.

"You had to have gotten up before dawn to manage this." Juliana dismounted and hitched Tecumseh to a wagon wheel.

Cass lifted her up to sit beside the basket and leaned in for another kiss. "Best way I know of to start the day." He took the cover off the basket. "Of course the second-best way is with Ma's cooking."

"Don't let Martha hear you say that," Juliana teased. She looked around them. "This is a lovely spot."

"I bought it a few weeks ago. Can you envision tree-lined streets and new homes?"

"Not as well as you can," Juliana said, "but I believe it'll happen."

He pulled a set of drawings from beneath the corner of the quilt behind him and lay them down between them.

"Anyone would love this." Juliana pointed to the broad front porch. "That's just begging for rocking chairs and iced tea on summer evenings. And this side entry. . .protection from the weather? I wish we'd had that this past winter."

311

"The architect calls it a 'country doctor's residence.'" Cass pointed to the group of rooms along one side of the main floor designated *waiting room*, *consultation room*, and *office*. "But I'm thinking this could just as easily be a separate apartment. For elderly relatives, for example. Putting it on the main floor this way would solve the problem of stairs—if stairs became too much of a challenge." He paused. "Of course a person would have to be careful about stating it that way. Some older people might take offense. If they were anything like Miss Theodora, for example."

Juliana nodded. Although at the moment she was having trouble concentrating on Aunt Theodora's feelings.

"There's something else I wanted to talk with you about." He paused. "I haven't wanted to complain, but it's becoming increasingly difficult to work for you."

Juliana frowned. "But why?"

"You come down to the office and distract me. You drive by the job site and the work at hand fades into oblivion. It's dangerous working for a woman you can't stop thinking about."

"Wh–what can't you stop thinking about?"

"This." He kissed her cheek. "And this." He bent down to kiss the spot on her neck just below her left ear. "And this," he whispered, sliding his hands about her waist and pulling her close. "And a great many other things far too scandalous to mention."

"I have a solution." She closed her eyes, and for the first time noticed the sweet aroma of his cologne. "You're fired. Now propose."

He smiled down at her. "My new favorite way to start the day."

EPILOGUE

May 1908

My favorite way to start the day. . .even after twenty years."

At the sound of her husband's voice, Juliana turned onto her side, then reached out to tap him on his chin. "It's been twenty-four years, Mr. Gregory."

"Can't be." He grinned. "You don't look a day older."

"You'd better have your eyes checked on the way to the office this morning. We can't have the boys reporting for their first day on the job site to a half-blind father. It would be embarrassing for them—not to mention dangerous." She leaned in to kiss his cheek. "Quilters are coming today. I should get downstairs and help Martha in the kitchen."

He caught her hand. "Didn't you tell me Mother was coming early to help Martha—and providing dessert? I distinctly remember something about my sister coming to town for a meeting and then helping Ma raid our gooseberry patch."

Juliana relented and stayed put. "And you should have heard what Sadie had to say about that meeting. I wouldn't be surprised to see her organizing a parade down O Street one of these days. She's that frustrated with the lack of progress."

"If she raided our gooseberry patch, at least she went home with something to show for the day's trip." He kissed Juliana's forehead and pulled her close.

"She and Lydia had quite the interesting conversation."

"Our Lydia or Aunt Lydia?"

"Our Lydia."

"Oh, no. Please tell me our daughter isn't going to end up parading in the streets, demanding votes for women."

"And what's wrong with votes for women?"

"Not a thing," Cass said quickly. He nuzzled her ear.

"Don't change the subject."

"Why not? I don't think our bedroom is the right place for a suffrage discussion." He kissed her cheek. "At least not this morning."

She looked up at him. . .at the familiar glint in those hazel eyes, the certain smile. And then. . .the knowing touch. She caught her breath. "Agreed." She leaned in.

⁓

By the time Juliana had made her way past the former nursery—how could the children have grown up so quickly—and down to the kitchen, Margaret had already arrived, and between her and Martha there wasn't a thing left to do but sit down at the breakfast table and enjoy poached eggs and toast with the aunts—who had also preceded Juliana to the kitchen.

"You missed the boys," Margaret said with a smile. "They looked ready to get their hands dirty—overalls and flannel shirts."

Cass's voice sounded from the doorway. He stepped into the kitchen and kissed his mother on the cheek. "And work gloves, I hope. I told Jessup he wasn't to be easy on them just because they're the boss's boys." He gazed about the table. "And where is the youngest blossom in my ladies' bouquet?"

"Alfred drove her over to the church," Martha said as she poured him coffee. "More organ practice, she said. I think she's more than a little nervous about her debut Sunday morning."

Aunt Lydia chimed in. "Of course it's only coincidence that this is the morning David Saunders said he was going to plant those trees the Grounds Improvement Committee ordered from Frey's."

"Sister," Aunt Theodora said, "let's not marry the child off quite yet."

"Hear, hear," Cass said, toasting the air with his coffee cup.

"Who's getting married besides Johnny?" Caroline Harrison came in the back door.

"No one!" Cass said firmly. "I forbid it. At least until she's graduated university."

Theodora wagged a finger in Cass's direction. "You might wish to rethink that word *forbid*, dear boy. Young ladies of Lydia's bent for independence don't accept being *forbidden* very well."

"Listen to what she's telling you," Aunt Lydia said. "It's the voice of experience."

Theodora sighed. "The reform dress movement made some very important points about women's roles in our society. And honestly, Sister, that was seventy years ago. Haven't we beaten that topic to death by now?"

"At our age," Aunt Lydia said, "do you think it wise to remind Death that we are still alive and kicking?"

"When the talk turns to ladies' garments and the Grim Reaper, that's my cue to leave." Cass kissed Juliana on the cheek and headed out the back door.

Aunt Theodora waved Caroline toward the empty chair at the kitchen table. "Join us."

Caroline sat, slipping the small basket on her arm into her lap and pulling out a stack of quilt blocks. "I've finished all the piecing. I hope Helen doesn't take me to task for not doing it all by hand." She placed her hand atop the stack of indigo-and-white blocks. "But I'm worried about getting it finished by August as it is." She glanced at Aunt Theodora. "You are still willing to write the names for us? You have such a fine hand. And Johnny was especially pleased when I told him we were going to have his Auntie-T do that."

"His doddering Auntie-T," Aunt Theodora said.

"Nonsense," Aunt Lydia insisted. "Your handwriting is just as fine as it was when you were a girl."

Aunt Theodora reached for the stack of quilt blocks. "You've made a list of names, I hope?"

Caroline nodded and laid the list before her on the table.

"I'll get you a sharpened pencil from my desk in the parlor," Juliana said.

Caroline followed her into the hall and then to the parlor before saying, "I hope this isn't too strange for you."

"Why would it be?"

Caroline cleared her throat. "Helen mentioned the other quilt. When she found out John and Clara wanted a signature quilt for their wedding. She was concerned it might be...difficult for you."

"It's fine. Truly."

"You and Cass have been so good to Johnny all these years. The scholarship—"

"Was well deserved. The foundation awarded it on merit. There was no favoritism in that. John has always been an exemplary student. And Dr. Gilbert is thrilled to have him join the practice. As to the quilt—it's what we do for one another."

"I knew you'd say that." She paused. "It was very kind of you to send congratulations—and such a generous graduation gift. Tears came to his eyes when he read your note."

Juliana smiled. "I only wrote the truth. His father would be very proud of him."

"Hail, hail, the gang's all here," Aunt Lydia called from the kitchen, as Helen Duncan and Lutie Gleason drove up the drive.

"It's fine, Caroline. You and Helen are both dears for your concern, but it's fine." Juliana delivered the pencil to Aunt Theodora, who bent to the task of writing names on the white rectangle at the center of each blue-and-white album quilt block. As she finished one, she handed it to a waiting quilter until, finally, the ladies had all gathered in the parlor to take up the task of embroidering over the penciled lines.

Helen sighed as she settled in. "These windows let in such exquisite light!" She glanced over at Juliana. "That really is the only thing I don't like about your former home. I told George we're going to have to add a sunroom this year. To the south."

"A sunroom is an excellent idea." Juliana nodded. "Those shade trees you planted out back should be large enough to give you nice shade from the summer sun, too."

"Blue floss, correct?" Lutie asked.

Caroline nodded and passed her a length of floss. "Clara loves the idea of all blue and white."

Talk turned to the spring fashions and the most recent issue of *The Delineator* which touted something called a *bolero*. Aunt Theodora labeled it yet another useless appendage nearly as ridiculous as the season's "hideously full sleeves" and the Cluny lace and embroidered net being set into lawn and batiste shirtwaists. "Impractical," she called them. "Designers continue to treat women like dress-up dolls. And white shoes?" She shook her head. "Ridiculous."

At lunch, the ladies exclaimed with delight over Martha's dainty sandwiches and Margaret's gooseberry pie. Juliana smiled as her mother-in-law accepted accolades. Margaret and Martha had long ago called a truce in their pie competition. They alternated making dessert for quiltings now, and all was well.

When the talk turned back to John and Clara's wedding quilt, Caroline mentioned setting the signature blocks on point. "I brought a sample with me of what I think I'll use for the joining blocks. It's in the basket I left in the kitchen."

"I'll get it." Juliana hopped up to retrieve the basket. She reached in and pulled out a square of dark blue fabric dotted with tiny white stars. "This is lovely." A lone quilt block caught her eye. "You've forgotten one." She reached in.

"Oh, did I drop that? Here," Caroline said. "I'll do that one. I'm just about ready for another."

Juliana looked back down at the name. *Jenna Pamelia Lindermann.* She glanced at Caroline, who looked. . .well, concerned. And she would. Caroline would do anything within her power to keep from causing another person pain. Such a dear woman.

317

As the sample of setting fabric was passed about the room, Juliana sat down, pondering the name on the quilt block still in her lap, while the others talked about how to quilt the top once Caroline had assembled the blocks.

Had it really been twenty-five years ago when she'd done everything she could to erase even the shadow of that name from her life? It didn't seem possible. She glanced up. At Aunt Theodora, ninety-five years old and still alternately delighting and frustrating them with her acerbic wit and ever-strong opinions. Aunt Lydia, beloved as ever for her gentle ways. Lutie Gleason, widowed five years ago and pouring her grief into service projects. Helen Duncan, making do with a so-so marriage but not letting it sap the joy out of her life. Cass's mother, whose marriage to Pastor James Taylor a few years ago had delighted the congregation who had come to love Margaret Nash for her servant's heart. Goodness, but the women in this room had lived a life. They had enough stories between them to fill more novels than Aunt Theodora would ever allow in the library out at Friendship Home.

And *Jenna Pamelia Lindermann,* mother of Dr. John Harrison, who would soon be practicing alongside the beloved Dr. Miles Gilbert. How many lives would Jenny's boy, Johnny, save? Only God knew. Juliana looked over at her open desk. At the cabinet photos of her three children. Three miracles, as far as she was concerned. At her wedding photo. Another miracle. A husband who still took her breath away. She smiled, remembering this morning. Cass might not remember how many years they'd been married, but he remembered everything that mattered.

She thought back to a night long ago when she'd asked God to show her what to do and then awakened to the sound of Aunt Theodora playing the piano. *"My faith looks up to Thee, Thou Lamb of Calvary, Savior divine. . . ."*

Tears gathered in her eyes. She looked over at Caroline, who was still glancing at her every few minutes, a concerned look on her dear face.

She smiled. Nodded. *It's all right.* And it was. More than all right. She picked up her needle and began to embroider the name.

The lines are fallen unto me in pleasant places;
yea, I have a goodly heritage.
PSALM 16:6

Stephanie Grace Whitson, bestselling author and two-time Christy finalist, pursues a full-time writing and speaking career from her home studio in southeast Nebraska. Her husband and blended family, her church, quilting, and Kitty—her motorcycle—all rank high on her list of "favorite things." Learn more at www.stephaniewhitson.com

Other titles by
Stephanie Grace Whitson

The Key on the Quilt

Coming Soon

The Message on the Quilt